Praise for

T E S S
GERRITSEN

"Tess Gerritsen is an automatic must-read in my house."
—Stephen King

"Tess Gerritsen...throws one twist after another
until the excitement is almost unbearable."
—San Jose Mercury News

"Ms. Gerritsen is a master!"
—Romantic Times BOOKreviews

"Gerritsen's romances are thrillers from beginning to end."
—Portland Press Herald

"Tess Gerritsen brings us action, adventure,
and compelling romance."
—Romantic Times BOOKreviews

"Riveting... Gerritsen knows how to fashion credible,
dimensional characters."
—Los Angeles Times

TESS GERRITSEN

PRESUMED GUILTY & KEEPER OF THE BRIDE

MIRA®

ISBN-13: 978-0-7783-2706-6
ISBN-10:   0-7783-2706-X

PRESUMED GUILTY
Copyright © 1993 by Tess Gerritsen

KEEPER OF THE BRIDE
Copyright © 1996 by Tess Gerritsen

www.MIRABooks.com

Printed in U.S.A.

CONTENTS

To Terrina and Mike, with aloha

One

He called at ten o'clock, the same time he always did.

Even before Miranda answered it, she knew it was him. She also knew that if she ignored it the phone would keep on ringing and ringing, until the sound would drive her crazy. Miranda paced the bedroom, thinking, *I don't have to answer it. I don't have to talk to him. I don't owe him a thing, not a damn thing.*

The ringing stopped. In the sudden silence she held her breath, hoping that this time he would relent, this time he would understand she'd meant what she told him.

The renewed jangling made her start. Every ring was like sandpaper scraping across her raw nerves.

Miranda couldn't stand it any longer. Even as she picked up the receiver she knew it was a mistake. "Hello?"

"I miss you," he said. It was the same whisper, resonant with the undertones of old intimacies shared, enjoyed.

"I don't want you to call me anymore," she said.

"I couldn't help it. All day I've wanted to call you. Miranda, it's been hell without you."

Tears stung her eyes. She took a breath, forcing them back.

"Can't we try again?" he pleaded.

"No, Richard."

"Please. This time it'll be different."

"It'll never be different."

"Yes! It will—"

"It was a mistake. From the very beginning."

"You still love me. I know you do. God, Miranda, all these weeks, seeing you every day. Not being able to touch you. Or even be alone with you—"

"You won't have to deal with that any longer, Richard. You have my letter of resignation. I meant it."

There was a long silence, as though the impact of her words had pummeled him like some physical blow. She felt euphoric and guilty all at once. Guilty for having broken free, for being, at last, her own woman.

Softly he said, "I told her."

Miranda didn't respond.

"Did you hear me?" he asked. "I told her. Everything about us. And I've been to see my lawyer. I've changed the terms of my—"

"Richard," she said slowly. "It doesn't make a difference. Whether you're married or divorced, I don't want to see you."

"Just one more time."

"No."

"I'm coming over. Right now—"

"No."

"You have to see me, Miranda!"

"I don't have to do anything!" she cried.

"I'll be there in fifteen minutes."

Miranda stared in disbelief at the receiver. He'd hung

up. Damn him, he'd hung up, and fifteen minutes from now he'd be knocking on her door. She'd managed to carry on so bravely these past three weeks, working side by side with him, keeping her smile polite, her voice neutral. But now he was coming and he'd rip away her mask of control and there they'd be again, spiraling into the same old trap she'd just managed to crawl out of.

She ran to the closet and yanked out a sweatshirt. She had to get away. Somewhere he wouldn't find her, somewhere she could be alone.

She fled out the front door and down the porch steps and began to walk, swiftly, fiercely, down Willow Street. At ten-thirty, the neighborhood was already tucked in for the night. Through the windows she passed she saw the glow of lamplight, the silhouettes of families in various domestic poses, the occasional flicker of a fire in a hearth. She felt that old envy stir inside her again, the longing to be part of the same loving whole, to be stirring the embers of her own hearth. Foolish dreams.

Shivering, she hugged her arms to her chest. There was a chill in the air, not unseasonable for August in Maine. She was angry now, angry about being cold, about being driven from her own home. Angry at *him*. But she didn't stop; she kept walking.

At Bayview Street she turned right, toward the sea.

The mist was rolling in. It blotted out the stars, crept along the road in a sullen vapor. She headed through it, the fog swirling in her wake. From the road she turned onto a footpath, followed it to a series of granite steps, now slick with mist. At the bottom was a wood bench—she thought of it as her bench—set on the beach of stones. There she sat, drew her legs up against her chest and stared out toward the sea. Somewhere, drifting on the bay, a buoy was clanging. She could dimly make out the green channel light, bobbing in the fog.

By now he would be at her house. She wondered how long he'd knock at the door. Whether he'd keep knocking until her neighbor Mr. Lanzo complained. Whether he'd give up and just go home, to his wife, to his son and daughter.

She lowered her face against her knees, trying to blot out the image of the happy little Tremain family. *Happy* was not the picture Richard had painted. *At the breaking point* was the way he'd described his marriage. It was love for Phillip and Cassie, his children, that had kept him from divorcing Evelyn years ago. Now the twins were nineteen, old enough to accept the truth about their parents' marriage. What stopped him from divorce now was his concern for Evelyn, his wife. She needed time to adjust, and if Miranda would just be patient, would just love him enough, the way he loved her, it would all work out….

Oh, yes. Hasn't it worked out just fine?

Miranda gave a little laugh. She raised her head, looked out to sea and laughed again, not a hysterical laugh but one of relief. She felt as if she'd just awakened from a long fever, to find that her mind was sharp again, clear again. The mist felt good against her face, its chill touch sweeping her soul clean. How she needed such a cleansing! The months of guilt had piled up like layers of dirt, until she thought she could scarcely see herself, her real self, beneath the filth.

Now it was over. This time it was really, truly over.

She smiled at the sea. *My soul is mine again,* she thought. A calmness, a serenity she had not felt in months, settled over her. She rose to her feet and started for home.

Two blocks from her house she spotted the blue Peugeot, parked near the intersection of Willow and Spring Streets. So he was still waiting for her. She paused by the car, gazing in at the black leather upholstery, the sheepskin seat covers, all of it too familiar. *The scene of the crime,* she thought. *The first kiss. I've paid for it, in pain. Now it's his turn.*

She left the car and headed purposefully to her house. She climbed the porch steps; the front door was unlocked, as she'd left it. Inside, the lights were still on. He wasn't in the living room.

"Richard?" she said.

No answer.

The smell of coffee brewing drew her to the kitchen. She saw a fresh pot on the burner, a half-filled mug on the countertop. One of the kitchen drawers had been left wide open. She slammed it shut. *Well. You came right in and made yourself at home, didn't you?* She grabbed the mug and tossed the contents into the sink. The coffee splashed her hand; it was barely lukewarm.

She moved along the hall, past the bathroom. The light was on, and water trickled from the faucet. She shut it off. "You have no right to come in here!" she yelled. "It's my house. I could call the police and have you arrested for trespassing."

She turned toward the bedroom. Even before she reached the doorway she knew what to expect, knew what she'd have to contend with. He'd be sprawled on her bed, naked, a grin on his face. That was the way he'd greeted her the last time. This time she'd toss him out, clothes or no clothes. This time he'd be in for a surprise.

The bedroom was dark. She switched on the lights.

He was sprawled on the bed, as she'd predicted. His arms were flung out, his legs tangled in the sheets. And he was naked. But it wasn't a grin she saw on his face. It was a frozen look of terror, the mouth thrown open in a silent scream, the eyes staring at some fearful image of eternity. A corner of the bed sheet, saturated with blood, sagged over the side. Except for the quiet tap, tap of the crimson liquid slowly dripping onto the floor, the room was silent.

Miranda managed to take two steps into the room before nausea assailed her. She dropped to her knees, gasping, retching. Only when she managed to raise her head again did she see the chef's knife lying nearby on the floor. She didn't have to look twice at it. She recognized the handle, the twelve-inch steel blade, and she knew exactly where it had come from: the kitchen drawer.

It was her knife; it would have her fingerprints on it.

And now it was steeped in blood.

Chase Tremain drove straight through the night and into the dawn. The rhythm of the road under his wheels, the glow of the dashboard lights, the radio softly scratching out some Muzak melody all receded to little more than the fuzzy background of a dream—a very bad dream. The only reality was what he kept telling himself as he drove, what he repeated over and over in his head as he pushed onward down that dark highway.

Richard is dead. Richard is dead.

He was startled to hear himself say the words aloud. Briefly it shook him from his trancelike state, the sound of those words uttered in the darkness of his car. He glanced at the clock. It was four in the morning. He had been driving for four hours now. The New Hampshire-Maine border lay ahead. How many hours to go? How many miles? He wondered if it was cold outside, if the air smelled of the sea. The car had become a sensory deprivation box, a self-contained purgatory of glowing green lights and elevator music. He switched off the radio.

Richard is dead.

He heard those words again, mentally replayed them from the hazy memory of that phone call. Evelyn hadn't bothered to soften the blow. He had scarcely registered the fact it was his sister-in-law's voice calling when she hit him with the news. No preambles, no are-you-sitting-down warnings. Just the bare facts, delivered in the familiar Evelyn half whisper. *Richard is dead,* she'd told him. *Murdered. By a woman....*

And then, in the next breath, *I need you, Chase.*

He hadn't expected that part. Chase was the outsider, the Tremain no one ever bothered to call, the one who'd picked up and left the state, left the family, for good. The brother with the embarrassing past. Chase, the outcast. Chase, the black sheep.

Chase, the weary, he thought, shaking off the cobwebs of sleep that threatened to ensnare him. He opened the window, inhaled the rush of cold air, the scent of pines and sea. The smell of Maine. It brought back, like nothing else could, all those boyhood memories. Scrabbling across the beach rocks, ankle deep in seaweed. The freshly gathered mussels clattering together in his bucket. The foghorn, moaning through the mist. All of it came back to him in that one whiff of air, that perfume of childhood, of good times, the early days when he had thought Richard was the boldest, the cleverest, the very best brother anyone could have. The days before he had understood Richard's true nature.

Murdered. By a woman.

That part Chase found entirely unsurprising.

He wondered who she was, what could have ignited an anger so white-hot it had driven her to plunge a knife into his brother's chest. Oh, he could make an educated guess. An affair turned sour. Jealousy over some new mistress. The inevitable abandonment. And then rage, at being used, at being lied to, a rage that would have overwhelmed all sense of logic or self-preservation. Chase could sketch in the whole scenario. He could even picture the woman, a woman like all the others who'd drifted through Richard's life. She'd be attractive, of course. Richard would insist on that much. But there'd be something a little desperate about her. Perhaps her laugh would be too loud or her smile too automatic, or the lines around her eyes would reveal a woman on the downhill slide. Yes, he could see the woman clearly, and the image stirred both pity and repulsion.

And rage. Whatever resentment he still bore Richard, nothing could change the fact they were brothers. They'd shared the same pool of memories, the same lazy afternoons drifting on the lake, the strolls on the breakwater, the quiet snickerings in the darkness. Their last falling-out had been a serious one, but in the back of his mind Chase had always assumed they'd smooth it over. There was always time to make things right again, to be friends again.

That's what he had thought until that phone call from Evelyn.

His anger swelled, washed through him like a full-moon tide. Opportunities lost. No more chances to say, *I care about you.* No more chances to say, *Remember when?* The road blurred before him. He blinked and gripped the steering wheel tighter.

He drove on, into the morning.

By ten o'clock he had reached Bass Harbor. By eleven he was aboard the *Jenny B,* his face to the wind, his hands clutching the ferry rail. In the distance, Shepherd's Island rose in a low green hump in the mist. *Jenny B*'s bow heaved across the swells and Chase felt that familiar nausea roil his stomach, sour his throat. *Always the seasick one,* he thought. In a family of sailors, Chase was the landlubber, the son who preferred solid ground beneath his feet. The racing trophies had all gone to Richard. Catboats, sloops, you name the class, Richard had the trophy. And these were the waters where he'd honed his skills, tacking, jibbing, shouting out orders. Spinnaker up, spinnaker down. To Chase it had all seemed a bunch of frantic nonsense. And then, there'd been that miserable nausea….

Chase inhaled a deep breath of salt air, felt his stomach settle as the *Jenny B* pulled up to the dock. He returned to the car and waited his turn to drive up the ramp. There were eight cars before him, out-of-state license plates on every one. Half of Massachusetts seemed to come north every summer. You could almost hear the state of Maine groan under the the weight of all those damn cars.

The ferryman waved him forward. Chase put the car in gear and drove up the ramp, onto Shepherd's Island.

It amazed him how little the place seemed to change over the years. The same old buildings faced Sea Street: the Island Bakery, the bank, FitzGerald's Café, the five-and-dime, Lappin's General Store. A few new names had sprung up in old places. The Vogue Beauty Shop was now Gorham's Books, and Village Hardware had been replaced by Country Antiques and a realty office. Lord, what changes the tourists wrought.

He drove around the corner, up Limerock Street. On his

left, housed in the same brick building, was the *Island Herald*. He wondered if any of it had changed inside. He remembered it well, the decorative tin ceiling, the battered desks, the wall hung with portraits of the publishers, every one a Tremain. He could picture it all, right down to the Remington typewriter on his father's old desk. Of course, the Remingtons would be long gone. There'd be computers now, sleek and impersonal. That's how Richard would run the newspaper, anyway. Out with the old, in with the new.

Bring on the next Tremain.

Chase drove on and turned onto Chestnut Hill. Half a mile up, near the highest point on the island, sat the Tremain mansion. A monstrous yellow wedding cake was what it used to remind him of, with its Victorian turrets and gingerbread trim. The house had since been repainted a distinguished gray and white. It seemed tamer now, subdued, a faded beauty. Chase almost preferred the old wedding-cake yellow.

He parked the car, grabbed his suitcase from the trunk and headed up the walkway. Even before he'd reached the porch steps the door opened and Evelyn was standing there, waiting for him.

"Chase!" she cried. "Oh, Chase, you're here. Thank God you're here."

At once she fell into his arms. Automatically he held her against him, felt the shuddering of her body, the warmth of her breath against his neck. He let her cling to him as long as she needed to.

At last she pulled away and gazed up at him. Those brilliant green eyes were as startling as ever. Her hair, shoulder length and honey blond, had been swept back into a French braid. Her face was puffy, her nose red and pinched. She'd tried to cover it with makeup. Some sort of pink powder caked her nostril and a streak of mascara had left a dirty shadow on her cheek. He could scarcely believe this was his beautiful sister-in-law. Could it be she truly was in mourning?

"I knew you'd come," she whispered.

"I left right after you called."

"Thank you, Chase. I didn't know who else to turn to…." She stood back, looked at him. "Poor thing, you must be exhausted. Come in, I'll get you some coffee."

They stepped into the foyer. It was like stepping back into childhood, so little had changed. The same oak floors, the same light, the same smells. He almost thought that if he turned around and looked through the doorway into the parlor, he'd see his mother sitting there at her desk, madly scribbling away. The old girl never did take to the type-writer; she'd believed, and rightly so, that if a gossip column was juicy enough, an editor would accept it in Swahili. As it turned out, not only had the editor acquired her column, he'd acquired *her* as well. All in all, a practical marriage.

His mother never did learn to type.

"Hello, Uncle Chase."

Chase looked up to see a young man and woman standing at the top of the stairs. Those couldn't be the twins! He watched in astonishment as the pair came down the steps, Phillip in the lead. The last time he'd seen his niece and nephew they'd been gawky adolescents, not quite grown into their big feet. Both of them were tall and blond and lean, but there the resemblance ended. Phillip moved with the graceful assurance of a dancer, an elegant Fred Astaire partnered with—well, certainly not Ginger Rogers. The young woman who ambled down after him bore a closer resemblance to a horse.

"I can't believe this is Cassie and Phillip," said Chase.

"You've stayed away too long," Evelyn replied.

Phillip came forward and shook Chase's hand. It was the greeting of a stranger, not a nephew. His hand was slender, refined, the hand of a gentleman. He had his mother's stamp of aristocracy—straight nose, chiseled cheeks, green eyes. "Uncle Chase," he said somberly. "It's a terrible reason to come home, but I'm glad you're here."

Chase shifted his gaze to Cassie. When he'd last seen his niece she was a lively little monkey with a never-ending supply of questions. He could scarcely believe she'd grown into this sullen young woman. Could grief have wrought such changes? Her limp hair was pulled back so tightly it seemed to turn her face into a collection of jutting angles: large nose, rabbity overbite, a square forehead unsoftened by even a trace of bangs. Only her eyes held any trace of that distant ten-year-old. They were direct, sharply intelligent.

"Hello, Uncle Chase," she said. A strikingly business-like tone for a girl who'd just lost her father.

"Cassie," said Evelyn. "Can't you give your uncle a kiss? He's come all this way to be with us."

Cassie moved forward and planted a wooden peck on Chase's cheek. Just as quickly she stepped back, as though embarrassed by this false ceremony of affection.

"You've certainly grown up," said Chase, the most charitable assessment he could offer.

"Yes. It happens."

"How old are you now?"

"Almost twenty."

"So you both must be in college."

Cassie nodded, the first trace of a smile touching her lips. "I'm at the University of Southern Maine. Studying journalism. I figured, one of these days the *Herald*'s going to need a—"

"Phillip's at Harvard," Evelyn cut in. "Just like his father."

Cassie's smile died before it was fully born. She shot a look of irritation at her mother, then turned and headed up the stairs.

"Cassie, where are you going?"

"I have to do my laundry."

"But your uncle just got here. Come back and sit with us."

"Why, Mother?" she shot back over her shoulder. "You can entertain him perfectly well on your own."

"Cassie!"

The girl turned and glared down at Evelyn. "What?"

"You are embarrassing me."

"Well, that's nothing new."

Evelyn, close to tears, turned to Chase. "You see how things are? I can't even count on my own children. Chase, I can't deal with this all alone. I just can't." Stifling a sob, she turned and walked into the parlor.

The twins looked at each other.

"You've done it again," said Phillip. "It's a lousy time to fight, Cassie. Can't you feel sorry for her? Can't you try and get along? Just for the next few days."

"It's not as if I *don't* try. But she drives me up a wall."

"Okay, then at least be civil." He paused, then added, "You know it's what Dad would want."

Cassie sighed. Then, resignedly, she came down the steps and headed into the parlor, after her mother. "I guess I owe him that much…."

Shaking his head, Phillip looked at Chase. "Just another episode of the delightful Tremain family."

"Has it been like this for a while?"

"Years, at least. You're just seeing them at their worst. You'd think, after last night, after losing Dad, we could pull together. Instead it seems to be driving us all apart."

They went into the parlor and found mother and daughter sitting at opposite ends of the room. Both had regained their composure. Phillip took a seat between them, reinforcing his role as perpetual human buffer. Chase settled into a corner armchair—his idea of neutral territory.

Sunshine washed in through the bay windows, onto the gleaming wood floor. The silence was filled by the ticking of the clock on the mantelpiece. It all looked the same, thought Chase. The same Hepplewhite tables, the same Queen Anne chairs. It was exactly the way he remembered it from childhood. Evelyn had not altered a single detail. For that he felt grateful.

Chase launched a foray into that dangerous silence. "I drove by the newspaper building, coming through town," he said. "Hasn't changed a bit."

"Neither has the town," said Phillip.

"Just as thrilling as ever," his sister deadpanned.

"What's the plan for the *Herald?*" asked Chase.

"Phillip will be taking over," said Evelyn. "It's about time, anyway. I need him home, now that Richard…" She swallowed, looked down. "He's ready for the job."

"I'm not sure I am, Mom," said Phillip. "I'm only in my second year at college. And there are other things I'd like to—"

"Your father was twenty when Grandpa Tremain made him an editor. Isn't that right, Chase?"

Chase nodded.

"So there's no reason you couldn't slip right onto the masthead."

Phillip shrugged. "Jill Vickery's managing things just fine."

"She's just a hired hand, Phillip. The *Herald* needs a real captain."

Cassie leaned forward, her eyes suddenly sharp. "There are others who could do it," she said. "Why does it have to be Phil?"

"Your father wanted Phillip. And Richard always knew what was best for the *Herald*."

There was a silence, punctuated by the steady ticking of the clock on the mantelpiece.

Evelyn let out a shaky breath and dropped her head in her hands. "Oh, God, it all seems so cold-blooded. I can't believe we're talking about this. About who's going to take his place…."

"Sooner or later," said Cassie, "we have to talk about it. About a lot of things."

Evelyn nodded and looked away.

In another room, the phone was ringing.

"I'll get it," said Phillip, and left to answer it.

"I just can't *think*," said Evelyn, pressing her hands to her head. "If I could just get my mind working again…."

"It was only last night," said Chase gently. "It takes time to get over the shock."

"And there's the funeral to think of. They won't even tell me when they'll release the—" She winced. "I don't see why it takes so long. Why the state examiner has to go over and over it. I mean, can't they *see* what happened? Isn't it obvious?"

"The obvious isn't always the truth," said Cassie.

Evelyn looked at her daughter. "What's that supposed to mean?"

Phillip came back into the room. "Mom? That was Lorne Tibbetts on the phone."

"Oh, Lord." Evelyn rose unsteadily to her feet. "I'm coming."

"He wants to see you in person."

She frowned. "Right this minute? Can't it wait?"

"You might as well get it over with, Mom. He'll have to talk to you sooner or later."

Evelyn turned and looked at Chase. "I can't do this alone. Come with me, won't you?"

Chase didn't have the faintest idea where they were going or who Lorne Tibbetts was. At that moment what he really wanted was a hot shower and a bed to collapse onto. But that would have to wait.

"Of course, Evelyn," he said. Reluctantly he stood, shaking the stiffness from his legs, which felt permanently flexed by the long drive from Greenwich.

Evelyn was already reaching for her purse. She pulled out the car keys and handed them to Chase. "I—I'm too upset to drive. Could you?"

He took the keys. "Where are we going?"

With shaking hands Evelyn slipped on her sunglasses. The swollen eyes vanished behind twin dark lenses. "The police," she said.

Two

The Shepherd's Island police station was housed in a converted general store that had, over the years, been chopped up into a series of hobbit-size rooms and offices. In Chase's memory, it had been a much more imposing structure, but it had been years since he'd been inside. He'd been only a boy then, and a rambunctious one at that, the sort of rascal to whom a police station represented a distinct threat. The day he'd been dragged in here for trampling Mrs. Gordimer's rose bed—entirely unintentional on his part—these ceilings had seemed taller, the rooms vaster, every door a gateway to some unknown terror.

Now he saw it for what it was—a tired old building in need of paint.

Lorne Tibbetts, the new chief of police, was built just right to inhabit this claustrophobic warren. If there was a height minimum for police work, Tibbetts had somehow slipped right under the requirement. He was just a chunk of a man, neatly decked out in official summer khaki, complete with height-enhancing cap to hide what Chase suspected was a bald spot. He reminded Chase of a little Napoleon in full dress uniform.

Though short on height, Chief Tibbetts was long on the social graces. He maneuvered through the clutter of desks and filing cabinets and greeted Evelyn with the overweening solicitousness due a woman of her local status.

"Evelyn! I'm so sorry to have to ask you down here like this." He reached for her arm and gave it a squeeze, an intended gesture of comfort that made Evelyn shrink away. "And it's been a terrible night for you, hasn't it? Just a terrible night."

Evelyn shrugged, partly in answer to his question, partly to free herself from his grasp.

"I know it's hard, dealing with this. And I didn't want to bother you, not today. But you know how it is. All those reports to be filed." He looked at Chase, a deceptively casual glance. The little Napoleon, Chase noted, had sharp eyes that saw everything.

"This is Chase," said Evelyn, brushing the sleeve of her blouse, as though to wipe away Chief Tibbetts's paw print. "Richard's brother. He drove in this morning from Connecticut."

"Oh, yeah," said Tibbetts, his eyes registering instant recognition of the name. "I've seen a picture of you hanging in the high school gym." He offered his hand. His grasp was crushing, the handshake of a man trying to compensate for his size. "You know, the one of you in the basketball uniform."

Chase blinked in surprise. "They still have that thing hanging up?"

"It's the local hall of fame. Let's see, you were class of '71. Star center, varsity basketball. Right?"

"I'm surprised you know all that."

"I was a basketball player myself. Madison High School, Wisconsin. Record holder in free throws. And points scored."

Yes, Chase saw it clearly. Lorne Tibbetts, rampaging midget of the basketball court. It would fit right in with that bone-crushing handshake.

The station door suddenly swung open. A woman called out, "Hey, Lorne?"

Tibbetts turned and wearily confronted the visitor, who looked as if she'd just blown in from the street. "You back again, Annie?"

"Like the proverbial bad penny." The woman shifted her battered shoulder bag to her other side. "So when am I gonna get a statement, huh?"

"When I have one to make. Now scram."

The woman, undaunted, turned to Evelyn. The pair of them could have posed for a magazine feature on fashion make-overs. Annie, blowsy haired and dressed in a lumpy sweatshirt and jeans, would have earned the label Before. "Mrs. Tremain?" she said politely. "I know this is a bad time, but I'm under deadline and I just need a short quote—"

"Oh, for Chrissakes, Annie!" snapped Tibbetts. He turned to the cop manning the front desk. "Ellis, get her out of here!"

Ellis popped up from his chair like a spindly jack-in-the-box. "C'mon, Annie. Get a move on, 'less you wanna write your story from the inside lookin' out."

"I'm going. I'm going." Annie yanked open the door. As she walked out they heard her mutter, "Geez, they won't let a gal do her job around here…."

Evelyn looked at Chase. "That's Annie Berenger. One of Richard's star reporters. Now a star pest."

"Can't exactly blame her," said Tibbetts. "That's what you pay her for, isn't it?" He took Evelyn's arm. "Come on, we'll get started. I'll take you into my office. It's the only private place in this whole fishbowl."

Lorne's office was at the far end of the hallway, past a series of closet-size rooms. Almost every square inch was crammed with furniture: a desk, two chairs, a bookcase, filing cabinets. A fern wilted, unnoticed, in a corner. Despite the cramped space, everything was tidy, the shelves dusted, all the papers stacked in the Out box. On the wall, prominently displayed, hung a plaque: *The smaller the dog, the bigger the fight.*

Tibbetts and Evelyn sat in the two chairs. A third chair was brought in for the secretary to take accessory notes. Chase stood off to the side. It felt good to stand, good to straighten those cramped legs.

At least, it felt good for about ten minutes. Then he found himself sagging, scarcely able to pay attention to what was being said. He felt like that wretched fern in the corner, wilting away.

Tibbetts asked the questions and Evelyn answered in her usual whispery voice, a voice that could induce hibernation. She gave a detailed summary of the night's events. A typical evening, she said. Supper at six o'clock, the whole family. Leg of lamb and asparagus, lemon soufflé for dessert. Richard had had a glass of wine; he always did. The conversation was routine, the latest gossip from the paper. Circulation down, cost of newsprint up. Worries about a possible libel suit. Tony Graffam upset about that last article. And then talk about Phillip's exams, Cassie's grades. The lilacs were lovely this year, the driveway needed resurfacing. Typical dialogue from a family dinner.

At nine o'clock Richard had left the house to do some work at the office—or so he'd said. And Evelyn?

"I went upstairs to bed," she said.

"What about Cassie and Phillip?"

"They went out. To a movie, I think."

"So everyone went their separate ways."

"Yes." Evelyn looked down at her lap. "And that's it. Until twelve-thirty, when I got the call…."

"Let's go back to that dinner conversation."

The account went into replay. A few extra details here and there, but essentially the same story. Chase, his last reserves of alertness wearing thin, began to drift into a state of semiconsciousness. Already his legs were going numb, sinking into a sleep that his brain longed to join. The floor began to look pretty good. At least it was horizontal. He felt himself sliding….

Suddenly he jerked awake and saw that everyone was looking at him.

"Are you all right, Chase?" asked Evelyn.

"Sorry," he muttered. "I guess I'm just more tired than I thought." He gave his head a shake. "Could I, uh, get a cup of coffee somewhere?"

"Down the hall," said Tibbetts. "There's a full pot on, plus a couch if you need it. Why don't you wait there?"

"Go ahead," said Evelyn. "I'll be done soon."

With a sense of relief Chase fled the office and went in search of the blessed coffeepot. Moving back down the hall, he poked his head into the first doorway and discovered a washroom. The next door was locked. He moved on and glanced into the third room. It was unlit. Through the shadows he saw a couch, a few chairs, a jumble of furniture off in a corner. In the sidewall there was a window. It was that window that drew his attention because, unlike a normal window, it didn't face the outside; it faced an adjoining room. Through the pane of glass he spied a woman, sitting alone at a small table.

She was oblivious to him. Her gaze was focused downward, on the table before her. Something drew him closer, something about her utter silence, her stillness. He felt like a hunter who has quite unexpectedly come upon a doe poised in the forest.

Quietly Chase slipped into the darkness and let the door close behind him. He moved to the window. A one-way mirror—that's what it was, of course. He was on the observing side, she on the blind side. She had no idea he was standing here, separated from her by only a half inch of glass. It made him feel somehow contemptible to be standing there, spying on her, but he couldn't help himself. He was drawn in by that old fantasy of invisibility, of being the fly on the wall, the unseen observer.

And it was the woman.

She was not particularly beautiful, and neither her clothes nor her hairstyle enhanced the assets she did have. She was wearing faded blue jeans and a Boston Red Sox T-shirt a few sizes too big. Her hair, a chestnut brown, was gathered into a careless braid. A few strands had escaped and drooped rebelliously about her temples. She wore little or no makeup, but she had the sort of face that needed none, the sort of face you saw on those Patagonia catalog models, the ones raking leaves or hugging lambs. Wholesome, with just a hint of sunburn. Her eyes, a light color, gray or blue, didn't quite fit the rest of the picture. He could see by the puffiness around the lids that she'd been crying. Even now, she reached up and swiped a tear from her cheek. She glanced around the table in search of something. Then, with a look of frustration, she tugged at the edge of her T-shirt and wiped her face with it. It seemed a helpless gesture, the sort of thing a child would do. It made her look all the more vulnerable. He wondered why she was in that room, sitting all alone, looking for all the world like an abandoned soul. A witness? A victim?

She looked straight ahead, right at him. He instinctively drew away from the window, but he knew she couldn't see him. All she saw was a reflection of herself staring back. She seemed to take in her own image with passive weariness. Indifference. As though she was thinking, *There I am, looking like hell. And I couldn't care less.*

A key grated in the lock. Suddenly the woman sat up straight, her whole body snapping to alertness. She wiped her face once more, raised her chin to a pugnacious angle. Her eyes might be swollen, her T-shirt damp with tears, but she had determinedly thrown off that cloak of vulnerability. She reminded Chase of a soldier girded for battle, but scared out of her wits.

The door opened. A man walked in—gray suit, no tie, all business. He took a chair. Chase was startled by the loud sound of the chair legs scraping the floor. He realized there must be a microphone in the next room, and that the sound was coming through a small speaker by the window.

"Ms. Wood?" asked the man. "Sorry to keep you waiting. I'm Lieutenant Merrifield, state police." He held out his hand and smiled. It said a lot, that smile. It said *I'm your buddy. Your best friend. I'm here to make everything right.*

The woman hesitated, then shook the offered hand.

Lieutenant Merrifield settled into the chair and gave the woman a long, sympathetic look. "You must be exhausted," he said, maintaining that best-friend voice. "Are you comfortable? Feel ready to proceed?"

She nodded.

"They've read you your rights?"

Again, a nod.

"I understand you've waived the right to have an attorney present."

"I don't have an attorney," she said.

Her voice was not what Chase expected. It was soft, husky. A bedroom voice with a heartbreaking quaver of grief.

"We can arrange for one, if you want," said Merrifield. "It may take some time, which means you'll have to be patient."

"Please. I just want to tell you what happened…."

A smile touched Lieutenant Merrifield's lips. It had the curve of triumph. "All right, then," he said. "Let's begin." He placed a cassette recorder on the table and pressed the button. "Tell me your name, your address, your occupation."

The woman sighed deeply, a breath for courage. "My name is Miranda Wood. I live at 18 Willow Street. I work as a copy editor for the *Island Herald.*"

"That's Mr. Tremain's newspaper?"

"Yes."

"Let's go straight to last night. Tell me what happened. All the events leading up to the death of Mr. Richard Tremain."

Chase felt his whole body suddenly go numb. *The death of Mr. Richard Tremain.* He found himself pressing forward, against that cold glass, his gaze fixed on the face of Miranda Wood. Innocence. Softness. That's what he saw when he looked at her. What a lovely mask she wore, what a pure and perfect disguise.

My brother's mistress, he thought with sudden compre-hension.

My brother's murderer.

In terrible fascination he listened to her confession.

"Let's go back a few months, Ms. Wood. To when you first met Mr. Tremain. Tell me about your relationship."

Miranda stared down at her hands, knotted together on the table. The table itself was a typically ugly piece of in-stitutional furniture. She noticed that someone had carved the initials JMK onto the surface. She wondered who JMK was, if he or she had sat there under similar circumstances, if he or she had been similarly innocent. She felt a sudden bond with this unknown predecessor, the one who had sat in the same hot seat, fighting for dear life.

"Ms. Wood? Please answer my question."

She looked up at Lieutenant Merrifield. The smiling de-stroyer. "I'm sorry," she said. "I wasn't listening."

"About Mr. Tremain. How did you meet him?"

"At the *Herald.* I was hired about a year ago. We got to know each other in the course of business."

"And?"

"And…" She took a deep breath. "We got involved."

"Who initiated it?"

"He did. He started asking me out to lunch. Purely business, he said. To talk about the *Herald.* About changes in the format."

"Isn't it unusual for a publisher to deal so closely with the copy editor?"

"Maybe on a big city paper it is. But the *Herald*'s a small-town paper. Everyone on the staff does a little of everything."

"So, in the course of business, you got to know Mr. Tremain."

"Yes."

"When did you start sleeping with him?"

The question was like a slap in the face. She sat up straight. "It wasn't like that!"

"You didn't sleep with him?"

"I didn't—I mean, yes, I did, but it happened over the course of months. It wasn't as if we—we went out to lunch and then fell into bed together!"

"I see. So it was a more, uh, *romantic* thing. Is that what you're trying to say?"

She swallowed. In silence she nodded. It all sounded so stupid, the way he'd phrased it. A more romantic thing. Now, hearing those words said aloud in that cold, bare room, it struck her how foolish it all had been. The whole disastrous affair.

"I thought I loved him," Miranda whispered.

"What was that, Ms. Wood?"

She said, louder, "I thought I loved him. I wouldn't have slept with him if I didn't. I don't *do* one-night stands. I don't even do affairs."

"You did this one."

"Richard was different."

"Different than what?"

"Than other men! He wasn't just—just cars and football. He cared about the same things I cared about. This island, for instance. Look at the articles he wrote—you could see how much he loved this place. We used to talk for hours about it! And it just seemed the most natural thing in the world to…" She gave a little shudder of grief and looked down. Softly she said, "I thought he was different. At least, he seemed to be…."

"He was also married. But you knew that."

She felt her shoulders droop. "Yes."

"And did you know he had two children?"

She nodded.

"Yet you had an affair with him. Did it mean so little to you, Ms. Wood, that three innocent people—"

"Don't you think I thought about that, every waking moment?" Her chin shot up in rage. "Don't you think I hated myself? I never *stopped* thinking about his family! About Evelyn and the twins. I felt evil, dirty. I felt—I don't know." She gave a sigh of helplessness. "Trapped."

"By what?"

"By my love for him. Or what I thought was love." She hesitated. "But maybe—maybe I never really *did* love him. At least, not the real Richard."

"And what led to this amazing revelation?"

"Things I learned about him."

"What things?"

"The way he used people. His employees, for instance. The way he treated them."

"So you saw the real Richard Tremain and you fell out of love."

"Yes. And I broke it off." She let out a deep breath, as though relieved that the most painful part of her confession was finished. "That was a month ago."

"Were you angry at him?"

"I felt more…betrayed. By all those false images."

"So you must have been angry."

"I guess I was."

"So for a month you walked around mad at Mr. Tremain."

"Sometimes. Mostly I felt stupid. And then he wouldn't

leave me alone. He kept calling, wanting to get back together."

"And that made you angry, as well."

"Yes, of course."

"Angry enough to kill him?"

She looked up sharply. "No."

"Angry enough to grab a knife from your kitchen drawer?"

"No!"

"Angry enough to go into the bedroom—your bedroom, where he was lying naked—and stab him in the chest?"

"No! No, no, no." She was sobbing now, screaming out her denials. The sound of her own voice echoed like some alien cry in that stark box of a room. She dropped her head into her hands and leaned forward on the table. "No," she whispered. She had to get away from this terrible man with his terrible questions. She started to rise from the chair.

"Sit down, Ms. Wood. We're not finished."

Obediently she sank back into the chair. "I didn't kill him," she cried. "I told you, I found him on my bed. I came home and he was lying there…."

"Ms. Wood—"

"I was on the beach when it happened. Sitting on the beach. That's what I keep telling all of you! But no one listens. No one believes me…."

"Ms. Wood, I have more questions."

She was crying, not answering, not able to answer. The sound of her sobs was all that could be heard.

At last Merrifield flicked off the recorder. "All right, then. We'll take a break. One hour, then we'll resume."

Miranda didn't move. She heard the man's chair scrape back, heard Merrifield leave the room, then the door shut. A few moments later the door opened again.

"Ms. Wood? I'll take you back to your cell."

Slowly Miranda rose to her feet and turned to the door. A young cop stood waiting, nice face, friendly smile. His name tag said Officer Snipe. Vaguely she remembered him from some other time, from her life before jail. Oh, yes. Once, on a Christmas Eve, he'd torn up her parking ticket. It had been a kind gesture, gallantry offered to a lady. She wondered what he thought of the lady now, whether he saw *murderer* stamped on her face.

She let him lead her into the hall. At one end she saw Lieutenant Merrifield, huddled in conference with Chief Tibbetts. The polite Officer Snipe guided her in the opposite direction, away from the pair. Miranda had gone only a short distance when her footsteps faltered, stopped.

A man was standing at the far end of the hall, watching her. She had never seen him before. If she had, she certainly would have remembered him. He stood like some unbreachable barrier, his hands jammed in his pockets, his shoulders looming before her in the cramped corridor. He didn't look like a cop. Cops had standards of appearance, and this man was on the far edge of rumpled—unshaven, dark hair uncombed, his shirt a map of wrinkles. What disturbed her the most was the way he looked at her. That wasn't the passive curiosity of a bystander. No, it was something far more hostile. Those dark eyes were like judge and jury, weighing the facts, pronouncing her guilty.

"Keep moving, Ms. Wood," said Officer Snipe. "It's right around the corner."

Miranda forced herself to move forward, toward that forbidding human barrier. The man moved aside to let her pass. As she did, she felt his gaze burning into her and heard his sharp intake of breath, as though he was trying not to breathe the same air she did, as if her very presence had somehow turned the atmosphere to poison.

For the past twelve hours she'd been treated like a criminal, handcuffed, fingerprinted, intimately searched. She'd had questions fired at her, humiliations heaped upon her. But never, until this man had looked at her, had she felt like a creature worthy of such disgust, such loathing. Rage suddenly flared inside her, a rage so fierce it threatened to consume her in its flames.

She halted and stared up at him. Their gazes locked. *There, damn you!* she thought. *Whoever you are, take a look at me! Take a good, long look at the murderess. Satisfied?*

The eyes staring down at her were dark as night, stony with condemnation. But as they took each other in, Miranda saw something else flicker in those depths, a hint of uncertainty, almost confusion. As if the picture he saw was all wrong, as if image and caption were terribly mismatched.

Just down the hall, a door swung open. Footsteps clicked out and stopped dead.

"Dear God," whispered a voice.

Miranda turned.

Evelyn Tremain stood frozen in the washroom doorway. "Chase," she whispered. "It's her...."

At once the man went to Evelyn and offered her his steadying arm. Evelyn gripped it with both hands, as if holding on to her only lifeline. "Oh, please," she murmured helplessly. "I can't stand to look at her."

Miranda didn't move. She felt paralyzed by guilt, by what she'd done to this woman, to the whole family.

Though her crime might not be murder, still she had committed a sin against Evelyn Tremain and for that she would always be tormented.

"Mrs. Tremain," she said quietly. "I'm sorry...."

Evelyn buried her face against the man's shoulder. "Chase, please. Get her out of here."

"He loved you," said Miranda. "I want you to know that. I want you to know that he never stopped loving—"

"Get her out of here!" cried Evelyn.

"Officer," said Chase quietly. "Please. Take her away."

Officer Snipe reached for Miranda's arm. "Let's go."

As she was led away Miranda called over her shoulder, "I didn't kill him, Mrs. Tremain! You have to believe that—"

"You tramp!" shouted Evelyn. "You filthy whore! You ruined my life."

Miranda glanced back and saw the other woman had pulled away from Chase and was now facing her like some avenging angel. Strands of blond hair had fallen free and her face, always pale, was now a stark white.

"You ruined my life!" Evelyn screamed.

That accusing shriek echoed in Miranda's ears all the way down that long walk to the jail.

Drained of resistance, she quietly entered the cell. She stood there, frozen, as the door clanged shut. Officer Snipe's footsteps faded away. She was alone, trapped in this cage.

Suddenly she felt as if she were suffocating, as if she would smother without fresh air. She scrambled over to the one small window and tried to pull herself up by the bars, but it was too high. She ran to the cot, dragged it across the cell and climbed on top. Even then she was barely tall enough to peek over the sill, to gulp in a tantalizing taste of freedom. Outside the sun was shining. She could see maple trees beyond the fenced yard, a few rooftops, a sea gull soaring in the sky. If she breathed in deeply, she could almost smell the sea. Oh, Lord, how sweet it all seemed! How unattainable! She gripped the window bars so tightly they dug into her palms. Pressing her face against the sill, she closed her eyes and willed herself to stay in control, to keep panic at bay.

I am innocent. They have to believe me, she thought.

And then, *What if they don't?*

No, damn it. Don't think about that.

She forced herself to concentrate on something else, anything else. She thought of the man in the hallway, the man with Evelyn Tremain. What had Evelyn called him? Chase. The name stirred a memory; Miranda had heard it before. She snatched desperately at that irrelevant strand of thought, concentrated hard on dredging up the memory, anything to crowd the fears from her mind. Chase. Chase. Someone had said it. She tried to bring back the voice, to match it to the utterance of that name.

The memory hit her like a blow. It was Richard who'd said it. *I haven't seen my brother in years. We had a falling-out when my father died. But then, Chase was always the problem kid in the family....*

Miranda's eyes flew open with the revelation. Was it possible? There'd been no resemblance, no hint of familial ties in that face. Richard had had blue eyes, light brown hair, a weathered face always on the verge of sunburn. This man called Chase was all darkness, all shadow. It was hard to believe they were brothers. But that would explain the man's coldness, his look of condemnation. He thought she'd murdered Richard, and repulsion was exactly what he would feel, coming face-to-face with his brother's killer.

Slowly she sank onto the cot. Lying there beneath the window she could catch glimpses of blue sky and cloud. August. It would be a hot day. Already her T-shirt was damp with sweat.

She closed her eyes and tried to imagine soaring like a sea gull in that bright blue sky, tried to picture the island far below her.

But all she could see were the accusing eyes of Chase Tremain.

Three

He truly was the ugliest dog on earth.

Miss Lila St. John regarded her pet with a mixture of affection and pity. Sir Oscar Henry San Angelo III, otherwise known as Ozzie, was a rare breed known as a Portuguese Water Dog. Miss St. John was not quite clear as to the attributes of this particular breed. She suspected it was some sort of geneticists' joke. Her niece had presented the dog to her—"to keep you company, Auntie"—and Miss St. John had been trying to remember ever since what that niece could hold against her. Not that Ozzie was entirely without redeeming value. He didn't bite, didn't bother the cat. He was a passable watchdog. But he ate like a horse, twitched like a mouse and was absolutely unforgiving if you neglected to take him on his twice-daily walk. He would stand by the door and whine.

The way he was doing now.

Oh, Miss St. John knew that look. Even if she couldn't actually see the beast's eyes under all that fur, she knew what the look meant. Sighing, she opened the door. The black bundle of fur practically shot down the porch steps and took off for the woods. Miss St. John had no choice but to follow him, and so off into the woods she went.

It was a warm evening, one of those still, sweet twilights that seem kissed with midsummer magic. She would not be surprised to see something extraordinary tonight. A doe and fawn, perhaps, or a fox cub, or even an owl.

She moved steadily through the trees in pursuit of the dog. She noticed they were headed in a direct line toward Rose Hill Cottage, the Tremains' summer camp. Such a tragedy, Richard Tremain's death.

She hadn't particularly liked the man, but theirs were the last two cottages on this lonely road, and on her walks here she had occasionally seen him through his window, his head bent in concentration at his desk. He'd always been polite to her, and deferential, but she'd suspected much of it was automatic and not, in any sense, true respect. He'd had no use for elderly women; he simply tolerated them.

But as for young women, well, she'd heard that was a different story.

It troubled her, these recent revelations about his death. Not so much the fact of his murder, but the identity of the one accused. Miss St. John had met Miranda Wood, had spoken to her on several occasions. On this small island, in the dead of winter, only green thumb fanatics braved the icy roads to attend meetings of the local garden club. That's where Miss St. John had met Miranda. They'd sat together during a lecture on triploid marigolds, and again at the talk on gloxinia cultivation. Miranda was polite and deferential, but genuinely so. A lovely girl, not a hint of dishonesty in her eyes. It seemed to Miss St. John that any woman who cared so passionately about flowers, about living, growing things, could simply not be a murderess.

It bothered her, all that cruel talk flying about town these days. Miranda Wood, a killer? It went against Miss St. John's instincts, and her instincts were always, always good.

Ozzie bounded through the last stand of trees and shot off toward Rose Hill Cottage. Miss St. John resignedly followed suit. That's when she saw the light flickering through the trees. It came from the Tremain cottage. Just as quickly, it vanished.

At once she froze as an eerie thought flashed to mind. *Ghosts?* Richard was the only one who ever used that cottage. *But he's dead.*

The rational side of her brain, the side that normally guided Miss St. John's day-to-day existence, took control. It must be one of the family, of course. Evelyn, perhaps, come to wrap up her husband's affairs.

Still, Miss St. John couldn't shake off her uneasiness.

She crossed the driveway and went up the front porch steps. "Hello?" she called. "Evelyn? Cassie?" There was no answer to her knock.

She tried to peer in the window, but it was dark inside. "Hello?" she called again, louder. She thought she heard, from somewhere in the cottage, a soft thud. Then—silence.

Ozzie began to bark. He danced around on the porch, his claws tip-tapping on the wood.

"Oh, hush!" snapped Miss St. John. "Sit!"

The dog whined, sat, and gave her a distinctly wounded look.

Miss St. John stood there a moment, listening for more sounds, but she heard nothing except the whap-whap of Ozzie's tail against the porch.

Perhaps she should call the police. She debated that move all the way back to her cottage. Once there, in her cheery little kitchen, the very idea seemed so silly, so alarmist. It was a good half-hour drive out here to the north shore. The local police would be reluctant to send a man all the way out here, and for what? A will-o'-the-wisp tale? Besides, what could there possibly be in Rose Hill Cottage that would interest any burglars?

"It's just my imagination. Or my failing eyesight. After all, when one's seventy-four, one has to expect the faculties to get a little screwy."

Ozzie walked in a tight circle, lay down and promptly went to sleep.

"Good Lord," said Miss St. John. "I'm talking to my dog now. What part of my brain will rot next?"

Ozzie, as usual, offered no opinion.

The courtroom was packed. Already, a dozen people had been turned away at the door, and this wasn't even a trial, just a bail review hearing, a formality required by law to be held forty-eight hours after arrest.

Chase, who sat in the second row with Evelyn and her father, suspected the proceedings would be brief. The facts were stark, the suspect's guilt indisputable. A few words by the judge, a bang of the gavel and they'd all be out of there.

And the murderess would slink back to her cell, where she belonged.

"Damned circus, that's what it is," growled Evelyn's father, Noah DeBolt. Silver haired and gravel throated, at sixty-six he was still as formidable as ever. Chase felt the automatic urge to sit up straight and mind his manners. One did not slouch in the presence of Noah DeBolt. One was always courteous and deferential, even if one was an adult.

Even if one was the chief of police, Chase noted, as Lorne Tibbetts stopped and politely tipped his hat at Noah.

The principals were settling in their places. The deputy D.A. from Bass Harbor was seated at his table, flipping through a sheaf of papers. Lorne and Ellis, representing half the local police force, sat off to the left, their uniformed spines ramrod straight, their hair neatly slicked down. They had even parted it on the same side. The defense attorney, a youngster wearing a suit that looked as if it cost twice his annual salary, was fussing with the catch on his leather briefcase.

"They should clear this place out," grunted Noah. "Who the hell let all these spectators in? Invasion of privacy, I call it."

"It's open to the public, Daddy," said Evelyn wearily.

"There's public, and then there's *public*. These people don't belong here. It's none of their damn business." Noah rose and waved for Lorne's attention, but the chief of police's brilliantined head was facing forward. Noah glanced around for the bailiff, but the man had disappeared through a side door. In frustration, Noah sat back down. "Don't know what this town's coming to," he muttered. "All these new people. No sense of what's proper anymore."

"Quiet, Daddy," murmured Evelyn. Then, fuming, she muttered, "Where are the twins? Why aren't they here? I want the judge to see them. Poor kids without a father."

Noah snorted. "They're full-grown adults. They won't impress anyone."

"There. I see them," said Chase, spotting Cassie and

Phillip a few rows back. They must have slipped in later, with the other spectators.

So the audience is in place, he thought. *All we need now are the two main players. The judge. And the accused.*

As if on cue, a side door opened. The ape-size bailiff reappeared, his hand gripping the arm of the much smaller prisoner.

At his second glimpse of Miranda Wood, Chase was struck by how much paler she appeared than he remembered. And how much more fragile. The top of her head barely reached the bailiff's shoulder. She was dressed unobtrusively, in a blue skirt and a simple white blouse, an outfit no doubt chosen by her attorney to make her look innocent, which she did. Her hair was gathered back in a neat but trim ponytail. No wanton-woman looks here. Those lush chestnut highlights were carefully restrained by a plain rubber band. She wore no jewelry, no makeup. The pallor of those cheeks came without the artifice of face powder.

On her way to the defendant's table she looked once, and only once, at the crowd. Her gaze swept the room and came to rest on Chase. It was only a few seconds of eye contact, a glimpse of her brittle mask of composure. Pride, that's what he saw in her face. He could read it in her body language: the straight back, the chin held aloft. Everyone else in this room would see it, too, would resent that show of pride. The brazen murderess, they'd think. A woman without repentance, without shame. He wished *he* could feel that way about her. It would make her guilt seem all the more assured, her punishment all the more justified.

But he knew what lay beneath the mask. He'd seen it in those eyes two days before, when they'd gazed out at him through a one-way mirror. Fear, pure and simple. She was terrified.

And she was too proud to show it.

From the instant Miranda walked into the courtroom, none of it seemed real. Her feet, her legs felt numb. She was actually grateful for the firm grip of the bailiff's hand around her arm as they stepped in the side door. She caught a kaleidoscopic glimpse of all those faces in the audience—if that's what you called a courtroom full of spectators. What else could you call them? An audience here to watch her performance, an act in the theater of her life. Half of them had come to hang her; the other half were here to watch. As her gaze slowly swept the room she saw familiar faces. There were her colleagues from the *Herald:* Managing Editor Jill Vickery, looking every bit the sleek professional, and staff reporters Annie Berenger and Ty Weingardt, both of them dressed à la classic rumpled writer. It was hard to tell that they were—or had been— friends. They all wore such carefully neutral expressions.

As her gaze shifted, she took in a single friendly face in the crowd—old Mr. Lanzo, her next-door neighbor. He was mouthing the words *I'm with you, sweetie!* She found herself almost smiling back.

Then her gaze shifted again, to settle on Chase Tremain's stony face. The smile instantly died on her lips. Of all the faces in the room, his was the one that most made her feel like shrinking into some dark, unreachable crevice, anywhere to escape his gaze of judgment. The faces beside him were no less condemning. Evelyn Tremain, dressed in widow's black, looked like a pale death's mask. Next to Evelyn was her father, Noah DeBolt, town patriarch, a man who with one steely look could wither the spirit of any who dared offend him. He was now aiming that poisonous gaze at Miranda.

The tug of the bailiff's hand redirected Miranda toward the defendant's table. Meekly she sat beside her attorney, who greeted her with a stiff nod. Randall Pelham was Ivy League and impeccably dressed for the part, but all Miranda could think of when she saw his face was how young he looked. He made her feel, at twenty-nine, positively middle-aged. Still, she'd had little choice in the matter. There were only two attorneys in practice on Shepherd's Island. The other was Les Hardee, a man with experience, a fine reputation and a fee to match. Unfortunately, Hardee's client list happened to include the names DeBolt and Tremain.

Randall Pelham had no such conflict of interest. He didn't have many clients, either. As the new kid in town, he was ready and willing to represent anyone, even the local murderess.

She asked softly, "Are we okay, Mr. Pelham?"

"Just let me do the talking. You sit there and look innocent."

"I am innocent."

To which Randall Pelham offered no response.

"All rise for His Honor Herbert C. Klimenko," said the bailiff.

Everyone stood.

The sound of shuffling feet announced the arrival of Judge Klimenko, who creaked behind the bench and sank like a bag of old bones into his chair. He fumbled around in his pockets and finally managed to perch a pair of bifocals on his nose.

"They brought him out of retirement," someone whispered in the front row. "You know, they say he's senile."

"They also say he's deaf!" shot back Judge Klimenko. With that, he slammed down the gavel. "Court is now in session."

The hearing convened. She followed her attorney's advice and let him do the talking. For forty-five minutes she didn't say a word as two men, one she barely knew, one she knew not at all, argued the question of her freedom. They weren't here to decide guilt or innocence. That was for the trial. The issue to be settled today was more immediate: should she be set free pending that trial?

The deputy D.A. ticked off a list of reasons the accused should remain incarcerated. Weight of evidence. Danger to the community. Undeniable flight risk. The savage nature of the crime, he declared, pointed to the defendant's brutal nature. Miranda could not believe that this monster he kept referring to was *her. Is that what they all think of me?* she wondered, feeling the gaze of the audience on her back. *That I'm evil? That I would kill again?*

Only when she was asked, twice, to stand for Judge Klimenko's decision did her attention shift back to the present. Trembling, she rose to her feet and gazed up at the pair of eyes peering down at her over bifocals.

"Bail is set at one hundred thousand dollars cash or two hundred thousand dollars secured property." The gavel slammed down. "Court dismissed."

Miranda was stunned. Even as the audience milled around behind her, she stood frozen in despair.

"It's the best I could do," Pelham whispered.

It might as well have been a million. She would never be able to raise it.

"Come on, Ms. Wood," said the bailiff. "Time to go back."

In silence she let herself be escorted across the room, past the gazes of all those prying eyes. Only for a second did she pause, to glance back over her shoulder at Chase Tremain. As their gazes locked she thought she saw, for an instant, a flicker of something she hadn't seen before. Compassion. Just as quickly, it was gone.

Fighting tears, she turned and followed the bailiff through the side door.

Back to jail.

"That will keep her locked away," said Evelyn.

"A hundred thousand?" Chase shook his head. "It doesn't seem out of reach."

"Not for us, maybe. But for someone like her?" Evelyn snorted. The look of satisfaction on her flawlessly made-up face was not becoming. "No. No, I think Ms. Miranda Wood will be staying right where she belongs. Behind bars."

"She hasn't budged an inch," said Lorne Tibbetts. "We've been questioning her for a week straight now and she sticks to that story like glue."

"It doesn't matter," said Evelyn. "Facts are facts. She can't refute them."

They were sitting outside, on Evelyn's veranda. At mid-morning they'd been driven from the house by the heat; the sun streaming in the windows had turned the rooms into ovens. Chase had forgotten about these hot August days. In his memory, Maine was forever cool, forever immune to the miseries of summer. So much for childhood memories. He poured another glass of iced tea and handed the pitcher over to Tibbetts.

"So what do you think, Lorne?" asked Chase. "You have enough to convict?"

"Maybe. There are holes in the evidence."

"What holes?" demanded Evelyn.

Chase thought, *my sister-in-law is back to her old self again. No more hysterics since that day at the police station.* She looked cool and in control, which is how he'd always remembered her from their childhood. Evelyn the ice queen.

"There's the matter of the fingerprints," said Tibbetts.

"What do you mean?" asked Chase. "Weren't they on the knife?"

"That's the problem. The knife handle was wiped clean. Now, that doesn't make a lot of sense to me. Here's this crime of passion, see? She uses her own knife. Pure impulse. So why does she bother to wipe off the fingerprints?"

"She must be brighter than you think," Evelyn said, sniffing. "She's already got you confused."

"Anyway, it doesn't go along with an impulse killing."

"What other problems do you have with the case?" asked Chase.

"The suspect herself. She's a tough nut to crack."

"Of course she is. She's fighting for her life," said Evelyn.

"She passed the polygraph."

"She submitted to one?" asked Chase.

"She insisted on it. Not that it would've hurt her case if she flunked. It's not admissible evidence."

"So why should it change *your* mind?" asked Evelyn.

"It doesn't. It just bothers me."

Chase stared off toward the sea. He, too, was bothered. Not by the facts, but by his own instincts.

Logic, evidence, told him that Miranda Wood was the killer. Why did he have such a hard time believing it?

The doubts had started a week ago, in that police station hallway. He'd watched the whole interrogation. He'd heard her denials, her lame explanations. He hadn't been swayed. But when they'd come face-to-face in the hall, and she'd looked him straight in the eye, he'd felt the first stirrings of doubt. Would a murderess meet his gaze so unflinchingly? Would she face an accuser with such bald courage? Even when Evelyn had appeared, Miranda hadn't ducked for cover. Instead, she'd said the unexpected. *He loved you. I want you to know that.* Of all the things a murderess might have said, that was the most startling. It was an act of kindness, an honest attempt to comfort the widow. It earned her no points, no stars in court. She could simply have walked past, ignoring Evelyn, leaving her to her grief. Instead, Miranda had reached out in pity to the other woman.

Chase did not understand it.

"There's no question but that the weight of the evidence is against her," said Tibbetts. "Obviously, that's what the judge thought. Just look at the bail he set. He knew she'd never come up with that kind of cash. So she won't be walking out anytime soon. Unless she's been hiding a rich uncle somewhere."

"Hardly," said Evelyn. "A woman like that could only come from the wrong side of the tracks."

Wrong side of the tracks, thought Chase. Meaning poor. But not trash. He'd been able to see that through the one-way mirror. Trash was cheap, easily bent, easily bought. Miranda Wood was none of those.

A car marked Shepherd's Island Police pulled up in the driveway.

Tibbetts sighed. "Geez, they just won't leave me alone. Even on my day off."

Ellis Snipe, spindly in his cop's uniform, climbed out. His boots crunched toward them across the gravel. "Hey, Lorne," he called up to the veranda. "I figured you was here."

"It's Saturday, Ellis."

"Yeah, I know. But we sort of got us a problem."

"If it's that washroom again, just call the plumber. I'll okay the work order."

"No, it's that—" Ellis glanced uneasily at Evelyn. "It's that Miranda Wood woman."

Tibbetts rose to his feet and went over to the veranda railing. "What about her?"

"You know that hundred thousand bail they set?"

"Yeah."

"Well, someone paid it."

"What?"

"Someone's paid it. We just got the order to release her."

There was a long silence on the veranda. Then, in a low voice laced with venom, Evelyn said, *"Who* paid it?"

"Dunno," said Ellis. "Court says it was anonymous. Came through some Boston lawyer. So what do we do, huh, Lorne?"

Tibbetts let out a deep breath. He rubbed his neck, shifted his weight back and forth a few times. Then he said, "I'm sorry, Evelyn."

"Lorne, you can't do this!" she cried.

"I don't have a choice." He turned back to the other cop. "You got the court order, Ellis. Let her walk."

"I don't understand," said Miranda, staring in bewilderment at her attorney. "Who would do this for me?"

"A friend, obviously," was Randall Pelham's dry response. "A very *good* friend."

"But I don't have any friends with that kind of money. No one with a hundred thousand to spare."

"Well, someone's putting up the bail. My advice is, don't look a gift horse in the mouth."

"If I just knew who it was—"

"It's been handled through some Boston attorney who says his client wishes to stay anonymous."

"Why?"

"Maybe the donor's embarrassed."

To be helping a murderess, she thought.

"It's his—or her—right to remain anonymous. I say, take it. The alternative is to stay in jail. Not exactly the most comfortable spot to be in."

She let out a deep breath. "No, it isn't." In fact, it had been horribly bleak in that cell. She'd spent the past week staring at the window, longing for the simple pleasure of a walk by the sea. Or a decent meal. Or just the warmth of the sunshine on her face. Now it was all within reach.

"I wish I knew who to thank," she said softly.

"Not possible, Miranda. I say, just accept the favor." He snapped his briefcase shut.

Suddenly he irritated her, this kid barely out of braces, so smart and snazzy in his gray suit. Randall Pelham, Esquire.

"The arrangements are made. You can leave this afternoon. Will you be staying at your house?"

She paused, shuddering at the memory of Richard's body in her bed. The house had since been cleaned, courtesy of a housekeeping service. Her neighbor Mr. Lanzo had arranged it all, had told her the place looked fine now. It would be as if nothing had happened in that bedroom. There would be no signs of violence at all.

Except in her memory.

But where else could she go?

She nodded. "I—I suppose I'll go home."

"You know the drill, right? Don't leave the county. Bass Harbor's as far as you can go. Stay in touch at all times. And don't, I repeat don't, go around discussing the case. My job's tough enough as it is."

"And we wouldn't want to tax your abilities, would we?" she said under her breath.

He didn't seem to hear the comment. Or maybe he was ignoring her. He strode out of the cell, then turned to gaze at her. "We can still try a plea bargain."

She looked him in the eye. "No."

"That way we could limit the damage. You could walk out of here in ten years instead of twenty-five."

"I didn't kill him."

For a moment Pelham returned her gaze. With a shrug of impatience, he turned. "Plea bargain," he said. "That's my advice. Think about it."

She *did* think about it, all afternoon as she sat in that stark cell waiting for the release papers.

But as soon as she stepped out of the building and walked, as a free woman, into the sunshine, all thoughts of trading away even ten years of her life seemed unimaginable. She stood there on the sidewalk, gazing up at the sky, inhaling the sweetest air she'd ever breathed in her life.

She decided to walk the mile to her house.

By the time she came within sight of her front yard, her cheeks were flushed, her muscles pleasantly tired. The house looked the same as it always had, shingled cottage, trim lawn—which someone had obviously watered in her absence—brick walkway, a hedge of hydrangea bushes sprouting fluffy white clouds of flowers. Not a large house, but it was hers.

She started up the walkway.

Only when she'd mounted the porch steps did she see the vicious words someone had soaped on her front window. She halted, stung by the cruelty of the message.

Killer.

In sudden fury she swiped at the glass with her sleeve. The accusing words dissolved into soapy streaks. Who could have written such a horrible thing? Surely none of her neighbors. Kids. Yes, that's who it must have been. A bunch of punks. Or summer people.

As if that made it easier to dismiss. No one much cared what the summer people thought. The ones who lived on the island year round—those were the ones whose opinions counted. The ones you had to face every day.

She paused at the front door, almost afraid to go in. At last she reached for the knob and entered.

Inside, to her relief, everything seemed orderly, just the way things should be. A bill, made out by the Conscientious Cleaners Company, lay on the end table. "Complete cleaning," read the work order. "Special attention to the master bedroom. Remove stains." The work order was signed by her neighbor, Mr. Lanzo, bless him. Slowly she made a tour of inspection. She glanced in the kitchen, the bathroom, the spare bedroom. Her bedroom she left for last, because it was the most painful to confront. She stood in the doorway, taking in the neatly made bed, the waxed floor, the spotless area rug. No signs of murder, no signs of death. Just a sunny bedroom with plain farmhouse fur-

niture. She stood there, taking it all in, not budging even
when the phone rang in the living room. After a while the
ringing stopped.

She went into the bedroom and sat on the bed. It seemed
like a bad dream now, what she'd seen here. She thought,
*If I just concentrate hard enough, I'll wake up. I'll find it
was a nightmare.* Then she stared down at the floor and
saw, by the foot of the bed, a brown stain in the oak planks.

At once she rose and left the room.

She walked into the living room just as the phone rang
again. Automatically she picked up the receiver. "Hello?"

"Lizzie Borden took an ax and gave her mother forty
whacks. When she saw what she had done, she gave her
father forty-one!"

Miranda dropped the receiver. In horror she backed
away, staring at the dangling earpiece. The caller was
laughing now. She could hear the giggles, cruel and child-
like, emanating from the receiver. She scrambled forward,
grabbed the earpiece and slammed it down on the cradle.

The phone rang again.

She picked it up.

"Lizzie Borden took an ax—"

"Stop it!" she screamed. "Leave me alone!"

She hung up and again the phone rang.

This time she didn't answer it. In tears, she ran out the
kitchen door and into the garden. There she sank into a
heap on the lawn. Birds chirped overhead. The smell of
warm soil and flowers drifted sweetly in the afternoon. She
buried her face in the grass and cried.

Inside, the phone kept on ringing.

Four

Miranda stood alone and unnoticed outside the cemetery gates. Through the wrought-iron grillwork she could see the mourners grouped about the freshly dug grave. It was a large gathering, as befitted a respected member of the community. *Respected, perhaps,* she added to herself. *But was he beloved?* Did any among them, including his wife, truly love him? *I thought I did. Once….*

The voice of Reverend Marriner was barely a murmur. Much was lost in the rustle of the lilac branches overhead. She strained to hear the words. "Loving husband…always be missed…cruel tragedy…Lord, forgive…"

Forgive.

She whispered the word, as though it were a prayer that could somehow pull her from the jaws of guilt. But who would forgive her?

Certainly not anyone in that gathering of mourners.

She recognized almost every face there. Among them were her neighbors, her colleagues from the newspaper, her friends. *Make that former friends,* she thought with bitterness. Then there were those too lofty to have made her acquaintance, the ones who moved in social circles to which Miranda had never gained entrance.

She saw the grim but dry-eyed Noah DeBolt, Evelyn's father. There was Forrest Mayhew, president of the local bank, attired in his regulation gray suit and tie. In a category all to herself was Miss Lila St. John, the local flower and garden nut, looking freeze-dried at the eternal age of seventy-four. And then, of course, there were the Tremains. They formed a tragic tableau, poised beside the open grave. Evelyn stood between her son and Chase Tremain, as though she needed both men to steady her. Her daughter, Cassie, stood apart, almost defiantly so. Her flowered peach dress was in shocking contrast to the background of grays and blacks.

Yes, Miranda knew them all. And they knew her.

By all rights she should be standing there with them. She had once been Richard's friend; she owed it to him to say goodbye. She should follow her heart, consequences be damned.

But she lacked the courage.

So she remained on the periphery, a lone and voiceless exile, watching as they laid to rest the man who had once been her lover.

She was still there when it was over, when the mourners began to depart in a slow and steady procession through the gates. She saw their startled glances, heard the gasps, the murmurs of "Look, it's her." She met their gazes calmly. To flee would have seemed an act of cowardice. *I may not be brave,* she thought, *but I am not a coward.* Most of them quickly passed by, averting their eyes. Only Miss Lila St. John returned Miranda's gaze, and the look she gave her was neither friendly nor unfriendly. It was merely thoughtful. For an instant Miranda thought she saw a flicker of a smile in those searching eyes, and then Miss St. John, too, moved on.

A sharp intake of breath made Miranda turn.

The Tremains had halted by the gate. Slowly Evelyn raised her hand and pointed it at Miranda. "You have no right," she whispered. "No right to be here."

"Mom, forget it," said Phillip, tugging her arm. "Let's just go home."

"She doesn't belong here."

"Mom—"

"Get her away from here!" Evelyn lunged toward Miranda, her hands poised to claw.

At once Chase stepped between the two women. He pulled Evelyn against him, trapping her hands in his. "Evelyn, don't! I'll take care of it, okay? I'll talk to her. Just go home. Please." He glanced at the twins. "Phillip, Cassie! Come on, take your mother home. I'll be along later."

The twins each took an arm and Evelyn allowed herself to be led away. But when they reached their car she turned and yelled, "Don't let the bitch fool you, Chase! She'll twist you around, the way she did Richard!"

Miranda stumbled back a step, physically reeling from the impact of those accusing words. She felt the gate against her back swing away, found herself grabbing at it for support. The cold wrought iron felt like the only solid thing she could cling to and she held on for dear life. The squeal of the gate hinges suddenly pierced her cloud of confusion. She found she was standing in a clump of daisies, that the others had gone, and that she and Chase Tremain were the only people remaining in the cemetery.

He was watching her. He stood a few feet away, as though wary of approaching her. As though she was some sort of dangerous animal. She could see the suspicion in his dark eyes, the tension of his pose. How aristocratic he looked today, so remote, so untouchable in that charcoal suit. The jacket showed off to perfection his wide shoulders and narrow waist. Tailored, of course. A real Tremain wouldn't consider any off-the-rack rag.

Still, she had trouble believing this man, with his Gypsy eyes and his jet black hair, was a Tremain.

For a year she had gazed up at those portraits in the newspaper building. They'd hung on the wall opposite her desk, five generations of Tremain men, all of them ruddy faced and blue eyed. Richard's portrait, just as blue eyed, had fit right in. Hang a portrait of Chase Tremain on that same wall and it would look like a mistake.

"Why did you come here, Ms. Wood?" he asked.

She raised her chin. "Why shouldn't I?"

"It's inappropriate, to say the least."

"It's very appropriate. I cared about him. We were—we were friends."

"Friends?" His voice rose in mocking disbelief. "Is that what you call it?"

"You don't know anything about it."

"I know that you were more than friends. What shall we call your relationship, Ms. Wood? An affair? A romance?"

"Stop it."

"A hot little tumble on the boss's couch?"

"Stop it, damn you! It wasn't like that!"

"No, of course not. You were just *friends.*"

"All right! All right…." She looked away, so he wouldn't see her tears. Softly she said, "We were lovers."

"At last. A word for it."

"And friends. Most of all, friends. I wish to God it had stayed that way."

"So do I. At least he'd still be alive."

She stiffened. Turning back to him she said, "I didn't kill him."

He sighed. "Of course you didn't."

"He was already dead. I found him—"

"In your house. In your bed."

"Yes. In my bed."

"Look Ms. Wood. I'm not the judge and jury. Don't waste your breath with me. I'm just here to tell you to stay away from the family. Evelyn's gone though enough hell. She doesn't need constant reminders. If we need to, we'll get a restraining order to keep you away. One false move and you'll be back in jail. Right where you belong."

"You're all alike," she said. "You Tremains and DeBolts. All cut from the same fancy silk. Not like the rest of us, who can be shoved out of sight. Right where we belong."

"It's not a matter of which cloth we're cut from. It's a matter of cold-blooded murder." He took a step toward her. She didn't move. She couldn't; her back was against the gate. "What happened, exactly?" he said, moving closer. "Did Richard break some sacred promise? Refuse to leave his wife? Or did he just come to his senses and decide he was walking out on you?"

"That's not what happened."

"So what did happen?"

"I walked out on *him!*"

Chase gazed down at her, skepticism shadowing every line of his face. "Why?"

"Because it was over. Because it was all wrong, everything between us. I wanted to get away. I'd already left the paper."

"He fired you?"

"I quit. Look in the files, Mr. Tremain. You'll find my letter of resignation. Dated two weeks ago. I was going to leave the island. Head somewhere I wouldn't have to see him every day. Somewhere I wouldn't be constantly reminded of what a disaster I'd made of things."

"Where were you planning to go?"

"It didn't matter. Just away." She looked off, past the gravestones. Far beyond the cemetery lay the sea. She could catch glimpses of it through the trees. "I grew up just fifty miles from here. Right across the water. This bay is my home. I've always loved it. Yet all I could think about was getting away."

She turned to look at him. "I was already free of him. Halfway back to happiness. Why should I kill Richard?"

"Why was he in your house?"

"He insisted on meeting me. I didn't want to see him. So I left and went for a walk. When I came back, I found him."

"Yes, I've heard your version. At least your story's consistent."

"It's also the truth."

"Truth, fiction." He shrugged. "In your case it all blends together, doesn't it?" Abruptly he turned and headed up the cemetery drive.

"What if it's *all* truth?" she called after him.

"Stay away from the family, Ms. Wood!" he yelled over his shoulder. "Or I'll have to call in Lorne Tibbetts."

"Just for a moment, consider the possibility that I didn't kill him! That someone else did!"

He was still walking away.

"Maybe it's someone you know!" she shouted. "Think about it! Or do you already know and you want me to take the blame? Tell me, Mr. Tremain! Who *really* killed your brother?"

That brought Chase to a sudden halt. He knew he should keep walking. He knew it was a mistake to engage the woman in any more of this insane dialogue. It *was* insane. Or she was insane. Yet he couldn't break away, not yet. What she'd just said had opened up too many frightening possibilities.

Slowly he turned to face her. She stood absolutely still, her gaze fixed on him. The afternoon sun washed her head with a coppery glow. All that beautiful hair seemed to overwhelm her face. She looked surprisingly fragile in that black dress, as though a strong gust might blow her away.

Was it possible? he wondered. Could this woman really have picked up a knife? Raised the blade over Richard's body? Plunged it down with so much rage, so much strength, that the tip had pierced straight through to his spine?

Slowly he moved toward her. "If you didn't kill him," he said, "who did?"

"I don't know."

"That's a pretty disappointing answer."

"He had enemies—"

"Angry enough to kill him?"

"He ran a newspaper. He knew things about certain people in this town. And he wasn't afraid to print the truth."

"Which people? What sort of scandal are we talking about?"

He saw her hesitate, wondered if she was dredging up some new lie.

"Richard was writing an article," she said. "About a local developer named Tony Graffam. He runs a company called Stone Coast Trust. Richard said he had proof of fraud—"

"My brother had paid reporters on his staff. Why would he bother to do his own writing?"

"It was a personal crusade of his. He was set on ruining Stone Coast. He needed just one last piece of evidence. Then he was going to print."

"And did he?"

"No. The article was supposed to appear two weeks ago. It never did."

"Who stopped it?"

"I don't know. You'd have to talk to Jill Vickery."

"The managing editor?"

Miranda nodded. "She knew the article was in the works and she wasn't crazy about the idea. Richard was the driving force behind the story. He was even willing to risk a libel suit. In fact, Tony Graffam has already threatened to sue."

"So we have one convenient suspect. Tony Graffam. Anyone else?"

She hesitated. "Richard wasn't a popular man."

"Richard?" He shook his head. "I doubt that. I was the brother with the popularity problem."

"Two months ago he cut salaries at the *Herald.* Laid off a third of the staff."

"Ah. So we have more suspects."

"He hurt people. Families—"

"Including his own."

"You don't know how hard it is these days! How desperate people are for work. Oh, he talked a good story. About how sorry he was to be laying people off. How it hurt him just as much as it hurt everyone else. It was *garbage*. I heard him talking about it later, to his accountant. He said, 'I cut the deadwood, just as you advised.' Deadwood. Those employees had been with the *Herald* for years. Richard had the money. He could have carried the loss."

"He was a businessman."

"Right. That's exactly what he was." Her hair, tossed by the wind, was like flames dancing. She was a wild and blazing fire, full of anger at him, at Richard, at the Tremains.

"So we've added to the pool of suspects," he said. "All those poor souls who lost their jobs. And their families. Why don't we toss in Richard's children? His father-in-law? His wife?"

"Yes! Why not Evelyn?"

Chase snorted in disgust. "You're very good, you know that? All that smoke and mirrors. But you haven't convinced me. I hope the jury is just as smart. I hope to hell they see through you and make you pay."

She looked at him mutely, all the fire, all the spirit suddenly drained from her body.

"I've already paid," she whispered. "I'll pay for the rest of my life. Because I'm guilty. Not of killing him. I didn't kill him." She swallowed and looked away. He could no longer see her face, but he could hear the anguish in her voice. "I'm guilty of being stupid. And naive. Guilty of having faith in the wrong man. I really thought I loved your brother. But that was before I knew him. And then, when I did know him, I tried to walk away. I wanted to do it while we were still…friends."

He saw her hand come up and stroke quickly across her face. It suddenly struck him how very brave she was. Not brazen, as he'd first thought upon seeing her today, but truly, heartbreakingly courageous.

She raised her head again, her gaze drawing level to his. The tears she'd tried to wipe away were still glistening on her lashes. He had a sudden, crazy yearning to touch her face, to wipe away the wetness of those tears. And with that yearning came another, just as insane, a man's hunger to know the taste of her lips, the softness of her hair. At once he took a step back, as though retreating from some dangerous flame. He thought, *I can see why you fell for her, Richard. Under different circumstances I might have fallen for her myself.*

"Oh, hell," she muttered in disgust. "What does it matter now, what I felt? To you or to anyone else?" Without looking back she left him and started up the driveway. Her abrupt departure seemed to leave behind an unfillable vacuum.

"Ms. Wood!" he yelled. She kept walking. He called out, "Miranda!" She stopped. "I have one question for you," he said. "Who bailed you out?"

Slowly she turned and looked at him. "You tell me," she said.

And then she walked away.

It was a long walk to the newspaper building. It took Miranda past familiar streets and storefronts, past people she knew. That was the worst part. She felt them staring at her through the shop windows. She saw them huddle in groups and whisper to each other. No one came right out and said anything to her face. They didn't have to. *All I lack,* she thought, *is a scarlet letter sewn on my chest. M for murderess.*

She kept her gaze fixed straight ahead and walked up Limerock Street. The *Herald* building stood before her, a brick-and-slate haven against all those watching eyes. She ducked through the double glass doors, into the newsroom.

Inside, all activity came to a dead halt.

She felt assaulted by all those startled looks.

"Hello, Miranda," said a cool voice.

Miranda turned. Jill Vickery, the managing editor, glided out of the executive office. She hadn't changed clothes since the funeral. On dark-haired, ivory-skinned Jill, the color black looked quite elegant. Her short skirt hissed against her stockings as she clipped across the floor.

"Is there something I can do for you?" Jill asked politely.

"I—I came to get my things."

"Yes, of course." Jill shot a disapproving glance at the other employees, who were still gawking. "Are we all so efficient that we've no more work to do?"

At once everyone redirected their attention to their jobs.

Jill looked at Miranda. "I've already taken the liberty of cleaning out your desk. It's all in a box downstairs."

Miranda was so grateful for Jill's simple civility she scarcely registered annoyance that her desk had been cold-bloodedly emptied of her belongings. She said, "I've also a few things in my locker."

"They should still be there. No one's touched it." There was a silence. "Well," said Jill, a prelude to escape from a socially awkward situation. "I wish you luck. Whatever happens." She started back toward her office.

"Jill?" called Miranda.

"Yes?"

"I was wondering about that article on Tony Graffam. Why it didn't run."

Jill looked at her with frank puzzlement. "Why does it matter?"

"It just does."

Jill shrugged. "It was Richard's decision. He pulled the story."

"Richard's? But he was working on it for months."

"I can't tell you his reasons. I don't know them. He just pulled it. And anyway, I don't think he ever wrote the story."

"But he told me it was nearly finished."

"I've checked his files." Jill turned and walked toward her office. "I doubt he ever got beyond the research stage. You know how he was, Miranda. The master of overstatement."

Miranda stared after her in bewilderment. The master of overstatement. It hurt to admit it, but yes, there was a lot of truth in that label.

People were staring at her again.

She headed down the stairwell and pushed into the women's lounge. There she found Annie Berenger, lacing up running shoes. Annie was dressed in her usual rumpled-reporter attire—baggy drawstring pants, wrinkled cotton shirt. The inside of her locker looked just as disorderly, a mound of wadded-up clothes, towels and books.

Annie glanced up and tossed her head of gray-streaked hair in greeting. "You're back."

"Just to clean out my things." Miranda found the cardboard box with her belongings stuffed under one of the benches. She dragged it out and carried it to her locker.

"I saw you at the funeral," said Annie. "That took guts, Mo."

"I'm not sure guts is the word for it."

Annie shoved her locker door shut and breathed a sigh of relief. "Comfortable at last. I just had to change out of that funeral getup. Can't think in those stupid high heels. Cuts the blood supply to my brain." She finished lacing up her running shoe. "So what's going to happen next? With you, I mean."

"I don't know. I refuse to think beyond a day or two." Miranda opened her locker and began to throw things into the box.

"Rumor has it you have friends in high places."

"What?"

"Someone bailed you out, right?"

"I don't know who it was."

"You must have an idea. Or is this your lawyer's advice, to plead ignorance?"

Miranda gripped the locker door. "Don't, Annie. Please."

Annie cocked her head, revealing all the lines and freckles of too many summers in the sun. "I'm being a jerk, aren't I? Sorry. It's just that Jill assigned me to the trial. I don't like having to drag an old colleague across the front page." She watched as Miranda emptied the locker and shut the door. "So. Can I get a statement from you?"

"I didn't do it."

"I've already heard that one."

"Want to earn a Pulitzer?" Miranda turned, squarely faced her. "Help me find out who killed him."

"You'll have to give me a lead, first."

"I don't have one."

Annie sighed. "That's the problem. Whether or not you did it, you're still the obvious suspect."

Miranda picked up the box and headed up the stairs. Annie trailed behind her.

"I thought real reporters went after the truth," said Miranda.

"This reporter," said Annie, "is basically lazy and angling for early retirement."

"At your age?"

"I turn forty-seven next month. I figure that's a good age to retire. If I can just get Irving to pop the question, it'll be a life of bonbons and TV soaps."

"You'd hate it."

"Oh, yeah." Annie laughed. "I'd be just miserable."

They walked into the newsroom. At once Miranda felt all those gazes turn her way. Annie, oblivious to their audience, went to her desk, threw her locker keys in her drawer and pulled out a pack of cigarettes. "You happen to have a light?" she asked Miranda.

"You always ask me, and I never have one."

Annie turned and yelled, "Miles!"

The summer intern sighed resignedly and tossed her a cigarette lighter. "Just give it back," he said.

"You're too young to smoke, anyway," snapped Annie.

"So were you once, Berenger."

Annie grinned at Miranda. "I love these boy wonders. They're so damn petulant."

Miranda couldn't help smiling. She sat on the desktop and looked at her ex-colleague. As always, Annie wore a wreath of cigarette smoke. It was part addiction, part prop, that cigarette. Annie had earned her reporter's stripes in a Boston newsroom where the floor was said to be an inch deep in cigarette butts.

"You do believe me, don't you?" asked Miranda softly. "You don't really think…"

Annie looked her straight in the eye. "No. I don't. And I was kidding about being lazy," said Annie. "I've been digging. I'll come up with something. It's not like I'm doing it out of friendship or anything. I mean, I could find out things that could hurt you. But it's what I have to do."

Miranda nodded. "Then start with this."

"What?"

"Find out who bailed me out."

Annie nodded. "A reasonable first step."

The back office door swung open. Jill Vickery came out and glanced around the newsroom. "Marine distress call. Sailboat's taking on water. Who wants the story?"

Annie slunk deep in her chair.

Miles sprang to his feet. "I'll take it."

"Coast Guard's already on the way. Hire a launch if you have to. Go on, get going. You don't want to miss the rescue." Jill turned and looked at Annie. "Are you busy at the moment?"

Annie shrugged. "I'm always busy."

Jill nodded toward Miles. "He'll need help. Go with the kid." She turned back to her office.

"I can't."

Jill stopped, turned to confront Annie. "Are you refusing my assignment?"

"Yeah. Sort of."

"On what grounds?"

Annie blew out a long, lazy puff of smoke. "Seasickness."

"I knew she'd confuse you, Chase. I just knew it. You don't understand her the way I do."

Chase looked up from the porch chair where he'd been brooding for the past hour. He saw that Evelyn had changed out of her black dress and was now wearing an obscenely bright lime green. He knew he should feel sorry for his sister-in-law, but at the moment Evelyn looked more in need of a stiff drink than of pity. He couldn't help comparing her to Miranda Wood. Miranda, with her ill-fitting black dress and her windblown hair, so alone on that cemetery hillside. He wondered if Richard ever knew how much damage he'd done to her, or if he'd ever cared.

"You haven't said a word since you got home," complained Evelyn. "What is going on with you?"

"Just how well did you know Miranda Wood?" he asked.

She sat down and fussily arranged the folds of her green dress. "I've heard things. I know she grew up in Bass Harbor. Went to some—some state university. Had to do it all on scholarship. Couldn't afford it otherwise. Really, not a very good family."

"Meaning what?"

"Mill workers."

"Ah. Dregs of the earth."

"What is the matter with you, Chase?"

He rose to his feet. "I need to take a walk."

"Oh. I'll go with you." She jumped to her feet, instantly wreaking havoc on all those nicely arranged folds of her dress.

"No. I'd like to be alone for a while. If you don't mind."

Evelyn looked as if she minded very much, but she managed to cover it gracefully. "I understand, Chase. We all need to mourn in our own way."

He felt a distinct sense of relief as he walked away from that front porch. The house had started to feel oppressive, as though the weight of all those memories had crowded out the breathable air. For a half hour he walked aimlessly. Only as his feet carried him closer to town did he begin to move with a new sense of purpose.

He headed straight for the newspaper building.

He was greeted by Jill Vickery, the sleekly attractive managing editor. It was just like Richard to surround himself with gorgeous women. Chase had met her earlier that day, at the funeral. Then, as now, she played the part of the professional to the hilt.

"Mr. Tremain," she said, offering her hand. "What a pleasure to see you again. May I show you around?"

"I was just wondering..." He glanced around the newsroom, which was currently occupied by only a bare-bones staff: the layout man arranging ads, another one staring at a computer screen, and that sloppy reporter puffing on a cigarette as she talked on the phone.

"Yes?" asked Jill.

"If I could go over some of my brother's files."

"Business or personal files?"

"Both."

She hesitated, then led him into the back office and through a door labeled Richard Tremain, Owner and Publisher. "These aren't all his files, you understand. He kept most of them here, but some he kept at home or at the cottage."

"You mean Rose Hill?"

"Yes. He liked to work out there, on occasion." She pointed to the desk. "The key's in the top drawer. Please let me know if you take anything."

"I wasn't planning to."

She paused, as though uncertain whether to trust him. But what choice did she have? He was, after all, the publisher's brother. At last she turned and left.

Chase waited for the door to shut, then he unlocked the file cabinet. He flipped immediately to the *W*'s.

He found a file on Miranda Wood.

Chase carried it to the desk and spread it open. It appeared to be a routine personnel record. The employment application was dated one year ago, when Miranda was twenty-eight. Her address was listed as 18 Willow Street. In the attached photograph she was smiling; it was the face of a confident young woman with her whole life ahead of her. It almost hurt to see how happy she looked. Her university record was outstanding. If anything, she was overqualified for her job as copy editor. Under the question "Why do you want this job?" she had written, "I grew up near Penobscot Bay. I want, more than anything, to live and work in the place I've always called home." He flipped through the pages and scanned the semiannual employee evaluation, filled out by Jill Vickery. It was excellent. He turned to the last page.

There was a letter of resignation, dated two weeks ago.

To: Richard Tremain, Publisher, *Island Herald*.
Dear Mr. Tremain,
I hereby notify you of my resignation from my position as copy editor. My reasons are personal. I would greatly appreciate a letter of reference, as I plan to seek employment elsewhere.

That was all. No explanations, no regrets. Not even a hint of recrimination.

So she told me the truth, he thought. *She really did walk off the job.*

"Mr. Tremain?" It was Jill Vickery, back again. "Are you looking for anything in particular? Maybe I can help you."

"Maybe you can."

She came in and gracefully settled into the chair across from him. Her gaze at once took in the file on the desk. "I see you have Miranda's employee record."

"Yes. I'm trying to understand what happened. Why she did it."

"I think you should know she was here just a short while ago."

"In the building?"

"She came to collect her things. I'm glad you two avoided a, uh…unexpected encounter."

He nodded. "So am I."

"Let me say this, Mr. Tremain. I'm very sorry about your brother. He was a wonderful man, an exceptional writer. He truly believed in the power of the printed word. We're going to miss him."

It was a canned speech, but she delivered it with such sincerity he was almost convinced she meant it. Jill Vickery certainly had the PR down flat.

"I understand Richard had a story in the pipeline," he said. "Something about a company called Stone Coast Trust. You familiar with it?"

Jill sighed. "Why does this particular article keep coming up?"

"Someone else interested?"

"Miranda Wood. She just asked about it. I told her that as far as I know, the story was never written. At least, I never saw it."

"But it was scheduled to run?"

"Until Richard canceled it."

"Why?"

She sat back and smoothly flicked her hair off her face.

"I wouldn't know. I suspect he didn't have enough evidence to go to print."

"What, exactly, is the story on Stone Coast Trust?"

"Small-town stuff, really. Not very interesting to outsiders."

"Try me."

"It had to do with developers' rights. Stone Coast has been buying up property on the north shore. Near Rose Hill Cottage, as a matter of fact, so you know how lovely it is up there. Pristine coastline, trees. Tony Graffam—he's president of Stone Coast—claimed he was out to preserve the area. Then we heard rumors of a high-class development in the works. And then, a month ago, the zoning on those lots was abruptly changed from conservation to resort. It's now wide open to development."

"That's all there is to the article?"

"In a nutshell. May I ask the reason for your interest?"

"It was something Miranda Wood told me. About other people having motives to kill my brother."

"In this case, she's stretching the point." Jill rose to her feet. "But one can hardly blame her for trying. She hasn't much else to grab onto."

"You think she'll be convicted?"

"I wouldn't want to hazard a guess. But from what my news staff tells me, it sounds likely."

"You mean that reporter? Annie something?"

"Annie Berenger. Yes, she's assigned to the story."

"Can I talk to her?"

Jill frowned. "Why?"

He shook his head. "I don't know. I guess I'm just trying to understand who this Miranda Wood really is. Why she would kill." He sat back, ran his hand through his hair. "I still can't quite fit the pieces together. I thought, maybe someone who's been watching the case—someone who knew her personally…"

"Of course. I understand." The words were sympathetic but her eyes were indifferent. "I'll send Annie in to talk to you."

She left. A moment later Annie Berenger appeared.

"Come in," said Chase. "Have a seat."

Annie shut the door and sat in the chair across from him. She looked like a reporter: frizzy red hair streaked with gray, sharp eyes, wrinkled slacks. She also reeked of cigarettes. It brought back memories of his father. All she needed was a splash of whiskey on her breath. A good old newsman's smell.

She was watching him with clear suspicion. "Boss lady says you want to talk about Miranda."

"You knew her pretty well?"

"The word is *know*. Present tense. Yes, I do."

"What do you think of her?"

Her mouth twitched into a smile. "This is your own private investigation?"

"Call it my quest for the truth. Miranda Wood denies killing my brother. What do you think?"

Annie lit a cigarette. "You know, I used to cover the police beat in Boston."

"So you're familiar with murder."

"In a manner of speaking." Leaning back, she thoughtfully exhaled a cloud of smoke. "Miranda had the motive. Oh, we all knew about the affair. It's hard to hide something like that in this newsroom. I tried to, well, advise her against it. But she follows her heart, you know? And it got her into trouble. That's not to say she did it. Killed him." Annie flicked off an ash. "I don't think she did."

"Then who did?"

Annie shrugged.

"You think it's tied to the Tony Graffam story?"

Annie's eyebrow shot up. "You dig stuff up fast. Must run in the family, that newsman's nose."

"Miranda Wood says Richard had a story about to break. True?"

"He said he did. I know he was writing it. He had a few more details to check before it went to print."

"What details?"

"Financial data, about Stone Coast Trust. Richard had just got his hands on some account information."

"Why didn't the article get to print?"

"Honest opinion?" Annie snorted. "Because Jill Vickery didn't want to risk a libel suit."

Chase frowned. "But Jill says the article doesn't exist. That Richard never wrote it."

Annie blew out a last breath of smoke and stubbed out her cigarette in the ashtray. "Here's a piece of wisdom for you, Mr. T," she said. She looked him in the eye. "Never trust your editor."

Did the article exist or didn't it?

Chase spent the next hour searching the files in Richard's office. He found nothing under *G* for Graffam or *S* for Stone Coast Trust. He tried a few more headings, but none of them panned out. Did Richard keep the file at home?

It was late afternoon when he finally returned to the house. To his relief, Evelyn and the twins were out. He had the place to himself. He went straight into Richard's home office and continued his search for the Graffam file.

He didn't find it. Yet Miranda claimed it existed. So did Annie Berenger.

Something strange was going on, something that added to all his doubts about Miranda's guilt. He mentally played back all the holes in the prosecution's case. The lack of fingerprints on the murder weapon. The fact she had passed the polygraph test. And the woman herself—proud, unyielding in her protestations of innocence.

He gave up trying to talk himself out of his next move. There was no way around it. Not if he wanted to know more. Not if he wanted to shake these doubts.

He had to talk to Miranda Wood.

He pulled on his windbreaker and headed out into the dusk.

Five blocks later he turned onto Willow Street. It was just the way he'd remembered it, a tidy, middle-class neighborhood with inviting front porches and well-tended lawns. Through the fading light he could just make out the address numbers. A few more houses to go....

Farther up the street a screen door slammed shut. He saw a woman come down her porch steps and start toward him along the sidewalk. He recognized her silhouette, the thick cloud of hair, the slim figure clad in jeans. She'd taken only a few steps when she spotted him and stopped dead in her tracks.

"I have to talk to you," he said.

"I made a promise, remember?" she answered. "Not to go near you or your family. Well, I'm keeping that promise." She turned and started to walk away.

"This is different. I have to ask you about Richard."

She kept walking.

"Will you listen to me?"

"That's how I got into this mess!" she shot back over her shoulder. "Listening to a Tremain!"

He watched in frustration as she headed swiftly up the street. It was useless to pursue her. She was already a block away now, and by the set of her shoulders he could tell she wasn't going to change her mind. In fact, she had just stepped off the sidewalk and was crossing the street, as though to put the width of the road between them.

Forget her, he thought. *If she's too stubborn to listen, let her go to jail.*

Chase turned and had started in the opposite direction when a car drove past. He would scarcely have noticed it except for one detail: its headlights were off. A few paces was all it took for Chase to register that fact. He stopped, turned. Far ahead, Miranda's slender figure was crossing the street.

By then the car had moved halfway down the block.

The driver'll see her in time, he thought. *He has to see her.*

The car's engine suddenly revved up in a threatening growl of power. Tires screeched. The car leaped forward in a massive blur of steel and smoke, and roared ahead through the shadows.

It was aiming straight for Miranda.

Five

The headlights sprang on, trapping its insubstantial victim in a blaze of light.

"Look out!" Chase shouted.

Miranda whirled and found her eyes flooded with a terrible, blinding brightness. Even as the car shot closer and those lights threatened to engulf her, she was paralyzed by disbelief, by the detached sense of certainty that this was not really happening. She had no time to reason it out. An instant before that ton of steel could slam into her body, her reflexes took over. She flung herself sideways, out of the path of the onrushing headlights.

Suddenly she was flying, suspended for an eternity in the summer darkness as death rushed past her in a roar of wind and light.

And then she was lying on the grass.

She didn't know how long she had been there. She knew only that the grass was damp, that her head hurt and that gentle hands were stroking her face. Someone called her name, again and again. It was a voice she knew, a voice she thought, in that confused moment, she must have known all her life. Its very timbre seemed to blanket her with the warmth of safety.

Again he called her name, and this time she heard panic in his voice. *He's afraid. Why?*

She opened her eyes and dazedly focused on his face. That's when she registered exactly who he was. All illusion of safety fell away.

"Don't." She brushed his hand aside. "Don't touch me."

"Lie still."

"I don't need you!" She struggled to sit up, but found herself unable to move under his restraining hands. He had her pinned by her shoulders to the grass.

"Look," he said, his voice maddeningly reasonable. "You took a mean tumble. You might have broken something—"

"I said, don't touch me!" Defiantly she shoved him away and sat up. Pure rage propelled her to her knees. Then, as the night wavered before her eyes, she found herself sinking back to the grass. There she sat and clutched her spinning head. "Oh, God," she groaned. "Why can't you just—just go away and leave me alone."

"Not on your life," came the answer, grim and resolute.

To her amazement she was suddenly, magically lifted up into the air. Through her anger she had to admit it felt good to be carried, good to be held, even if the man holding her was Chase Tremain. She was floating, borne like a featherweight through the darkness. *Toward what?* she wondered with sudden apprehension.

"That's enough," she protested. "Let me down."

"Only a few more steps."

"I hope you get a hernia."

"Keep up the damn wiggling and I will."

He swept her up the porch steps and in the front door. With unerring instinct he carried her straight to the bedroom and managed to flick on the wall switch. The room—the bed—sprang into view. The bed where she'd found Richard. Though the blood was gone, the mattress new and unstained, this room would always remind her of death. She hadn't slept here since that night, would never sleep here again.

She shuddered against him. "Please," she whispered, turning her face against his chest. "Not here. Not this room."

For a moment he paused, not understanding. Then, gently he answered, "Whatever you say, Miranda."

He carried her back to the living room and lowered her onto the couch. She felt the cushions sag as he sat beside her. "Does anything hurt?" he asked. "Your back? Your neck?"

"My shoulder, a little. I think I fell on it."

She flinched at the touch of his hands. Carefully he maneuvered her arm, checking its range of motion. She was scarcely aware of the occasional twinges he evoked from her muscles. Her attention was too acutely focused on the face gazing down at her. Once again she was struck by how unlike Richard he was. It wasn't just the blackness of his hair and eyes. It was his calmness under fire, as though he held any emotions he might be feeling under tight rein. This was not a man who'd easily reveal himself, or his secrets, to anyone.

"It seems all right," he said, straightening. "Still, I'd better call a doctor. Who do you see?"

"Dr. Steiner."

"Steiner? Is that old goat still in practice?"

"Look, I'm okay. I don't need to see him."

"Let's just be on the safe side." He reached for the telephone.

"But Dr. Steiner doesn't make house calls," she protested. "He never has."

"Then tonight," Chase said grimly, dialing the phone, "I guess we're going to make history."

Lorne Tibbetts poured himself a cup of coffee and turned to look at Chase. "What I want to know is, what in blazes are you doing here?"

Chase, leaning over Miranda's kitchen table, wearily rubbed his face. "To tell you the truth, Lorne," he muttered, "I don't know."

"Oh."

"I guess I thought I could…figure things out. Make sense of what's happened."

"That's our job, Chase. Not yours."

"Yeah, I know. But—"

"You don't think I'm doing a good job?"

"I just get this feeling there's more than meets the eye. Now I know there is."

"You mean that car?" Lorne shrugged. "Doesn't prove a thing."

"He was *aiming* for her. I saw it. As soon as she stepped into the street he hit the gas."

"He?"

"He, she. It was dark. I didn't see the driver. Just the license plate. And the taillights. Big car, American. I'm pretty sure."

"Color?"

"Dark. Black, maybe blue."

Lorne nodded. "You're not a bad witness, Chase."

"What do you mean?"

"I had Ellis check on that license number. Matches a brown '88 Lincoln, registered to an island resident."

"Who?"

"Mr. Eddie Lanzo. Ms. Wood's next-door neighbor."

Chase stared at him. "Her neighbor? Have you brought him in yet?"

"The car was stolen, Chase. You know how it is around here. Folks leave their keys in the ignition. We found the car over by the pier."

Chase sat back, stunned. "So the driver's untraceable," he said. "That makes it even more likely he was trying to kill her."

"It just means it was some crazy kid out for a joyride. Got his hands on that wheel, got a little overwhelmed by all that power, pushed too hard on the gas pedal."

"Lorne, he was out to kill her."

Lorne sat down and looked him in the eye. "And what are you out to do?"

"Learn the truth."

"You don't believe she did it?"

"I've been hearing some things, Lorne. Other names, other motives. Tony Graffam, for instance."

"We've looked into that. Graffam was off the island when your brother was killed. I have half a dozen witnesses who'll say so."

"He could have hired someone."

"Graffam was in big enough trouble with that north shore development. Charges of bribing the land planning commission. That article would've simply been the last nail in the coffin. Anyway, how does this tie in with what happened tonight? Why would he go after Miranda Wood?"

Chase fell silent at that question. He couldn't see a motive, either. Other people in town might dislike Miranda, but who would go to the trouble of killing her?

"Maybe we're looking at this the wrong way," said Chase. "Let's ask a more basic question. Who put up the bail money? Someone wanted her out so badly he put up a hundred thousand dollars."

"A secret admirer?"

"In jail she's safe. Out here she's a sitting duck. You have any idea who bailed her out, Lorne?"

"No."

"The money could be traced."

"A lawyer handled the transfer of funds. All cash. Came from some Boston account. Only the bank knows the account holder's identity. And they aren't talking."

"Subpoena the bank. Get the name on that account."

"It'll take time."

"Do it, Lorne. Before something else happens."

Lorne went to the sink and rinsed his coffee cup. "I still don't see why you're getting into this," he said.

Chase himself didn't know the answer. Just this morning he'd wanted Miranda Wood put behind bars. Now he wasn't sure what he wanted. That innocent face, her heartfelt denials of guilt had him thoroughly confused.

He looked around the kitchen, thinking it didn't *look* like the kitchen of a murderess. Plants hung near the window, obviously well tended and well loved. The wallpaper had dainty wildflowers scattered across an eggshell background. Tacked to the refrigerator were snapshots of two little towheaded boys—nephews, maybe?—a schedule of the local garden club meetings and a shopping list. At the bottom of the list was written "cinnamon tea." Was that the sort of beverage a murderess would drink? He couldn't picture Miranda holding a knife in one hand and a cup of herbal tea in the other.

Chase looked around as Dr. Steiner shuffled into the kitchen. Some things on the island never changed, and this old grouch was one of them. He looked exactly the same as Chase remembered from his boyhood, right down to the wrinkled brown suit and the alligator medical bag. "All this to-do," the doctor said disapprovingly. "For nothin' but a muscle strain."

"You sure about that?" asked Chase. "She was sort of dazed for a minute. Right after it happened."

"I looked her over good. She's fine, neurologically speaking. You just keep an eye on her tonight, young man. Make sure she doesn't get into trouble. You know, headache, double vision, confusion—"

"I can't."

"Can't what?"

"I can't stay and watch her. It's awkward. Considering…"

"No kidding," muttered Lorne.

"She's not my responsibility," said Chase. "What do I do?"

Dr. Steiner grunted and turned for the kitchen door. "You figure it out. By the way," he said, pausing in the doorway, "I don't do house calls." The door slammed shut.

Chase turned to find Lorne looking at him. "What?"

"Nothing," said Lorne. He reached for his hat. "I'm going home."

"And what the hell am I supposed to do?"

"That," said Lorne with an I-told-you-so look, "is your problem."

* * *

Miranda lay on the living-room couch and stared at the ceiling. She could hear voices from the kitchen, the sound of the door opening and closing. She wondered what Chase had told them, whether Tibbetts believed any of it. She herself couldn't believe what had happened. But all she had to do was close her eyes and it came back to her: the roar of the car engine, the twin headlights rushing at her.

Who hates me so much they want me dead?

It wasn't hard to come up with an answer. The Tremain family. Evelyn and Phillip and Cassie....

And Chase.

No, that wasn't possible. His shout of warning had saved her life. If not for him, she would be lying right now on a slab in Ben LaPorte's Funeral Home.

That thought made her shudder. Hugging herself, she burrowed deeper into the couch cushions, seeking some safe little nook in which to hide. She heard the kitchen door open and shut again, then footsteps creaked into the living room and approached the couch. She looked up and saw Chase.

Weariness was what she read in his eyes, and uncertainty, as though he hadn't quite made up his mind what should be done next. Or what should be said next. He'd shed his windbreaker. His chambray shirt was the comfortably faded blue of a well-worn, well-loved garment. That shirt reminded her of her father, of how it used to feel to nestle her face against his shoulder, of those wondrous childhood scents of laundry soap and pipe tobacco and safety. That was what she saw in that faded blue shirt, what she longed for.

What she'd never find with this man.

Chase sat in the armchair. A prudent distance away, she noted. *Keeping me at arm's length.*

"Feeling better?" he asked.

"I'll be fine." She kept her voice like his—detached, neutral. She added, "You can leave if you want."

"No. Not yet. I'll wait here awhile, if that's okay. Until Annie gets here."

"Annie?"

"I didn't know who else to call. She said she'd be over to spend the night. You should have someone here to keep an eye on you. Make sure you don't slide into a coma or something."

She gave a tired laugh. "A coma would feel pretty good right now."

"That's not very funny."

She looked up at the ceiling. "You're right. It isn't."

There was a long silence.

Finally he said, "That wasn't an accident, Miranda. He was trying to kill you."

She didn't answer. She lay there fighting back the sob swelling in her throat. *Why should it matter to you?* she thought. *You, of all people.*

"Maybe you haven't heard," he said. "The car belonged to your neighbor. Mr. Lanzo."

She looked at him sharply. "Eddie Lanzo would never hurt me! He's the only one who's stood by me. My one friend in this town."

"I didn't say it was him. Lorne thinks the driver stole Mr. Lanzo's car. They found it abandoned by the pier."

"Poor Eddie," she murmured. "Guess that's the last time he leaves his keys in the car."

"So if it wasn't Eddie, who does want you dead?"

"I can make a wild guess." She looked at him. "So can you."

"Are you referring to Evelyn?"

"She hates me. She has every right to hate me. So do her children." She paused. "So do you."

He was silent.

"You still think I killed him. Don't you?"

Sighing, he raked his fingers through his hair. "I don't know what to think anymore. About you, about anyone. All I can be sure of is what I saw tonight. It's all tied in, this whole bloody mess. It has to be."

He looks so tired, so confused, she thought. *Almost as confused as I am.*

"Maybe you should move out of here for a few days," he said. "Until things get sorted out."

"Where would I go?"

"You must have friends."

"I did." She looked away. "At least, I thought I did. But everything's changed. I pass them on the street and they don't even say hello. Or they cross to the other side. Or they pretend they don't see me. That's the worst of all. Because I begin to think I don't exist." She looked at him. "It's a very small town, Chase. You either fit in, or you don't belong. And there's no way a murderess could ever fit in." She lay back against the cushions and stared at the ceiling. "Besides, this is my house. *My* house. I saved like crazy for the down payment. I won't leave it. It's not much, but at least it's mine."

"I can understand that. It's a nice house."

He sounded sincere enough, but his words struck her as patronizing. The lord of the manor extolling the charms of the shepherd's hovel.

Suddenly annoyed, she sat up. The abrupt movement made the room spin. She clutched her head for a moment, waiting for the spell to pass.

"Look, let's be straight with each other," she muttered through her hands. "It's only a two-bedroom cottage. The basement's damp, the water pipes screech and there's a leak in the kitchen roof. It's not Chestnut Street."

"To be honest," he said quietly, "I never felt at home on Chestnut Street."

"Why not? You were raised there."

"But it wasn't really a home. Not like this house."

Puzzled, she looked up at him. It struck her then how rough around the edges he seemed, a dark, rumpled stranger hulking in her mauve armchair. No, this man didn't quite fit on Chestnut Street. He belonged on the docks, or on the windswept deck of a schooner, not in some stuffy Victorian parlor.

"I'm supposed to believe you'd prefer a cottage on Willow Street to the family mansion?"

"I guess it does sound—I don't know. Phony. But it's true. Know where I spent most of my time as a kid? In the turret, playing around all the trunks and the old furniture. That was the only place in the house where I felt comfortable. The one room no one else cared to visit."

"You sound like the family outcast."

"In a way, I was."

She laughed. "I thought all Tremains were, by definition, *in*."

"One can have the family name and still not be part of the family. Or didn't you ever feel that way?"

"No, I was always very much part of my family. What there was of it." Her gaze drifted to the spinet piano, where the framed photo of her father was displayed. It was a grainy shot, one of the few she still had of him, taken with her old Kodak Brownie. He was grinning at her over the hood of his Chevy, a bald little gnome of a man dressed in blue overalls. She found herself smiling back at the image.

"Your father?" asked Chase.

"Yes. Stepfather, really. But he was every bit as wonderful as any real father."

"I hear he worked for the mill."

She frowned at him. It disturbed her that Chase was obviously acquainted with that detail of her life. A detail that was none of his business. "Yes," she said. "Both my parents did. What else have you heard about me?"

"It's not that I've been checking up on you."

"But you have, haven't you? You and your family have probably run my name through some computer. Criminal check. Family history. Credit report—"

"We've done no such thing."

"Personal life. All the hot and juicy details."

"Where would I find those?"

"Try my police record." In irritation she rose from the couch and moved to the fireplace. There she stood focused on the clock over the mantelpiece. "It's getting late, Mr. Tremain. Annie should be here any minute. You're free to leave, so why don't you?"

"Why don't you sit back down? It makes me nervous, having you up and about."

"I make *you* nervous?" She turned to him. "You hold all the cards. You know everything about me. What my parents did for a living. Where I went to school. Who I slept with. I don't like that."

"Were there that many?"

His retort struck her like a physical blow. She could think of no response to such a cruel question. She was reduced to staring at him in speechless fury.

"Don't answer," he said. "I don't want to know. Your love life's none of my business."

"You're right. It's none of your damn business." She turned away, angrily clutching the mantelpiece with both hands. "No matter what you learn about me, it'll all fit right in with your image of the mill worker's daughter, won't it? Well, I'm not ashamed of where I came from. My parents made an honest living. They didn't have some trust fund to keep them in caviar. Like some families I know," she added, leaving no doubt by the tone of her voice just which family she was referring to.

He acknowledged the insult with a brief silence.

"I'm surprised you fell for Richard," he said. "Considering your attitude toward trust-funders."

"Before I knew Richard, I didn't *have* an attitude problem." She turned to confront him. "Then I got to know him. I saw what the money did to him. For him. He never had to struggle. He always had that green buffer to protect him. It made him careless. Immune to other people's pain." Her jaw came up in a pose of proud disdain. "Just like you."

"Now you're making the assumptions about me."

"You're a Tremain."

"I'm like you. I have a job, Miranda. I work."

"So did Richard. It kept him amused."

"Okay, maybe you're right about Richard. He didn't need to work. The *Herald* was more of a hobby to him, a reason to get up in the morning. And he got a kick out of telling his friends in Boston that he was a publisher. But that was Richard. You can't slap that rich-boy label on me because it won't stick. I was booted out of the family years ago. I don't have a trust fund and I don't own a mansion.

But I do have a job that pays the bills. And, yes, keeps me *amused*."

His anger was tightly controlled but evident all the same. *I've touched a nerve,* she thought. An acutely sensitive one. Chastened, she sat in a chair by the fireplace. "I guess—I guess I assumed a few too many things."

He nodded. "We both did."

In silence they gazed at each other across the room. A truce, however uneasy, had at last settled between them.

"You said you were booted out of the family. Why?" she asked.

"Simple. I got married."

She looked at him in puzzlement. He had said the words without emotion, with the tone of voice one used to describe the weather. "I take it she wasn't a suitable bride."

"Not according to my father."

"The wrong side of the tracks?"

"In a manner of speaking. My father, he was attuned to that sort of thing."

Naturally, she thought. "And was your father right? About those girls from the wrong side of the tracks?"

"That wasn't why we got divorced."

"Why did you?"

"Christine was too…ambitious."

"Hardly a flaw."

"It is when I'm just the rung on the social ladder she's trying to climb."

"Oh."

"And then we had some lean years. I was working all the time, and…" He shrugged. Another silence stretched between them.

"Richard never told me what kind of work you do."

He leaned back, the tension easing away from his face. Unexpectedly he laughed. "Probably because what I do struck him as so damn boring. My partners and I design office buildings."

"You're an architect?"

"Structural engineer. My architect partners do the creative work. I make sure the walls don't come crashing down."

An engineer. Not exactly a fluff career, she thought, but a real, honest job. Like her father had.

She shook her head. "It's strange. When I look at you, I can't quite believe you're his brother. I always assumed…"

"That we'd be a matched set? No, we were definitely different. In more ways than you'll ever know."

Yes, the more she knew about Chase, the less he seemed like a Tremain. And the more she thought she could like him.

"What did you ever see in my brother?" he asked.

His question, voiced so softly, was jarring all the same. It reminded her of the ghosts that still hovered in this house.

She sighed. "I saw what I wanted to see."

"Which was?"

"A man who needed me. A man I could play savior to."

"Richard?"

"Oh, it *seemed* as if he had everything going for him. But he also had this…this vulnerability. This need to be saved. From what, I don't know. Maybe himself."

"And you were going to save him."

She gave a bitter laugh. "I don't know. You don't think about these things. You just feel. And you fall into it…."

"You mean you followed your heart."

She looked up at him. "Yes," she whispered.

"Didn't it seem wrong to you?"

"Of course it did!"

"But?"

Her whole body sagged with the weight of her unhappiness. "I couldn't…see my way out of it. I cared about him. I wanted to be there for him. And he'd string me along. He'd tell me things would work out, as long as we both had faith." She looked down at her hands, clasped together in her lap. "I guess I lost my faith first."

"In him? Or the situation?"

"Him. I began to see the flaws. It came out, after a while. How he manipulated people, used people. If he didn't need you, he'd ignore you. A user, that's what he was. An expert at making people do what he wanted."

"Then you broke it off. How did he react?"

"He couldn't believe it. I don't think anyone ever left *him.* He kept calling me, bothering me. And every day, at work, I'd have to face him. Pretend nothing was going on between us."

"Everyone knew, though."

She shrugged. "Probably. I'm not very good at hiding things. Annie knew, because I told her. And everyone else must have guessed." She sighed. The truth was, she hadn't cared at the time. Love, and then pain, had made her indifferent to public opinion.

They said nothing for a moment. She wondered what he thought of her now, whether any of it made a difference. Suddenly it mattered what he *did* think of her. He was scarcely more than a stranger, and a hostile one, but it mattered very much.

"You're not the first one, you know," he said. "There were other women."

It was a cruel revelation to spring on her, and Chase didn't know why he did it. He only knew that he wanted to give her a good, hard shaking. To shatter any rose-colored illusions she might still harbor about Richard. She might say the feelings were gone, but deep inside, might a few warm memories still linger?

He saw, by the look in her eyes, that his words had had their intended effect. Instantly he regretted the wounds he'd inflicted. Still, shouldn't she know? Shouldn't she be told just how naive she'd been?

"Were there many?" she asked softly.

"Yes."

She looked away, as though to hide the pain from view. "I—I think I knew that. Yes, I must have known that."

"It's just the way he was," said Chase. "He liked being admired. He was like that as a boy, too."

She nodded. And he realized, yes, she did know that about Richard. On some level she must have sensed his unquenchable thirst for admiration. And tried to satisfy it.

Chase had done damage enough. Here she was, demoralized and wounded. *And I pour on the salt.*

I should get out of here, leave her alone.

Where the hell was Annie Berenger?

Miranda seemed to shake herself back to life. She brushed her hair off her face, sat up and looked at him. So much torment in those eyes, he thought. And, at the same time, so much courage.

"You never told me why you're here," she said.

"The doctor thought someone should watch you—"

"No. I mean, why did you come in the first place?"

"Oh." He sat back. "I was at the *Herald* this afternoon. Talked to Jill Vickery, about the Stone Coast Trust article you mentioned. She says it was never written. That Richard never got that far with it."

Miranda shook her head. "I don't understand. I know he had at least a few pages written. I saw them on his desk, at the *Herald*."

"Well, I couldn't find any article. I thought maybe you'd know where to look. Or maybe you'd have it."

She looked at him in bewilderment. "Why would I?"

"I assume Richard was a frequent visitor here."

"But he didn't bring his work. Have you checked the house?"

"It's not there."

She thought about it a moment. "Sometimes," she said, "he'd drive up to the north shore, to write. He had a cottage…"

"You mean Rose Hill. Yes, I suppose I should check there tomorrow."

Their gazes intersected, held. She said, "You're starting to believe me. Aren't you?"

He heard, in her voice, the stirring of hope—however faint. He found himself wanting to respond, to offer her some small scrap of a chance that he might believe her. It was hard *not* to believe her, especially when she looked at him that way, her gaze unwavering, those gray eyes bright and moist. They could rob a man of his common sense, those eyes, could sweep self-control right out from under him. They awakened other sensations as well, disturbing ones. She was sitting more than half a room away, but even at that distance her presence was like some heady perfume, impossible to ignore.

She asked again, softly, "Do you believe me?"

Abruptly he rose to his feet, determined to shake off the

dangerous spell she was weaving around him. "No," he said. "I can't say that I do."

"But don't you see there's something more to this than just a—a crime of passion?"

"I admit, things don't feel quite right. But I'm not ready to believe you. Not by a long shot."

There was a knock on the door. Startled, Chase turned to see the door swing open and Annie Berenger poke her head in.

"Hello, cavalry's here," she called. She came in dressed in an old T-shirt and sweatpants. Blades of wet grass clung to her running shoes. "What's the situation?"

"I'm fine," said Miranda.

"But she needs watching," said Chase. "If there are any problems, Dr. Steiner's number is by the phone."

"Leaving already?" asked Annie.

"They'll be expecting me at home." He went to the door. There he paused and glanced back at Miranda.

She hadn't moved. She just sat there. He had the urge to say something comforting. To tell her that what he'd said earlier wasn't quite true. That he *was* starting to believe her. But he couldn't admit it to her; he could scarcely admit it to himself. And there was Annie, watching everything with her sharp reporter's eyes.

So he merely said, "Good night, Miranda. I hope you're feeling better. And Annie, thanks for the favor." Then he turned and walked out the door.

Outside, it took him a few seconds to accustom his eyes to the darkness. By the time he'd reached the edge of the front yard he could finally make out the walkway under his feet.

He could also see the silhouette of a man standing stoop-shouldered before him on the sidewalk.

Chase halted, instantly tense.

"She okay?" asked the man.

"Who are you?" demanded Chase.

"I could ask the same o' you," came the cranky reply.

"I'm…visiting," said Chase.

"So, is Mo gonna be all right, or what?"

"Mo? Oh, you mean Miranda. Yes, she'll be fine, Mr…."

"Eddie Lanzo. Live next door. Like to keep an eye on her, y'know? Not good, a nice young woman livin' all by herself. And all these crazies runnin' around here, peekin' in windows. Not safe to be female these days."

"Someone's staying with her tonight, so you needn't worry."

"Yeah. Okay. Well, I won't bother her none, then." Eddie Lanzo turned to go back to his house. "Whole island's going to pot, I tell ya," he muttered. "Too many crazies. Last time I leave my keys in the car."

"Mr. Lanzo?" called Chase.

"Yeah?"

"Just a question. I was wondering if you were home the night Richard Tremain was killed?"

"Me?" Eddie snorted. "I'm always home."

"Did you happen to see or hear anything?"

"I already tol' Lorne Tibbetts. I go to bed at nine o'clock sharp, and that's it till morning."

"Then you're a sound sleeper? You didn't hear anything?"

"How can I with my hearing aid turned off?"

"Oh." Chase watched as the man shuffled back to his house, still muttering about Peeping Toms and car thieves. It somehow surprised Chase that a grouchy old geezer like Lanzo would show such concern about Miranda Wood. *A nice young woman,* Lanzo had called her.

What the hell does he know? thought Chase. *What do we ever know about anyone? People have their secrets. I have mine, Miranda Wood has hers.*

He turned and headed for Chestnut Street.

It was a twenty-minute walk, made invigorating by the brisk night air. When at last he stepped in the front door he found that, except for the lamp in the foyer, all the lights were out. Had no one else come home?

Then he heard Evelyn call out his name.

He found her sitting all alone in the darkened parlor. He could barely make out her shadow in the rocking chair. The dim glow of the street lamp through the window framed her silhouette.

"At last you're home," she said.

He started toward one of the lamps. "You need some light in here, Evelyn."

"No, Chase. Don't. I like the dark. I always have."

He paused, uncertain of what to say, what to do. He lingered in the shadows, watching her.

"I've been waiting for you," she murmured. "Where did you go, Chase?"

He paused. "To see Miranda Wood."

Her reaction was cold, dead silence. Even the creak of her rocking chair had stilled.

"She has you in her spell. Doesn't she?" Evelyn whispered.

"There's no spell. I just had some questions to ask her, about Richard." He sighed. "Look, Evelyn, it's been a long day for you. Why don't you go up and get some sleep?"

Still the figure did not move. She sat like a black statue against the window. "That night I called you," she said, "the night he died—I was hoping…"

"Yes?"

Another silence. Then, "I've always liked you, Chase. Since we were kids. I always hoped you'd be the one to propose. Not Richard, but you." The rocking chair began to creak again, softly. "But you never did."

"I was in love with Christine. Remember?"

"Oh, Christine." She hissed out the name in disgust. "She wasn't good enough for you. But you found that out."

"We were mismatched, that's all."

"So were Richard and I."

He didn't know what to say. He knew what she was leading up to, and he wanted to avoid that particular path of conversation. In all those years of growing up together he had never been able to picture himself and Evelyn DeBolt as a couple. Certainly she was attractive enough. And she was closer to his age than she was to Richard's. But he had seen, early on, that she had a talent for manipulating people, for twisting minds and hearts. The same talent Richard had possessed.

And yet, he felt so very sorry for her.

He said gently, "You're just tired, Evelyn. You've had a terrible week. But the worst of it's over now."

"No. The worst part is just beginning. The loneliness."

"You have your children—"

"You'll be leaving soon, won't you?"

"A few more days. I have to. I have a job in Greenwich."

"You could stay. Take over the *Herald*. Phillip's still too young to run it."

"I'd be a lousy publisher. You know that. And I don't belong here anymore. Not on this island."

For a moment they regarded each other through the shadows.

"So that's it, then," she whispered. "For us."

"I'm afraid so."

He saw the silhouette nod sadly.

"Will you be all right?"

"Fine." She gave a soft laugh. "I'll be just fine."

"Good night, Evelyn."

"Good night."

He left her sitting there by the window. Only as he moved toward the stairwell did he suddenly notice the sour odor lingering in the hall. An empty glass sat on the foyer table, near the telephone. He picked up the glass and sniffed it.

Whiskey.

We all have our secrets. Evelyn does, too.

He set the glass back down. Then, deep in thought, he climbed the stairs to bed.

Six

"So where were you two last night?" Chase asked.

The twins, busy attacking sausage and eggs, simultaneously looked up at their uncle.

"I was over at Zach Brewer's," said Phillip. "You remember the Brewers, don't you? Over on Pearl Street."

"What little Phil really means is, he was checking out Zach's sister," said Cassie.

"At least I wasn't holed up in some cave, pining for a date."

"I wasn't pining for a date. I was busy."

"Oh, sure," snorted Phillip.

"Busy? Doing what?" asked Chase.

"I was over at the *Herald,* trying to get a handle on things," said Cassie. "You know, Dad left things such a mess. No written plans for succession. Not a clue as to which direction he wanted the paper to go. Editorially speaking."

"Let Jill Vickery take care of it," said Phillip with a shrug. "That's what we pay her for."

"I'd think at least you'd care, Phil. Seeing as you're the heir apparent."

"These transitions need to be handled gradually." Phil nonchalantly shoveled another forkful of eggs into his mouth.

"In the meantime, the *Herald* drifts around rudderless. I don't want it to be just another church and social rag. We should turn it into a muckraking journal. Shake things up along the coast, get people mad. The way Dad got 'em mad a few months ago."

"Got who mad?" asked Chase.

"Those stooges on the planning board. The ones who voted to rezone the north shore. Dad made 'em out to look pretty greasy. I bet Jill was quaking in her shiny Italian shoes, waiting for that libel suit to pop."

"You seem to know a lot about what goes on at the *Herald*," said Chase.

"Of course. Second best tries harder."

She said it lightly, but Chase couldn't miss the note of resentment in her voice. He understood exactly how she felt. He, too, had been the second-best sibling, had spent his childhood trying harder, to no avail. Richard had been the anointed one. Just as Phillip was now.

The doorbell rang. "That'll be Granddad," said Phillip. "He's early."

Chase stood. "I'll get it."

Noah DeBolt was standing on the front porch. "Good morning, Chase. Is Evelyn ready for her appointment?"

"I think so. Come in, sir."

That "sir" was automatic. One simply didn't call this man by his first name. As Noah walked in the door, Chase marveled at the fact that the years hadn't stooped the shoulders in that tailored suit, nor softened the glare of those ice blue eyes.

Noah paused in the foyer and glanced critically around

the house. "It's about time we made some changes in here. A new couch, new chairs. Evelyn's put up with this old furniture long enough."

"They're my mother's favorites," said Chase. "Antiques—"

"I know what the hell they are! Junk." Noah's gaze focused on the twins, who were staring at him through the doorway. "What, are you two still eating breakfast? Come on, it's eight-thirty! With the fees lawyers charge, we don't want to be late."

"Really, Mr. DeBolt," said Chase. "I can drive us all to the lawyer. You didn't have to bother—"

"Evelyn asked me to come," said Noah. "What my girl asks for, I deliver." He glanced up the stairs. Evelyn had just appeared on the landing. "Right, sweetheart?"

Head held high, Evelyn came down the stairs. It was the first Chase had seen of her since the night before. No tremor, no effects of whiskey were apparent this morning. She looked cool as aspic. "Hello, Daddy," she said.

Noah gave her a hug. "Now," he said softly, "let's go finish this unpleasant business."

They drove in Noah's Mercedes, Evelyn and her father in the front seat, Chase crammed in the back with the twins. How had Richard tolerated it all these years, he wondered, living in the same town with this bully of a father-in-law? But that was the price one paid for marrying Noah DeBolt's only daughter: eternal criticism, eternal scrutiny.

Now that Richard was dead, Noah was back in control of his daughter's life. He drove them to Les Hardee's office. He escorted Evelyn through the front door. He led her by the arm right up to the reception desk.

"Mrs. Tremain to see Les," said Noah. "We're here to review the will."

The receptionist gave them a strange look—something Chase could only read as panic—and pressed the intercom button. "Mr. Hardee," she said. "They're here."

Instantly Les Hardee popped out of his office. His suit and tie marked him as a dapper man; his sweating brow did not match the image. "Mr. DeBolt, Mrs. Tremain," he said, almost painfully. "I would have called you earlier, but I only just— That is to say, we…" He swallowed. "There seems to be a problem with the will."

"Nothing that can't be fixed," said Noah.

"Actually…" Hardee opened the conference-room door. "I think we should all sit down."

There was another man in the room. Hardee introduced them to Vernon FitzHugh, an attorney from Bass Harbor. FitzHugh looked like a working-class version of Hardee, articulate enough, but rough around the edges, the sort of guy who probably had had to sling hash to pay his way through law school. They all sat at the conference table, Hardee and FitzHugh at opposite ends.

"So what's this little problem with Richard's will?" asked Noah. "And what do you have to do with all this, Mr. FitzHugh?"

FitzHugh cleared his throat. "I'm afraid I'm the bearer of bad news. Or, in this case, a new will."

"What?" Noah turned to Hardee. "What's this garbage, Les? *You* were Richard's attorney."

"That's what I thought," said Hardee morosely.

"Then where did this other will come from?"

Everyone looked at FitzHugh.

"A few weeks ago," explained FitzHugh, "Mr. Tremain came to my office. He said he wanted to draw up a new will, superseding the will drawn up previously by Mr.

Hardee. I advised him that Mr. Hardee was the one who should do it, but Mr. Tremain insisted I draw it up. So I honored his request. I would have brought it to your attention earlier, but I've been out of town for a few weeks. I didn't hear of Mr. Tremain's death until last night."

"This is bizarre," said Evelyn. "Why would Richard draw up a new will? How do we even know it was really him?"

"It was him," confirmed Hardee. "I recognize his signature."

There was a long silence.

"Well," said Evelyn. "Let's hear it, Les. What's been changed."

Hardee slipped on his glasses and began to read aloud. "I, Richard D. Tremain, being of sound mind and body—"

"Oh, skip the legal gobbledygook!" snapped Noah. "Get to the basics. What's different about the new will?"

Hardee looked up. "Most of it is unchanged. The house, joint accounts, contents therein, all go to Mrs. Tremain. There are generous trust accounts for the children, and a few personal items left to his brother."

"What about Rose Hill Cottage?" asked Noah.

Here Hardee shifted in his chair. "Perhaps I should just read it." He flipped ahead six pages and cleared his throat. "That parcel of land on the north shore comprising approximately forty acres, inclusive of the access road, as well as the structure known as Rose Hill Cottage, I bequeath to…" Here Hardee paused.

"What about Rose Hill?" pressed Evelyn.

Hardee took a deep breath. "I bequeath to my dear friend and companion, Miranda Wood."

"Like hell," said Noah.

* * *

On the street outside Hardee's office, Noah and Evelyn sat side by side in the car. Neither one spoke. Neither was comfortable with the silence. The others had chosen to walk home, much to Noah's relief. He needed this time alone with Evelyn.

Noah said softly, "Is there anything you want to tell me, Evelyn?"

"What do you mean, Daddy?"

"Anything at all. About Richard."

She looked at her father. "Am I supposed to say something?"

"You can tell me, you know. We're family, that's what matters. And family stick together. Against the whole world, if they have to."

"I don't know what you're talking about."

Noah looked into his daughter's eyes. They were the same shade of green as his wife's eyes had been. Here was the one link he had left to his darling Susannah. Here was the one person in the world he still cared about. She returned his gaze calmly, without even the tiniest flicker of uneasiness. Good. Good. She could hold her own against anyone. In that way, she truly was a DeBolt.

He said, "I'd do anything for you, Evelyn. Anything. All you have to do is ask."

She looked straight ahead. "Then take me home, Daddy."

He started the engine and turned the car toward Chestnut Street. She didn't say a word during the entire drive. She was a proud girl, his daughter. Though she'd never ask for it, she needed his help. And she'd get it.

Whatever it takes, he thought. *It'll be done.*

After all, Evelyn was his flesh and blood, and he couldn't let flesh and blood go to prison.

Even if she was guilty.

Her garden had always been her sanctuary. Here Miranda had planted hollyhocks and delphiniums, baby's breath and columbine. She hadn't bothered with color schemes or landscape drawings. She'd simply sunk plants into the earth, scattered seeds and let the jungle of vines and flowers take over her backyard. They'd been neglected this past week, poor things. A few days of no watering had left the blooms bedraggled. But now she was home and her babies looked happier. Strangely enough, *she* was happy, as well. Her back was warmed by the sun, her hands were working the rich loam. This was all she needed. Fresh air and freedom. *How long will I have it?*

She put that thought firmly aside and swung the pickax into the hardened earth. She'd turn a little more soil, expand the perennial bed another two feet. She leaned the pickax against the house and knelt to loosen up the clods, sift out the stones.

The sun was making her drowsy.

At last, unable to resist the promise of a nap, she stretched out on the lawn. There she lay, her hands and knees caked with soil, the grass cushioning her bare legs. A perfect summer day, just like the days she remembered from her childhood. She closed her eyes and thought about all those afternoons when her mother was still alive, when her father would stand at the barbecue, singing as he grilled hamburgers….

"What a sharp game you play," said a voice.

Miranda sat up with a start and saw Chase standing at

her white picket fence. He shoved open the gate and came into the yard. As he approached, it occurred to her how filthy she must look in her gardening shorts and T-shirt. Framed against the glare of sun and blue sky, Chase looked immaculate, untouchable. She squinted to see his expression, but all she could make out was a dark oval, the flutter of his windblown hair.

"You knew, didn't you?" he said.

She rose to her feet and clapped the dirt from her hands. "Knew what?"

"How did you manage it, Miranda? A few sweet whispers? Write me into the will and I'll be yours forever?"

"I don't know what you're talking about."

"I just came from our family attorney. We found a nasty surprise waiting for us. Two weeks ago Richard made out a new will. He left Rose Hill Cottage to you."

Her immediate reaction was stunned silence. In disbelief she stared at him.

"Nothing to say? No denials?"

"I never expected—"

"I think it's exactly what you expected."

"No!" She turned away, confused. "I never wanted a thing—"

"Oh, come on!" He reached for her arm and pulled her around to face him. "What was it, blackmail? A way to keep you quiet about the affair?"

"I don't know anything about a will! Or the cottage! Besides, how could he leave it to me? Doesn't it go to his wife? Evelyn owns half—"

"No, she doesn't."

"Why not?"

"Rose Hill came through my mother's family. An inheritance that went directly to Richard, so Evelyn had no claim on it. It was Richard's to pass on any way he chose. And he chose to give it to you."

She shook her head. "I don't know why."

"That cottage was the one place on this island he really cared about. The one place we both cared about."

"All right, then!" she cried. "*You* take it! It's yours. I'll sign a statement today, handing it over. I don't want it. All I want is to be left *alone*." She stared straight up at his coldly immobile face. "And to never, ever see another Tremain for as long as I live."

She broke away and ran up the back porch steps, into the house. The screen door slammed shut behind her. She headed straight into the kitchen, where she suddenly halted. There was nowhere else to run. In agitation she went to the sink and turned on the faucet. There, surrounded by her beloved ferns, she scrubbed furiously at the dirt caked on her hands.

She was still scrubbing when the screen door opened, then softly swung shut again. For a long time he didn't say a word. She knew he was standing behind her, watching her.

"Miranda," he said.

Angrily she turned off the faucet. "Go away."

"I want to hear your side of it."

"Why? You wouldn't believe me. You don't *want* to believe me. But you know what? I don't care anymore." She grabbed a dish towel and blotted her hands. "I'll go to the lawyer's this afternoon. Sign a statement of refusal, or whatever it's called. I would never accept it. Anything I received from him would be tainted. Just like I'm tainted."

"You're wrong, Miranda. I do want to believe you."

She stood very still, afraid to turn, to look at him. She sensed his approach as he moved toward her across the kitchen. And still she couldn't turn, couldn't face him. She could only stare down at the clumps of wet garden dirt in the sink.

"But you can't, can you?" she said.

"The facts argue against it."

"And if I tell you the facts are misleading?" Slowly she turned and found he was right there, so close she could reach up and touch his face. "What then?"

"Then I'd be forced to trust my instincts. But in this particular case, my instincts are shot all to hell."

She stared at him, suddenly confused by the signals he was sending. By the signals her body was sending. He had her closed off from all retreat, her back pinned against the kitchen sink. She had to tilt her head up just to meet his gaze, and the view she had of him, towering above her, was more than a little frightening. Yet it wasn't fear that seemed to be pumping through her veins. It was the warm and unexpected pulse of desire.

She slid away and paced across the kitchen, as far as she could get from him and still be in the same room. "I meant what I said. About refusing all rights to Rose Hill Cottage. In fact, I think we should do it right now. Go to the lawyer."

"Is that really what you want?"

"I know I don't want anything of his. Anything to remind me of him."

"You'd give up the cottage, just like that?"

"It doesn't mean a thing to me. I've never even seen the place."

Chase looked surprised. "He never took you to Rose Hill?"

"No. Oh, he told me about it. But it was his own private retreat. Not the sort of place he'd share with me."

"You could be handing back a fortune in real estate, sight unseen."

"It's not my fortune. It never was."

He regarded her with narrowed eyes. "I can't figure you out. Every time I think I have, you throw me a curve ball."

"I'm not all that complicated."

"You managed to intrigue Richard."

"I was hardly the first woman to do that."

"But you're the first one who ever left him."

"And look where it got me." She gave a bitter laugh. "You may not believe this, but I used to think of myself as a person with high morals. I paid my taxes. Stopped at every red light. Followed all the rules." She turned and stared out the window. Softly she said, "Then I fell for your brother. Suddenly I didn't know what the rules were anymore. I was slipping around in strange territory. God, it scared me. At the same time I felt…exhilarated. And that scared me even more." She turned to him. "I'd give anything to turn back the clock. To feel…innocent again."

Slowly he came toward her. "Some things we can't recapture, Miranda."

"No." She stared down, her cheeks flushed with guilt. "Some things we lose forever."

His touch, so unexpected, made her flinch. It was the gentlest of strokes, just his hand tracing the curve of her cheek. Startled, she looked up to find a gaze so searching it left her nowhere to hide. She hated feeling so nakedly exposed but she found she could not break away. The hand cupping her face was warm and so very compelling.

Here I am, falling into the same old trap, she thought.

With Richard I lost my innocence. What will I lose to this man? My soul?

She said, "I learned my lesson from your brother, Chase. I'm no longer fair game." She turned and walked away, into the living room.

"I'm not Richard."

She looked back. "It doesn't matter who you are. What matters is that I'm not the same dumb, trusting soul I used to be."

"He really hurt you, didn't he?" He was watching her from the kitchen threshold. His shoulders seemed to fill the doorway.

She didn't answer. She sank into an armchair and stared at her dirt-stained knees.

Chase studied her from across the room. All his anger toward her, which had built up since that morning in Les Hardee's office, suddenly evaporated. In its place was a fury toward Richard. Golden boy Richard, who had always gotten what he wanted. Richard the firstborn, the one with the classic Tremain fair hair and blue eyes, had bought everything he ever coveted with the coin of wit and charm. But once he'd attained his goal, he'd lose interest.

That was his pattern with women. Once, Richard had wanted Evelyn DeBolt, and he'd won her. He'd had to marry her, of course. You didn't play games with the only child of Noah DeBolt. But after the prize was his he'd grown bored with his wife. That was Richard, always coveting, never satisfied.

And here was the one woman, the one prize, he hadn't been able to keep. Such an unassuming female, thought Chase, feeling a strange ache in his throat. Was it pity or sympathy? He couldn't tell the difference.

He sat in the chair across from her. "You…seem to have recovered from last night."

"Just some sore muscles. That's all." She shrugged, as though she knew he couldn't possibly be interested. Whatever turmoil was swirling in her head, she kept it carefully concealed. "I sent Annie home this morning. I couldn't see the point of her staying."

"Safety's sake?"

"Safety from what?"

"What if it wasn't an accident?"

She looked up. "At the moment I'm not terrifically popular in this town. But I can't see one of our upstanding citizens turning hit-and-run driver."

"Still, one of our upstanding citizens did steal Mr. Lanzo's car."

"Poor Eddie." She shook her head. "It'll just reinforce his paranoia. Now he'll add car thieves to that list of crazies he imagines cruising the street."

"Yes, he mentioned that last night. Something about Peeping Toms."

She smiled. "Eddie grew up in Chicago. He never did shake those big-city jitters. He swears he spotted some mob car watching my…" She suddenly paused, frowning. "You know, I never paid much attention to his stories. But now that I think about it…"

"When did he tell you about that car?"

"Maybe a month or two ago."

"Before Richard's murder, then."

"Yes. So it's probably not related." She sighed. "It's just poor, crazy Eddie." She stood. "I'll change clothes. I can't go to the lawyer looking like this."

"You really want to go right now?"

"I have to. Until I do, I won't feel clean. Or free of him."

"I'll call ahead, then." He glanced at his watch. "We can just make the ferry to Bass Harbor."

"Bass Harbor? I thought Les Hardee was Richard's lawyer."

"He is. But this last will was drawn up by some lawyer named Vernon FitzHugh. Do you know him?"

"No, thank God." She turned and headed up the hall. "Or you'd probably accuse Mr. FitzHugh and me of fraud." She vanished into the bedroom.

Chase watched the door swing shut behind her. "As a matter of fact," he muttered, "the thought did cross my mind."

Vernon FitzHugh was expecting them. What he didn't anticipate was the purpose of their visit.

"Have you really thought this through, Ms. Wood? This is prime real estate we're talking about. The north shore has just been rezoned for development. I expect your piece of property, in a few years, will be worth well over—"

"It should never have come to me," said Miranda. "It belongs to the Tremain family."

FitzHugh glanced uneasily at Chase, one of those sidelong looks that reveal so much. "Perhaps we should discuss this in private, Ms. Wood. If Mr. Tremain would care to wait outside…"

"No, I want him to stay. I want him to hear every word." She looked meaningfully at FitzHugh. "So he can't accuse us of collusion."

"Collusion?" FitzHugh, alarmed, sat up straight. "Mr. Tremain, you don't think I wanted to get involved in this, do you? It's a messy situation. Two lawyers, two wills. And then, the complicating circumstances of the client's death."

He assiduously avoided looking at Miranda. "I'm just trying to carry out Mr. Tremain's instructions. Which are to ensure that Rose Hill Cottage goes to Ms. Wood."

"I don't want it," said Miranda. "I want to give it back."

FitzHugh looked troubled. He removed his glasses and set them on the desk. It seemed, with that one gesture, he simultaneously shed the role of the detached professional. Now he was speaking to her as a friend, an adviser. The flat accent of a working-class Mainer slipped into his voice. This man knew only too well what it was like to be poor. And here was this stubborn young woman, throwing away the promise of security.

"Richard Tremain," he began, "came to me with a request. I'm bound to honor it. It's not my job to decide whether you're innocent or guilty. I just want to see that the intent of the will is carried out. I made very sure that this was what he wanted, and he wanted that land to go to you. If you're convicted, then the point will be moot—you can't inherit. But let's say you're found innocent. Then Rose Hill goes to you, no question about it. Wait a few days, Ms. Wood. If this is really what you want, come back and I'll draw up the papers. But I won't do it today. I have to think of Mr. Tremain's last request. After all, he was my client."

"Why *did* he come to you?" Chase asked. "Mr. Hardee has been Richard's attorney for years."

FitzHugh studied Chase for a moment, weighing the man's motives. Coercion was what he suspected, the wealthy Tremain family putting pressure on this woman, this outsider, to surrender her inheritance. It wasn't right. Someone had to take the woman's side, even if she refused to stand up for herself.

"Richard Tremain came to me," FitzHugh said, "because he *didn't* want Les Hardee involved."

"Why not?"

"Mr. Hardee is' also Noah DeBolt's attorney. I think Mr. Tremain was worried this would leak out to his father-in-law."

"And what a riot that would have caused," said Chase.

"Having met Mr. DeBolt this morning, yes, I can imagine there would've been fireworks."

Chase leaned forward, his gaze narrowing on the attorney. "The day Richard was here to change his will, how did he seem to you? I mean, his state of mind. People don't just walk in and change their wills for no good reason."

FitzHugh frowned. "Well, he seemed…upset. He didn't mention any fear of dying. Said he just wanted to straighten out his affairs…." He glanced at Miranda and reddened at the unintentional double entendre.

Miranda flushed, as well, but she refused to shrink from his gaze. *I'm through with being punished,* she thought. *Through with cringing at the looks people give me.*

"You said he was upset. What do you mean?" asked Chase.

"He seemed angry."

"At whom?"

"We didn't discuss it. He just came in and said he didn't want the cottage to go to Mrs. Tremain."

"He was specific about Evelyn?"

"Yes. And he was concerned only about Rose Hill Cottage. Not the bank account or the other assets. I assumed it was because those other assets were joint marital property, and he couldn't redirect those. But Rose Hill was his, through inheritance. He could dispose of it as he wished." FitzHugh looked at Miranda. "And he wanted you to have it."

She shook her head. "Why?"

"I assume, because he cared about you. Giving you Rose Hill was his way of telling you how much."

In silence Miranda bowed her head. She knew both men were watching her. She wondered what expression she'd see in Chase's eyes. Cynicism? Disbelief? *You can't imagine that your brother would feel love, not just lust, for a woman like me?*

"So, Ms. Wood?" asked FitzHugh. "You agree this isn't a move you should make?"

She raised her head and looked across the desk at the attorney. "Draw up the papers. I want to do it now."

"Maybe you don't," said Chase quietly.

Miranda looked at him in disbelief. "What?"

"Mr. FitzHugh has brought up some points I hadn't considered. You should think about it, just for a few days." His gaze met Miranda's. She could see that he was baffled by something he'd heard here today.

"Are you saying I should keep Rose Hill Cottage?"

"All I'm saying is this. Richard had a reason for changing the will. Before we go changing things back, let's find out why he did it."

Vernon FitzHugh nodded. "My thoughts exactly," he said.

They exchanged scarcely a word on the ferry back to Shepherd's Island. Only when they'd driven off the pier and turned onto Shore Circle Road did Miranda stir from her silence. "Where are we going?" she asked.

"The north shore."

"Why?"

"I want you to see Rose Hill. It's only fair you know exactly what you're handing back to Evelyn."

"You enjoy this, don't you?" she said. "Running me around in circles. Playing your little mind games. One minute you say I'm stealing Tremain property. The next, you're trying to talk me into playing thief. What's the point of it all, Chase?"

"I'm bothered by what FitzHugh told us. That Richard wanted to keep the cottage away from Evelyn."

"But it *should* go to her."

"Rose Hill came from my mother's side. The Pruitts. Evelyn has no claim to it."

"He could have left it to you."

Chase laughed. "Not likely."

"Why not?"

"We weren't exactly the closest of brothers. I was lucky just to get his collection of rusty Civil War swords. No, he wanted Rose Hill to go to someone he loved. You were his first choice. Maybe his only choice."

"He didn't love me, Chase," she said softly. "Not really."

They drove north, winding past summer cottages, past granite cliffs jagged with pines, past stony beaches where waves broke into white foam. Gulls circled and swooped at the blue-gray sea.

"Why did you say that?" he asked. "About Richard not loving you?"

"Because I knew. I think I always knew. Oh, maybe he *thought* he loved me. But for Richard, love was a lot of moonlight and madness. A fever that eventually breaks. It was just a matter of time."

"That sounds like Richard. As a kid, he was always in pursuit of the never-ending high."

"Are all you Tremains like that?"

"Hardly. My father was married to his work."

"And what are you married to?"

He glanced at her. She was struck by the intensity of his gaze, the gaze of a man who's not afraid to tell the truth. "Nothing and no one. At least, not anymore. Not since Christine."

"Your wife?"

He nodded. "It didn't last very long. I was just a kid, really, only twenty. Doing my share of wild and crazy things. It was a handy way to get back at my father, and it worked."

"What happened to Christine?"

"She found out I wasn't going to inherit the Tremain fortune and she walked out. Smart girl. She, at least, was using her head."

He focused on the road, which he obviously knew well. Miranda noticed how easily he handled the curves, guiding the car skillfully around each treacherous bend. Whatever wildness he'd displayed in his youth had since been reined in. Here was a man in tight control of his life, his emotions, not a man in pursuit of the ephemeral moonlight and madness.

A twenty-minute drive brought them to the last stretch of paved road. The asphalt gave way to a dirt access road flanked by birch and pine. Rustic signs proclaimed the different camps hidden among the tress. Mom and Pop's. Brandywine Cottage. Sanity Camp. Here and there, dirt tracks led off to the dozen or so summer retreats of prominent island families, most of whom had held their cottages for generations.

The access road began to climb, winding a half mile up the contours of the hillside. They passed a stone marker labeled St. John's Wood. Then they came to the last sign, every bit as rustic as the others: Rose Hill. A final bend in the road took them through the last stand of trees, and then a broad, sloping field lay before them. It sat at the very crest of the hill—a weathered cottage facing north, to the sea. Vines of purple clematis clung lovingly about the veranda railings. Rosebushes, overgrown with weeds but still valiantly blooming, crouched like thorny sentinels beside the porch steps.

They parked in the gravel turnaround and stepped out into an afternoon fragrant with the scent of flowers and sun-warmed grass. For a moment Miranda stood motionless, her face turned to the sky. Not a cloud marred that perfect blue. A single gull, riding the wind off the hillside, drifted overhead.

"Come on," said Chase. "Let me show you inside."

He led her up the porch steps. "I haven't seen the place in at least ten years. I'm almost afraid to go in."

"Afraid of what?"

"The changes. Of what they might've done to it. But I guess that's how it is with your childhood home."

"Especially if you were happy there."

He smiled. "Exactly."

For a moment they stood and regarded the old porch swing, creaking back and forth in the breeze.

"Do you have a key?" she asked.

"There should be one under here." He crouched down beneath one of the windowsills. "There's this little crack in the wood where Mom always kept a spare key…." He sighed and straightened. "Not anymore. Well, if the door's locked, maybe we can find a window open somewhere." Tentatively he reached for the knob. "How do you like that?" He laughed, pushing open the door. "It's not even locked."

As the door creaked open, the front room swung into view—a faded Oriental carpet stretched across the threshold, a stone fireplace, wide pine floors. Miranda stepped inside and suddenly halted in surprise.

At her feet lay a jumble of papers. A rolltop desk stood in the corner, its drawers wide open, their contents strewn across the floor. Books had been pulled off a nearby shelf and tossed haphazardly among the papers.

Chase stepped inside and came to a halt beside her. The screen door slammed shut.

"What the hell?" he said.

Seven

In silence they took in the ransacked desk, the scattered papers. Without a word Chase moved quickly toward the next room.

Miranda followed him into the kitchen. There were no signs of disturbance here. The pots and pans were hung on a beam rack, the flour and sugar canisters lined up neatly on the butcher block counters.

She was right on his heels as he headed for the stairs. They ran up the steps and looked first in the small guest bedroom. Everything appeared in order. Quickly Chase circled the room, opening closets, glancing in drawers.

"What are you looking for?" she asked.

He didn't answer. He moved across the hall, into the master bedroom.

Here double windows, flanked by lace curtains, faced the sea. A cream coverlet draped the four-poster bed. Motes of dust drifted in the sun-warmed stillness.

"Doesn't look like they touched this room, either," said Miranda.

Chase went to the dresser, picked up a silver hairbrush, and set it back down. "Obviously not."

"What on earth is going on here, Chase?"

He turned and glanced in frustration about the room. "This is crazy. They left the paintings on the walls. The furniture…"

"Nothing's missing?"

"Nothing valuable. At least, nothing your ordinary thief would go after." He opened a dresser drawer and glanced through the contents. He opened a second drawer and paused, staring inside. Slowly he withdrew a pair of women's panties. It was scarcely more than a few strips of black lace and silk. He pulled out a matching bra, equally skimpy, equally seductive.

He looked at Miranda, his gaze flat and unreadable. "Yours?" he asked quietly.

"I told you, I've never been here. They must belong to Evelyn."

He shook his head. "I don't think so."

"How would you know?"

"She never comes out here. Despises the rustic life, or so she claims."

"Well, they're not mine. I don't own anything like— like that."

"There's more inside here. Maybe you'll recognize something else."

She went to the dresser and pulled out an emerald-and-cream bra. "Well, it's obvious this isn't mine."

"How so?"

"This is a 36C. I'm…" She cleared her throat. "Not that big."

"Oh."

Quickly she turned away, before he could confirm her

statement. Not that he hadn't had the chance to look. He had eyes, didn't he?

And he sees too damn much, she thought. She turned toward the window and stood with her back to Chase, all the while struggling to regain her composure. Outside, the fading light of day slanted across the treetops. A long summer dusk. In the field below there would be fireflies and the hum of insects in the grass. And the chill. Even on these August evenings there was always the chill that rose from the sea. She hugged herself and shivered.

His approach was gentle, silent. She couldn't hear him, but she knew, without looking, that he was right behind her.

Chase was standing so close, in fact, that he could smell the scent of her hair—clean and sweet and intoxicating. The fading daylight from the window brought out its glorious chestnut hues. He wanted to reach out and run his fingers through those shimmering strands, to bury his face in the tangled silk. A mistake, a mistake. He knew it before it happened, and yet he couldn't help himself.

She shivered at his touch. Just the tiniest tremble, the softest sigh. He ran his hands down her shoulders, down the cool smoothness of her bare arms. She didn't pull away. No, she leaned back, as though melting against him. He wrapped his arms around her, enfolding her in their warmth.

"When I was a boy," he whispered, "I used to think there were magical creatures in that field down there. Elves and fairies hiding among the toadstools. I'd see their lights flitting about at night. It was only fireflies, of course. But to a kid, they might have been anything. Elvish lanterns, Dragon lights. I wish…"

"What do you wish, Chase?"

He sighed. "That I still had some of that child inside me.

That we could have known each other then. Before all this happened. Before…"

"Richard."

Chase fell silent. His brother would always be there, his life and his death like a darkness hovering over them. What could possibly thrive in such shadow? Not friendship; certainly not love. *Love?* No, what Chase felt, standing there behind her, hugging her slim, warm body to his, had far more to do with lust. *Well, what the hell. Maybe it runs in my family,* he thought, *in my tainted bloodline. This propensity for reckless, hopeless affairs. Richard had it. My mother had it. Is it my turn to succumb?*

Miranda shifted in his embrace, turned to face him. One look at that soft, upturned mouth and he was lost.

She tasted of summer and warmth and sweet amber honey. At the first touch of their lips he wanted more, more. He felt like a man who has fallen drunk at his first sip of nectar and now craves nothing else. His hands found their way into that silken mass of hair, were buried in it, lost in it. He heard her murmur, "please," and was too fevered to think it anything but a request for more. Only when she said it again, and then, "Chase, no," did he finally pull away.

They stared at each other. The confusion he felt was mirrored in her eyes. She retreated a step, nervously shoving back her hair.

"I shouldn't have let you do that," she said. "It was a mistake."

"Why?"

"Because you—you'll say I led you on. That's what you'll tell Evelyn, isn't it? You think it's how I got hold of Richard. Temptation. Seduction. It's what everyone else believes."

"But is it true?"

"You've just proved it. Get me alone in a room and look what happens! Another Tremain male bites the dust." Her voice took on a cold edge. "What I want to know is, who's really seducing whom?"

She's all motion, all skittishness, he thought. In another moment she would shatter and fly into pieces.

"Neither of us did any seducing, any tempting. It just happened, Miranda. The way it usually happens. Nature tugs on our strings and we can't always resist."

"This time I will. This time I know better. Your brother taught me a few things. The most important thing is not to be so damn gullible when it comes to men."

That last word was still hanging in the air between them when they heard footsteps thump onto the porch below. Someone rapped on the front door.

Chase turned and left the room.

Miranda, suddenly weak, leaned against the window-sill. She clutched it tightly, as though drawing strength from the wood. *Too close,* she thought. *I let down my guard, let him slip right past my defenses.*

She would have to be more careful. She would have to remind herself that Chase and Richard were variations on a theme, a theme that had already wreaked havoc on her life. She took a deep breath and slowly let it out, willing the turmoil, the confusion, to flow out of her body. *Back in control,* she thought. She released the sill. She stood straight. Then, with a new semblance of calmness, she followed Chase down the stairs.

He was in the front room with the visitor. Miranda recognized her old acquaintance from the garden club, Miss Lila St. John, local expert on flowering perennials. Miss

St. John was dressed in her signature black dress. Summer or winter, she always wore black, set off with a touch of white lace here and there. Today it was a black walking dress of crinkled linen. It did not quite match her brown boots or her straw hat, but on Miss St. John it all seemed to look just right.

She turned at the sound of Miranda's footsteps. If she was surprised to see Miranda she didn't show it. She simply nodded, then turned her sharp gray eyes back to the ransacked desk. On the front porch a dog whined. Through the screen door Miranda saw what looked like a large black fur ball with a red tongue.

"It's all my fault, you know," said Miss St. John. "I can't believe I was such an imbecile."

"How is it your fault?" asked Chase.

"I sensed something was wrong last week. We were taking our walk, you see, Ozzie and I. We walk every evening around dusk. That's when the deer come out, the pests, though I do love to see them. Anyway, I saw a light through the trees, somewhere in this direction. I came up to the cottage and knocked on the door. No one answered, so I left." She shook her head. "I shouldn't have, you know. I should have looked into it. I *knew* it didn't feel right."

"Did you see a car?"

"If you were coming to loot the joint, would *you* park your car out front? Of course not. I know I'd park down the road a bit, in the trees. Then I'd sneak up here on foot."

It was hard to imagine Miss St. John doing any such thing.

"It's a good thing you didn't get involved," said Chase. "You could have gotten yourself killed."

"At my age, Chase, getting killed is not a major concern." She used her walking stick, a knobby affair with a duck's head handle, to prod among the papers on the floor. "Any idea what he was after?"

"Not a clue."

"Not valuables, obviously. That's a Limoges on that shelf over there, isn't it?"

Chase glanced sheepishly at the hand-painted vase. "If you say so."

Miss St. John turned to Miranda. "Have you any thoughts on the matter?"

Miranda found herself under the gaze of two very intense gray eyes. Miss St. John might be dismissed by many as little more than a charming eccentric, but Miranda could see the intelligence in that gaze. While their previous conversations had tended more toward delphiniums and daffodils, even then, Miss St. John had made her feel like some sort of new plant species under a magnifying glass. "I'm not sure I know what to think, Miss St. John," she said.

"Take a look at the mess. What does it tell you?"

Miranda glanced at the papers, the scattered books. Then her gaze shifted to the bookcases. Only a top shelf had been emptied. Two full bookcases were undisturbed. "He didn't look through all the books. So whoever broke in here must have been interrupted. By you, maybe."

"Or he found what he was looking for," said Chase.

Miss St. John turned to him. "And what might that be?"

"A guess?" Chase and Miranda glanced at each other. "The file on Stone Coast Trust," Chase ventured.

"Ah." Miss St. John's eyes took on a gleam of interest. "Your brother's little campaign against Tony Graffam. Yes, Richard seemed to do quite a bit of writing out here. At that desk, in fact. On my evening walks I'd see him through the window."

"Did you ever stop to talk to him? About what he was working on?"

"Oh, no. That's why we come out here, isn't it? To get away from all those prying townies." She glanced at Miranda. "I never saw *you* out here."

"I've never been here," she said, shifting uneasily under that thoughtful gaze. This matter-of-fact reference to her link with Richard had taken her by surprise. And yet, Miss St. John's bluntness was far preferable to the delicate avoidance with which so many others treated the subject.

Miss St. John bent down for a closer look at the papers. "He must have done a prodigious amount of work here, judging by this mess. What is all this, anyway?"

Chase bent and sifted through the papers. "Looks like a lot of old article files.... Financial records from the *Herald...* And here we've got a collection of local personality profiles. Why, here's one of you, Miss St. John."

"Me? But I was never interviewed for anything."

Chase grinned. "Must be the unauthorized version, then."

"Does it mention all my sexy secrets?"

"Well, let's just take a good look here—"

"Oh, *give* me the damn thing." Miss St. John snatched the page out of his hands and scanned the typewritten notes. She read them aloud. "Age seventy-four...holds title to lot number two, St. John's Wood, and cottage thereon...rabid member of local garden club." Here she glanced up huffily. *"Rabid?"* She continued reading. "Eccentric recluse, never married. Engaged once, to an Arthur Simoneau, killed in action...Normandy...." Her voice trailed off. Slowly she sat down, still clutching the piece of paper in both hands.

"Oh, Miss St. John," said Miranda. "I'm sorry."

The elderly woman looked up, still shaken. "It…was a very long time ago."

"I can't believe he went digging into your personal life, without you even knowing about it. Why would he do that?"

"You're saying it was Richard?" asked Miss St. John.

"Well, these are his papers."

Miss St. John frowned at the page for a moment. "No," she said slowly. "I don't believe he wrote this. There's an error in here. It says my cottage lies in St. John's Wood. But it lies three feet over the line, on Tremain property. A surveyor's mistake from seventy years past. Richard knew that."

Chase frowned. "I never heard that, about your cottage."

"Yes, your family land goes past the second stone wall. It includes the entire access road. So, technically, all the rest of us are trespassers on your private road. Not that it ever mattered. It always felt like a giant family out here. But now…" She shook her head. "So many strangers on the island. All those tourists from *Massachusetts.*" She made it sound like an invasion from hell.

"Did Stone Coast Trust approach you?" Miranda asked her. "About selling St. John's Wood?"

"They approached everyone on this road. I, of course, refused. So did Richard. That effectively squelched the project. Without Rose Hill, Stone Coast would own a dis-connected patchwork of little lots. But now…" Sadly she sighed. "I imagine Evelyn, at this very moment, has her pen poised over the sales contract."

"Actually, she does not," said Chase. "Rose Hill didn't go to Evelyn. Richard left the property to Miranda."

Miss St. John stared at them. "Now that," she said after a long pause, "is an entirely unexpected development."

"For me, as well," said Miranda.

While Miss St. John sat back in thought, Miranda and Chase gathered up the rest of the papers. They found more article files, a few miscellaneous clippings, an old financial report from the *Herald.* Obviously Richard had used the cottage as another office. Was this where he had stored his most sensitive papers? Miranda wondered about this when she came across a whole bundle of personality profiles. Like the page on Miss St. John, the information contained in these files was highly private.

In some cases it was downright shocking. She was startled to read that Forrest Mayhew, the local bank president, had been arrested for drunk driving in Boston. That town selectman George LaPierre, married thirty years, had been treated last year for syphilis. That Dr. Steiner—*her* doctor—was under investigation for medicare fraud.

She handed the papers to Chase. "Look at these! Richard was collecting dirt on everyone in town!"

"Here, what's this?" he asked. There was a yellow adhesive note attached to the back cover of the folder. On it was the handwritten scrawl, "Mr. T., do you want more? Let me know." It was signed "W.B.R."

"So Richard *didn't* write these," said Miranda. "This person W.B.R.—whoever he was—must've done the reporting."

"You have anyone on staff with those initials?"

"No. At least, not at the moment." She reached for a manila folder lying on the floor. "Look, there's another note from W.B.R." This time the note was paper-clipped to the top cover. "All I could get. Sorry—W.B.R."

"What's inside?" asked Miss St. John.

Miranda opened the file and stared. "This is it! The file on Stone Coast Trust!"

"Jackpot," said Chase.

"There's no profile of Tony Graffam. But here's his tax return. A list of bank account numbers and assets…" She nodded. "We hit pay dirt."

"I think not," said Miss St. John.

They both looked at her.

"If that file is so important, why did the burglar leave it here?"

In silence they considered that question.

"Maybe our burglar wasn't interested in Stone Coast Trust at all," said Miss St. John. "I mean, look at all this nasty information Richard's been gathering. Snoopy reports on drunk driving. Medicare fraud. Syphilis. George LaPierre, of all people! And at his age, too. These files could destroy some fine reputations. Now, I tell you, isn't that a motive for burglary?"

Or murder, thought Miranda. Why had Richard gathered such information in the first place? Was he planning an exposé on island residents? Or was there some darker reason? Coercion, for instance. Blackmail.

"If someone broke in to steal his own file, then we can assume it's now gone," said Chase. "Which means George LaPierre, Dr. Steiner, all the others in this pile didn't do it."

"Not necessarily," said Miss St. John. "What if he broke in and simply substituted a milder version? Mine, for instance. There's not a thing in my profile that qualifies as scandalous. How do you know I didn't come in here and destroy a far more venomous version?"

Chase smiled. "I will duly place you on the list of suspects, Miss St. John."

"Don't you discount me, Chase Tremain. Age alone does not take one out of the running. I have more up here—" she tapped her head "—than that imbecile George LaPierre had in his prime. If he ever *had* a prime."

"What you're saying, Miss St. John," said Miranda, "is that we can't count out any name in this pile. Or any name *not* in this pile."

"Correct."

Miranda frowned at the books. "One thing doesn't make sense. First, our burglar searches the desk. He throws around some papers, looking for some incriminating file. Why would he then search the bookcase? That's not the sort of place Richard would keep papers."

After a pause Miss St. John said, "You're right, of course. That doesn't make sense."

"Well," said Chase, "I guess we should call Lorne. Though I'm not sure he'd be much help at this point." He turned to the phone.

He'd already picked up the receiver when Miss St. John suddenly said, "Wait. Perhaps you should hold off on that call." She was staring at a loose page near her feet. Thoughtfully she picked up the paper and smoothed it across her knee.

Frowning, Chase hung up the receiver. "Why?"

"This is a profile of Valerie Everhard. You remember her, Chase. Our local librarian. And a married lady. According to this, Valerie has taken on a lover."

"So?"

"The man she's seeing is our chief of police." Miss St. John looked up and her eyes had lost all trace of humor. "Lorne Tibbetts."

"Why did he have these awful reports?" asked Miranda. "What was he planning to do with them?"

They were driving through darkness back to town. The fog had rolled in from the sea and curtained off all view beyond the dim haze of their headlights. Nothing seemed real in this mist, nothing seemed familiar. They were driving through a strange land, through a swirling cloud that seemed as if it would never lift.

"It doesn't sound like Richard," said Chase. "Snooping around in his neighbors' private lives. He committed enough sins of his own. If anyone was vulnerable to blackmail, it was Richard. Besides, who cares if Lorne is having a little fling with the librarian?"

"The librarian's husband?"

"Okay, but why would Richard care?"

She shook her head, unable to come up with an answer. "I wonder if any of these people knew about these files. Miss St. John didn't." She looked down at the papers on her lap and thought of the terrible secrets they contained. She had the sudden urge to shove the pile away, to throw off that unclean burden. "Chase?" she asked. "How do we know any of this is true?"

"We don't." He gave a short laugh. "And we can't exactly knock on George LaPierre's door and ask if he's had syphilis."

Miranda frowned at the note clipped to the folder. "I wonder who this is. This W.B.R. who got the information."

"The initials don't ring any bells?"

"None at all."

As the darkness flew past their windshield, Miranda thought of all the secrets revealed in these files. The banker's weakness for whiskey. The doctor's white-collar fraud. The husband and wife who conversed with their fists. All of it concealed beneath the glaze of respectability. *What private pains we nurse in silence.*

"Why *these* particular people?" she asked suddenly.

"Because they have the most to lose?" Chase suggested. "We're talking old island families here. LaPierre, Everhard, St. John. All of them respected names."

"Except for Tony Graffam."

"That's true. I guess he has a file in there, too..." He paused. "Wait. There's our link."

"What?"

"The north shore. You haven't lived here long enough to know all these families. But I grew up with them. I remember the summers I used to play with Toby LaPierre. And Daniel Steiner. And Valerie Everhard. Their families all have summer cottages out there."

"It could be coincidental."

"Or it could mean everything."

Chase frowned at the highway. The fog was thinning. "When we get back to your house," he said, "let's take a good look at those names. See if my hunch holds up."

An hour and a half later they sat at Miranda's dining table, the pages spread out before them. The remains of a hastily prepared supper—mushroom omelets and toast—had been pushed aside and they were now on their second cup of coffee. It was such a domestic scene, she thought with a twinge of longing, almost like newlyweds lingering at the dinner table. Except that the man sitting across from her could never, would never, fit into the picture. He was a temporary apparition, a visitor passing through her dining room.

She forced herself to focus on the sheet of paper, where he'd just checked off the final name.

"Okay, here's the list," said Chase. "Everyone in Richard's file. I'm almost certain they all own property on the north shore."

"Are any names missing?"

Chase sat back and mentally ticked off the camps along the access road. "There's Richard, of course. Then there's old man Sulaway's property, down the road. He's a retired lobsterman, sort of a recluse. And then there's Frenchman's Cottage. I think it was sold some years back. To hippies, I heard. They come up for the summers."

"So they'd be living there now."

"If they still own the place. But they're not from this area. I can't see Richard bothering to dig up information on them. And as for old Sully, well, an eighty-five-year-old sounds like a pretty unlikely victim for blackmail."

Blackmail. Miranda gazed at the papers on the table. "What was Richard thinking of?" she wondered. "What did he have against these people?"

"Something to do with the rezoning? Were any of these names on the land commission?"

"They couldn't have voted, anyway. They would've been disqualified. You know, conflict of interest." She sat back. "Maybe our burglar was looking for something entirely different."

"Then the question is, did he—or she—find it?"

From somewhere in the house came a sound that made them both glance up. It was the soft tinkle of breaking glass.

Miranda jerked to her feet in alarm. At once Chase grabbed her hand, signaled her to be silent. Together they moved from the dining room into the living room. A quick glance around told them the windows were all intact. They paused for a moment, listening, but heard no other sounds. Chase started toward the bedrooms.

They were moving up the hall when they heard, louder this time, the distinct crash of shattering glass.

"That came from the cellar!" said Miranda.

Chase wheeled and headed back into the kitchen. He flicked on a wall switch and yanked open the cellar door. A single bare bulb shone over the narrow stairway. A strange mist seemed to swirl in the shadows, obscuring the bottom of the stairs. They had taken only two steps down when they both smelled smoke.

"You've got a fire in here!" said Chase, moving down the steps. "Where's your extinguisher?"

"I'll get it!" Miranda scrambled into the kitchen, pulled the extinguisher from the pantry shelf and dashed back down the cellar steps.

By now the smoke was thick enough to make her eyes burn. Through the whirling haze she saw the source: a bundle of flaming rags. Nearby, just beneath a shattered basement window, lay a red brick. At once she understood what had happened, and her panic gave way to fury. *How dare they smash my window? How dare they attack me in my own home?*

"Stay back!" Chase yelled, plunging forward through the smoke. His shoes crunched over broken glass as he crossed the concrete floor. He aimed the extinguisher; a stream of white shot out and hissed over the flames. A few sweeps of the nozzle and the fire faltered and died under a smothering blanket of powder. Only the smoke remained, a stinking pall that hung like a cloud around the bare light bulb.

"It's out!" said Chase. He was prowling the basement now, searching for new flames. He didn't notice that

Miranda had gone rigid with fury, didn't see that she was staring, white-faced, at the broken glass on the floor.

"Why can't they leave me *alone?*" she cried.

Chase turned and looked at her with sudden intensity. He said, dead quiet, "You mean this has happened before?"

"Not—not this. But phone calls, really cruel ones. Again and again. And messages, written on my window."

"What sort of messages?"

"What you'd expect." She swallowed and looked away. "You know, to the local murderess."

He took a step toward her. "You know who's doing it?"

"I told myself it was just—just some kids. But kids, they wouldn't set fire to my house…."

Chase glanced down at the brick, then up at the shattered window. "It's a crazy way to burn down a house," he said. He went to her, took her by the shoulders, gently rubbed her arms. She felt warmth in his touch, and strength. Courage. He framed her face with his hands and said quietly, "I'm going to call the police."

She nodded. Together they started up the steps to the kitchen. They were halfway up the stairs when the door above them suddenly slammed shut. An instant later the bolt squealed home.

"They've shut us in!" cried Miranda.

He dashed past her up the stairs and began pounding on the door. In frustration he threw himself against it. His shoulder slammed into the wood.

"It's solid!" said Miranda. "You can't break it down."

Chase groaned. "I think I just found that out."

Footsteps creaked across the floor overhead. Miranda froze, tracing with her gaze the intruder's movements.

"What's he doing?" she whispered.

As if in answer to her question, the single light bulb suddenly went out. The basement was plunged into darkness.

"Chase?" she cried.

"I'm here! Right here. Give me your hand."

She reached up blindly toward him; at once he found her wrist. "It's all right," he murmured, pulling her toward him, gathering her tightly against his chest. Just the unyielding support of that embrace was enough to take the edge off her panic. "We'll be okay," he murmured. "We just have to find a way out. We can't make it through the window. You have a cellar door? A coal hatch?"

"There's—there's an old loading hatch near the furnace. It opens to the side yard."

"All right. Let's see if we can get it open. Just move us in the right direction."

Together they felt their way down the steps, to the cellar floor. Shards of glass skittered before their feet as they inched their way through the darkness. It seemed like a journey across eternity, through a blackness so thick it might have been firm to the touch. At last Miranda's extended hand touched pipes, then the cold, damp granite of the cellar wall.

"Which way to the hatch?" asked Chase.

"I think it's to the left."

Upstairs, the creaking moved across the floor, then a door slammed shut. *They've left the house,* Miranda thought in relief. *They're not going to hurt us.*

"I found the oil tank!" said Chase.

"Then the coal hatch should be just above. There are some steps—"

"Right here." He released her hand. Though she knew he was right beside her, that break in contact left her hovering at the edge of panic. If only she could see something, anything! She could hear Chase shoving up against the wood, could hear the crack and groan of the hatch as he struggled to swing it open. Straining to see through the darkness, she could make out, little by little, the vague outline of his head, then the gleam of sweat on his face. More details seemed to emerge out of darkness: the hulking shadow of the furnace, the oil tank, the reddish glint of the copper pipes. It was all visible now.

Too visible. Where was the light coming from?

With new apprehension she turned and stared up at the basement window. Reflected in the shattered glass was a flickering dance of orange light. Firelight. "Oh, my God," she whispered. "Chase..."

He turned and stared.

Even as they watched, the glow in the window shards leaped to a new and horrifying brilliance.

"We have to get out of here!" she cried.

He shoved against the hatch. "I can't get it open!"

"Here, let me help you!"

They both pushed up against the wood, pounded it with their bare fists. Already, smoke was swirling in through the broken window. Overhead, through the cracks in the floorboards, they could see the terrible glow of flames consuming the house above. Most of the heat was funneled up, toward the roof, but soon the timbers would give way. They would be trapped beneath falling debris.

The hatch was immovable.

Chase snatched up the fire extinguisher and began to

pound it against the wood. "I'll keep trying to break through!" he yelled. "You get to the window—yell for help!"

Miranda scrambled over to the window. Smoke was billowing in, a thick, suffocating black cloud. She could barely reach the opening. She glanced around in panic for a crate, a chair, something to stand on. Nothing was in sight.

She screamed louder than she had ever screamed in her life.

Even then, she knew help wouldn't reach them in time. The basement window faced the back of the house, toward the garden. She was too far below the opening for her voice to carry any distance. She glanced up, at the floor beams. Already, the evil glow of heat shone through. She could hear the groan of the wood as it sagged. How long before those beams gave way? How long before she and Chase collapsed under that smothering blackness of smoke? The air had grown unbearably close.

It's already an oven, she thought. *And it will only get hotter....*

Eight

Chase pounded desperately at the hatch. A board splintered, but the barrier held. "Someone's nailed it shut!" he yelled. "Keep calling for help!"

She screamed, again and again, until her voice cracked, until she had almost no voice left.

She heard, in the distance, the sound of a dog barking, and Mr. Lanzo's far-off shouts. She tried to shout back. All she could manage was a pitifully weak cry. There was no answering call. Had she imagined the voice? Or couldn't he hear her?

Even if he did, would he track her screams to this small opening facing the garden? Safety lay so close, yet was so unreachable. If she stood on tiptoe she could actually poke her hand through the shards of broken glass, could feel the soil beneath her fingertips. Just inches away would be her beloved delphiniums, her newly planted violas....

An image of her garden, of rich, moist earth and a freshly tilled flower bed suddenly flashed into her mind. Hadn't she just expanded that bed? Hadn't she used a pickax to break up the sod? The pickax—where did she leave it? She remembered laying it against the side of the house—

Near the cellar window.

With her bare fist she broke away the last shards of glass. Something warm ran down her arm. Blood, she thought with a strange sense of detachment. But no pain— she was too panicked to feel anything but the desperate need to escape the flames. She reached through the open window and ran her fingers along the outside wall. Nothing on the right, just the rough clapboard shingles above a granite foundation. She shifted to the left side of the window, swept her hand along the outside frame and touched warm metal. The pickax head!

She gripped it so tightly her fingers cramped. Painfully she managed to slide the heavy iron head sideways, in front of the window. With a little wriggling she maneuvered first the sharp point, then the blade end, through the window opening.

The pick landed with a hard clang on the concrete floor.

Coughing and gasping, she dragged the tool into the blinding smoke. Already, flames were engulfing the floorboards above her head. "Chase!" she cried. "Where are you?"

"I'm here!"

She started toward the sound of Chase's voice but halfway across she lost her bearings. The whole room seemed to be moving around her like some crazy circus ride. *I can't faint now,* she thought. *If I do, I'll never wake up.* Already her knees were giving way. How she needed a breath of fresh air, just one! She sank to the floor. The concrete felt blessedly damp and cool against her face.

"Miranda!"

The sound of Chase's voice seemed to jump-start some last internal surge of strength. She struggled back to her knees. "I can't—can't see you...."

"I'll find you! Keep talking!"

"No, we'll both get lost! Stay by the hatch!" She began to crawl, moving in the direction of his voice, dragging the pickax behind her. The sound of the fire above them had grown to a roar. Fallen embers lay scattered and glowing on the concrete. Blinded by smoke, she put her hand on one and the pain that seared her skin brought a sob to her throat.

"I'm coming for you!" Chase shouted.

His voice seemed far away, as though he were calling from some distant room. She realized she was fading, and that the room had grown dark, and that this inferno was where she would die. She clawed her way forward, dragging herself and the pickax a few more precious inches.

"Miranda!" His voice seemed even more distant now, another world, another universe. And that seemed most terrible of all—that she would die without the comfort of his touch.

She reached out to drag herself one last time—

And found his hand. Instantly his fingers closed around her wrist and he hauled her close. His touch was like some wondrous restorative. She found the strength to rise once again to her knees.

"Here," she said with a cough, dragging the pickax toward him. "Will this work?"

"It has to!" He staggered to his feet. "Stay low," he commanded. "Keep your head down!"

She heard him grunt as he swung the pickax, heard the

thunk of the metal slamming into the wood. Another swing, another blow. Splinters flew, raining into her hair. He was coughing, weaving. Against the backlight of flames she could see him struggle to stay on his feet.

He swung again.

The hatch gave way. A blast of cool air flew in through the jagged opening. The inrush of fresh oxygen was like throwing fuel on the fire. Everywhere, timbers seemed to explode into flame. Miranda dropped to the ground, her face buried in her arms. An ember fell hissing onto her head. She brushed it away, shuddering at the smell of her own burning hair.

Chase gasped in one last breath of air, then, grunting from the effort, he heaved the pickax against the wood.

The hatch flew apart.

Miranda felt herself yanked upward, through some long, dark tunnel. She could see no light at the other end, could see no end at all. There was just that black passage, the dizzying sense of motion, the clawlike grasp of fingers against her flesh.

Then, suddenly, there was the grass.

And there was Chase, cradling her in his arms, stroking her face, her hair.

She took in a breath. The rush of air into her lungs was almost painful. She coughed, drew in more air, more! She felt drunk on its sweetness.

The night was a whirlwind of noise, sirens, shouting voices and the crackle of fire. She gazed up in horror at the flames; they seemed to fill the heavens.

"Oh, God," she whispered. "My house…"

"We made it out," said Chase. "That's all that matters. We're alive."

She focused on his face. It was a mask of soot, lit by the hellish glow of the fire. They stared at each other, a look of shared wonder that they were both still breathing.

"Miranda," he murmured. He bent and pressed his lips to her forehead, her eyelids, her mouth. He tasted of smoke and sweat and desperation. All at once, they were both shaking and clutching each other in wild relief.

"Mo! Honey! You all right?"

Mr. Lanzo, dressed in his pajamas, scuttled toward them across the lawn. "I was afraid you were inside! Kept tellin' those idiot firemen I heard you screaming!"

"We're okay," Chase said. He took Miranda's face in his hands and kissed her. "We're fine."

Somewhere, a window shattered in the heat of the flames.

"Hey! You people move back!" a fireman yelled. "Everyone get back!"

Chase pulled Miranda to her feet. Together they retreated across Mr. Lanzo's lawn and onto the street. They watched as the fire hoses unleashed a torrent of spray. Water hissed onto the flames.

"Aw, honey," said Mr. Lanzo sadly. "It's too late. She's gone."

Even as he said it, the roof collapsed. Miranda watched in despair as a sheet of flame shot up, turning the night sky into a blazing dawn. *It's all gone,* she thought. *Everything I owned. I've lost it all.*

She wanted to scream out her fury, her anguish, but the violence of those flames held her in a trance. She could only watch as a strange numbness took hold.

"Ms. Wood?"

Slowly she turned.

Lorne Tibbetts was standing beside her. "What happened here?" he asked.

"What the hell do you *think* happened?" Chase shot back. "Someone torched her house. While we were in it."

Lorne looked at Miranda, who stared back at him with dazed eyes. He looked at the burning house, which had already collapsed into little more than a heap of firewood.

"You'd better come with me," he said. "I'll need a statement. From both of you."

"Now do you believe it?" asked Chase. "Someone's trying to kill her."

Lorne Tibbetts's gaze, in the best poker player tradition, revealed absolutely nothing. He began to doodle in the margin of his notepad. Nothing artistic there, not even a few healthy free-form loops. These were tight little triangles linked together like crystals. The geometric creation of a geometric mind. He clicked his pen a few times, then he turned and yelled, "Ellis?"

Ellis poked his head in the door. "Yo, Lorne."

"You finished with Ms. Wood?"

"Got it all down."

"Okay." Lorne rose to his feet and started out of the room.

"Wait," said Chase. "What happens now?"

"I talk to her. Ellis talks to you."

"You mean I have to tell it all over again?"

"It's the way we do things around here. Independent questioning. Routine police procedure." He tucked his shirt into his trousers, smoothed back his hair and walked out the door.

Ellis Snipe sat in Lorne's vacated seat and grinned at Chase. "Hey, Mr. T. How ya doing?"

Chase looked at that moronic, gap-toothed smile and wondered, *Was Mayberry ever this bad?*

"Why don't we start at the beginning," said Ellis.

"Which beginning?" Chase shot back.

Ellis looked confused. "Uh, you choose."

Chase sighed. He glanced at the door, wondering how Miranda was holding up. No matter what Dr. Steiner had said, a hospital bed was where she belonged. But the old quack had simply dressed her glass cuts, examined her lungs and declared hospitalization unnecessary. What Dr. Steiner had neglected to consider was her emotional state. She'd lost her house, her possessions; she was left with no sense of order to her life. What she needed was a safe place, a cocoon where no one could hurt her....

"Uh, Mr. Tremain? You think you could maybe try and cooperate?"

Chase looked at Ellis. What was the point of fighting? he thought wearily. Ellis Snipe looked like the kind of robot who'd follow orders to the letter. If he had to, he'd sit there all night, waiting for Chase to talk.

For the second time that night Chase told the story. He took it back to the cottage, the evidence of a break-in, the secret files. This time he left out the information about Lorne Tibbetts and his fling with the librarian. Some things, he thought, should remain private.

Ellis wrote it all down in a weird, spidery script that couldn't possibly be produced by a normal personality.

When Chase was finished, Ellis asked one and only one question. "Was there anything in those secret files about me?"

"Not a thing," said Chase.

Ellis looked disappointed.

After Ellis had left, Chase sat alone at the table, wondering what came next. A third cop, another go-around with the story? The whole affair had taken on a surreal quality, like some never-ending nightmare. For ten minutes he waited for something to happen. Then, fed up with being ignored, he shoved his chair back and went in search of Miranda.

He found her in the same interrogation room where he'd first laid eyes on her over a week before. She was sitting alone. A smudge of soot blackened her cheek, and her hair was dusted with ash.

She gazed at him with a look of utter exhaustion. "The cop station from hell," she murmured.

He smiled. Then he saw her hand. It was encased in bandages. "Is it as serious as it looks?"

"The doctor just believes in doing a thorough job." She looked in wonder at the free-form sculpture of surgical gauze and tape. "I was afraid he'd amputate."

"A hand as nice as yours? I wouldn't have let him."

She tried to return the smile, but couldn't quite manage it.

"You have to leave the island," he said.

"I can't. The terms of my bail—"

"To hell with the bail terms! You can't wait around for the next accident, the next fire."

"I can't leave the county."

"This time you were lucky. Next time—"

"What am I *supposed* to do?" She looked at him in sudden anger. "Run and hide?"

"Yes."

"From *what?* I don't even know who's trying to kill me!" Her cry echoed in the stark room. At once she flushed, as though shamed by the sound of her own hysteria.

"If I leave, I'll never know what I'm running from," she said quietly. "Or if I'm still being hunted. What kind of life is that, Chase? Never knowing if I'm safe. Always waking up at night, listening for footsteps. Wondering if that creak on the stairs is someone coming for me…." She shuddered and stared down at the table.

Lord, he thought. *How did I ever get involved with this woman? She's not my problem. I'm not her white knight. I should get up and walk right out of this room. Who would blame me?*

And then a voice inside him said, *I would.*

He pulled out a chair and sat across from her. She didn't look up. She just kept staring at the ugly tabletop.

"If you won't leave, then what are you going to do?"

She shrugged. It hurt him to see the hopelessness in that gesture. "Does it matter?"

"It matters to me."

"Why?" The look she gave him made him want to say things he knew he'd regret. That he cared whether she lived or died. He cared what happened to her. He cared too much.

He said, with unassailable logic, "Because what happened tonight is somehow tied in with Richard. The break-in at Rose Hill. The fire. And you."

She gave a dispirited laugh. "Yes, somewhere in all this mess, I seem to fit in. And I haven't the faintest idea why."

The door opened. Ellis said, "There you are, Mr. T. Lorne says you both can go. Says he can't think of any more questions."

I hope I never see this place again, thought Chase as they followed Ellis down the hall, into the front office. Lorne was sitting at one of the desks, talking on the phone.

He glanced up as Chase and Miranda walked past, and motioned to them to wait.

"Oh, hell." Chase sighed. "He just thought of another question."

Lorne hung up and said to Ellis, "Bring the car around. We got us another call."

"Man, oh, man," Ellis whined as he headed out to the garage. "This is one heck of a Thursday night."

Lorne looked at Miranda. "You got a place to stay?"

"I'll drive her to the hotel," said Chase.

"I was thinking along the lines of someplace safer," Lorne said. "A friend's house, maybe?"

"There's always Mr. Lanzo," said Miranda.

"No, I'll take you over to Annie's house," said Chase. "At least *her* faculties are still intact."

"Yeah, that'd be better," said Lorne, reaching for his hat. "Considering."

"Considering what?" said Chase.

"The two empty gas cans we found over by Ms. Wood's house. Plus the two-by-fours nailed over the cellar hatch."

Miranda stared at him. There it was. Undeniable proof someone was trying to kill her. Her body seemed to sag against Chase. "Then you believe me," she whispered.

Lorne reached for his hat. "Well, I'll tell you what I believe, Ms. Wood. I do believe this is one of the weirdest nights we've ever had here on this island. And I do not like the trend."

"What else is going on?" asked Chase.

"An assault. On Miss Lila St. John, if you can believe it. She just called in the report."

"Someone attacked her?" said Chase, shocked. "Why?"

"She claims she tried to stop a break-in." Lorne, obviously skeptical, started for the door. "At Rose Hill Cottage."

"So," said Annie Berenger, pouring out three tall whiskeys. "Do I get to write all about the juicy details? Or is this baby-sitting job another gratis deal?"

"I thought you and Miranda were friends," said Chase.

"Oh, we are. But I'm a reporter, too." She handed Chase a glass. "It's my job to take advantage of the situation." She glanced at the closed door to the bathroom, where Miranda was showering. "You know, Chase, she looked pretty beat-up. Shouldn't she be in a hospital or something?"

"She'll be fine right here, Annie. As long as you keep your eagle eye on her."

"Terrific. What I always wanted to be. A mommy." She tossed back a quick slug of whiskey. "Oh, don't get me wrong. I like Miranda. I used to be a lot like her. About a century ago." She poured herself a second glass. "But women grow up fast these days. We have to. It's the men who age us. Take my boyfriend, Irving. Please. I've been waiting a year for him to pop the question. It's giving me gray hairs." She took a sip of whiskey, then turned and looked at Chase. "So how much trouble is she in?"

"It could get dangerous. Are you ready for that?"

"Ready?" She went to an end table and opened the drawer. Casually she pulled out a revolver. "Little souvenir I picked up in Boston. I'm a lousy shot, but sometimes I get lucky." She tossed the gun back into the drawer. "Good enough?"

"I'm impressed."

Annie laughed. "Men always are when they see my pistol's bigger than theirs." She glanced over her shoulder as the bathroom door opened. "Hi. Feeling better?"

"Just cleaner," said Miranda, walking barefoot into the living room. She was wearing one of Annie's huge T-shirts. It hung like a dress over her slim hips.

Annie held out a glass of whiskey. "Join us in a toast."

"To what?"

"Just drink it. We'll think of something."

Miranda came toward them and took the glass. She brought with her those fresh shower smells, the scent of flowers and soap and feminine warmth. Her hair, still damp, was a mass of unruly waves. The sight of her sent Chase's head swimming. Or was it the whiskey?

"So what happens now?" asked Annie.

Chase turned away and set his glass on the nearest table. "The police are handling it."

"Look, I've been covering that beat for five years. I wouldn't be too optimistic."

"Lorne's a bright guy. He can figure it out."

"But whose side is he on? I'm not saying Lorne's corrupt, or anything. But you did find that page about him and Valerie Everhard."

"A fling with the local librarian?" Chase shrugged. "I'd consider that only a minor scandal."

"Did you ask Lorne about it?"

"Yes. He didn't deny it. And he didn't seem bothered by it."

"Annie, did you know Richard had those files?" Miranda asked.

Annie shrugged. "We had a number of files on local personalities. Jill did the interviews, wrote the pieces. Every summer we'd run a few profiles. But nothing that'd make tongues twitter." She set her glass down. "Well, whatever was in those files, it's all up in smoke now. A pity you didn't have copies. You've lost your only clues."

"I don't think so," said Chase. "Those were the papers the burglar left behind. Whatever he's really after is still at Rose Hill."

"How do you know?"

"Because he went back there tonight."

"What he didn't count on," said Miranda, "was tangling with Miss Lila St. John. Again."

Annie shook her head and laughed. "That is one poor, unfortunate burglar."

Miss Lila St. John was, at that moment, holding a bag of ice to a nasty-looking goose egg on the back of her head. "What do you mean, did I get a good look at him?" she snapped. "Does it seem likely I got a look at him? Considering where he whacked me?"

"It was just a routine question, ma'am," whimpered Ellis.

"That is the problem with you police people. You are so tied up with your routine questions you never bother to think."

"Miss St. John," Lorne politely interjected, "allow me to rephrase Ellis's question. What, exactly, *did* you see?"

"Precious little."

"A figure? A face?"

"Just a light. I told you, I was sitting here reading. *Death Becomes You.*

"Excuse me?"

"The name of the book. It features a police detective with a genius IQ." She paused. "Obviously, a novel with no basis in reality."

Lorne let that one slide by. Miss St. John deserved a

little leeway tonight. After all, a blow on the head—even a head as hard as hers—would make anyone cranky. "Go on," he said.

"Well, I put the book aside to make tea. And as I did, I happened to look out that window. It faces south, toward Rose Hill Cottage. That's when I saw the light."

"A car headlight?"

"No, much dimmer. A flashlight, I think. Moving through the woods. I knew it was headed for Rose Hill. That's all that lies in that direction. So I decided to check on it."

"Why didn't you call us?"

"Because it might simply have been one of the Tremains. Now, how would it look if I dragged you men all the way out here, just to confront the rightful owner?"

"The rightful owner seems to be in doubt."

"Let's not confuse ourselves with that issue. Anyway, I went out—"

"Alone?"

"If only! I would have been just fine if Ozzie hadn't followed me."

"Ozzie?" inquired Ellis.

As if on cue, an enormous black dog sauntered across the room and eyed Ellis.

"Yes, you certainly made a racket," said Miss St. John to the dog. "All that yowling and thrashing in the bushes. No wonder you never catch anything." She looked at Lorne. "It's *his* fault. He followed me up the road. Somewhere along the way I lost track of the light. I was trying to see through the dark and shoo off Ozzie at the same time. He was making such unattractive noises. I turned around and gave him a slap. And that's when he whacked me."

"Ozzie?" asked Ellis.

"No! The man. Or woman. It was dark, so I couldn't tell you which."

"Did you black out?"

"I'm not sure. Things got a little confused at that point. I remember being on my knees in the bushes. Hearing footsteps run away. And feeling mad as hell." She glared at Ozzie. "Yes, and I do mean at *you.*"

The dog, unperturbed, began to lick Lorne's brand-new boot. Gingerly, Lorne gave the dog a little shove. Ozzie, looking insulted, redirected his affectionate overtures toward a more agreeable target—Ellis's leg.

"Then you never saw your attacker?" Lorne asked.

"No, I can't say I did."

"What happened then?"

"I came back here. Oh, I got a little turned around in the dark, but I found my way back, eventually. And I called you."

"So the attack happened—when?"

"It would be about two hours ago."

About the same time the flames were consuming the last of Miranda Wood's house, thought Lorne. It seemed unlikely that the same culprit could have set fire to the house, then raced out here in time to knock Miss St. John on the head. Two crimes, two criminals. Too bad.

Lorne preferred simple solutions.

"Are you certain your attacker was headed for Rose Hill?" he asked.

"I know he was. And he'll be back."

"Why?"

"Because he didn't get what he wanted."

"You're referring to the scandal sheets?"

Miss St. John gave him a look of pure innocence. "Oh. You know about that?"

"Yes. And for your information, Miss St. John, I didn't come on to Valerie Everhard. She came on to me."

Ellis looked up from the dog now nuzzling his knee. "What was that about Valerie Everhard?"

"Never mind," snapped Lorne and Miss St. John simultaneously.

"There was a report on me, too," said Miss St. John with a faint note of pride. "As well as almost everyone on this road. I had no idea Richard Tremain was such a busybody."

"Any idea why?"

"I'll give the man the benefit of the doubt and attribute it to mere curiosity. As opposed to less benign motives."

Blackmail was what she meant. Lorne couldn't see that such a scheme made much sense. First of all, none of those secrets was particularly nasty. Embarrassing, perhaps, but nothing that couldn't be lived down. And that included his own penchant for married librarians. Second, the would-be victims ranged from the moderately well-to-do Forrest Mayhew to the outright cash-strapped Gordimers. Why blackmail a family that can scarcely pay their grocery bills?

Unless money was not the sought-after payment.

He wondered about this all the way back to town. Wondered why Richard Tremain would want those secrets. Wondered if he was even the one who'd collected them in the first place. The cottage, after all, had been open to others in the family. Cassie. Phillip.

Evelyn.

No, not Evelyn, he thought. She wouldn't dirty her hands in this filth.

"You and Valerie Everhard," Ellis muttered as he drove. "I never woulda guessed."

"Look, I felt sorry for her," said Lorne. "She needed some male attention."

"Oh." Ellis kept staring straight ahead at the road and nodding to himself.

"What the hell's that supposed to mean?" Lorne demanded.

"Oh, I was just thinking."

"About what?"

"How awful sorry you must be feeling for that woman right now."

"Valerie Everhard?"

"No." said Ellis. "The widow Tremain."

"It's a matter of loyalty, Chase," said Noah. "To the family. To your brother. To the people who *matter.*"

Chase said nothing. He simply continued slicing his ham, albeit with more concentrated vigor than usual. He knew they were all watching him. Noah and Evelyn. The twins. They were waiting for him to respond. But he kept on slicing that meat, mangling it, really, into smaller and smaller pieces.

"Never mind, Daddy," said Evelyn. "Can't you see? He's so wrapped up with that witch, he can't see the trap he's—"

"Please, Evelyn." Chase set down his knife.

"She's twisted you around, Chase! She has a talent for that! Among other things. But you can't be bothered with the facts anymore. No, all you want to believe are her lies."

"I want to believe the truth," he said quietly.

"The truth is, she's a whore."

"Evelyn," cut in Noah. "That is quite enough."

Evelyn turned on her father. "Whose side are you on?"

"You know damn well I'm on your side. I always have been."

"Then why don't you back me up?"

"Because this conversation doesn't become you. You've forgotten all I taught you about dignity. Pride."

"Well, *excuse me,* Daddy. It's not every day one's husband gets murdered." She glanced around at the sideboard. "Where's that wine? It's not too early for a drink."

"You will get over the murder. You'll get beyond it. And you will remember who you are."

"Who I am?" She rose to her feet. "Who I am is more of an embarrassment every day." She shoved her chair back against the table and left the room.

There was a long silence.

"She does have a point, Chase," said Noah, sounding quite reasonable. "The family should stick together. No matter what attractions this Miranda Wood person offers, don't you think it's best you stand by us?"

"What attraction *does* she offer?" asked Cassie.

"That's irrelevant," snapped Chase.

Noah raised an eyebrow. "Is it?"

Chase met Noah's gaze with a look of sheer indifference. Which, at that moment, wasn't at all what he was feeling. He had plenty of feelings when it came to Miranda Wood, and indifference wasn't one of them. All night he'd dreamt about her. He'd awakened sweating, remembering the fire, feeling once again the panic of not being able to find her in that well of smoke and flames. He'd drop back to sleep, only to sink yet again into the same nightmare. Some time during his fitful tossing and turning, he'd come to several realizations. That he was incapable of logical thought where Miranda Wood was concerned. That the attraction he felt for her was growing more dangerous every day.

And that, no matter what his instincts told him, the weight of evidence still pointed to her guilt.

This morning he'd risen from bed exhausted but absolutely clearheaded. He knew what he had to do. He had to put some distance between them. As he should have done from the very beginning.

He said, "You don't have to worry, Noah. I don't plan to see her again."

"I always thought you were the smarter Tremain," said Noah. "I was right."

Chase shrugged. "Not really a flattering comment. Considering how little you thought of Richard."

Noah glanced at the twins. "You two! Don't you have something better to do?"

"Not really," said Phillip.

"Well, clear the table, then. Go on."

"It's not as if we didn't know," said Cassie.

Noah frowned at her. "Know what?"

"That you and Dad didn't get along."

"For that matter, young lady, he didn't get along with you, either."

"Normal father-daughter disagreements. Not like you two, always at each other's throats. All that yelling and name-calling—"

"That's enough!" Noah's face had turned an ugly red. He rose partway out of his chair, his gaze targeted on his insolent granddaughter. "The day you were born, Cassandra, I took one look at you and I said, 'Watch out for that one. She's going to be trouble.'"

"Yes, it runs in our family, doesn't it?"

Instantly Phillip was on his feet, tugging at Noah's arm. "Come on, Granddad. Let's go outside, you and me. Walk around the block. I wanted to tell you about my year at Harvard—"

"Damn nursery for snooty rich boys."

"Just a walk, Granddad. It'll do you good."

Noah harrumphed and shoved his chair against the table. "Let's go, then. Hell, I could use the fresh air."

The two men walked out, slamming the front door behind them.

Cassie looked at Chase and smiled ironically. "One big happy family."

"What was that you said? About Noah and Richard."

"They despised each other. You knew that."

"*Despised* wasn't the word that came to mind. Disliked, maybe. You know, the usual rivalry between father and son-in-law."

"This wasn't just your usual rivalry." Cassie began to slice her ham into dainty pieces. For the first time Chase found himself actually seeing his niece. Before, she'd always seemed lost from view, the colorless sister skulking in the shadow of her brother. Now he took a new and closer look, and what he saw was a young woman with a square jaw and eyes like a ferret's. The resemblance to Noah was startling. No wonder the old man didn't get along with her. He probably saw too much of himself in that face. She looked him straight in the eye. No squirming, no discomfort, just that steady gaze.

"What did they argue about? Noah and your father?"

"Anything. Everything. Oh, they never let it get beyond these walls. Dad was weird that way. We could all be screaming at each other in this house, but once we stepped out the door he insisted we look like the perfect family. It was so phony. In public Dad and Noah would make like old buddies. And all the time there was that rivalry between them."

"Over your mother?"

"Of course. Noah's darling. And Dad could never be a good enough husband." She snorted. "Not that he tried very hard."

Chase paused, wondering how to phrase his next question. "Did you know your father was having… affairs?"

"He's been at it for years," Cassie said with a wave of her hand. "Lots of women."

"Which ones?"

She shrugged. "I figured that was his business."

"You two weren't very close, were you?"

"Daughters just weren't his thing, Uncle Chase. While I was working my butt off, getting straight A's, he was planning for Phillip's Harvard education. Grooming him to take over the *Herald.*"

"Phillip doesn't seem exactly thrilled by the prospect."

"You noticed that? Dad never did." She took a few bites of ham, then gave Chase a thoughtful look. "And what was the problem between *you* two?"

"Problem?" He resisted the urge to look away, to avoid her gaze. She would probably know immediately that he was hiding something. As it was, she'd probably already detected the flicker of discomfort in his eyes.

"The last time I saw you, Uncle Chase, I was ten years old. That was at Grandpa Tremain's funeral. Now, Greenwich isn't that far away. But you never came back for a visit, not once."

"Lives get complicated. You know how it is, Cassie."

She gave him a searching look, then said, "It's not easy, is it? Being the ignored sibling in the family?"

Damn this sharp-eyed brat, he thought. He gathered up his empty dishes and rose to his feet.

"You don't think she did it. Do you?" Cassie asked. They didn't have to mention names. They both knew exactly what they were talking about.

"I haven't decided," he said. He carried the dishes toward the kitchen. In the doorway he stopped. "By the way, Cassie," he said. "I called here last night about seven, to say I wouldn't be home for dinner. No one answered the phone. Where was your mother?"

"I really wouldn't know." Cassie picked up a slice of toast and calmly began to spread marmalade on it. "You'd have to ask her."

Chase drove directly to Rose Hill. No detours, no little side trips to pick up suspected murderesses. He had no intention of being distracted by Miranda Wood today. What he needed was a dose of coolheaded logic, and that meant keeping his distance. Today he had other things on his mind, the first item being: Who kept trying to break in to the cottage, and what was he searching for?

The answer lay somewhere in Rose Hill.

So that was where he headed. He drove with the window rolled down, the salt air whistling past his cheek. It brought back all those summer days of his childhood, riding with his mother along this very road, the smell of the sea in his face, the cry of the gulls echoing off the cliffs. How she had loved this drive! His mother had been a daredevil behind the wheel, screeching around these curves, laughing as the wind tangled her dark hair. They'd both laughed a lot those days, and he'd wondered if anyone else in the world had a mother so wild, so beautiful. So free.

Her death had left him devastated.

If only, before she'd died, she'd told him the truth.

He turned onto the access road and bumped along past all the old camp signs, past the cottages of families whose kids he'd once played with. Good memories, bad memories—they all returned as he drove up that road. He remembered twirling in the tire swing until he was so dizzy he threw up. Kissing buck-toothed Lucy Baylor behind the water tower. Hearing that awful crash of a breaking window and knowing it was *his* baseball they'd find lying in the shattered glass. The memories were so vivid he didn't notice that he'd already rounded the last bend and was just now turning onto the gravel driveway.

There was a car parked in front of the cottage.

He pulled up beside it and climbed out. He saw no sign of the driver. Could their burglar have turned desperate enough to pay a visit in broad daylight?

He hurried up the porch steps and was startled to hear the whistling of a kettle from the kitchen. Who the hell would be brazen enough to not only break in, but also make himself right at home? He shoved open the door and came face-to-face with the guilty party.

"I've just made some tea," said Miranda. She gave him a tight smile, not unfriendly, just nervous. Perhaps afraid. She nodded down at the tea tray she was carrying. "Would you like some?"

Chase glanced around the room, at the books arranged in neat piles on the floor. The desk had been cleared, the drawers' contents emptied into a series of cardboard boxes.

Slowly his gaze shifted and took in the three bookcases. One was already two-thirds empty.

"We spent the morning going through Richard's papers," Miranda explained. "I'm afraid we haven't turned up anything yet, but—"

He shook his head. "We?"

"Miss St. John and I."

"Is she here?"

"She went back to her house, to feed Ozzie."

Their gazes met. *I try to stay away from you,* he thought, *and damn it, here you are. Here we are, alone in this house.*

The possibilities flooded his mind. Temptation, enemy of reason, danced its devil dance, the way it did every time he was in the same room with her. He thought of Richard, thought of her, thought of the two of them together. It hurt. Maybe that's why he chose to think of it. To quell the rising need he felt when he looked at her now.

"She—Miss St. John—thought it made sense to get started without you," Miranda said in a rush, as though suddenly frantic to fill the silence. "We didn't know when you'd get here, and we didn't want to call the house. I suppose we're trespassing, in a way, but…" Her voice trailed off.

"Technically speaking," he said after a pause, "you are."

She set down the tea tray, then straightened to face him. Her nervousness was gone. In its place was calm determination. "Maybe so. But it's what I have to do. We can search together. Or we can search separately. But I am going to search." She raised her chin, met his gaze without flinching. "So, Chase. Which way shall it be?"

Nine

His gaze was neutral, as unrevealing as that blank wall behind him. More revealing to Miranda was her acute sense of disappointment. She'd hoped to see at least a trace of gladness in his eyes, that he'd be pleased to find her here today. What she hadn't expected was this…indifference. *So that's how it is between us,* she thought. *What's happened since I saw you last? What did Evelyn say to you? That's it, isn't it? They've gotten to you. Richard's family. Your family.*

He shrugged. "It does make sense, I suppose. Working together."

"Of course it does."

"And you've already gotten off to a good start, I see."

In silence she poured a cup of tea, then carried it to the bookcase. There she calmly continued the task she'd been working on earlier—pulling down the books, riffling through the pages for any loose papers. She felt him watching her, sensed his gaze like a prickling in her back. "You can start on the other bookcase," she said without looking at him.

"What have you found so far?"

"No surprises." She reached for another book. "Unless you count Richard's rather weird taste in reading material." She looked at a book jacket. *The Advanced Physics of Ocean Waves.* "This one, for instance. I never knew he was interested in physics."

"He wasn't. When it came to science, he was functionally illiterate."

She opened the cover. "Well, this *is* his book. I see someone's written him a dedication in the front…." Glancing at the title page, she suddenly flushed.

"What is it?"

"You know the old saying?" Miranda murmured. "About not judging a book by its cover?"

Chase moved behind her and read over her shoulder. "*One Hundred and One Sexual Positions.* Fully illustrated?"

Miranda flipped open to a random page and instantly flushed. "They meant what they said about fully illustrated."

He reached around her to take the book. His breath grazed her neck; it left her skin tingling.

"Obviously a dummy jacket," said Chase. "I wonder how many other disguised books are in that stack?"

"I didn't really check," Miranda admitted. "I was looking for loose papers. I wasn't paying much attention to the books themselves."

Chase flipped to the title page and read aloud the handwritten dedication. "To my darling Richard. Can we try number forty-eight again? Love, M." Chase glanced at Miranda.

"I didn't give him that thing!" she protested.

"Then who's M?"

"Someone else. Not me."

He frowned at the dedication. "I wonder what number forty-eight is." He flipped to the page.

"Well?"

Chase took a discreet peek. "You don't want to know," he muttered and let the page riffle shut.

A slip of paper flew out and landed on the floor. They both stared at it in surprise. Chase was the first to snatch it up.

"Dearest love," he read aloud. "I'm thinking of you every day, every hour. I've given up caring about propriety or reputation or hellfire. There's only you and me and the time we have together. That, my darling, is my new definition of heaven." Chase glanced at her, one eyebrow raised in a cynical slant.

Miranda looked straight at him. "In case you're wondering," she said evenly, "I didn't write that note, either." In irritation she took the book and set it down on the nearest pile.

"Then I guess we'll just file it under 'interesting stuff,'" said Chase. "And continue with the rest of these books."

Miranda settled onto the rug. Chase sat in front of the other bookcase. They didn't touch, didn't look at each other. *Safer that way,* she thought. *For both of us.*

For half an hour they flipped through books, slapped them shut, threw clouds of dust in the air. Miranda was the one who found the next piece of the puzzle. It was tucked away in a financial ledger, in an envelope labeled Deductible Expenses.

"It's a receipt," she said, frowning at the slip of paper. "A month ago Richard paid four hundred dollars to this company."

"For what services?" asked Chase.

"It doesn't say. It's just made out to the Alamo Detective Agency in Bass Harbor."

"A detective agency? I wonder what Richard was after."

"Chase." She handed him the slip of paper. "Look at the name of the payee."

"William B. Rodell?" He glanced at her quizzically.

At least you're looking at me again, she thought. *At least we're connecting.* "Don't you remember?" she said. "That note attached to Richard's files."

Chase stared at the receipt, revelation suddenly brightening his dark features.

"Of course," he said softly. "William B. Rodell…"

W.B.R.

It was easy to see how the Alamo Detective Agency got its name. Willie Rodell was a good ol' boy transplant from San Antonio who split his time between Maine and Florida. Summertime was for Maine, and here he was, sitting behind his old steel desk, books and papers piled up in front of him like the battlements of a fort. The office was strictly a solo affair—one phone, one desk, one man. But what a man. Willie Rodell had enough flesh on his bones to fill the suits of two six-footers. *This must be what they mean by Texas-size,* thought Miranda.

"Yeah, I mighta done some work for Mr. Tremain now and again," said Rodell, leaning back in his equally Texas-size chair.

"Meaning you did or you didn't?" asked Chase.

"Well, you're holdin' one of my receipts there, so I guess it means I did."

"What sort of job?"

Willie shrugged. "Routine stuff."

"What *is* your routine stuff?"

"Mostly I do domestic affairs, if you catch my drift.

Who's doin' what to whom, that sorta thing." His smirk re-arranged the folds of his face into something vaguely obscene.

"But that's not the sort of thing you did for Richard, was it?"

"Nope. Though I hear tell there was more than enough dirt to dig in his particular case."

Cheeks burning, Miranda stared down fixedly at Willie's desk, a battle zone of broken pencils and twisted paper clips scattered among a bizarre assortment of magazines. *Hot Ladies. National Locksmith. Car and Driver.*

Chase got right to the point. "He hired you to compile files on his neighbors. Didn't he?"

Willie looked at him blandly. "Files?"

"We saw them, Mr. Rodell. They were among Richard's papers. Detailed reports on almost every resident along the access road. Each one containing sensitive information."

"Dirt sheets."

"That's right."

Willie shrugged. "I didn't write 'em."

"There was a note attached to one of the reports. It said, 'Want more? Let me know.' It was signed with the initials W.B.R." Chase reached over and plucked one of Willie's business cards from the desk. "Which just happens to be your initials."

"Helluva coincidence, hey?"

"He wanted dirt on his neighbors. Why?"

"He was snoopy?"

"So he paid you to write those reports."

"I told you, I didn't write 'em." Willie held up one fat hand. "Scout's honor."

"Then who did?"

"Dunno. But I admire his work."

Miranda, who'd been sitting quietly, focused on one of the magazines on the desk. *National Locksmith.* "You stole them," she said. She looked up at Willie's moonlike face. "That's what Richard hired you for. To steal those files from someone else."

Willie reached up and smoothed back a nonexistent strand of hair.

"You were paid to be a burglar," said Miranda. "What else were you paid for?"

"Look," said Willie, holding up both fat hands in a gesture of mock surrender. "Folks pay me to gather info, okay? That's all I do. Clients don't care how I get it, long as I get it."

"And where did you get those dirt sheets?" asked Chase.

"They were part of a bunch o' papers I sorta picked up."

"What else did you sort of pick up?"

"Financial records, bank statements. Hey, I didn't exactly *steal* 'em. I just, well, borrowed 'em for a few minutes. Long enough to run 'em through ol' man Xerox. Then I put 'em right back where I found 'em."

"The office of Stone Coast Trust," said Miranda.

Willie gave her a man-in-the-moon grin. "Betcha you're real good at Twenty Questions."

"So those were Tony Graffam's files," said Chase. "Not Richard's."

"Mr. T. didn't even know they existed till I handed 'em over. Thought for sure he was gonna want more. You know how it is. Get a taste of appetizer, you want the main course. Well, those papers were just the appetizer. I coulda got more."

"Why didn't you?"

"He fired me."

They frowned at him. "What?" said Miranda.

"That's right," said Willie. "Two days after I hand him those papers, he calls and says, thanks, he won't be needin' my services no more and how much do I owe you? That was that."

"Did he say why he fired you?"

"Nope. Just told me to keep it under my hat, and that he wasn't interested in Stone Coast no more."

"When was this?"

"Oh, about a week before he died."

"The same time he told Jill to kill the article," said Miranda. She looked at Chase. "Maybe he saw what Tony Graffam had on him. And decided to drop the whole investigation."

"But I looked over those papers, 'fore I handed 'em over," said Willie. "There wasn't any report on Tremain. Far as I could tell, wasn't nothin' in there to blackmail him with."

"Did you keep copies?"

"Mr. T. took it all. Didn't want loose papers floatin' around." Willie folded his hands behind his neck and stretched. Blots of sweat showed in his cavernous armpits. "Naw, I don't think it was the files. I think someone went and offered him a little, you know, incentive payment to forget the whole thing. So that's what he did."

"But Richard didn't need the money," said Miranda. "They couldn't bribe him."

"Sweetie, you can bribe just about anyone," said Willie, obviously an authority on such matters. "All it takes is the right price. And even a fella as rich as Tremain had his price."

"The lazy man's method of investigative journalism," said Chase. "Hire a thug to steal the evidence."

"I had no idea he'd do such a thing," said Miranda, gazing ahead in quiet disbelief. It was just after noon, a time when Main Street in Bass Harbor should have been bustling with tourists. Today, though, a cold summer drizzle had cooled the ardor of even the most inveterate sightseers. Miranda and Chase, hunched in their jackets, walked alone.

"And I thought it was just talent," she said softly. "The way he could pull a story together. Come up with evidence that surprised everyone. All that time he was paying someone to do the dirty work."

"It was just Richard's way," said Chase. "Meaning the easy way."

She looked at him. His hair, dampened by mist, was a cap of black, unruly waves. He stared straight ahead, his profile unrevealing. "Is that how he was as a boy?" she asked.

"He was good at finding shortcuts. For a few bucks he'd get someone to write his book report. Or help him cram for tests. He even found some idiot to finish his math homework for him." Chase grinned sheepishly. "Me."

"He bribed you into doing his homework?"

"It was more like, well, blackmail."

"What did he have on you?"

"Lots. Broken windows. Trampled flower beds. I was a pretty bad kid."

"But good at math, obviously."

Chase laughed. "When someone threatened exposure, I was good at a lot of things."

"And Richard took advantage of it."

"He was older. In a lot of ways, smarter. Everyone liked him, wanted to believe the best of him. And the worst of me." He shook his head. "I can see the same thing happening with his kids now. Phillip's the golden boy. And Cassie, she'll be trying all her life to match up."

"Will you be trying all *your* life to match up?"

He looked at her, then looked away. "No. I don't particularly care to make the same mistakes Richard did."

Meaning me, she thought.

The day suddenly seemed colder, darker. It was more than just her sagging spirits. The drizzle had turned to rain.

"Let's duck in someplace and get lunch," said Chase. "We've got another hour and a half till the ferry leaves."

They found a café tucked into an alley off Main Street. From the outside it seemed an unassuming little place with a name to match: Mary Jane's. It was the whiff of rich coffee and grilled meat that finally drew them in. Nothing fancy served here, just good plain food, roast chicken and red potatoes and crisp green beans, accompanied by freshly brewed coffee. Miranda's spirits might be sagging, but her appetite was in fine shape. She moved on to a slice of peach pie and a third round of coffee. A good thing she didn't normally react to stress by overeating. By now she'd be twenty pounds overweight.

"In a way," said Chase, "I'm relieved to learn the truth about those files."

"Relieved to learn Richard paid for an out-and-out burglary?"

"At least he wasn't the one snooping on his neighbors. The one planning blackmail."

She set down her fork. "Yes, I suppose you could talk yourself into thinking that breaking into Stone Coast Trust was somehow, well, morally correct."

"I'm not saying it was. But I can see how Richard might justify it. He's seen the coast eaten away by development. Then it hits close to home and he figures it's time to play dirty. Find out what you can about the developer. Steal a few files, financial records. Throw it back in the other guy's face."

"But he didn't. That's the strange part. He paid Rodell to steal those files. Then, after he gets hold of them, he drops the whole crusade. Kills the article, fires Rodell." She paused, and added softly, "And changes his will."

Chase frowned. "I don't see how that's related."

"The timing fits. Maybe he found something in those papers that got him angry at Evelyn. Made him decide to keep her from ever getting Rose Hill."

"You think there was a file on Evelyn? We didn't see one."

"He might've destroyed it. Or it could have been taken from the cottage. After his death."

They both fell silent at the implications of that statement. Who but Evelyn herself would bother to take such a file?

"This is crazy," said Chase. "Why would Evelyn steal it? It was her own damn cottage. She could walk in and out without anyone raising an eyebrow." He reached for his coffee cup, took a deliberate sip. "I can't see her breaking in and trashing the place."

You can't see her killing anyone, either. Can you? she thought. She wondered about Chase and his sister-in-law. Was their relationship merely cordial? Or did it run deeper than that? He'd stubbornly resisted the possibility that Evelyn might be guilty of wrongdoing, be it theft or murder. Miranda could understand why. Evelyn was a beautiful woman.

Now a free woman.

There was, after all, an appealing tidiness to a match between Chase and Evelyn. It would keep the money in the family, the same last name on the checkbook. Everyone would slip into their new roles with a minimum of muss and fuss. Chase had spent his boyhood trying to live up to his brother's image. Now he could slip right into Richard's place. Much as Miranda hated to admit it, such a mating would have a certain symmetry, a social correctness.

Something I'd never be able to give him.

The waitress came by with the check. Miranda reached for it, but Chase snatched it up first. "I'll take care of it," he said.

Miranda took a few bills from her pocket and laid them on the table.

"What's that for?" asked Chase.

"Call it pride," she said, rising to her feet, "but I always pay my way."

"With me you don't have to."

"I have to," she said flatly. "Especially with you." She grabbed her jacket and headed out the door.

He caught up with her outside. The rain had stopped but the sun had not yet emerged and the sky was a cold monochrome of gray. They walked side by side for a moment, not quite friends, not quite strangers.

"I'll be honest," he said. "I wasn't planning to see you today. Or ever again."

"It's a small town, Chase. It's hard to avoid a person here."

"I was going to drive back to Greenwich tomorrow."

"Oh." She lowered her eyes, willing herself not to feel

disappointment. Or hurt. All those emotions she'd vowed never to feel for another Tremain. The emotions she was feeling now.

"But I've been thinking," he said.

Those four words made her halt and look up at him. *He's watching me, waiting for me to reveal myself. Give myself away as beguiled and bedazzled.*

Which, damn it, I am.

"I've been thinking," he said, "of staying a few more days. Just to clear up those questions about Richard."

She said nothing.

"Anyway, that's why I'm staying in town. It's the only reason."

Her chin came up. "Did I imply otherwise?"

"No." He let out a breath. "No, you didn't."

They walked on, another block, another silence.

"You'll be looking for the same answers, I expect," he said.

"I don't have much choice, do I? It's my future. My freedom."

"Look, I know it makes sense, in a way, for you and I to work together. But it's not exactly…"

"Seemly," she finished for him. "That's what you mean, isn't it? That it's embarrassing for you to be consorting with a woman like me."

"I didn't say that."

"Never mind, Chase." In irritation she turned and continued walking. "You're right, of course. We can't work together. Because we don't really trust each other. Do we?"

He didn't answer. He simply walked beside her, his hands thrust deep in his pockets. And that, more than anything he could have said, was what hurt her most.

* * *

They might not trust each other. They might not want anything to do with each other. But the simple fact was, if they wanted answers, the cottage was where they both had to look. So when Miranda pulled into the gravel driveway of Rose Hill the next morning she was not surprised to see Chase's car already parked there. Ozzie was sprawled on the front porch, looking dejected. He managed a few half-hearted wags of his tail as she came up the steps, but when he saw she wasn't going to invite him inside he flopped back down into a whimpering imitation of a shag rug.

Miss St. John and Chase had already gone through the second bookcase. The place was looking more and more like a disaster zone, with cardboard boxes filled with papers, books precariously stacked in towers, empty coffee cups and dirty spoons littering the end tables.

"I see you started without me," said Miranda, careful to avoid looking at Chase. He was just as carefully avoiding her gaze. "What have you found?"

"Odds and ends," said Miss St. John, thoughtfully eyeing them both. "Shopping lists, receipts. Another love note from M. And a few quite literate college term papers."

"Phillip's?"

"Cassandra's. She must have done some writing out here. A few of the books are hers, as well."

Miranda picked up a bundle of papers and glanced through the titles. "A political analysis of the Boer conflict." "Doom foretold: the French colonialists in Vietnam." "The media and presidential politics." All were authored by Cassandra Tremain.

"A smart cookie," said Miss St. John. "A pity that slick brother of hers always steals the spotlight."

Miranda dug deeper in the box and pulled out the latest note from M. It was typewritten.

> I waited till midnight—you never came. Did you forget? I wanted to call, but I'm always afraid she'll pick up the phone. She has you every weekend, every night, every holiday. I get the dregs.
> How can you say you love me, when you leave me here, waiting for you? I'm worth more than this. I really am.

Quietly Miranda let the note flutter back into the box. Then she went to the window and stood staring out, toward the sea. Pity stirred inside her, for the woman who had written that note, for the pain she'd suffered. *The price we both paid for loving the wrong man.*

"Miranda?" Chase asked. "Is something wrong?"

"No." She cleared her throat and turned to him. "I'm fine. So…where should I start looking?"

"You could help me finish with this shelf. I'm finding papers here and there, so it's going slower than I expected."

"Yes, of course." She went to the shelf, pulled out a book and sat on the floor beside him. Not too close, not too far. *Neither friends nor enemies,* she thought. Just two people sharing the same rug, the same purpose. *For that, we don't even have to like each other.*

For an hour they flipped through pages, brushed away dust. Most of the books, it seemed, hadn't been opened in ages. There were old postcards dated twenty years earlier, addressed to Chase's mother. There was a hand-scrawled list of bird species sighted at Rose Hill, and a library notice from twelve years before, still stuck in the overdue book.

Over the years, so many bits and pieces of the Tremain and Pruitt families had ended up on these shelves. It took time to sort out the vital from the trivial.

An oversize atlas of the state of Maine provided the next clue. Chase pulled it off the shelf and glanced in the front cover. Then he turned and called, "Miss St. John? You ever heard of a place called Hemlock Heights?"

"No. Why?"

"There's a map of it tucked in here." Chase pulled the document out of the atlas and spread it out on the rug. It was a collection of six photocopied pages taped together to form a site map. The pages looked fairly fresh. Property lines had been sketched in, and the lots were labeled by number. At the top was the development's name: Hemlock Heights. "I wonder if Richard was thinking of investing in real estate."

Miss St. John crouched down for a closer look. "Wait. This looks rather familiar. Isn't this our access road? And this lot at the end—lot number one. That's Rose Hill. I recognized that little jag up the mountain."

Chase nodded. "You're right. That's exactly what this is. Here's St. John's Wood. And the stone wall."

"It's the Stone Coast Trust map," said Miranda. "See? Most of the lots are labeled Sold."

"Good heavens," said Miss St. John. "I had no idea so many of the camps have changed hands. There are only four of us who haven't sold out to Tony Graffam."

"What kind of offer did he make for St. John's Wood?" asked Miranda.

"It was a very good price at the time. When I refused to sell he bumped it up even higher. That was a year ago. I couldn't understand why the offer was so generous. You see, this was all conservation land. These old camps were grandfathered in, built before the days of land commissions. The cottages were allowed to stand, but you couldn't develop any of it. From a commercial standpoint the land was worthless. Then suddenly it's all been rezoned for development. And now I'm sitting on a gold mine." She looked at the other unsold lots on the map. "So is old Sulaway. And the hippies in Frenchman's Cottage."

"And Tony Graffam," said Miranda.

"But what if the zoning decision was a sham?" said Chase. "What if there were payoffs? If that fact became public knowledge…"

"My guess is, there'd be such protest, the zoning would be reversed," said Miss St. John. "And Mr. Graffam would be the proud owner of a lot of worthless property."

"But it's worthless to him right now, Miss St. John," said Miranda, studying the map. "Graffam needs that access road to get to his lots. And you said the road belongs— belonged—to Richard."

"Yes, we keep coming back to that, don't we?" said Chase softly. "That link between Richard and Stone Coast Trust. The link that refuses to go away…." He stood, clapping the dust from his trousers. "Maybe it's time we paid a visit to our neighbors."

"Which ones?" asked Miranda.

"Sulaway and the hippies. The other two on this road who didn't sell. Let's find out if Graffam put any pressure to bear. Like a blackmail note or two."

"He didn't try to blackmail Miss St. John," pointed out Miranda. "And she didn't sell."

"Ah, but my property's scarcely worth the effort," said Miss St. John. "I'm just a tiny patch off to the side. And as for trying to blackmail me, well, you saw for yourself he doesn't have a thing on me worth mentioning. Not that I wouldn't mind generating a whiff of scandal at my age."

"The others could be more vulnerable," said Chase. "Old Sulaway, for instance. We should at least talk to him."

"A good idea," said Miss St. John. "Since you thought of it, Chase, *you* do it."

Chase laughed. "You are a coward, Miss St. John."

"No, I'm just too old for the aggravation."

Without warning, Chase reached for Miranda's hand and with one smooth motion pulled her up in an arc that almost, but not quite, ended in his arms. She reached out to steady herself and found her palms pressing against his chest. At once she stepped back.

"Is this a request for me to come along?" she said.

"It's more along the lines of a plea. To help me soften up old Sulaway."

"Does he need softening up?"

"Let's just say he hasn't taken kindly to me since I batted a baseball through his window. And that was twenty-five years ago."

Miranda laughed in disbelief. "You sound like you're afraid of him. Both of you."

"Obviously she's never met old Sulaway," said Miss St. John.

"Is there something I should know about him?"

Chase and Miss St. John glanced at each other.

"Just be careful when you walk into his front yard," said Miss St. John. "Give him lots of warning. And be ready to get out of there fast."

"Why? Does he have a dog or something?"

"No. But he does have a shotgun."

Ten

"You're that boy who broke my window!" yelled Homer Sulaway. "Yeah, I recognize you." He stood on the front porch, his skinny arms looped around a rifle, his lobsterman's dungarees rolled up at the ankles. Chase had told Miranda the man was eighty-five. The toothless, prune-faced apparition on that porch looked about a century older. "You two go on, now! Leave me alone. Can't afford to fix no more broken windows."

"But I paid for it, remember?" said Chase. "Had to mow lawns for six months, but I did pay for it."

"Damn right," said Sully. "Or I'd 'a got it outta your old man's hide."

"Can we talk to you, Mr. Sulaway?"

"What about?"

"Stone Coast Trust. I wanted to know if—"

"Not interested." Sully turned and shuffled back across the porch.

"Mr. Sulaway, I have a young lady here who'd like to ask—"

"Don't have no use for young ladies. Or old ladies, either." The screen door slammed shut behind him.

There was a silence. "Well," muttered Chase. "The old boy's definitely mellowed."

"I think he's afraid," said Miranda. "That's why he's not talking to us."

"Afraid of what?"

"Let's find out." She approached the cottage and called, "Mr. Sulaway? All we want to know is, are they trying to blackmail you? Has Stone Coast threatened you in some way?"

"Those are lies they're spreading!" Sulaway yelled through the screen door. "Vicious lies! Not true, any of it!"

"That's not what Tony Graffam says."

The door flew open and Sully stormed out onto the porch. "What's Graffam got to say about me? What's he tellin' people now?"

"We could stand out here and yell about it. Or we could talk in private. Which do you prefer?"

Sulaway glanced around, as though searching for watchers in the woods. Then he snapped, "Well? You two need an engraved invitation, or what?"

They followed him inside. Sully's kitchen was a dark little space, the windows closed in by trees, every shelf and countertop crammed full with junk and knickknacks. Newspapers were stacked in piles about the floor. The kitchen table was about the only unoccupied surface. They sat around it, in old ladder-back chairs that look dangerously close to collapse.

"Your brother's the one they was really pressurin'," Sully told Chase. "But Richard, he wasn't about to give in, no sir. He tells us, we gotta stick together. Says we can't sell, no matter how many letters they send us, how many lies they tell." Sully shook his head. "Didn't do no good. Just about everybody on this road went and signed on Graffam's dotted line, just like that. And Richard, look what went and happened to him. Hear he got himself poked with a knife."

Miranda saw Chase glance in her direction. Old Sully was so out of touch he didn't realize he was sitting with the very woman accused of plunging that knife into Richard Tremain.

"You said something about a letter," said Chase. "Telling you to sell. Did Graffam send it?"

"Wasn't signed. I hear none of 'em were."

"So Richard got a letter, as well?"

"I figure. So did Barretts down the way. Maybe everyone did. People wouldn't talk about 'em."

"What did the letter say? The one you got?"

"Lies. Mean, wicked lies…."

"And the one they sent Richard?"

Sully shrugged. "I wasn't privy to that."

Miranda glanced around the kitchen with its overflowing shelves. A pack rat, this Mr. Sulaway was. He kept things, junk and treasure both. She said, "Do you still have that letter?"

Sully hunched his shoulders, like a hermit crab about to retreat into its shell. He grunted. "Maybe."

"May we see it?"

"I dunno." He sighed, rubbed his face. "I dunno."

"We know they're lies, Mr. Sulaway. We just want to see what tactics they're using. We have to stop Graffam before he does any more damage."

For a moment Sully sat hunched and silent. Miranda

thought he might not have heard what she said. But then he creaked to his feet and shuffled over to the kitchen counter. From the flour canister he pulled out a folded sheet of paper. He handed it to Miranda.

She laid it flat on the table.

"What really happened to Stanley? The Lula M knows. So do we."

Below those cryptic words was a handwritten note, penciled in. "Sell, Sully."

"Who's Stanley?" asked Miranda.

Sully had shrunk into his chair and was staring down at his leathery hands.

"Mr. Sulaway?"

The answer came out in a whisper. "My brother."

"What does that note refer to?"

"It was a long time ago…." Sully wiped his eyes, as though to clear away some mist clouding his vision. "Just an accident," he murmured. "Happens all the time out there. The sea, you can't trust her. Can't turn yer back on her…."

"What happened to Stanley?" asked Miranda gently.

"Got…got his boot caught in the trap line. Pulled him clean over the side. Water's cold in December. It'll freeze yer blood. I was aboard the *Sally M,* didn't see it." He turned, stared at the window. The trees outside seemed to close in upon the house, shutting it off from light, from warmth.

They waited.

He said softly. "I was the one found him. Draggin' in the water off *Lula*'s stern. I cut him loose…hauled him aboard…brought him to port." He shuddered. "That was it. Long time ago, fifty years. Maybe more…."

"And this note?"

"It's a lie, got spread around after..."

"After what?"

"After I married Jessie." He paused. "Stanley's wife."

There it is, thought Miranda. The secret. The shame.

"Mr. Sulaway?" asked Chase quietly. "What did they have on Richard?"

Sully shook his head. "Didn't tell me."

"But they did have something?"

"Whatever it was, it didn't make him sell. Had a hard head, your brother. That's what got him in the end."

"Why didn't *you* sell, Mr. Sulaway?" Miranda asked.

The old man turned to her. "Because I won't," he said. She saw in his eyes the look of a man who's been backed into the last corner of his life. "Ain't no way they can scare me. Not now."

"Can't they?"

He shook his head. "I got cancer."

"Do you think he killed his brother?" asked Miranda.

They were walking along the road, through the dappled shade of pine and birch. Chase had his hands in his pockets, a frown on his brow. "What does it matter now, whether he did it or not?"

Yes, what did it matter? she wondered. The old man was about to face his final judgment. Innocent or guilty, he'd already lived fifty years with the consequences.

"It's hard to believe Graffam was able to dig up that story," said Miranda. "He's a newcomer to the island. What he had on Sully was fifty years old. How did Graffam find out about it?"

"Hired investigator?"

"And he used the name 'Sully' in that note. Remember? Only a local person would use that nickname."

"So he had a local informant. Someone with his finger on the island's pulse."

"Or someone in the business of knowing what goes on in this town," she added, thinking of Willie B. Rodell and the Alamo Detective Agency.

They came to a sign that read Harmony House.

"Used to be called Frenchman's Cottage," said Chase. "Until the hippies bought it." Down a rutted road they walked. They heard the tinkle of wind chimes before they saw the cottage. The sound floated through the trees, dancing on the breeze. The chimes were of iridescent glass, sparkling as they swayed from the porch overhang. The cottage door hung wide open.

"Anyone home?" called Chase.

At first only the wind chimes answered. Then, faintly, they heard the sound of laughter, approaching voices. Through the trees they saw them—two men and a woman, walking toward them.

None of the three was wearing a stitch.

The trio, spotting unexpected visitors, didn't seem in the least perturbed. The woman had wild hair generously streaked with gray, and an expression of placid indifference. The two men flanking her were equally shaggy and serene. One of the men, silver haired and weathered, seemed to be the official spokesperson. As his two companions went into the cottage, he came forward with his hand held out in greeting.

"You've found Harmony House," he said. "Or is this just a fortunate accident?"

"It's on purpose," said Chase, shaking the man's hand.

"I'm Chase Tremain, Richard's brother. He owned Rose Hill Cottage, up the road."

"Ah, yes. The place with the weird vibes."

"Weird?"

"Vanna feels it whenever she gets close. Disharmonic waves. Tremors of dissonance."

"I must have missed it."

"Meat eaters usually do." The man looked at Miranda. He had pale blue eyes and a gaze that was far too direct for comfort. "Does my natural state bother you?"

"No," she said. "It's just that I'm not used to..." Her gaze drifted downward, then snapped back to his face.

The man looked at her as though she were a creature to be pitied. "How far we've fallen from Eden," he said, sighing. He went to the porch railing and grabbed a sarong that had been hanging out to dry. "But the first rule of hospitality," he said, wrapping the cloth around his waist, "is to make your guests comfortable. So we'll just cover the family jewels." He motioned them into the cottage.

Inside, the woman, Vanna, now also draped in a sarong, sat cross-legged beneath a stained glass window. Her eyes were closed; her hands lay palm up on her knees. The other man knelt at a low table, rolling what appeared to be brown rice sushi. Potted plans were everywhere, thick as weeds. They blended right in with the Indonesian hangings, the dangling crystals, the smell of incense. The whole effect was jarred only by the fax machine in the corner.

Their host, who went by the surprisingly mundane name of Fred, poured rose hip tea and offered them carob cookies. They came to Maine every summer, he said, to reconnect with the earth. New York was purgatory, a place with one foot in hell. False people, false values. They worked there only because it kept them in touch with the common folk. Plus, they needed the income. For most of the year they tolerated the sickness of city life, breathing in the toxins, poisoning their bodies with refined sugars. Summers were for cleansing. And that was why they came here, why they left their jobs for two months every year.

"What *are* your jobs?" asked Miranda.

"We own the accounting firm of Nickels, Fay and Bledsoe. I'm Nickels."

"I'm Fay," said the man rolling sushi.

The woman, undoubtedly Bledsoe, continued to meditate in silence.

"So you see," said Fred Nickels, "there is no way we can be persuaded to sell. This land is a connection to our mother."

"Was it hers?" asked Chase.

"Mother Earth owns everything."

Chase cleared his throat. "Oh."

"We refuse to sell. No matter how many of those ridiculous letters they send us—"

Both Miranda and Chase sat up straight. "Letters?" they said simultaneously.

"We three have lived together for fifteen years. Perfect sexual harmony. No jealousy, no friction. All our friends know it. So it would hardly upset us to have our arrangement announced to the world."

"Is that what the letters threatened to do?" asked Miranda.

"Yes. 'Expose your deviant lifestyle' was the phrase, I think."

"You're not the only ones to get a letter," said Chase. "My hunch is, everyone on this road—everyone who didn't want to sell—got one in the mail."

"Well, they threatened the wrong people here. Deviant lifestyles are exactly what we wish to promote. Am I right, friends?"

The man with the sushi looked up and said, "Ho."

"He agrees," said Fred.

"Was the letter signed?" asked Miranda.

"No. It was postmarked Bass Harbor, and it came to our house in New York."

"When?"

"Three, four months ago. It advised us to sell the camp. It didn't say to whom, specifically. But then we got the offer from Mr. Graffam, so I assumed he was behind it. I had Stone Coast Trust checked out. A few inquiries here and there, just to find out what I was dealing with. My sources say there's money involved. Graffam's just a front for a silent investor. My bet is it's organized crime."

"What would they want with Shepherd's Island?" asked Chase.

"New York's getting uncomfortable for 'em. Hotdog D.A.'s and all that. I think they're moving up the coast. And the north shore's just the foothold they'd want. Tourist industry's already booming up here. And look at this place! Ocean. Forest. No crime. Tell me some poor schlump from the city wouldn't pay good money to stay at a resort right here."

"Did you ever meet Graffam?"

"He paid us a visit, to talk land deal. And we told him, in no uncertain terms, to—" Fred stopped, grinned "—fornicate with himself. I'm not sure he knew the meaning of the word."

"What kind of man is he?" asked Miranda.

Fred snorted. "Slick. Dumb. I mean, we're talking *really* stupid. The IQ of an eggplant. What idiot names a development Hemlock Heights? Might as well call it Poison Oak Estates." He shook his head. "I can't believe he got those other suckers to sell." He laughed. "You should meet him, Tremain. Tell me if you don't agree he's a throwback to our paramecium ancestors."

"A paramecium," said the woman, Bledsoe, briefly opening her eyes, "is far more advanced."

"Unfortunately," said Fred, "I'm afraid the rezoning is a fait accompli. Soon we'll be surrounded. Condos here, a Dunkin' Donuts there. The Cape Codification of Shepherd's Island." He paused. "And you know what? *That's* when we'll sell! My God, what a profit! We could buy a whole damn county up in the Allagash."

"The project could still be stopped," said Miranda. "They won't get their hands on Rose Hill. And the zoning could be reversed."

"Not a chance," said Fred. "We're talking tax income here. Conservation land brings in zilch for the island. But a nice little tourist resort? Hey, I'm a CPA. I know the powers of the almighty buck."

"There are people who'll fight it."

"Makes no difference." Fred sniffed appreciatively at his rose hip tea. The edges of his sarong had slipped apart and he sat with thighs naked. Incense smoke wafted about his grizzled head. "They can scream, protest. Lay their bodies before the bulldozers. But it's hopeless. There are things people just can't stop."

"A cynical answer," said Miranda.

"For cynical times."

"Well, they can't buy Rose Hill," said Miranda, rising to her feet. "And if organized crime's behind these purchases, you can bet the island will fight back. People here don't take well to mobsters. They don't take to outsiders, period."

Fred gazed up at her with a smile. "But *you* are an outsider, aren't you, Ms. Wood?"

"I'm not from this island. I came here a year ago."

"Yet they accepted *you*."

"No, they didn't." Miranda turned toward the door. She stood there for a moment, staring through the screen. Outside, the trees were swaying under a canopy of blue sky. "They never accepted me," she said softly. "And you know what?" She let out a long sigh of resignation. "I've only now come to realize it. They never will."

There was a third car parked in the driveway at Rose Hill.

They saw it as they walked up the last bend of the road—a late-model Saab with a gleaming burgundy finish. A glance through the car window revealed a spotless interior, not even a loose business card or candy wrapper on the leather upholstery.

The screen door squealed open and Miss St. John came out on the porch. "There you are," she said. "We have a visitor. Jill Vickery."

Of course, thought Miranda. Who else would manage to keep such an immaculate car?

Jill was standing amidst all the books, holding a box in her arms. She glanced at Miranda with a look of obvious surprise, but made no comment about her presence. "Sorry to pop in unannounced," she said. "I had to get a few records. Phillip and I are meeting the accountant tomorrow. You know, working out any tax problems for the transfer of the *Herald*."

Chase frowned. "You found the financial records here?"

"Just last month's worth. I couldn't find them back in the office, so I figured he'd brought them out here to work on. I was right."

"Where were they?" asked Chase. "We've combed all through his files. I never saw them."

"They were upstairs. The nightstand drawer." How she knew where to look was something she didn't bother to explain. She glanced around the front room. "You've certainly torn the place apart. What are you looking for? Hidden treasure?"

"Any and all files on Stone Coast Trust," said Chase.

"Yes, Annie mentioned you were dogging that angle. Personally, I think it's a dead end." Coolly she turned to look at Miranda. "And how are things going for you?" It was merely a polite question, carrying neither warmth nor concern.

"Things are…difficult," said Miranda.

"I can imagine. I hear you're staying with Annie these days."

"Only temporarily."

Jill flashed her one of those ironic smiles. "It's rather inconvenient, actually. The trial was going to be Annie's story. And now you're living with her. I'll have to pull her off it. Objective reporting and all."

"No one at the *Herald* could possibly be objective," Chase pointed out.

"I suppose not." Jill shifted the box in her arms. "Well, I'd better be going. Let you get on with your search."

"Ms. Vickery?" called Miss St. John. "I wonder if you could shed some light on an item we found here."

"Yes?"

"It's a note, from someone named M." Miss St. John

handed her the slip of paper. "Miranda here didn't write it. Do you know who did?"

Jill read the note without any apparent emotion, not even a twitch of her perfect eyebrow. Miranda thought, *If only I had an ounce of her style, her poise.*

"It's not dated. So..." Jill looked up. "I can think of several possibilities. None of them had that particular initial. But M could stand for a nickname. Or just the word *me.*"

"Several possibilities?"

"Yes." Jill glanced uneasily at Miranda. "Richard, he...had his attractions. Especially for the female summer interns. There was that one we had last year. Before you were hired, Miranda. Her name was Chloe something or other. Couldn't write worth a damn, but she was good decoration. And she picked up interviews no one else could get, which drove poor Annie up a wall." Jill looked again at the note. "This was typed on a manual typewriter. See? The *e* loop's smudged, key needs to be cleaned. If I remember right, Chloe always worked on an old manual. The only one in the office who couldn't compose on a computer keyboard." She gave the note back to Miss St. John. "It could have been her."

"Whatever happened to Chloe?" asked Chase.

"What you'd expect to happen. Some hot and heavy flirting. A few fireworks. And then, just another broken heart."

Miranda felt her throat tighten, her face flush. None of them was looking directly at her, but she knew she was the focus of their attention, as surely as if they were staring. She went to the window and found herself gripping the curtain, fighting to keep her head erect, her spine straight. Another broken heart. It made her feel like some object on an assembly line, just another stupid, gullible woman. It's what they thought of her.

It's what she thought of herself.

Jill again shifted her box of papers. "I'd better get back to the office or the mice will play." She went to the door, then stopped. "Oh, I almost forgot to tell you, Chase. Annie just heard the news."

"What news?" asked Chase.

"Tony Graffam's back in town."

Miranda didn't react. She heard Jill go down the porch steps, heard the Saab's engine roar to life, the tires crunch away across the gravel. She felt Chase and Miss St. John's gaze on her back. They were watching her in silence, an unbearable, pitying silence.

She pushed open the screen door and fled from the cottage.

Halfway across the field Chase caught up to her. He grabbed her arm and pulled her around to face him. "Miranda—"

"Leave me alone!"

"You can't run away from it—"

"If only I could!" she cried. "Jill said it! I'm just another broken heart. Another dumb woman who got exactly what she deserved."

"You didn't deserve it."

"Damn you, Chase, don't feel sorry for me! I can't stand that, either." She broke free and started to turn away. He pulled her back. This time he held on, got a tight grip on each wrist. She found herself staring into his dark, in-escapable eyes.

"I don't feel sorry for you," he shot back. "You don't get my pity, Miranda. Because you're too good for it. You've got more going for you than any woman I've met. Okay, you're naive. And gullible. We all start out that way. You've learned from it, fine. You should. You want to kick yourself, and maybe it's well deserved. But don't overdo it. Because I think Richard fell just as hard for you as you fell for him."

"Is that supposed to make me feel better?"

"I'm not trying to make you feel better. I'm just telling you what I think."

"Right." Her laughter was self-mocking. "That I'm one notch above a bimbo?" Again she tried to pull free. Again he held her tight.

"No," he said quietly. "What I'm saying is this. I know you're not the first. I know Richard had a lot of women. I've met a few of them through the years. Some of them were gorgeous. Some of them were talented, even brilliant. But out of all those women—and they were, each and every one of them, exceptional—you're the only one I could see him really falling for."

"Out of all those *gorgeous* women?" She shook her head and laughed. "Why me?"

Quietly he said, "Because you're the one *I'd* fall for."

At once she went still. He stared down at her, his dark hair stirring in the wind, his face awash in sunlight. She heard her own quick breaths, heard her heartbeat pounding in her ears. He released her wrists. She didn't move, even when his arms circled behind her, even as he drew her hard against him. She scarcely had the breath to whimper before he settled his mouth firmly on hers.

At the first touch of his lips she was lost. The sun seemed to spin overhead, a dizzying view of brightness against a field of blue. And then there was only him, all rough edges and shadows, his dark head blotting out the sky, his mouth stealing away her breath. She wavered for an instant between resistance and surrender. Then she found herself reaching up and around his neck, opening her lips to his eager assault, pressing more eagerly against the bite of his teeth. She drank him in, his taste, his warmth. Through the roaring in her ears she heard his low groans of satisfaction and need, ever more need. How quickly she had yielded, how easily she had fallen—the woman mastered first by one brother, and now the other.

The day's unbearable brightness seemed to flood her eyes as she pulled away. Her cheeks were blazing. The buzz of insects in the field and the rustle of grass in the wind were almost lost in the harsh sound of her own breathing.

"I won't be passed around, Chase," she said. "I won't."

Then she turned and stalked across the field. She headed back to the cottage, her feet stirring the perfume of sun-warmed grass. She knew he was following somewhere behind, but this time he made no attempt to catch up. She walked alone, and the brightness of the afternoon, the dancing wildflowers, the floating haze of dandelion fuzz only seemed to emphasize her own wretchedness.

Miss St. John was standing on the porch. With scarcely a nod to the other woman, Miranda walked right past her and into the cottage. Inside, she went straight to the bookcase, grabbed another armful of books from the shelf and sat on the floor. She was single-mindedly flipping through the pages when she heard footsteps come up the porch.

"It's not a good time for an argument, Chase," she heard Miss St. John say.

"I'm not planning to argue."

"You have that look in your eye. For heaven's sake, cool down. Stop. Take a deep breath."

"With all due respect, Miss St. John, you're *not* my mother."

"All right, I'm not your mother!" Miss St. John snapped. As she stomped away down the steps, she muttered, "But I can see when a man sorely needs my advice!"

The screen door slapped shut. Chase stood just inside the threshold, gazing at Miranda. "You took it the wrong way," he said.

Miranda looked up at him. "Did I?"

"What happened between you and Richard is a separate issue. A dead issue. It has nothing to do with you and me."

She snapped the book shut. "It has everything to do with you and me."

"But you make it sound like I'm just—just picking up the affair where he left off."

"Okay, maybe it's not that bald. Maybe you're not even aware you're doing it." She reached for another book and stubbornly focused on the pages as she flipped through it. "But we both know Richard was the golden boy of the family. The one who had it all, inherited everything. You were the Tremain who didn't even get a decent trust fund. Well, if you can't inherit a newspaper or a fortune, at least you can inherit your brother's cast-off mistress. Or, gee, maybe even his wife. Just think. Evelyn wouldn't even have to go to the trouble of changing her last name."

"Are you finished?"

"Definitely."

"Good. Because I don't think I can stand here and listen to that garbage any longer. First of all, I'm not in the least bit interested in my sister-in-law. I never was. When Richard married her, I had to stop myself from sending him my condolences. Second, I don't give a damn who gets the *Herald*. I sure as hell never wanted the job. The paper was Richard's baby, from the start. And third—" He paused and took a deep breath, as though drawing the courage to say what had to be said. "Third," he said quietly, "I'm not a Tremain."

She looked up at him sharply. "What are you saying? You're Richard's brother, aren't you?"

"His half brother."

"You mean…" She stared into those Gypsy eyes, saw herself reflected in irises dark as coals.

Chase nodded. "My father knew. I don't think Mother ever told him, exactly. She didn't have to. He could just look at me and see it." He smiled, a bitter, ironic smile. "Funny that I myself never did. All the time I was growing up, I didn't understand why I couldn't match up to Richard. No matter how hard I tried, he was the one who got Dad's attention. My mother tried to make up for it. She was my very best friend, right up until she died. And then it was just the three of us." He sank into a chair and rubbed his forehead, as though trying to massage away the memories.

"When did you learn?" Miranda asked softly. "That he wasn't your father?"

"Not until years later, when Dad was dying. He had one of those cliché deathbed confessions. Only he didn't tell *me.* He told Richard. Even at the very end, Richard was the privileged one." Wearily Chase leaned back, his head pressed against the cushions, his gaze focused on the ceiling. "Later they read the will. I couldn't understand why I'd been essentially cut out. Oh, he left me enough to get me started in business. But that was it. I thought it had to do with my marriage, the fact Dad had opposed it from the start. I was hurt, but I accepted it. My wife didn't. She got in a shouting match with Richard, started yelling that it wasn't fair. Richard lost his cool and let it all out. The big secret. The fact his brother was a bastard."

"Is that when you left the island?"

He nodded. "I came back once or twice, to humor my wife. After we got divorced it seemed like my last link to this place had been cut. So I stayed away. Until now."

They fell silent. He seemed lost in bad memories, old hurts. *No wonder I could never find any hint of Richard in his face,* she thought. *He's not a Tremain at all. He's his own man, the sort of man Richard could never be.*

The sort of man I could love.

He felt her studying him, sensed she was reaching out to him. Abruptly he rose to his feet and moved with studied indifference toward the screen door. There he stood looking out at the field. "Maybe you were right," he said.

"About what?"

"That what happened between you and Richard is still hanging over us."

"And if it is?"

"Then this is a mistake. You, me. It's the wrong reason to get involved."

She looked down, unwilling to reveal, even to the stiffly turned back, the hurt in her eyes. "Then we shouldn't, should we?" she murmured.

"No." He turned to face her. She found her gaze drawn, almost against her will, to meet his. "The truth is, Miranda, we have too many reasons not to. What's happened between us has been..." He shrugged. "It was an attraction, that's all."

That's all. Nothing, really, in the larger context of life. Not something you risked your heart on.

"Still..." he said.

"Yes?" She looked up with a sudden, insane leap of hope.

"We can't walk away from each other. Not with all that's happened. Richard's death. The fire." He gestured about the book-strewn room. "And this."

"You don't trust me. Yet you want my help?"

"You're the only one with stakes high enough to see this through."

She gave a tired laugh. "You got that part right." She wrapped her arms around herself. "So, what comes next?"

"I'll go have a talk with Tony Graffam."

"Shall I come?"

"No. I want to check him out on my own. In the meantime, you can finish up here. There's still the upstairs."

Miranda gazed around the room, at the dusty piles of books, the stacks of papers, and she shook her head. "If I just knew what I was looking for. What the burglar was looking for."

"I have a hunch it's still here somewhere."

"Whatever *it* is."

Turning, Chase pushed open the door. "When you find it, you'll know."

Eleven

Fred Nickels had said Tony Graffam was slick and dumb. He was right on both counts. Graffam wore a silk suit, a tie in blinding red paisley and a gold pinkie ring. The office, like the man, was all flash, little substance: plush carpet, spanking new leather chairs, but no secretary, no books on the shelves, no papers on the desk. The wall had only one decoration—a map of the north shore of Shepherd's Island. It was not labeled as such, but Chase needed only a glance at the broad, curving bay to recognize the coastline.

"I tell you, it's a witch hunt!" Graffam complained. "First the police, now you." He stayed behind his desk, refusing to emerge even to shake hands, as though clinging to the polished barrier for protection. In agitation he slid his fingers through his tightly permed hair. "You think I'd go and waste someone? Just like that? And for what, a piece of property? Do I look dumb?"

Chase politely declined to answer that question. He said, "You were pressing an offer for Rose Hill Cottage, weren't you?"

"Well, of course. It's the prime lot up there."

"And my brother refused to sell."

"Look, I'm sorry about your brother. Tragedy, a real tragedy. Not that he and I were on good terms, you understand. I couldn't deal with him. He had a closed mind when it came to the project. I mean, he actually went and got hostile. I don't know why. It's only business, right?"

"But I was under the impression this wasn't a business deal, at all. Stone Coast Trust is billed as a conservation project."

"And that's exactly what it is. I offered your brother top dollar for that land, more than Nature Conservancy would've paid. Plus, he would've retained lifetime use of the family cottage. An incredible deal."

"Incredible."

"With the addition of Rose Hill, we could extend the park all the way back to the hillside. It would add elevation. Views. Access."

"Access?"

"For maintenance, of course. You know, for the hiking trails. Decent footpaths, so everyone could enjoy a taste of nature. Even the handicapped. I mean, mobility impaired."

"You thought of everything."

Graffam smiled. "Yes. We did."

"Where does Hemlock Heights come in?"

Graffam paused. "Excuse me?"

"Hemlock Heights. That is, I believe, the name of your planned development."

"Well, nothing was *planned*—"

"Then why did you apply for rezoning? And how much did you pay to bribe the land commission?"

Graffam's face had gone rigid. "Let me repeat myself, Mr. Tremain. Stone Coast Trust was formed to protect the north shore. I admit, we might have to develop a parcel here and there, just to maintain the trust. But sometimes we have to compromise. We have to do things we'd rather not."

"Does that include blackmail?"

Graffam sat up sharply. "What?"

"I'm talking about Fred Nickels. And Homer Sulaway. The names should be familiar to you."

"Yes, of course. Two of the property owners. They declined my offer."

"Someone sent them nasty letters, telling them to sell."

"You think I sent them?"

"Who else? Four people turned you down. Two of them got threatening letters. And a third—my brother—winds up dead."

"That's what you're leading up to, isn't it? Trying to make it look like I had something to do with his death."

"Is that what I said?"

"Look, I've taken enough heat on this deal. A year of putting up with this—this small-town crap. I've turned handsprings to make this project work, but I'm not going to be his fall guy."

Chase stared at Graffam in confusion. What was the man babbling about? Whose fall guy?

"I was out of state when it happened. I have witnesses who'll swear to that."

"Who are you working for?" Chase cut in.

Graffam's jaw suddenly snapped shut. Slowly he sat back, his expression hardening to stone.

"So you have a backer," said Chase. "Someone who's

put up the money. Someone who's doing the dirty work. Who are you fronting for? The mob?"

Graffam said nothing.

"You're scared, Graffam. I can tell."

"I don't have to answer any of your questions."

Chase pressed the attack. "My brother was set to blow the whistle on Stone Coast, wasn't he? So you sent him one of your threatening letters. But then you found out he couldn't be blackmailed. Or bought off. So what did you do? Pay someone to take care of the problem?"

"Meaning murder?" Graffam burst out laughing. "Come on, Tremain. A broad killed him. We both know that. Dangerous creatures, broads. Tick 'em off and they get ideas. They see red, grab a kitchen knife and that's it. Even the cops agree. It was a broad. She had the motive."

"And you had a lot of money to lose. So did your backer. Richard already had his hands on your account numbers. He traced your invisible partner. He could have exposed the deal—"

"But he didn't. He killed the article, remember? I had it on good authority it was gonna stay dead. So why should we go after him?"

Chase fell silent. That's what Jill had said, that Richard was the one who'd canceled the article, called off the crusade. It was the one detail that didn't make sense. Why had Richard backed down?

Did he back down? Or had Jill Vickery lied?

He brooded over that last possibility as he left Graffam's office and walked to the car. What did he know about Jill, really? Only that she'd been with the *Herald* for five years, that she kept it running smoothly. That she was bright, stylish and underpaid. She could land a better job anywhere on the East Coast. Why had she chosen to stay with this Podunk paper and work for slave wages?

He'd planned to return at once to Rose Hill Cottage. Instead, he drove to the *Herald.*

He found the office manned only by a skeleton crew: the summer intern, tapping at a computer keyboard, and the layout tech, stooped over a drawing table. Chase walked past them, into Richard's office, and went straight to the file cabinet.

He found Jill Vickery's employment file right where it should be. He sat at the desk and opened the folder.

Inside was a neatly typed résumé, three pages, all the right names and jobs. B.A., Bowdoin, 1977. Masters, Columbia, 1979. Stints on the city desk, *San Francisco Chronicle;* then obits, *San Diego Union;* police beat, *San Jose Times;* op-ed editor, *Portland Press Herald.* A solid résumé.

So why does she end up here?

Something about that résumé bothered him. Something that didn't seem quite right. It was enough to make him reach for the phone and dial the *Portland Press Herald,* her previous employer. He spoke to the current op-ed editor, a woman who vaguely recalled a Jill Vickery. It had been a while back, though.

Chase next called the *San Jose Times.* This time there was some uncertainty, a lot of yelling around the city room, asking if anyone remembered a reporter named Jill Vickery from seven years before. Someone yelled, wasn't there a Jill on the police beat years back? That was good enough for Chase. He hung up and considered letting it drop.

Still, that résumé. What was it that bothered him?

The obits. *San Diego Union.* That didn't make sense. Obits was the coal mine equivalent of the newspaper business. You worked your way up from there. Why had she gone from the city desk in San Francisco to a bottom-of-the-barrel position?

He dialed the *San Diego Union.* No one named Jill Vickery had ever worked there.

Ditto for San Francisco.

Half the résumé was a fraud. Was it just a case of padding a thin work history? And what was she doing during those eight years between college and her job with the *San Jose Times?*

Once again he reached for the phone. This time he called Columbia University, Department of Journalism. In any given year, how many students could possibly graduate with a master's degree? And how many of these students would have the first name Jill?

There was only one in 1979, they told him. But it wasn't a Jill Vickery who'd graduated. It was a Jill Westcott.

Once again, he called the *San Diego Union.* This time he asked about a Jill Westcott. This time they remembered the name. We'll fax you the article, they said.

A few minutes later it slid out of the fax machine, sharp and clear.

A photo of Jill Westcott, now named Jill Vickery. And with it was a tale of cold-blooded murder.

Miranda sat in the fading light of day and stared list-lessly at her surroundings. She'd spent the afternoon rum-maging through the bathroom and two bedrooms. Now she was hot, dusty and discouraged. Nothing of substance had turned up, only innocuous bits of paper—store receipts, a ten-year-old postcard from Spain, another typewritten note from M.

> …I am not the weak little nothing I used to be. I can live without you quite nicely, and I intend to do so. I don't need your pity. I am not like the others, those women with minds the size of walnut shells. What I want to know, what I don't understand, is what attracts you to creatures like that? Is it the jiggling flesh? The cow-eyed worship? Well, it doesn't mean a thing. It's empty devotion. Without your money, you wouldn't rate a second glance from those bimbos. I'm the only one who doesn't give a damn how much you have in the bank. And now you've lost me.

The bitterness, the pain of that letter seemed to rub off on her own mood. She put it back in the drawer, buried it among the silky underclothes. Another woman's lingerie. Another woman's anguish.

By the time she'd straightened up the room again the afternoon had slid toward twilight. She didn't turn on the lamp. It was soothing, the veil of semidarkness, the chirp of crickets through the open window. From the field came that indefinable scent of evening—the mist from the sea, the cooling grasses. She went to a chair by the window, sat down and leaned her head back to rest. So many doubts, so many worries weighed upon her. Always, looming over every tentative moment of joy, was that threat of prison. There were times, during these past few days of freedom, that she had almost been able to push the thought from mind. But in the moments like this, when the silence was deep and she was alone in her fears, the image of prison bars seemed to close around her. *How many years will they keep me? Ten, twenty, a lifetime?*

I would rather die.

She shuddered back to alertness.

Downstairs, the screen door had softly squealed open.

"Chase?" she called. "Is that you?" There was silence. She rose from the chair and went to the top of the stairs. "Chase?"

She heard the screen door softly tap shut, then there was nothing, only the distant chirp of crickets from the fields.

Her first instinct was to reach for the light switch. Just in time she stopped herself. Darkness was her friend. It would hide her, protect her.

She shrank away from the stairs. Trembling, she stood with her back pressed against the wall and listened. No new sounds drifted up from the first floor. All she heard was the hammering of her own heartbeat. Her palms were slick. Every nerve ending was scraped raw with fear.

There it was—a footstep. In the kitchen. An image shot through her mind. The cabinets, the drawers. The knives.

Her breath was coming in tight gasps. She shrank farther from the stairs, her thoughts flying frantically toward escape. Two upstairs bedrooms, plus a bathroom. And screens on all the windows. Could she make it through in time?

From below came more footsteps. The intruder had moved out of the kitchen. He was approaching the stairs.

Miranda fled into the master bedroom. Darkness obscured her path; she collided with a nightstand. A lamp wobbled, fell over. The clatter as it crashed to the floor was all the intruder needed to direct him toward this bedroom.

In panic she dashed to the window. Through the

darkness she saw a portion of gently sloping roof. From there it would be a twenty-foot drop to the ground. The sash was already up. Only the screen stood between her and freedom. She shoved at it—and it refused to push free. Only then did she see that the screen had been nailed to the window frame.

Frantic now, she began to kick at the steel mesh, sobbing as each blow met resistance. Again and again she kicked, and each time the wire sagged outward, but held.

A footstep creaked on the stairway.

She aimed a last desperate kick at the mesh.

The window frame splintered, and the whole screen fell away and thudded to the ground. At once she scrambled over the sill and dropped down onto the ledge of roof. There she hesitated, torn between the solid comfort of shingles beneath her feet and the free-fall of escape. She couldn't see what lay directly below. The rosebushes? She grabbed hold of the roof and lowered her body over the edge. For a few seconds she clung there, steeling herself for the impact.

She let go.

The night air rushed up at her. The fall seemed endless, a hurtling downward through space and darkness.

Her feet slammed into the ground. Instantly her legs buckled, and she fell sprawling to the gravel. For a moment she lay there as the sky whirled overhead like a kaleidoscope of stars. A frantic burst of adrenaline had masked all the sensation of pain. Her legs could be shattered. She wouldn't have felt it. She knew only that she had to escape, had to run.

She staggered to her feet and began to stumble down the road. She rounded the bend of the driveway—

And was instantly blinded by a pair of headlights leaping at her from the darkness. Instinctively she raised her arms to shield her eyes against the onslaught. She heard the car's brakes lock, heard gravel fly under the skidding tires. The door swung open.

"Miranda?"

With a sob of joy she stumbled forward into Chase's arms. "It's you," she cried. "Thank God it's you."

"What is it?" he whispered, pulling her close against him. "Miranda, what's happened?"

She clung to the solid anchor of his chest. "He's there—in the cottage—"

"Who?"

Suddenly, through the darkness, they both heard it: the slam of the back door, the thrash of running footsteps through the brush.

"Get in the car!" ordered Chase. "Lock the doors!"

"What?"

He gave her a push. "Just do it!"

"Chase!" she yelled.

"I'll be back!"

Stunned, she watched him melt into the night, heard his footsteps thud away. Her instinct was to follow him, to stay close in case he needed her. But already she'd lost sight of him and could make out nothing but the towering shadows of trees against the starry sky, and beneath them, a darkness so thick it seemed impenetrable.

Do what he says!

She climbed into the car, locked the doors and felt instantly useless. While she sat here in safety Chase could be fighting for his life.

And what good will I do him?

She pushed open the door and scrambled out of the car, around to the rear.

In the trunk she found a tire iron. It felt heavy and solid in her grasp. It would even the odds against any opponent. Any unarmed opponent, she was forced to amend.

She turned, faced the forest. It loomed before her, a wall of shadow and formless threat.

Somewhere in that darkness Chase was in danger.

She gripped the tire iron more tightly and started off into the night.

The crash of footsteps through the underbrush alerted Chase that his quarry had shifted direction. Chase veered right, in pursuit of the sound. Branches thrashed his face, bushes clawed at his trousers. The darkness was so dense under the trees that he felt like a blind man stumbling through a landscape of booby traps.

At least his quarry would be just as blind. *But maybe not as helpless,* he thought, ducking under a pine branch. *What if he's armed? What if I'm being led into a trap?*

It's a risk I have to take.

The footsteps moved to the left of him. By slivers of starlight filtering through the trees Chase caught a glimpse of movement. That was all he could make out, shadow moving through shadow. Heedless of the branches whipping his face he plunged ahead and found himself snagged in brambles. The shadow zigzagged, flitting in and out of the cover of trees. Chase pulled free of the thicket and resumed his pursuit. He was gaining. He could hear, through the pounding of his heart, the hard breathing of his quarry. The shadow was just ahead, just beyond the next curtain of branches.

Chase mustered a last burst of speed and broke through, into a clearing. There he came to a halt.

His quarry had vanished. There was no movement, no sound, only the whisper of wind through the treetops. A flutter of shadow off to his right made him whirl around. Nothing there. He halted in confusion as he heard the crackle of underbrush to his left. He turned, listening for footsteps, trying to locate his quarry. Was that breathing, somewhere close by? No, the wind….

Again, that crackle of twigs. He moved forward, one step, then another.

Too late he felt the rush of air, the hiss of the branch as it swung its arc toward his head.

The blow pitched him forward. He reached out to cushion the fall, felt the bite of pine needles, the slap of wet leaves as he scraped across the forest floor. He tried to cling to consciousness, to order his body to rise to its feet and face the enemy. It refused to obey. Already he saw the darkness thicken before his eyes. He wanted to curse, to rail in fury at his own helplessness. But all he could manage was a groan.

Pain. The pounding of a jackhammer in his head. Chase ordered it to stop, demanded it stop, but it kept beating away at his brain.

"He's coming around," said a voice.

Then another voice, softer, fearful. "Chase? Chase?"

He opened his eyes and saw Miranda gazing down at him. The lamplight shimmered in her tumbled hair, washed like liquid gold across her cheek. Just the sight of her seemed to quiet the aching in his head. He struggled to remember where he was, how he had gotten there. An image of darkness, the shadow of trees, still lingered.

Abruptly he tried to sit up, and caught a spinning view of other people, other faces in the room.

"No," said Miranda. "Don't move. Just lie still."

"Someone—someone out there—"

"He's gone. We've already searched the woods," said Lorne Tibbetts.

Chase settled back on the couch. He knew where he was now. Miss St. John's cottage. He recognized the chintz fabric, the jungle of plants. And the dog. The panting black mop sat near one end of the couch, watching him. Or was it? With all that hair, who could say if the beast even had eyes? Slowly Chase's gaze shifted to the others in the room. Lorne. Ellis. Miss St. John. And Dr. Steiner, wielding his trusty penlight.

"Pupils look fine. Equal and reactive," said Dr. Steiner.

"Take that blasted thing away," Chase groaned, batting at the penlight.

Dr. Steiner snorted. "Can't do much damage to a head as hard as his." He set a bottle of pills on the end table. "For the headache. May make you a little drowsy, but it'll cut the pain." He snapped his bag shut and headed for the door. "Call me in the morning. But not too early. And may I remind you—all of you—I do not, repeat, do *not* make house calls!" The door slammed shut behind him.

"What wonderful bedside manner," moaned Chase.

"You remember anything?" asked Lorne.

Chase managed to sit up. The effort sent a bolt of pain into his skull. At once he dropped his head into his hands. "Not a damn thing," he mumbled.

"Didn't see his face?"

"Just a shadow."

Lorne paused. "You sure there was someone there?"

"Hey, I didn't imagine the headache." Chase grabbed

the pill bottle, fumbled the cap off and gulped two tablets down, dry. "Someone hit me."

"A man? Woman?" pressed Lorne.

"I never saw him. Her. Whatever."

Lorne turned to Miranda. "He was unconscious when you found him?"

"Coming around. I heard his groans."

"Pardon me for asking, Ms. Wood. But can I see that tire iron you were carrying?"

"What?"

"The tire iron. You had it earlier."

Miss St. John sighed. "Don't be ridiculous, Lorne."

"I'm just being thorough. I have to look at it."

Without a word Miranda fetched the tire iron from the porch and brought it back to Lorne. "No blood, no hair," she said tightly. "I wasn't the one who hit him."

"No, I guess not," said Lorne.

"Jill Vickery," Chase muttered.

Lorne glanced at him. "Who?"

The pain in Chase's head suddenly gave way to a clear memory of that afternoon. "It's not her real name. Check with the San Diego police, Lorne. It may or may not tie in. But you'll find she has an arrest record."

"For what?"

Chase raised her head. "She killed her lover."

They all stared at him.

"Jill?" said Miranda. "When did you find this out?"

"This afternoon. It happened ten, eleven years ago. She was acquitted. Justifiable homicide. She claimed he'd threatened her life."

"How does this fit in with anything else?" asked Lorne.

"I'm not sure. All I know is, half her job résumé was

pure fiction. Maybe Richard found out. If he did—and confronted her…"

Lorne turned to Miss St. John. "I need to use your telephone."

"In the kitchen."

Lorne spent only a few minutes on the phone. He emerged from the kitchen shaking his head. "Jill Vickery's at home. Says she was home all evening."

"It's only a half-hour drive to town," said Miss St. John. "She could have made it, barely."

"Assuming her car was right nearby. Assuming she could slip right behind the wheel and take off." He looked at Ellis. "You checked up and down the road?"

Ellis nodded. "No strange cars. No one saw nothin'."

"Well," said Lorne, "whoever it was, I don't think he'll be back." He reached for his hat. "Take my advice, Chase. Don't drive anywhere tonight. You're in no shape to get behind a wheel."

Chase gave a tired laugh. "I wasn't planning to."

"I can take him up to the cottage," said Miranda. "I'll keep an eye on him."

Lorne paused and looked first at Miranda, then at Chase. If he had doubts about the arrangement, he didn't express them. He simply said, "You do that, Ms. Wood. You keep a *good* eye on him." Motioning to Ellis, he opened the door. "We'll be in touch."

Twelve

Light spilled from the hallway across the pine floor of the bedroom. Miranda pulled down the coverlet and said, "Come on, lie down. Doctor's orders."

"To hell with doctors. That doctor, anyway," growled Chase. He sat on the side of the bed and gave his head a shake, as though to clear it. "I'm okay. I feel fine."

She regarded his battered, unshaven face. "You look like a truck ran over you."

"The brutal truth!" He laughed. "Are you always so damn honest?"

There was a silence. "Yes," she said quietly. "As a matter of fact, I am."

He looked up at her. *What do you see in my eyes?* she wondered. *Sincerity? Or lies, bald, dangerous lies?*

It's still not there, is it? Trust. There'll always be that doubt between us.

She sat beside him on the bed. "Tell me everything you learned today. About Jill."

"Only what I read in the press file from San Diego." He

reached down and began to pull off his shoes. "The trial got a fair amount of coverage. You know, sex, violence. Circulation boosters."

"What happened?"

"The defense claimed she was an emotionally battered woman. That she was young, naive, vulnerable. That her boyfriend was an abusive alcoholic who regularly beat her up. The jury believed it."

"What did the prosecution say?"

"That Jill had a lifelong hatred of men. That she used them, manipulated them. And when her lover tried to leave her, she flew into a rage. Both sides agreed on the facts of the killing. That while her lover was passed out drunk she picked up a gun, put it to his head and pulled the trigger." Exhausted, Chase lay back on the pillows. The pills were taking effect. His eyelids were already drifting shut. "That was ten years ago," he said. "An era Jill conveniently left behind when she came to Maine."

"Did Richard know all this?"

"If he bothered to check, he did. Only the last half of her résumé was true. Richard may have been so dazzled by the whole package he didn't bother to confirm much beyond the last job or two. Or he may have found out the truth only recently. Who knows?"

Miranda sat thinking, trying to picture Jill as she must have been ten years ago. Young, vulnerable. Afraid.

Like me.

Or was the prosecution's description a more accurate image? A man hater, a woman of twisted passions?

That's how they'll try to portray me. As a killer. And some people will believe it.

Chase had fallen asleep.

For a moment she sat beside him, listening to his slow and even breaths, wondering if he could ever learn to trust her. If she could ever be more to him than just a piece of the puzzle—the puzzle of his brother's death.

She rose and pulled the coverlet over his sleeping form. He didn't move. Gently she smoothed back his hair, stroked the beard-roughened cheek. Still he didn't move.

She left him and went downstairs. The boxes of papers confronted her, other bits and pieces of that puzzle. She separated them into files. Article files. Financial records. Personal notes from M, as well as from other, unidentified women. The miscellaneous debris of a man's life. How little she had known Richard! What a vast part of him he had kept private, even from his family. That's why he had so jealously guarded this north shore retreat.

In the fabric of his life, I was just a single, unimportant thread. Will I ever stop hurting from that?

She rose and checked the doors, the windows. Then she went back upstairs, to the master bedroom.

Chase was still asleep. She knew she should use the other room, the other bed, but tonight she didn't want to lie alone in the darkness. She wanted warmth and safety and the comfort of knowing Chase was nearby.

She had promised to look after him tonight. What better place to watch over him than in the same bed?

She lay down beside him, not close but near enough to imagine his warmth seeping toward her through the sheets.

Sometime during the night the dreams came.

A man, a lover, was holding her. Protecting her. Then she looked up at his face and saw he was a stranger. She pulled away, began to run. She found she was in a crowd of people. She began to search for a familiar face, a pair of arms she could reach out to, but they were all strangers, all strangers.

And then there he was, standing far beyond her reach. She cried out to him, held her hands out for him to grab. He moved toward her and her hands connected with warm and solid flesh. She heard him say, "I'm here, Miranda. Right here...."

And he was.

Through the semidarkness she saw the gleam of his face, the twin shadows of his eyes. His gaze was so still, so very quiet. Her breath caught as he took her face in his hands. Slowly he pressed his lips to hers. That one touch sent a shudder of pleasure through her body. They stared at each other and the night seemed filled with the sounds of their breathing.

Again, he kissed her.

Again, that wave of pleasure. It crested to a wanting for more, more. Her sleep-drugged body awoke, alive with hunger. She pressed hard against him, willing their bodies to meld, their warmth to mingle, but that frustrating barrier of clothes still lay between them.

He reached for her T-shirt. Slowly he pulled it up and over her head, let it drop from the bed. She was not so patient. Already she was undoing his buttons, sliding back his shirt, fumbling at his belt buckle. No words were spoken; none were needed. The soft whispers, the whimpers, the moans said more than any words could have.

So did his hands. His fingers slid across, between, inside all the warm and secret places of her body. They teased her, inflamed her, brought her to the very edge of release. Then, with knowing cruelty, they abandoned her, leaving her unsatisfied. She reached out to him, silently pleading for more.

He grasped her hips and willingly thrust into her again, but this time not with his fingers.

She cried out, a sound of joy, of delight.

At the first ripple of her climax he let his own needs take over. Needs that made him drive deep inside her, again and again. As her last wave of pleasure washed through her, he found his own cresting, breaking. He rode it to the very end and collapsed, sweating and triumphant, into her welcoming arms.

And so they fell asleep.

Chase was the first to awaken. He found his arms looped around her, his face buried in the sweet-smelling strands of her hair. She was curled up on her side, facing away from him, the silky skin of her back pressed against his chest. The memory of their lovemaking was at once so vivid he felt his body respond with automatic desire. And why not, with this woman in his arms? She was life and lust and honeyed warmth. She was everything a woman should be.

And I'm treading on dangerous ground.

He pulled away and sat up. Morning light shone through the window, onto her pillow. So innocent she looked, so untouched by evil. It occurred to him that Jill Vickery once must have looked as pure.

Before she shot her lover.

Dangerous women. How could you tell them from the innocents?

He left the bed and went straight to the shower. Wash the magical spell away, he thought. Wash away the desire, the craving for Miranda Wood. She was like a sickness in his blood, making him do insane things.

Last night, for instance.

They had simply fallen into it, he told himself. A physical act, that was all, a chance collision of two warm bodies.

He watched her sleep as he dressed. With each layer of clothes he felt more protected, more invulnerable. But when she stirred and opened her eyes and smiled at him, he realized how thin his emotional armor really was.

"How are you feeling this morning?" she asked softly.

"Much better, thanks. I think I can drive myself back to town."

There was a silence. Her smile faded as she took in the fact he was already dressed. "You're leaving?"

"Yes. I just wanted to make sure you got out of here safely."

She sat up. Hugging the sheets to her chest, she watched him for a moment, as though trying to understand what had gone wrong between them. At last she said, "I'll be fine. You don't have to wait around."

"I'll stay. Until you get dressed."

A shrug was her response, as if it didn't matter to her one way or the other. *Good,* he thought. *No sticky emotions over last night. We're both too smart for that.*

He started to leave, then stopped. "Miranda?"

"Yes?"

He turned to look at her. She was still hugging her knees, still every bit as bewitching. To see her there could break any man's heart. He said, "It's not that I don't think you're a wonderful woman. It's just that…"

"Don't worry about it, Chase," she said flatly. "We both know it won't work."

He wanted to say, "I'm sorry," but somehow it seemed

too lame, too easy. They were both adults. They had both made a mistake.

There was nothing more to be said.

"It's not as if any of this is incriminating," said Annie, flipping through the notes from M that were arrayed on her kitchen table. "Just your routine desperate-woman language. Darling. If you'd only see me. If only this, if only that. It's pathetic, but it's not murderous. It doesn't tell us that M—whoever she is—killed him."

"You're right." Miranda sighed, leaning back in the kitchen chair. "And it doesn't seem to tie in with Jill at all."

"Sorry. The only M around here is you. I'd say these letters could cause you more damage than good."

"Jill said there was a summer intern a year ago. A woman who got involved with Richard."

"Chloe? Ancient history. I can't imagine she'd sneak back to town just to kill an ex-lover. Besides, there's no *M* in her name."

"The *M* could stand for a nickname. A name only Richard used for her."

"Muffin? Marvelous?" Laughing, Annie rose to her feet. "I think we're beating a dead horse. And I'm going to be late." She went to the closet and pulled out a warm-up jacket. "Irving hates to be kept waiting."

Miranda glanced with amusement at Annie's attire: a torn T-shirt, scruffy running shoes and sweatpants. "Irving likes the casual look?"

"Irving *is* the casual look." Annie slung her purse over her shoulder. "We're sanding the deck this week. Loads of fun."

"Will I ever get to meet this boat bum of yours?"

Annie grinned. "Soon as I can drag him to shore. I

mean, the yachting season's gotta end one of these days."
She waved. "See ya."

After Annie had left, Miranda scrounged together a
salad and sat down at the kitchen table for a melancholy
dinner. Irving and his boat didn't sound like much in the
way of companionship, but at least Annie had someone to
keep her company. Someone to keep away the loneliness.

Once, Miranda hadn't minded being alone. She'd even
enjoyed the silence, the peace of a house all to herself. Now
she craved the simple presence of another human being.
Even a dog would be nice. She'd have to think about
getting one, a large one. A dog wouldn't desert her the way
most of her friends had. The way Chase had.

She set down her fork, her appetite instantly gone. Where
was he now? Probably sitting in that house on Chestnut
Street, surrounded by all the other Tremains. He'd have
Evelyn and the twins to keep him company. He wouldn't
be alone or lonely. He would be just fine without her.

In anger she rose to her feet and slid the remains of her
salad into the trash. Then she started for the door, determined to get outside, to run around the block, anything to
escape the house.

At the front door she halted. A visitor stood on the
porch, hand poised to ring the bell.

"Jill," whispered Miranda.

This was not the cool, unflappable Jill she knew. This
Jill was white-faced and brittle.

"Annie's not here right now," said Miranda.
"She...should be back any minute."

"You're the one I came to see." Without warning Jill
slipped right past into the living room and shut the door
behind her.

"I—I was just on my way out." Miranda edged slowly for the door.

Jill took a sidestep, blocking her way. For a moment she stood there, regarding Miranda. "It's not as if I haven't been punished," she said softly. "I've done everything I could to put it behind me. Everything. I've worked like a madwoman these last five years. Built the *Herald* into a real newspaper. You think Richard knew what he was doing? Of course not! He relied on me. *Me.* Oh, he never admitted it, but he let me run the show. Five years. And now you've ruined it for me. You've already got the police shoveling up old dirt. You think the Tremains will keep me on? Now that they know? Now that everyone knows?"

"I wasn't the one. I didn't tell Lorne."

"*You're* the reason it's all come up! You and your pathetic denials! Why don't you just admit you killed him? And leave the rest of us out of it."

"But I didn't kill him."

Jill began to pace the room. "I've sinned, you've sinned. Everyone has. We're all equal. What sets us apart is how we live with our sins. I've done the best I could. And now I find it's not good enough. Not good enough to erase what happened…."

"Did Richard know? About San Diego?"

"No. I mean, yes, in the end. He found out. But it didn't matter to him—"

"It didn't matter that you killed a man?"

"He understood the circumstances. Richard was good that way." She let out a shaky laugh. "After all, he himself wasn't above a little sinning."

Miranda paused, gathered the courage for her next question. "You had an affair with him, didn't you?"

Jill's response was a careless shrug. "It didn't mean anything. It was years ago. You know, the new girl on the block. He got over it." She snapped her fingers. "Just like that. We stayed friends. We understood each other." She stopped pacing and turned to look at Miranda. "Now Lorne wants to know where I was the night Richard was killed. He's asking *me* to come up with an alibi! You're casting the blame all around, aren't you? To hell with who gets hurt. You just want off the hook. Well, sometimes that's not possible." She moved closer, her gaze fixed on Miranda, like a cat's on a bird. Softly she said, "Sometimes we have to pay for our sins. Whether it's an indiscreet affair. Or murder. We pay for it. I did. Why can't you?"

They stared at each other, caught in a binding fascination for each other's transgressions, each other's pain. *Killer and victim,* thought Miranda. *That's what I see in her eyes. Is that what you see in mine?*

The telephone rang, shattering the silence.

The sound seemed to rattle Jill. At once she turned and reached for the door. There she stopped. "You think you're the exception, Miranda. You think you're untouchable. Just wait. In a few years, when you're my age, you'll know just how vulnerable you are. We all are."

She walked out, closing the door behind her.

At once Miranda slid the bolt home.

The phone had stopped ringing. Miranda stared at it, wondering if it had been Chase, praying that he would call again.

The phone remained silent.

She began to pace the living room, hoping Chase, Annie, *anyone* would call. Starved for the sound of a human voice, she turned on the TV. Mindless entertainment, that's what she needed. For a half hour she sat on the couch among Annie's discarded socks and sweatshirts, flicking nervously between channels. Opera. Basketball. Game show. Opera again. In frustration she flicked it back to basketball.

Something clattered in the next room.

Startled, she left the couch and went into the kitchen. There she found herself staring down at a plastic saucer rolling around and around on its side across the linoleum floor. It collapsed, shuddered and fell still. Had it tumbled off the drainboard? She looked up at the sink and noticed, for the first time, that the window was wide open.

That's not the way I left it.

Slowly she backed away. The gun—Annie's gun. She had to get it.

In panic she turned to make a dash for the living room—

And found her head brutally trapped, her mouth covered by a wad of cloth. She flailed blindly against her captor, against the fumes burning her nose, her throat, but found her arms wouldn't work right. Her legs seemed to slide away from her, dissolving into some bottomless hole. She felt herself falling, caught a glimpse of the light as it receded into an impossibly high place. She tried to reach out for it but found her arms had gone numb.

The light wavered, shrank.

And then it winked out, leaving only the darkness.

Phillip was banging away at the piano. Rachmaninoff, Chase thought wearily. Couldn't the boy choose something a little more sedate? Mozart, for instance, or Haydn. Anything but this Russian thunder.

Chase headed out to the veranda, hoping to escape the racket, but the sound of the piano seemed to pound right through the walls. Resignedly he stood at the railing and stared toward the harbor. Already sunset. The sea had turned to red flame.

He wondered what Miranda was doing.

Wondered if he'd ever stop wondering.

This morning, when they'd driven off in their separate cars, their separate ways, he'd known their relationship had gone as far as it could. To go any further would require a level of trust he wasn't ready to give her. Their amateur detective work had come to a dead end; for now they had no reason to see each other. It was time to let the pros take over. The police, at least, would be objective. They wouldn't be swayed by emotions or hormones.

They still believed Miranda was guilty.

"Uncle Chase?" Cassie pushed through the screen door and came out to join him. "You can't stand the music, either, I see."

He smiled. "Don't tell your brother."

"It's not that he's a bad musician. He's just…loud." She leaned against one of the posts and looked up at the sky, at the first stars winking in the gathering darkness. "Think you could do me a favor?" she asked.

"What's that?"

"When Mom gets home, will you talk to her? About the *Herald.*"

"What about it?"

"Well, with all that's come up—about Jill Vickery, I mean—it's beginning to look like we'll need a strong hand on the helm. We all know Dad groomed Phillip to be the designated heir. And he's a bright kid—I'm not putting him down or anything. But the fact is, Phillip's just not that interested."

"He hasn't said much about it, one way or the other."

"Oh, he won't say anything. He'll never admit the truth. That he's not crazy about the job." She paused, then said with steel in her voice, "But I am."

Chase frowned at his niece. Not yet twenty, and she had the look of a woman who knew exactly what she wanted in life. "You think you have what it takes?"

"It's in my blood! I've been involved from the time I could put pen to paper. Or fingers to keyboard. I know how that office works. I can write, edit, lay out ads, drive the damn delivery truck. I can *run* that paper. Phillip can't."

Chase remembered Cassie's term papers, the ones he'd glanced through at the cottage. They weren't just the chewing up and spitting out of textbook facts, but thoughtful, critical analyses.

"I think you'd do a terrific job," he said. "I'll talk to your mother."

"Thanks, Uncle Chase. I'll remember to mention your name when I get my Pulitzer." Grinning, she turned to go back into the house.

"Cassie?"

"Yes?"

"What do you think of Jill Vickery?"

Cassie frowned at the change of subject. "You mean as a managing editor? She was okay. Considering what she got paid, we were lucky to keep her."

"I mean, on a personal level."

"Well, that's hard to say. You never really get to know Jill. She's like a closed book. I never had any idea about that stuff in San Diego."

"Do you think she had an affair with your father?"

Cassie shrugged. "Didn't they all?"

"Do you think she was hurt by it?"

Cassie thought this over for a moment. "I think, if she was, she got over it. Jill's a tough cookie. That's the way I'd like to be." She turned and went into the house.

Phillip was still playing Rachmaninoff.

Chase stood and watched the last glow of sunset fade from the sea. He thought about Jill Vickery, about Miranda, about all the women Richard had hurt, including his own wife, Evelyn.

We're lousy, we Tremain men, he thought. *We use women, then we hurt them.*

Am I any different?

In frustration he slapped the porch railing. *Yes, I am. I would be. If only I could trust her.*

Phillip's pounding on the piano had become unbearable.

Chase left the porch, walked down the steps and headed for his car.

He would talk to her one last time. He would look her in the eye and ask her if she was guilty. Tonight he would get his answer. Tonight he would decide, once and for all, if Miranda Wood was telling the truth.

No one answered Annie's front door.

The lights were on inside, and Chase could hear the TV. He rang the bell, knocked, called out Miranda's name. Still there was no answer. At last he tried the knob and found the door was unlocked. He poked his head inside.

"Miranda? Annie?"

The living room was deserted. A basketball game, unwatched, was playing out its last minute on the TV. A pair of Annie's socks lay draped over the back of the sofa. Everything seemed perfectly normal, yet not quite right. He stood there for a moment, as though expecting the former occupants of the room to magically reappear and confront him.

The basketball game went into its fifteen-second countdown. A last-ditch throw, across the court. Basket. The crowd cheered.

Chase crossed the room, into the kitchen, and halted.

Here things were definitely not right. A chair lay toppled on its side. On the floor a saucer lay upside down. Though the kitchen window was wide open, an odor hung in the room, something vaguely sharp, medicinal.

Quickly he searched the rest of the house. He found neither Miranda nor Annie.

With growing panic he hurried outside and glanced up and down the street. Except for the far-off barking of a dog, the evening was still.

No, not quite. Was that the sound of a car engine running? If seemed muffled or distant. He circled around the house and saw a small detached garage in back. The door was shut. The sound of the car engine, though still muffled, seemed closer.

He started toward the garage. Then, out of the corner of his eye, he sighted a flicker of movement. He turned just in time to spy a shadow slipping away, blending into the darkness.

This time, you bastard, Chase thought, *you don't get away from me.*

Chase sprinted off in pursuit.

He heard his quarry dodge left, toward a thick hedge of bushes. Chase, too, veered left, scrambled over a low stone wall and broke into a sprint.

The fleeing shadow burst through the hedge and made

a sharp right, into a neighboring yard littered with garden tools. Chase, intent on capture, didn't notice his quarry had swept up a rake. It came flying at him through the darkness.

Chase ducked. Tines first, it flew over his head, then clattered into a wheelbarrow behind him. Chase leaped back to his feet.

His quarry grabbed a pickax, flung it.

Again Chase dodged. He heard the whoosh of air as the lethal weapon looped past. By the time he'd recovered his balance the figure was off and running again, toward a stand of trees.

He'll be lost in the shadows! thought Chase. He mustered a final burst of speed, drew within reach. His quarry was tired. He could hear the other man's ragged breaths. Chase launched himself forward, grabbed a handful of shirt and held on.

His quarry, instead of trying to pull free, spun around and charged like a bull.

Chase was flung backward, into a tree. The shock lasted only an instant. Rage, not pain, was his first response. Shoving away from the tree, he flung himself at his attacker. Both men fell off balance, went skidding across the wet leaves. The attacker punched, and the blow caught Chase in the belly. With a new strength born of fury, Chase slammed his fist blindly at the squirming shadow. The man groaned, tried to lash out. Chase hit him again. And again.

The man went limp.

Chase rolled away from the body. For a moment he sat there, catching his breath, wincing at the pain in his knuckles. The other man was still alive—he could hear him breathing. Chase grabbed the inert figure by the legs and dragged him across the leaf-strewn lawn, toward a faint pool of light from a distant porch lamp. There he knelt to see who his prisoner was. In disbelief he stared at the face, now revealed.

It was Noah DeBolt. Evelyn's father.

Thirteen

The steady growl of an engine slowly penetrated Chase's numbed awareness. The car in the garage…the closed door…

That's when the realization hit him. He lurched to his feet. *Miranda.*

He sprinted across the yard to the garage. A cloud of fumes assailed him as he pushed through the door. Miranda's car was parked inside, its engine still running. In panic, he flung open the car door.

Miranda lay sprawled across the front seat.

He switched off the ignition. Coughing, choking, he dragged her roughly out of the car, out of the garage. It terrified him how lifeless she felt in his arms. He carried her to the lawn and laid her down on the grass.

"Miranda!" he yelled. He shook her hard, so hard her whole body shuddered. "Wake up," he pleaded. "Damn you, Miranda. Don't you give up on me. Wake up!"

Still she didn't move.

In panic he slapped her face. The brutality of that blow, the sting of her flesh against his, shocked him. He laid his ear to her breast. Her heart was beating. And there it was—a breath!

She groaned, moved her head.

"Yes!" he shouted. "Come on. Come on." She sank back into unconsciousness. He didn't want to do it, but he had no choice. He slapped her again.

This time she moved her hand, a reflexive gesture to ward off the savage blows. "No," she moaned.

"Miranda, it's me! Wake up." He brushed back her hair, gently took her face in his hands and kissed her forehead, her temples. "Please, Miranda," he whispered. "Look at me."

Slowly she opened her eyes. They were dazed and full of confusion. At once she lashed out blindly, as though still fighting for her life.

"No, it's me!" he cried. He held her, hugged her tightly against him. Her frantic thrashing grew weaker. He felt the panic melt from her body until she lay quietly in his arms.

"It's all over," he whispered. "All over."

She pulled away and stared up at him with a look of bewilderment. "Who…"

"It was Noah."

"Evelyn's *father?*"

Chase nodded. "He's the one who's been trying to kill you."

"You have no right to hold me, Lorne. You understand? *No right.*" Noah, his face bruised an ugly purple, stared at his accusers. Through the closed door came the sounds of the police station: the clack of a typewriter, the ringing phone, the voices of patrolmen headed out for night duty. But here, in the back room, there was dead silence.

Quietly Lorne said, "You're not in any position to pull rank, Noah. So talk to us."

"I don't have to say a thing," said Noah. "Not until Les Hardee gets here."

Lorne sighed. "Legally speaking, yeah, you're right. But it would sure make things easy if you'd just tell us why you tried to kill her."

"I didn't. I went to her house to talk to her. I heard the car running in the garage. I thought maybe she was trying to kill herself. I started to go in, to check on it. Then Chase showed up. I guess I panicked. That's why I ran."

"That's all you were doing there? Just paying Ms. Wood a visit?"

Noah gave him an icy nod.

"In a getup like that?" Lorne nodded at Noah's black shirt and trousers.

"What I wear happens to be my concern."

"Chase says differently. He says you dragged her in the garage, left her there and started the car."

Noah snorted. "Chase has a little trouble being objective. Especially where Miranda Wood is concerned. Besides, *he* attacked *me*. Who the hell's got the bruises, anyway? Look at my face. Look at it!"

"Seems to me you both got some pretty good bruises," said Lorne.

"Self-defense," claimed Noah. "I had to fight back."

"Chase thinks you're the one who's been going after her. That you set fire to her house. Drove at her with a stolen car. And what about tonight? Was that supposed to be a convenient little suicide?"

"She's got him all twisted around. Got him taking her side. The side of a murderer—"

"Who's the guilty party here, Noah?"

Noah, sensing he'd said too much already, said abruptly, "I'm not going to talk till Les gets here."

In frustration Lorne crumpled his paper coffee cup in his fist. "Okay," he said, dropping into a chair. "We can wait. As long as it takes, Noah. As long as it takes."

"It's not going to stick," said Miranda. "I know it won't."

They sat huddled together on a bench in the intake area. Ellis Snipe had brought them coffee and cookies. Perhaps it was his way of personally atoning for the ordeal the police had put them through. So many questions, so many reports to be filed. And then, halfway through the interrogation, Dr. Steiner had shown up, called in by Lorne to check on her condition. In the guise of a medical exam, he had practically assaulted her with his stethoscope. *Breathe deep, damn it! Gotta check your lungs. You think I like making all these house calls? This keeps up, you two will have to put me on retainer!*

The questions, the demands, had left her exhausted. It was all she could manage, to sit propped up against Chase's shoulder. Waiting—for what? For Noah to confess? For the police to tell her the nightmare was over?

She knew better than that.

"He'll get out of it," she said. "He'll find a way."

"This time he won't," said Chase.

"But I never saw his face. I can barely remember what happened. What can they charge him with? Trespassing?" Miranda shook her head. "This is Noah DeBolt we're talking about. In this town, a DeBolt can get away with murder."

"Not Richard's murder."

She stared at him. "You think he killed Richard? His own son-in-law?"

"It's starting to fall together, Miranda. Remember what that lawyer FitzHugh told us? The real reason Richard gave Rose Hill to you? It was to keep the land out of Evelyn's control."

"I don't see what you're getting at."

"Who's the one person in the world Evelyn listens to? Trusts? Her *father*. Noah could have talked her into selling the land."

"You think this is all for control of Rose Hill? That's not much of a motive for murder."

"But the threat of bankruptcy is. If his investment collapsed, Noah would be left holding acres of land he could never develop. Worthless land."

"The north shore? Then you think Noah was the money behind Stone Coast Trust."

"Which makes Tony Graffam nothing but a front man. A patsy, really. My guess is, Richard found out. He had those financial records from Stone Coast, remember? The account numbers, the tax returns. I think he matched one of those accounts to Noah."

"Richard could have ruined him right then and there," she pointed out. "All he had to do was run the story in the *Herald*. But he canceled it."

"It's the way their relationship worked, Richard and Noah. They were always out to cut each other down. But not in public, *never* in public. It was a private rivalry, just between them. That's why Richard didn't print the article. It would've exposed his own father-in-law. And brought the family's dirty linen out into the public eye."

Miranda shook her head. "We'll never prove it. Not

after Noah's lawyer gets through with the smoke and mirrors. You've been away from this island too long, Chase. You've forgotten how it is. The DeBolts, they're the equivalent of gods in this town."

"Not any longer."

"Then there's the matter of evidence. How do you prove he killed Richard?" She sighed, an admission of defeat. "No, *I'm* the convenient suspect. The one they'll convict." She sat back wearily. "The one they'll put away."

"That won't happen, Miranda. I won't let it happen."

Their gazes met. For the first time she saw what she'd been longing to see in his eyes. Trust. "Then you think I'm telling the truth."

"I know you're telling the truth." He touched her face. As his hand stroked down the curve of her cheek she closed her eyes and felt herself melting, flowing like warm liquid against him. "I think I've known it all along. But I was afraid to admit it. Afraid to consider the other possibilities...."

"It wasn't me, Chase. It wasn't." She slid into his arms and there she found warmth and courage, all the courage she'd somehow lost in these past soul-battering days. *Believe me,* she thought. *Never stop believing me.*

They were still locked in that embrace when Evelyn Tremain walked in the station door.

Miranda felt Chase stiffen against her, heard his sharp intake of breath. Slowly she raised her head and turned to see Evelyn and the DeBolt family attorney, Les Hardee, standing a few feet away.

"So it's come to this, has it?" Evelyn said quietly.

Chase said nothing.

"Where is my father?" said Evelyn.

"In the room down the hall," said Chase. "He's talking to Lorne."

"Without me?" cut in the attorney. He headed swiftly down the hall, muttering, "A clear violation of rights…."

Evelyn hadn't moved. She was still staring at them. "What sort of lies are you spreading about my father, Chase?"

Slowly Chase stood to face her. "Only the truth, Evelyn. It may be hard to take, but you'll have to accept it."

"The *truth?*" Evelyn let out a disbelieving laugh. "An officer calls me, tells me my father's been arrested for assault. Assault? *Noah DeBolt?* Who's lying, Chase? My father? You?" She looked at Miranda. "Or someone else?"

"Lorne will explain the charges. You'd better talk to him."

"Because you won't? Is that it? Oh, Chase." She shook her head. "You've turned your back on your own family. We love you. And look how you hurt us." She turned, faced the corridor. Softly she said, "I just hope Lorne has the good sense to know the truth when he hears it." Taking a deep breath, she started down the hall.

"Wait here," Chase said to Miranda.

"What are you going to do?"

He didn't answer. He just kept walking away, in pursuit of Evelyn.

Stunned, Miranda watched him vanish around the corner. She heard a door open, then close behind him, shutting her out. She wondered what was going on in that room, what words were being exchanged, what deals forged. She had no doubt there *would* be deals, declarations of Noah's innocence. His attorney would do his best to twist the story around, make it seem like some crazy misunderstanding. Somehow they'd manage to make Miranda look like the guilty party.

Please, Chase, she thought. *Don't let them sway you. Don't start doubting me again.*

She stared down the hall and waited.

And she feared the worst.

"The charges are preposterous," said Evelyn. "My father's never broken a law in his life. Why, if he gets too much change back from a clerk, he'll go across town to return it. How can you accuse him of assault, much less attempted murder?"

"Mr. Tremain here has the bruises to prove it," said Lorne.

"So does my client!" cut in Les Hardee. "All that proves is, they traded blows in the dark. A case of mistaken identity. Two men blindly duking it out. At the very worst, you can accuse my client of idiotic behavior."

"Thanks a lot, Les," grunted Noah.

"The point is," said Hardee, "you can't hold him. The damage—" he glanced at Chase's bruised face, then at Noah's face, even more bruised "—appears to be mutual. And as for that nonsense about trying to kill Miranda Wood, well, where's your evidence? She was facing a jail term. Of course she was depressed. Of course she'd consider suicide."

"What about the fire?" pointed out Chase. "The car that almost ran her down? I was there, I saw it. *Someone's* trying to kill her."

"Not Mr. DeBolt."

"Does he have alibis?"

"Do *you* have evidence?" Hardee shot back. He turned

to Lorne. "Look, let's call a halt to this farce. I'll take the responsibility. Release Mr. DeBolt."

Lorne sighed. "I can't."

Evelyn and Hardee stared at the diminutive chief of police.

"I'm afraid there *is* evidence," said Lorne, almost apologetically. "Ellis found a bottle of chloroform behind the garage. That kind of argues against suicide, doesn't it?"

"Nothing to do with me," said Noah.

"Then here's some more evidence," cut in Chase. It was time to gamble, time to shoot the wad. He was going to make a guess here; he only hoped it was the right one. "You know that money from the Bank of Boston? That hundred thousand dollars used to bail out Miranda Wood? Well, I had a banker friend of mine slip into the computer. Match that money transfer to an account."

"What?" Lorne turned to Chase in surprise. "You know who paid the bail?"

"Yes." *Here goes,* thought Chase. "Noah DeBolt."

It was Evelyn who reacted first, with a rage that transformed her face into an ugly mask. The look was directed at her father. "You did *what?*"

Noah said nothing. His silence was all Chase needed to back up his hunch. Right on target.

"It can be officially confirmed," said Chase. "Yes, it was your father who paid the bail."

Evelyn was still staring at Noah. "You let her out?"

Noah's head drooped. In an instant he'd been transformed into a very old, very tired-looking man. "I did it for you," he whispered.

"For me? For *me?*" Evelyn laughed. "What other favors have you done for me, Daddy?"

"It was for you. Everything was for you—"

"You crazy old man," muttered Evelyn. "You must be going senile."

"No." Noah's head shot up. "I would've done anything, don't you see? I was protecting you! My little girl—"

"Protecting me from what?"

"From yourself. From what you did…."

Evelyn turned away in disgust. "I don't know what the hell he's raving about."

"Don't turn your back on me, young lady!"

"You can see he needs a doctor, Lorne. Try a psychiatrist."

"This is the thanks I get!" Noah roared. "For keeping you out of *prison?*"

Instant silence. Evelyn, white-faced, turned to confront her father. "Prison? For what?"

"Richard." Noah, his rage suddenly spent, sank slowly back against the chair. Softly he said, "For Richard."

"You thought…that I—" Evelyn shook her head. "Why? You knew it was that—that bitch!"

Noah merely looked away. With that one gesture he gave his answer. An answer that lifted a weight so heavy from Chase's soul he felt he was floating. It was a burden he could only now acknowledge had been there all along, the burden of proof. With that one gesture, the last blot of suspicion was washed away.

"You know Miranda's innocent," said Chase.

Noah dropped his head in his hands. "Yes," he whispered.

"How?" cut in Lorne.

"Because I had her followed. Oh, I knew about the affair. I knew what he was up to. I'd had enough of it! I wasn't going to see him hurt Evelyn again. So I hired a man, told him to watch her. To follow her, take photos.

Catch 'em in the act. I wanted Evelyn to know, once and for all, what a bastard she'd married."

"And the night he was killed, you had Miranda under surveillance?" asked Lorne.

Noah nodded.

"What did your man see?"

"Of the murder? Nothing. He was busy following the woman. She left the house, walked to the beach. Sat there for an hour or so. Then she went home. By then my son-in-law was already dead."

Exactly what she said, thought Chase. *It was all the truth, right down to the last detail.*

"Then your man never saw the killer?" said Lorne.

"No."

"But you assumed your daughter…"

Noah shrugged. "It seemed…a logical guess. He had it coming. All these years of hurting her. You think he didn't deserve it? You think she wasn't justified?"

"But I didn't do it," said Evelyn.

Her words went ignored.

"Why did you bail out Miranda Wood?" asked Lorne.

"I thought if she went to trial, if her story held together, there was a chance they'd start to look at other suspects."

"You mean Evelyn."

"Better to have it over and done with!" blurted out Noah. "If there was an accident, that would end it. No more questions. No more suspects."

"So you wanted her out of jail," said Chase. "Out on the street, where you could reach her."

"That's enough, Noah!" cut in Hardee. "You don't have to answer these questions."

"Damn you, Les!" snapped Evelyn. "You should have

told him that earlier!" She looked at her father, her expression a mixture of pity and disgust. "Let me set your mind at rest, Daddy. I didn't kill Richard. The fact you thought I did only shows how little you know me. Or I you."

"I'm sorry about this, Evelyn," said Lorne quietly. "But now I'm going to have to ask you a few questions."

Evelyn turned to him. Her chin came up, a gesture of stubborn pride, newfound strength. For the first time in all the years he'd known her Chase felt a spark of admiration for his sister-in-law.

"Ask away, Lorne," she said. "You're the cop. And I guess I'm now your prime suspect."

Chase didn't stay to hear the rest. He left the room and headed down the hall to find Miranda. *Now it can be proved. It was true, every word you said.* They could start from the beginning, he thought. He suddenly strode ahead with new hope, new anticipation. The shadow of murder was gone, and they had a chance to do it over, to do it right.

He rounded the corner eagerly, expecting to see her sitting on the bench.

The bench was empty.

He went over to the clerk, who was typing out Noah's arrest report. "Did you see where she went?"

The clerk glanced up. "You mean Ms. Wood?"

"Yes."

"She left the station. About, oh, twenty minutes ago."

"Did she say where she was going?"

"Nope. Just got up and walked out."

In frustration Chase turned to the door. *You never make it easy for me, do you?* he thought. Then he pushed through the door and headed out into the night.

* * *

All day Ozzie had been restless. Last night, all that frantic running around and police activity had driven the beast nearly mad with excitement. A day later and the agitation still hadn't worn off. He was all nerved up, clawing at the door, whining and tip-tapping back and forth across the wood floor.

Maybe it's my fault, Miss St. John thought, gazing in disgust at her hysterical dog. *Maybe my mood has simply rubbed off on him.*

Ozzie crouched at the front door like a discarded fur coat, staring pitifully at his mistress.

"You," said Miss St. John, "are a tyrant."

Ozzie merely whimpered.

"Oh, all right," said Miss St. John. "Out, out!" She opened the door. The dog bounded out into the twilight.

Miss St. John followed the beast down the gravel driveway. Ozzie was dancing along, his fur bouncing like black corkscrews. Truly an ugly animal, thought Miss St. John, the same thought that occurred to her on every walk. That he was worth several thousand dollars for his pedigree alone only went to show you the worthlessness of pedigrees, be they for dogs or people. But what Ozzie lacked in beauty he made up in energy. Already he was trotting far ahead and veering up the path, toward Rose Hill.

Miss St. John, feeling more like dog than mistress, followed him.

The cottage was dark. Chase and Miranda had left that morning and now the place stood deserted and forlorn. A pity. Such charming cottages should not go empty, especially not in the summertime.

She climbed the steps and peered through the window. Shadows of furniture huddled within. The books were back in the shelves. She could see the gleam of their spines lined up against the wall. Though they'd combed those books and papers thoroughly, she still wondered whether they had missed something. Some small, easily overlooked item that held the answers to Richard Tremain's death.

The door was locked, but she knew where the key was kept. What harm would there be in another little visit? She'd always felt just a bit proprietary when it came to Rose Hill. After all, she'd played near here almost every day as a child. And as an adult she'd made a point of keeping an eye on the cottage, as a favor to the Tremains.

Ozzie seemed happy enough, padding about in the yard.

Miss St. John retrieved the key from the planter, unlocked the door and went inside.

It seemed very still, very sad in that living room. She turned on all the lamps and wandered about, her gaze combing the nooks and crannies of the furniture. They'd already made a search of those places. There was no point repeating it.

She went through the kitchen, through the upstairs bedrooms, came back down again. No hunches, no revelations.

She was turning to leave when her gaze swept past the area rug, set right in front of the door. That's when a memory struck her, of a scene from *Tess of the D'Urbervilles*. A confessional note, slipped under the closed door, only to be pushed accidentally under the adjacent rug. A note that was never found because it lay hidden from view.

So vivid was that image that when she bent and pulled

up the edge of the rug she was not at all startled to see a sealed envelope lying there.

The note was from M. The intended recipient had never found it, never read it.

…This pain is alive, like a creature gnawing at my organs. It won't die. It refuses to die. You put it there, you planted it, you gave the embryo all those years of nourishment.

And then you walked away.

You say you are doing me a kindness. You say it is better to break off now, because, if it goes on longer, it will only hurt more. You don't know what it is to hurt. Once you claimed to be love's walking wounded. Once, I thought to save you.

You were the serpent I hugged to my breast.

Now you say you've found a new savior. You think she'll make you happy. But she won't. It will be the same with her as it was with the others. You'll decide she isn't perfect. No one who's ever loved you, really loved you, has ever been good enough for you.

But you're getting old, flabby, and still you think that somewhere there's a young and perfect woman just longing to make love to your wrinkled old carcass.

She doesn't know you the way I do. I've had years to learn all your dirty little secrets. Your conceits and lies and cruelty. You'll use her, the way you've used all the others. And then she'll be tossed on the heap with the rest of us, another woman terribly hurt.

You should suffer where you've sinned. A good clean slice—

Miss St. John, still clutching the letter, abruptly left Rose Hill and hurried home.

With shaking hands she made two phone calls. The first was to Lorne Tibbetts.

The second was to Miranda Wood.

Fourteen

Miranda was near the point of exhaustion by the time she climbed up Annie's porch steps. It had been only a ten-minute walk from the police station, but the distance she had traveled had been emotional, not physical. Sitting alone on that bench, shut out from the fancy deal-making between attorneys and cops, she'd come to the sad realization that Noah DeBolt would never be charged with any crime worse than trespassing. That she, Miranda, was too convenient a suspect to be let off the hook. And that Chase, by walking down the corridor, by joining Evelyn and Noah behind that closed door, had made his choice.

Didn't they say that crisis brought families together? Well, the arrest of patriarch Noah DeBolt was one hell of a crisis. The family would rally.

Miranda was not, could never be, part of that family.

She stepped in the front door. Annie was still not home. Silence hung like a shroud over the house. When the phone suddenly rang, the sound was almost shocking to her ears.

She picked up the receiver.

"Miranda?" came a breathless voice.

"Miss St. John? Is something wrong?"

"Are you home alone?" was Miss St. John's bizarre reply.

"Well, yes, at the moment—"

"I want you to lock the door. Do it now."

"No, everything's all right. They've arrested Noah DeBolt—"

"Listen to me! I found another letter, at Rose Hill. That's what she was after, don't you see? The reason she kept going to the cottage! To get back all her letters!"

"Whose letters?"

"M."

"But Noah DeBolt—"

"This has nothing to do with Noah! It was a crime of passion, Miranda. The classic motive. Let me read you the letter…."

Miranda listened.

By the time Miss St. John had finished, Miranda's hands were numb from clutching the receiver.

"I've already called the police," said Miss St. John. "They've sent a man to pick up Jill Vickery. Until then, keep your doors locked. It's a sick letter, Miranda, written by a sick woman. If she comes to the house, *don't let her in.*"

Miranda hung up.

At once she missed the sound of a human voice, any voice, even one transmitted through telephone wires. *Annie, come home. Please.*

She stared at the phone, wondering if she should call someone. But who? It was only as she stood there, thinking, that she noticed several days' mail mounded haphazardly by the telephone, some of it threatening to spill over onto the floor. A half-dozen household bills mingled with ad circulars and magazines. Annie's book-keeping must be as sloppy as her housekeeping, she thought, straightening the pile. Only then did she notice the newsletter from the alumni association of Tufts University—Annie's old alma mater. It lay at the edge of the table, four photocopied pages stapled together, personal notes from the class of '68, with a mass-mailing label on front. Of no particular interest to Miranda—except for one detail.

It was addressed to Margaret Ann Berenger.

You're the only M I know, Annie had said.

And all the time, she'd known another.

It doesn't mean she's the one.

Miranda stood staring at that label. Margaret Ann Berenger. Where was the proof, where was the link between Annie and all those letters from M?

It suddenly occurred to her. *A typewriter.*

A manual model, Jill had said, with an *e* hammer in need of cleaning. It would be a large item, difficult to hide. A quick check of all the closets, all the cabinets, confirmed that there was no manual typewriter in the house. Could it be in the garage?

No, she'd been in the garage. It was barely large enough to hold a car, much less store household items.

She checked, anyway. No typewriter.

She went back into the house, her mind racing. By now Jill might already be under arrest. Annie would hear of it in no time, would know the search for the real M was on. Her first move would be to get rid of the incriminating typewriter, if she hadn't already done so. It was the one piece of evidence that could link Annie to Richard's murder.

It could prove my innocence. I have to find it, before she destroys it. I have to get it to the police.

There was one more place she had to look.

She ran from the house and got into her car.

Moments later she pulled up in front of the *Herald* building. It was dark inside. The latest issue had just been put to bed. No one would be working late tonight, so she'd have the building to herself.

She let herself in the front door with her key—the key she'd never gotten around to turning in. With a twinge of irony she remembered that it was Richard who'd told her to keep it. He was certain he could talk her into returning to the job.

Well, here she was, back again.

She moved up the aisle of desks and went straight to Annie's. She flicked on the lamp. The top drawer was unlocked. Among the jumble of pens and paper clips she found some loose keys. Which one would open Annie's locker? She gathered them all up and headed down the stairwell and into the women's room.

She turned on the light. A flowered couch, mauve wallpaper, Victorian prints sprang into view. Jill's decorative touch couldn't disguise the fact it was a closed-in dungeon of a room, without a single window. Miranda moved to the bank of lockers. There were six of them, extra wide to accommodate employees' heavy coats and boots during the winter months. She knew which one belonged to Annie. It had the sticker that said I've Got PMS. What's Your Excuse?

She inserted the first key into the lock. It didn't turn.

She tried the second key, then the third. The lock popped open.

She swung open the door and frowned at the contents.

On the top shelf were mittens, a pair of old running shoes, a wool scarf.

On the bottom shelf a sweater lay draped over a towel-wrapped bundle. Miranda took out the bundle. The object inside was heavy. She unwrapped the towel, revealed the contents.

It was an old blue-green Olivetti with pica type.

She slid in a scrap of paper and with shaking hands typed the name Margaret Ann Berenger. The *e* loop was smudged.

An overwhelming sense of relief, almost euphoria, at once washed over her. Quickly she shut the locker and re-wrapped the typewriter. As she gathered it up in her arms, a puff of air blew past her cheek. That was all the warning she had, that soft whisper of wind through the door as it opened and shut behind her.

Miranda turned.

The intruder stood in the doorway, her hair a mass of windblown waves, her face utterly devoid of emotion.

Miranda said softly, "Annie."

In silence Annie's gaze settled on the typewriter in Miranda's arms.

"I thought you were with Irving," said Miranda.

Annie's gaze slowly rose once again to meet Miranda's. Sadness now filled those eyes, a look of pain that seemed to spill from her very soul. *Why did I never see it before?* thought Miranda.

"There is no Irving," said Annie.

Miranda shook her head in confusion.

"There never was an Irving. I made him up. All the dates, all those evenings out. You see, I'd drive to the harbor. Park there and just sit. Hours, sometimes." Annie took a deep breath and, shuddering, let it out. "I couldn't take the pity, Miranda. All that sympathy for an old maid."

"I never thought that—"

"Of course you did. You all did. Then there was Richard. I wouldn't give him the satisfaction of knowing that—" Her voice broke. She wiped her hand across her eyes.

Slowly Miranda set the typewriter down on the bench. "Knowing what, Annie?" she asked softly. "How badly he hurt you? How alone you really were?"

A shudder racked Annie's body.

"He hurt us both," said Miranda. "Every woman he ever touched. Every woman who ever loved him. He hurt us all."

"Not the way he hurt me!" Annie cried. The echo of her pain seemed to reverberate endlessly against those stark walls. "Five years of my life, Miranda. That's what I gave him. Five years of secrets. I was forty-two when we met. I still had time for a baby. A few short years left. I kept hoping, waiting for him to make up his mind. To leave Evelyn." She wiped her eyes again, smearing a streak of mascara and tears across her cheek. "Now it's too late for me. It was my last chance and he took it from me. He *stole* it from me. And then he ended it." She shook her head, laughing through her tears. "He said he was only trying to be kind. That he didn't want me to waste any more years on him. Then he said the thing that hurt me most of all. He said, 'It was just your fantasy, Annie. I never really loved you the way you thought I did.'" The look she gave Miranda was the gaze of a tortured animal's. "Five years, and he tells me that. What he didn't tell me was the truth. He'd found someone younger. You." There was no hostility, no anger in her voice, only quiet resignation. "I never blamed you, Miranda. You didn't know. You were just another victim. He would have left you, the way he left us all."

"You're right, Annie. We were all his victims."

"I'm sorry. I'm so sorry, Miranda." Annie slid her hand into her jacket pocket. "But someone has to suffer for it." Slowly she withdrew the gun.

Miranda stared at the barrel, now pointed at her chest. She wanted to argue, to plead, anything to make Annie lower the gun. But her voice had frozen in her throat. She could only stare at the black circle of the barrel and wonder if she would feel the bullet.

"Come, Miranda. Let's go."

Miranda shook her head. "Where—where are we going?"

Annie opened the door and gestured for Miranda to move first. "Up the stairs. To the roof."

No one was home.

Chase circled around Annie's house to the garage and found that the car was gone. Miranda must have returned, then left again. He was standing in the driveway, wondering where to look next, when he heard the phone ringing inside the house. He ran up the porch steps and into the living room to answer the call.

It was Lorne Tibbetts. "Is Miranda there?" he asked.

"No, I'm looking for her."

"What about Annie Berenger?"

"Not here, either."

"Okay," said Lorne. "I want you to leave the house, Chase. Do it right now."

Chase was stunned by the unexpected command. He said, "I'm waiting for Miranda to show up."

He heard Lorne turn and say something to Ellis. Then,

"Look, we got evidence snowballing down here. If Annie Berenger shows up first, you keep things nice and casual, okay? Don't rattle her. Just calmly leave the house. Ellis is on his way over."

"What the hell's going on?"

"We think we know who M is. And it's not Jill Vickery. Now get out of there." Lorne hung up.

If it isn't Jill Vickery...

Chase went to the end table and opened the drawer. Annie's gun was missing.

He slammed the drawer shut.

Where are you, Miranda?

The next thought sent him running outside to his car. There might still be time to find them. He'd missed Miranda by only five, maybe ten minutes. They couldn't have gone far, not yet. If he circled around town, kept his eyes open, he might be able to find her car.

If they were still in the area.

I can't lose you. Now that we can prove your innocence. Now that we have a chance together.

He swung the car around. With tires screeching, he raced back toward town.

"Go on. Up the last flight."

Miranda paused, her foot on the next step. "Please, Annie..."

"Keep moving."

Miranda turned to face her. They were already on the third-floor landing. One more flight and then the door to the roof. Once she'd marveled at the beauty of this stairwell, at the carved mahogany banister, the gleaming wood finish. Now it had become a spiral death trap. She gripped the railing, drawing strength from the unyielding support of solid wood.

"Why are you doing this?" she asked.

"Go on. Go!"

"We were friends once—"

"Until Richard."

"But I didn't know! I had no idea you were in love with him! If only you'd told me."

"I never told anyone. I couldn't. It was his idea, you see. Keep it quiet, keep it our little secret. He said he wanted to protect me."

Then I'm the only one left who knows, thought Miranda. *The only one still alive.*

"Move," said Annie. "Up the stairs."

Miranda didn't budge. She looked Annie in the eye. Quietly she said, "Why don't you just shoot me now? Right here. If that's what you're going to do anyway."

"It's your choice." Calmly Annie raised the gun. "I'm not afraid of killing. They say that it's hardest the first time you do it. And you know what? It wasn't really hard at all. All I had to do was think about how much he hurt me. The knife seemed to move all by itself. I was just a witness."

"I'm not Richard. I never meant to hurt you."

"But you will, Miranda. You know the truth."

"So do the police. They found that letter, Annie. The last one you wrote."

Annie shook her head. "They arrested Jill tonight. But you're still the one they'll blame. Because they'll find the typewriter in your car. What a clever girl you'll seem, making up all those letters, planting them in the cottage. Throwing suspicion on poor innocent Jill. But then the guilt caught up with you. You got depressed. You knew jail was inevitable. So you chose the easy way out. You climbed to the roof of the newspaper building. And you jumped."

"I won't do it."

Annie gripped the gun with both hands and pointed it at Miranda's chest. "Then you'll die here. I had to kill you, you see. I found you planting the typewriter in Jill's office. You had a gun. You ordered me into the stairwell. I tried to grab the gun and it went off. A tidy end for everyone involved." Slowly she cocked back the pistol hammer. "Or would you rather it be the roof?"

I have to buy time, thought Miranda. *Have to wait for a chance, any chance, to escape.*

She turned and gazed up at the last flight of stairs.

"Go on," said Annie.

Miranda began to climb.

Fourteen steps, each one a fleeting eternity. Fourteen lifetimes, passing, gone. Frantically she tried to visualize the roof, the layout, the avenues of escape. She'd been up there only once, when the news staff had gathered for a group photo. She recalled a flat stretch of asphalt, punctuated by three chimneys, a heating duct, a transformer shed. Four stories down—that would be the drop. Would it kill her? Or was it just high enough to leave her crippled on the sidewalk, a helpless mound of broken bones, to be dispatched with a few blows by Annie?

The door to the roof loomed just above. If she could just get through that door and barricade it, she might be able to buy time, to scream for help.

Only a few steps more.

She stumbled and fell forward, catching herself on the stairs.

"Get up," said Annie.

"My ankle—"

"I said, get up!"

Miranda sat on the step and reached down to massage her foot. "I think I sprained it."

Annie took a step closer. "Then crawl if you have to! But get up those stairs!"

Miranda, her back braced firmly against the step, her legs wound up tight, calmly kept rubbing her ankle. And all the time she thought, *Closer, Annie. Come closer....*

Annie moved up another step. She was standing just below Miranda now, the gun frighteningly close. "I can't wait. Your time's run out." She raised the gun to Miranda's face.

That's when Miranda raised her foot—in a vicious, straight-out kick that thudded right into Annie's stomach. It sent Annie toppling backward down the stairs, to sprawl on the third-floor landing. But even as she fell she never released the gun. There was no opportunity to wrestle away the weapon. Annie was already rising to her knees, gun in hand. Her aim swept up toward her prey.

Miranda yanked open the rooftop door and dashed through just as Annie fired. She heard the bullet splinter the door, felt wood chips fly, sting her face. There was no latch, no way to bolt the door shut. So little time, so little time! Fourteen steps and Annie would be on the roof.

Miranda glanced wildly about her, could make out in the darkness the silhouette of chimneys, crates, other unidentifiable shapes.

Footsteps thudded up the stairs.

In panic Miranda took off into the shadows and slipped behind a transformer shed. She heard the door fly open, heard it bang shut again.

Then she heard Annie's voice, calling through the darkness. "There's nowhere to run, Miranda. Nowhere to go but straight down. Wherever you are, I'll find you...."

Chase spotted it from a block away: Miranda's old Dodge, parked in front of the *Herald* building. He pulled up behind it and climbed out. A glance through the window told him the car was unoccupied. Miranda—or whoever had driven it here—must be in the building.

He rattled the front door to the *Herald.* It was locked. Through the glass he saw a lamp burning on one of the desks. Someone had to be inside. He banged on the door and called, "Miranda?" There was no answer.

He rattled the door again, then started around to the back of the building. There had to be another way in, an unlocked window or a loading door. He had circled the corner and was moving down one of the alleys when he heard it. Gunfire.

It came from somewhere inside the building.

"Miranda?" he yelled.

He wasted no more time searching for unlocked entrances. He grabbed a trash can from the alley, carried it around to the front of the building and hurled it through the window. Glass shattered, flying like hail across the desks inside. He kicked in the last jagged fragments, scrambled over the sill and dropped onto a carpet littered with razorlike shards. At once he was running past the desks, moving straight for the back of the building. With every step he took he grew more terrified of what he might find. Images of Miranda raced through his head. He shoved through the first door and confronted the deserted print shop. Newspapers—the next issue—were bundled and stacked against the walls. No Miranda.

He turned, moved down the hall to the women's lounge. Again, that surge of terror as he pushed through the door.

Again, no Miranda.

He turned and headed straight into the women's rest room, pushing open stall doors. No one there.

Ditto for the men's room.

Where the hell had that gunshot come from?

He ran back into the hall and started up the stairwell. Two more floors to search. Offices on the second floor, storage and news file rooms on the third. Somewhere up there he'd find her.

Just let me find you alive.

Miranda hugged the side of the transformer shed and listened for the sound of footsteps. Except for the hammering of her own heart she heard nothing, not even the softest crunch of shoes on asphalt. *Where is she? Which way is she moving?*

Quickly Miranda glanced to either side of her. Her eyes had began to adjust to the darkness. She could make out, to the left, a jumble of crates. Right beside them were the handrails of a fire escape. A way off the roof! If she could just make it to that edge, without being seen.

Where was Annie?

She had to risk a look. She crouched down and slowly inched toward the corner. What she saw made her pull back at once in panic.

Annie was moving straight toward the transformer shed.

Miranda's instinct told her to run, to attempt a final dash for freedom. Logic told her she'd never make it. Annie was already too close.

In desperation she scrabbled for a few bits of gravel near her feet. She flung it high overhead, aiming blindly for the opposite end of the roof. She heard it clatter somewhere off in the darkness.

For a few terrifying seconds she listened for sounds— any sounds. Nothing.

Again she edged around the corner of the transformer. Annie was following the sound, toward the opposite edge of the roof, stalking slowly toward one of the chimneys. A few steps farther. One more…

Now was her chance—her only one! Miranda ran.

Her footsteps sounded like drumbeats across the asphalt roof. Even before she reached the fire escape she heard the first gunshot, heard the whine of the bullet as it hurtled past. No time to think, only move! She scrambled for the fire escape, swung her leg over onto the first metal rung.

Another gunshot exploded.

The bullet's impact was like a punch in the shoulder. Its force sent her toppling sideways, over the roof's edge. She caught a dizzying view of the night sky, then felt herself falling, falling. Instinctively she reach up, clawed blindly for a handhold. As she tumbled over the edge of the fire escape landing, her left hand closed around cold steel— the railing. Even as her legs slipped away, dangling beneath her like dead weights, her grip held. She tried to reach up with the other arm but it wouldn't seem to obey her commands. She could only raise it to shoulder height, and then her hand closed only weakly around the outside edge of the landing. For a second she clung there, her feet hanging uselessly. Then she managed to brace one foot against the brick face of the building. *Still alive, still here!*

she thought. *If I can just pull myself over the rail—get back onto the landing…*

The flicker of a shadow moving just above made her freeze. Slowly she lifted her gaze and stared into the gun barrel. Annie was standing at the roof's edge, aiming directly at Miranda's head.

"Now," said Annie softly. "Let go of the fire escape."

"No. No—"

"Just open your fingers. Lean back. A fast and easy way to die."

"It won't work. They'll find out! They'll know you did it!"

"Jump, Miranda. *Jump.*"

Miranda stared down at the ground. It was so far away, so very far.

Annie swung one leg over the roof's edge, aimed her heel at Miranda's hand gripping the rail and stamped down.

Miranda screamed. Still she held on.

Annie raised her heel, stamped again, then again, each blow crushing Miranda's left hand.

The pain was unbearable. Miranda's grip loosened. She lost her foothold, was left dangling free. Her left hand, throbbing in agony, could stand the abuse no longer. Her right hand, already weak and growing numb from the bullet wound, didn't have the strength to hold her weight. She gazed up in despair as Annie raised her heel and prepared to stamp down one last time.

The blow never fell.

Instead, Annie's body was jerked up and backward, like a puppet whose strings have been yanked all at once. She let out an unearthly screech of rage, of disbelief. And then there was a thud as her body, hurled aside, slammed onto the rooftop.

An instant later Chase appeared at the roof's edge. He leaned over and grabbed her left wrist. "Take my other hand! Take it!" he yelled.

Bracing her feet against the brick wall, Miranda managed to raise her right arm. "I can't…can't reach you…."

"Come on, Miranda!" He leaned farther, his body stretching over the edge. "You have to do it! I need both your hands! Just reach up, that's all! I'll grab it, darling. Please!"

Darling. That single word, one she'd never heard before on his lips, seemed to spark some new source of strength deep inside her. She took a breath and strained toward the heavens. *That's as far as I can go,* she thought in despair. *No farther.*

That's when his hand closed around her wrist. At once she was held in a grip so tight she never feared, even for an instant, that she would fall. He dragged her up and up, over the roof's edge.

Only then did her strength give out. She had no need of it now, not when Chase was here to lend her his. She tumbled into his arms.

No tree had ever felt so solid, so unbendable. Nothing, no one could hurt her in the fortress of those arms. He said, "My God, Miranda, I thought—"

Instantly he fell silent.

A pistol hammer clicked back.

They both spun around to see Annie standing a few feet away. She wobbled on unsteady legs. With both hands she clutched the gun.

"It's too late, Annie," said Chase. "The police know. They have your final letter. They know you killed Richard. Even now they're looking for you. It's over."

Annie slowly lowered the gun. "I know," she whispered. She took a deep breath and looked up at the sky. "I loved you," she said to the heavens. "Damn you, Richard. *I loved you!*" she screamed.

Then she raised the gun, put the barrel in her mouth and calmly pulled the trigger.

Fifteen

This time the ministrations of cranky Dr. Steiner were insufficient. Only a hospital—and a surgeon—would do. An emergency ferry run was ordered and Miranda was loaded aboard the *Jenny B* with Dr. Steiner in attendance. The hospital in Bass Harbor was alerted to an incoming patient: gunshot wound to the right shoulder, patient conscious and oriented, blood pressure stable, bleeding under control. The *Jenny B* pulled away from the dock with two passengers, a crew of three and a corpse.

Chase wasn't aboard.

He was at that moment fidgeting in a chair in Lorne Tibbetts's back office, answering a thousand and one questions. A command performance. A woman, after all, was dead; an investigation was called for; and as Lorne so succinctly put it, the choice was between talk or jail. All the time Chase sat there, he was wondering about the *Jenny B.* Had it reached Bass Harbor yet? Was Miranda stable?

Would Lorne ever finish with the damn questions?

It was two in the morning when Chase finally walked

out of the police station. The night was warm, warm for Maine, anyway, but he felt chilled as he walked to his car. No more ferries to Bass Harbor tonight. He was stranded on the island until morning. At least he knew that Miranda was out of danger. A phone call to the hospital had told him she was resting comfortably, and was expected to recover.

Now he wondered where to go, where to sleep.

Not Chestnut Street. He could never sleep under Evelyn's roof again, not after the damage he'd done to the DeBolt family. No, tonight he felt rootless, cut off from the DeBolts, from the Tremains, from the legacy of his rich and haughty past. He felt born anew. Cleansed.

He got in the car and drove to Rose Hill.

The cottage felt cold, devoid of life or spirit, as if any joy that had ever existed within had long since fled. Only the bedroom held any warmth. This was where he and Miranda had made love. Here the memory of that night, that one night, still lingered.

He lay on the bed and tried to conjure up the memory of her scent, her softness, but it was like trying to catch your own reflection in water. Every time you reach out to hold it, it slips from your grasp.

The way Miranda had slipped from his grasp.

She's not one of us, Evelyn had once said. *She's not our kind of people.*

Chase thought of Noah, of Richard, of Evelyn. Of his own father. And he thought, *Evelyn's right. Miranda's not our kind of people.*

She's far better.

"Happy endings," said Miss St. John, "are not automatic. Sometimes one has to work for them."

Chase took the advice, and the cup of coffee she handed him, in silence. The advice was something he already knew. Hadn't experience taught him that happy endings were what you found in fairy tales, not real life? Hadn't his own marriage proved the point?

But this time it will be different. I'll make it different. If only I could be certain I'm the one she wants.

He sipped his cup of coffee and absentmindedly scratched Ozzie's wild black mop of hair. He didn't know why he was petting the beast, except that Ozzie seemed so damn appreciative. A glance at his watch told Chase he had plenty of time to catch the twelve-o'clock ferry to Bass Harbor. To Miranda.

All night he'd lain sleepless in bed, wondering about their chances, their future. The specter of his brother couldn't be so easily dispelled. Just a few short weeks ago Richard had been the man she loved, or thought she loved. Richard had taken her innocence, used her, nearly destroyed her. *And now here I am, another Tremain. After what Richard did to her, why should she trust me?*

Events, emotions had moved at lightning speed these past few days. A week ago he had called her a murderess. Only hours ago he had come to accept her innocence as gospel truth. She had every right to resent him, to never forgive him for the things he'd once said to her. So many cruel and terrible words had passed between them. Could love, real love, grow from such poisoned beginnings?

He wanted to believe it could. He had to believe it could.

But those doubts kept tormenting him.

When Miss St. John had come knocking at the cottage door at ten o'clock with an offer of coffee and a morning chat, he'd almost welcomed the intrusion, though he suspected her invitation was inspired by more than neighborly kindness. Word of the night's goings-on must already be buzzing about town. Miss St. John, with her mile-long antennae, had no doubt picked up the signals and was probably curious as hell.

Now that she'd been brought up to date, she was going to offer an opinion, whether he wanted to hear it or not.

"Miranda's a lovely woman, Chase," she said. "A very kind woman."

"I know," was all he could answer.

"But you have doubts."

He sighed, a breath that seemed weighted with pain and uncertainty. "After all that's happened…"

"People are entitled to make mistakes, Chase. Miranda made one with your brother. It wasn't a terrible sort of mistake. It had nothing to do with cruelty or bad intentions. It had only to do with love. With misjudgment. The mistake was real. But the emotions were the right ones."

"But you don't understand," he said, looking up at her. "My doubts have nothing to do with her. It's *me,* whether she can forgive me. For being a Tremain. For being this symbol of everything, everyone who's ever hurt her."

"I think Miranda's the one who's searching for forgiveness."

He shook his head. "What should I forgive *her* for?"

"You have to answer that."

He sat in silence for a moment, rubbing the ugly head of that ugly dog. *What do I forgive you for? For showing me the real meaning of innocence. For making me question every stuffy notion I was brought up to believe in. For making me realize I've been an idiot.*

For making me fall in love with you.

With sudden determination he put down his coffee cup and rose to his feet. "I'd better get going," he said. "I've got a ferry to catch."

"And then what happens?" asked Miss St. John, walking him to the door.

Smiling, he took her hand—the hand of a very wise woman. "Miss St. John," he said, "when I find out, you'll be the first to know."

She waved as he headed out to his car. "I'll count on it!" she yelled.

Chase drove like a crazy man to the ferry landing. He arrived an hour early, only to find a long line of cars already waiting to board. Rather than risk missing the sail, he decided to leave his car and board as a foot passenger.

Two hours later he walked off onto the dock in Bass Harbor. No taxis here; he had to hitch a ride to the hospital. By the time he strode up to the patient information desk, it was already two-thirty.

"Miranda Wood," said the volunteer, setting down the phone receiver, "was discharged an hour ago."

"What?"

"That's what the floor nurse said. The patient left with Dr. Steiner."

Chase felt ready to punch the desk in frustration. "Where did they go?" he snapped.

"I wouldn't know, sir. You could ask upstairs, at the nurses' station, second floor."

Chase was about to head for the stairwell when he suddenly glanced up at the wall clock. "Miss—what time does the ferry return to Shepherd's Island?" he asked.

"I think the last one leaves at three o'clock."

Twenty minutes.

He hurried outside and glanced up and down the street for a taxi, a bus, anything on wheels that might take him to the landing. They *had* to be at the landing. Where else would she and Dr. Steiner go, except back to the island?

It was the last ferry of the day and he'd never catch it in time.

Happy endings are not automatic. Sometimes one has to work for them.

Okay, damn it, he thought. *I'm ready to work. I'm ready to do anything it takes to make this turn out right.*

He took off at a sprint down the street. It was two miles to the ferry landing.

He ran every step of the way.

The deckhand yelled, "All aboard!" and the engines of the *Jenny B* growled to life.

Standing at the rail, Miranda stared out over the gray-green expanse of Penobscot Bay. So many islands in the distance, so many places in the world to run to. Soon she'd be on her way, leaving memories, good and bad, behind her. There was just this one last journey to Shepherd's Island, to tie up all those loose ends, and then she could turn her back on this place forever. It was a departure she'd planned weeks ago, before Richard's murder, before the horrors of her arrest.

Before Chase.

"I still say it was an idiotic idea, young lady," said Dr. Steiner, hunched irritably on a bench beside her. "Checking out just like that. What if you start to bleed again? What if you get an infection? I can't handle those complications! I tell you, I'm getting too old for this business. Too old!"

"I'll be just fine, Doc," she said, her gaze focused on the bay. "Really," she said softly, "I'll be just fine…."

Dr. Steiner began to mutter to himself, a grumpy monologue about disobedient patients and how hard it was to be a doctor these days. Miranda scarcely listened. She had too many other things on her mind.

A quiet exit, some time alone—yes, all in all, it was better this way. Seeing Chase again would be too confusing. What she needed was escape, a chance to analyze what she really felt for him. Love? She thought so. Yes, she was *sure* of it. But she'd been wrong before, terribly wrong. *I don't want to make the same mistake, suffer the same consequences.*

And yet…

She gripped the railing and gazed off moodily at the islands. The wind had come up and it whistled across the water, blew its cold salt breath against her face.

I do love him, she thought. *I know I do.*

But it's not enough to make a future. Too much stood in the way. The ghost of Richard. The shadow of mistrust. And always, always, those metaphorical train tracks on whose wrong side she'd grown up. It shouldn't make a difference, but then, she was merely Miranda Wood. Perhaps, to a Tremain, it made *all* the difference.

"Bow line's free!" called the deckhand.

The engines of the *Jenny B* throttled up. Slowly she pivoted to starboard, to face the far-off green hillock that was Shepherd's Island. The deckhand strode the length of the boat and released the stern line. Just as it slipped free there came a shout from the dock.

"Wait! Hold the boat!"

"We're full up!" yelled the deckhand. "Catch the next one."

"I said *hold up!*"

"Too late!" barked the deckhand. Already the *Jenny B* was pulling away from the dock.

It was the deckhand's sharp and sudden oath that made Miranda turn to look. She saw, far astern, a figure racing toward the end of the pier. He took a flying leap across the growing gap of water and landed with only inches to spare on the deck of the *Jenny B*.

"Son of a gun," marveled the deckhand. "Are you nuts?"

Chase scrambled to his feet. "Have to talk to someone—one of your passengers—"

"Man, you must want to talk *real* bad."

Chase took a calming breath and glanced around the deck. His gaze stopped at Miranda. "Yeah," he said softly. "Real bad."

Miranda, caught standing against the rail, could only stare in astonishment as Chase walked toward her. The other passengers were all watching, waiting to see what would happen next.

"Young man," snapped Dr. Steiner. "If you sprained your ankle, don't expect me to fix it. You two and all your damn fool stunts."

"My ankle's fine," said Chase, his gaze never leaving Miranda. "I just want to talk to your patient. If it's all right with her."

Miranda gave a laugh of disbelief. "After a leap like that, how could I refuse?"

"Let's go up front." Chase reached for her hand. "For this, I don't need an audience."

They walked to the bow and stood by the rail. Here the

salt wind flew at them unremittingly, whipping at their clothes, their hair. Above, gulls swooped and circled, airborne companions of the plodding *Jenny B.*

Chase said, "They told me you checked out early. You should have stayed in the hospital."

Miranda hugged herself against the wind and stared down at the water. "I couldn't lie in that bed another day. Not with so many things hanging over me."

"But it's over, Miranda."

"Not yet. There's still that business with the police. And I have to settle with my lawyer."

"That can wait."

"But I can't." She raised her head and faced the wind. "I want to leave this place. As soon as I can. Any way I can."

"Where are you going?"

"I don't know. I've thought about heading west. Jill Vickery walked away from her past. Maybe I can, too."

There was a long silence. "Then you're not staying on the island," he said.

"No. There's nothing here for me now. I'll be getting the insurance money from the house. It will be enough to get me out of here. To go some place where they don't know me, or Richard, or anything that happened."

The water broke before the bow of the *Jenny B* and the spray flew up, misting their faces.

"It's not an easy thing," she said, "living in a town where they'll always wonder about you. I understand now why Jill Vickery left San Diego. She wanted to wash away the guilt. She wanted to get back her innocence. That's what I want back, Chase. My innocence."

"You never lost it."

"Yes, I did. That's what you thought. What you'll always think of me."

"I know better now. I have no more questions, Miranda. No more doubts."

She shook her head. Sadly she turned away. "It's not as easy as that, to bury the past."

"Okay, so it's not." He pulled her around to face him. "It's never easy, Miranda. Love. Life. You know, just this morning, Miss St. John said a very wise thing to me. She said happy endings aren't automatic. You have to work for them." He reached up and framed her face in his hands. "Don't you think this happy ending is worth working for?"

"But I don't know if I believe in anymore. Happy endings."

"Neither did I. But I'm beginning to change my mind."

"You'll always be wondering about me, Chase. About whether you can trust me—"

"No, Miranda. That's the one thing I'll *never* wonder about."

He kissed her then, a sweet and gentle joining that spoke not of passion but of hope. That one touch of his lips seemed to rinse away the terrible grime of guilt, of remorse, that had stained her soul.

The renewal of innocence. That's what he offered; that's what she found in his arms.

It seemed only a short time later when the gulls suddenly burst forth into a wild keening, a raucous announcement that land was close at hand. The couple standing at the bow did not stir from each other's arms. Even when the boat's whistle blew, even when the *Jenny B* glided into the harbor, they would still be standing there.

Together.

One

The wedding was off. Cancelled. Canned. Kaput.

Nina Cormier sat staring at herself in the church dressing room mirror and wondered why she couldn't seem to cry. She knew the pain was there, deep and terrible beneath the numbness, but she didn't feel it. Not yet. She could only sit dry-eyed, staring at her reflection. The picture-perfect image of a bride. Her veil floated in gossamer wisps about her face. The bodice of her ivory satin dress, embroidered with seed pearls, hung fetchingly off-shoulder. Her long black hair was gathered into a soft chignon. Everyone who'd seen her that morning in the dressing room—her mother, her sister, Wendy, her stepmother, Daniella—had declared her a beautiful bride.

And she *would* have been. Had the groom bothered to show up.

He didn't even have the courage to break the news to her in person. After six months of planning and dreaming, she'd received his note just twenty minutes before the ceremony. Via the best man, no less.

Nina,

I need time to think about this. I'm sorry, I really am. I'm leaving town for a few days. I'll call you.

Robert

She forced herself to read the note again.

I need time…. I need time….

How much time does a man need? she wondered.

A year ago, she'd moved in with Dr. Robert Bledsoe. It's the only way to know if we're compatible, he'd told her. Marriage was such a major commitment, a permanent commitment, and he didn't want to make a mistake. At 41, Robert had known his share of disastrous relationships. He was determined not to make any more mistakes. He wanted to be sure that Nina was the one he'd been waiting for all his life.

She'd been certain Robert was the man *she'd* been waiting for. So certain that, on the very day he'd suggested they live together, she'd gone straight home and packed her bags….

"Nina? Nina, open the door!" It was her sister, Wendy, rattling the knob. "Please let me in."

Nina dropped her head in her hands. "I don't want to see anyone right now."

"You need to be with someone."

"I just want to be alone."

"Look, the guests have all gone home. The church is empty. It's just me out here."

"I don't want to talk to anyone. Just go home, will you? Please, just go."

There was a long silence outside the door. Then Wendy said, "If I leave now, how're you going to get home? You'll need a ride."

"Then I'll call a cab. Or Reverend Sullivan can drive me. I need some time to think."

"You're sure you don't want to talk?"

"I'm sure. I'll call you later, okay?"

"If that's what you really want." Wendy paused, then added, with a note of venom that penetrated even through the oak door, "Robert's a jerk, you know. I might as well tell you. I've always thought he was."

Nina didn't answer. She sat at the dressing table, her head in her hands, wanting to cry, but unable to squeeze out a single tear. She heard Wendy's footsteps fade away, then heard only the silence of the empty church. Still no tears would come. She couldn't think about Robert right now. Instead, her mind seemed to focus stubbornly on the practical aspects of a cancelled wedding. The catered reception and all that uneaten food. The gifts she had to return. The nonrefundable airline tickets to St. John Island. Maybe she should go on that honeymoon anyway and forget Dr. Robert Bledsoe. She'd go by herself, just her and her bikini. Out of this whole heartbreaking affair, at least she'd come out with a tan.

Slowly she raised her head and once again looked at her reflection in the mirror. Not such a beautiful bride after all, she thought. Her lipstick was smeared and her chignon was coming apart. She was turning into a wreck.

With sudden rage she reached up and yanked off the veil. Hairpins flew in every direction, releasing a rebellious tumble of black hair. To hell with the veil; she tossed it in the trash can. She snatched up her bouquet of white lilies and pink sweetheart roses and slam-dunked it into the trash can as well. That felt good. Her anger was like some new and potent fuel flooding her veins. It propelled her to her feet.

She walked out of the church dressing room, the train of her gown dragging behind her, and entered the nave.

The pews were deserted. Garlands of white carnations draped the aisles, and the altar was adorned with airy sprays of pink roses and baby's breath. The stage had been beautifully set for a wedding that would never take place. But the lovely results of the florist's hard work was scarcely noticed by Nina as she strode past the altar and started up the aisle. Her attention was focused straight ahead on the front door. On escape. Even the concerned voice of Reverend Sullivan calling to her didn't slow her down. She walked past all the floral reminders of the day's fiasco and pushed through the double doors.

There, on the church steps, she halted. The July sunshine glared in her eyes, and she was suddenly, painfully aware of how conspicuous she must be, a lone woman in a wedding gown, trying to wave down a taxi. Only then, as she stood trapped in the brightness of afternoon, did she feel the first sting of tears.

Oh, no. Lord, no. She was going to break down and cry right here on the steps. In full view of every damn car driving past on Forest Avenue.

"Nina? Nina, dear."

She turned. Reverend Sullivan was standing on the step above her, a look of worry on his kind face.

"Is there anything I can do? Anything at all?" he asked. "If you'd like, we could go inside and talk."

Miserably she shook her head. "I want to get away from here. Please, I just want to get away."

"Of course. Of course." Gently, he took her arm. "I'll drive you home."

Reverend Sullivan led her down the steps and around

the side of the building, to the staff parking lot. She gathered up her train, which by now was soiled from all that dragging, and climbed into his car. There she sat with all the satin piled high on her lap.

Reverend Sullivan slid in behind the wheel. The heat was stifling inside the car, but he didn't start the engine. Instead they sat for a moment in awkward silence.

"I know it's hard to understand what possible purpose the Lord may have for all this," he said quietly. "But surely there's a reason, Nina. It may not be apparent to you at the moment. In fact, it may seem to you that the Lord has turned His back."

"Robert's the one who turned his back," she said. Sniffling, she snatched up a clean corner of her train and wiped her face. "Turned his back and ran like hell."

"Ambivalence is common for bridegrooms. I'm sure Dr. Bledsoe felt this was a big step for him—"

"A big step for *him?* I suppose marriage is just a stroll in the park for me?"

"No, no, you misunderstand me."

"Oh, please." She gave a muffled sob. "Just take me home."

Shaking his head, he put the key in the ignition. "I only wanted to explain to you, dear, in my own clumsy way, that this isn't the end of the world. It's the nature of life. Fate is always throwing surprises at us, Nina. Crises we never expect. Things that seem to pop right out of the blue."

A deafening boom suddenly shook the church building. The explosion shattered the stained glass windows, and a hail of multicolored glass shards flew across the parking lot. Torn hymn books and fragments of church pews tumbled onto the blacktop.

As the white smoke slowly cleared, Nina saw a dusting of flower petals drift gently down from the sky and settle on the windshield right in front of Reverend Sullivan's shocked eyes.

"Right out of the blue," she murmured. "You couldn't have said it better."

"YOU TWO, WITHOUT A DOUBT, are the biggest screwups of the year."

Portland police detective Sam Navarro, sitting directly across the table from the obviously upset Norm Liddell, didn't bat an eyelash. There were five of them sitting in the station conference room, and Sam wasn't about to give this prima donna D.A. the satisfaction of watching him flinch in public. Nor was Sam going to refute the charges, because they *had* screwed up. He and Gillis had screwed up big time, and now a cop was dead. An idiot cop, but a cop all the same. One of their own.

"In our defense," spoke up Sam's partner, Gordon Gillis, "we never gave Marty Pickett permission to approach the site. We had no idea he'd crossed the police line—"

"You were in charge of the bomb scene," said Liddell. "That makes you responsible."

"Now, wait a minute," said Gillis. "Officer Pickett has to bear some of the blame."

"Pickett was just a rookie."

"He should've been following procedure. If he'd—"

"Shut up, Gillis," said Sam.

Gillis looked at his partner. "Sam, I'm only trying to defend our position."

"Won't do us a damn bit of good. Since we're obviously the designated fall guys." Sam leaned back in his chair and eyed Liddell across the conference table. "What do you want, Mr. D.A.? A public flogging? Our resignations?"

"No one's asking for your resignations," cut in Chief Abe Coopersmith. "And this discussion is getting us nowhere."

"*Some* disciplinary action is called for," said Liddell. "We have a dead police officer—"

"Don't you think I know that?" snapped Coopersmith. "*I'm* the one who had to answer to the widow. Not to mention all those bloodsucking reporters. Don't give me this *us* and *we* crap, Mr. D.A. It was one of *ours* who fell. A cop. *Not* a lawyer."

Sam looked in surprise at his chief. This was a new experience, having Coopersmith on his side. The Abe Coopersmith he knew was a man of few words, few of them complimentary. It was because Liddell was rubbing them all the wrong way. When under fire, cops always stuck together.

"Let's get back to the business at hand, okay?" said Coopersmith. "We have a bomber in town. And our first fatality. What do we know so far?" He looked at Sam, who was head of the newly re-formed Bomb Task Force. "Navarro?"

"Not a hell of a lot," admitted Sam. He opened a file folder and took out a sheaf of papers. He distributed copies to the other four men around the table—Liddell, Chief Coopersmith, Gillis, and Ernie Takeda, the explosives expert from the Maine State Crime Lab. "The first blast occurred around 2:15 a.m. The second blast around 2:30 a.m. It was the second one that pretty much levelled the R. S. Hancock warehouse. It also caused minor damage to two adjoining buildings. The night watchman was the one who found the first device. He noticed signs of breaking and entering, so he searched the building. The bomb was left on a desk in one of the offices. He put in the call at 1:30 a.m.

Gillis got there around 1:50, I was there at 2:00 a.m. We had the blast area cordoned off and the top-vent container truck had just arrived when the first one went off. Then, fifteen minutes later—before we could search the building—the second device exploded. Killing Officer Pickett." Sam glanced at Liddell, but this time the D.A. chose to keep his mouth shut. "The dynamite was Dupont label."

There was a brief silence in the room. Then Cooper-smith said, "Not the same Dupont lot number as those two bombs last year?"

"It's very likely," said Sam. "Since that missing lot number's the only reported large dynamite theft we've had up here in years."

"But the Spectre bombings were solved a year ago," said Liddell. "And we know Vincent Spectre's dead. So who's making *these* bombs?"

"We may be dealing with a Spectre apprentice. Some-one who not only picked up the master's technique, but also has access to the master's dynamite supply. Which, I point out, we never located."

"You haven't confirmed the dynamite's from the same stolen lot number," said Liddell. "Maybe this has no con-nection at all with the Spectre bombings."

"I'm afraid we have other evidence," said Sam. "And you're not going to like it." He glanced at Ernie Takeda. "Go ahead, Ernie."

Takeda, never comfortable with public speaking, kept his gaze focused on the lab report in front of him. "Based on materials we gathered at the site," he said, "we can make a preliminary guess as to the makeup of the device. We believe the electrical action fuse was set off by an elec-tronic delay circuit. This in turn ignited the dynamite via

Prima detonating cord. The sticks were bundled together with two-inch-wide green electrical tape." Takeda cleared his throat and finally looked up. "It's the identical delay circuit that the late Vincent Spectre used in his bombings last year."

Liddell looked at Sam. "The same circuitry, the same dynamite lot? What the hell's going on?"

"Obviously," said Gillis, "Vincent Spectre passed on a few of his skills before he died. Now we've got a second generation bomber on our hands."

"What we still have to piece together," said Sam, "is the psychological profile of this newcomer. Spectre's bombings were coldbloodedly financial. He was hired to do the jobs and he did them, *bam, bam, bam.* Efficient. Effective. This new bomber has to set a pattern."

"What you're saying," said Liddell, "is that you expect him to hit again."

Sam nodded wearily. "Unfortunately, that's exactly what I'm saying."

There was a knock on the door. A patrolwoman stuck her head into the conference room. "Excuse me, but there's a call for Navarro and Gillis."

"I'll take it," said Gillis. He rose heavily to his feet and went to the conference wall phone.

Liddell was still focused on Sam. "So this is all that Portland's finest can come up with? We wait for *another* bombing so that we can establish a *pattern?* And then maybe, just *maybe,* we'll have an idea of what the hell we're doing?"

"A bombing, Mr. Liddell," said Sam calmly, "is an act of cowardice. It's violence in the absence of the perpetrator. I repeat the word—*absence.* We have no ID, no fingerprints, no witnesses to the planting, no—"

"Chief," cut in Gillis. He hung up the phone. "They've just reported another one."

"What?" said Coopersmith.

Sam had already shot to his feet and was moving for the door.

"What was it this time?" called Liddell. "Another warehouse?"

"No," said Gillis. "A church."

THE COPS ALREADY had the area cordoned off by the time Sam and Gillis arrived at the Good Shepherd Church. A crowd was gathered up and down the street. Three patrol cars, two fire trucks and an ambulance were parked haphazardly along Forest Avenue. The bomb disposal truck and its boiler-shaped carrier in the flatbed stood idly near the church's front entrance—or what was left of the front entrance. The door had been blown clear off its hinges and had come to rest at the bottom of the front steps. Broken glass was everywhere. The wind scattered torn pages of hymn books like dead leaves along the sidewalk. Gillis swore. "This was a big one."

As they approached the police line, the officer in charge turned to them with a look of relief. "Navarro! Glad you could make it to the party."

"Any casualties?" asked Sam.

"None, as far as we know. The church was unoccupied at the time. Pure luck. There was a wedding scheduled for two, but it was cancelled at the last minute."

"Whose wedding?"

"Some doctor's. The bride's sitting over there in the patrol car. She and the minister witnessed the blast from the parking lot."

"I'll talk to her later," said Sam. "Don't let her leave. Or the minister, either. I'm going to check the building for a second device."

"Better you than me."

Sam donned body armor, made of overlapping steel plates encased in nylon. He also carried a protective mask, to be worn in case a second bomb was identified. A bomb tech, similarly garbed, stood by the front door awaiting orders to enter the building. Gillis would wait outside near the truck; his role this time around was to fetch tools and get the bomb carrier ready.

"Okay," Sam said to the technician. "Let's go."

They stepped through the gaping front entrance.

The first thing Sam noticed was the smell—strong and faintly sweet. Dynamite, he thought. He recognized the odor of its aftermath. The force of the blast had caused the pews at the rear to topple backward. At the front, near the altar, the pews had been reduced to splinters. All the stained glass panels were broken, and where the windows faced south, hazy sunlight shone in through the empty frames.

Without a word between them, Sam and the tech automatically split up and moved along opposite sides of the nave. The site would be more thoroughly searched later; this time around, their focus was only on locating any second bombs. The death of Marty Pickett still weighed heavily on Sam's conscience, and he wasn't about to let any other officers enter this building until he had cleared it.

Moving in parallel, the two men paced the nave, their eyes alert for anything resembling an explosive device. All the debris made it a slow search. As they moved forward, the damage visibly worsened, and the odor of exploded dynamite grew stronger. Getting closer, he thought. The bomb was planted somewhere around here....

In front of the altar, at a spot where the first row of pews would have stood, they found the crater. It was about three feet across and shallow; the blast had ripped through the carpet and pad, but had barely chipped the concrete slab below. A shallow crater was characteristic of a low-velocity blast—again, compatible with dynamite.

They would take a closer look at it later. They continued their search. They finished with the nave and progressed to the hallways, the dressing rooms, the restrooms. No bombs. They went into the annex and surveyed the church offices, the meeting rooms, the Sunday school classroom. No bombs. They exited through a rear door and searched the entire outside wall. No bombs.

Satisfied at last, Sam returned to the police line, where Gillis was waiting. There he took off the body armor. "Building's clean," Sam said. "We got the searchers assembled?"

Gillis gestured to the six men waiting near the bomb carrier truck. There were two patrolmen and four crime lab techs, each one clutching empty evidence bags. "They're just waiting for the word."

"Let's get the photographer in there first, then send the team in. The crater's up front, around the first row of pews on the right."

"Dynamite?"

Sam nodded. "If I can trust my nose." He turned and eyed the crowd of gawkers. "I'm going to talk to the witnesses. Where's the minister?"

"They just took him off to the ER. Chest pains. All that stress."

Sam gave an exasperated sigh. "Did anyone talk to him?"

"Patrolman did. We have his statement."

"Okay," said Sam. "I guess that leaves me with the bride."

"She's still waiting in the patrol car. Her name's Nina Cormier."

"Cormier. Gotcha." Sam ducked under the yellow police line and worked his way through the gathering of onlookers. Scanning the official vehicles, he spotted a silhouette in the front passenger seat of one of the cars. The woman didn't move as he approached; she was staring straight ahead like some wedding store mannequin. He leaned forward and tapped on the window.

The woman turned. Wide dark eyes stared at him through the glass. Despite the smudged mascara, the softly rounded feminine face was undeniably pretty. Sam motioned to her to roll down the window. She complied.

"Miss Cormier? I'm Detective Sam Navarro, Portland police."

"I want to go home," she said. "I've talked to so many cops already. Please, can't I just go home?"

"First I have to ask you a few questions."

"A few?"

"All right," he admitted. "It's more like a lot of questions."

She gave a sigh. Only then did he see the weariness in her face. "If I answer all your questions, Detective," she said, "will you let me go home?"

"I promise."

"Do you keep your promises?"

He nodded soberly. "Always."

She looked down at her hands, clasped in her lap. "Right," she muttered. "Men and their promises."

"Excuse me?"

"Oh, never mind."

He circled around the car, opened the door, and slid in behind the wheel. The woman next to him said nothing; she just sat there in resigned silence. She seemed almost swallowed up by those frothy layers of white satin. Her hairdo was coming undone and silky strands of black hair hung loose about her shoulders. Not at all the happy picture of a bride, he thought. She seemed stunned, and very much alone.

Where the hell was the groom?

Stifling an instinctive rush of sympathy, he reached for his notebook and flipped it open to a blank page. "Can I have your full name and address?"

The answer came out in a bare whisper. "Nina Margaret Cormier, 318 Ocean View Drive."

He wrote it down. Then he looked at her. She was still staring straight down at her lap. Not at him. "Okay, Miss Cormier," he said. "Why don't you tell me exactly what happened?"

SHE WANTED TO GO HOME. She had been sitting in this patrol car for an hour and a half now, had talked to three different cops, had answered all their questions. Her wedding was a shambles, she'd barely escaped with her life, and those people out there on the street kept staring at her as though she were some sort of sideshow freak.

And this man, this cop with all the warmth of a codfish, expected her to go through it again?

"Miss Cormier," he sighed. "The sooner we get this over with, the sooner you can leave. What, exactly, happened?"

"It blew up," she said. "Can I go home?"

"What do you mean by blew up?"

"There was a loud boom. Lots of smoke and broken windows. I'd say it was your typical exploding building."

"You mentioned smoke. What color was the smoke?"

"What?"

"Was it black? White?"

"Does it matter?"

"Just answer the question, please."

She gave an exasperated sigh. "It was white, I think."

"You think?"

"All right. I'm sure." She turned to look at him. For the first time she really focused on his face. If he'd been smiling, if there'd been even a trace of warmth, it would have been a pleasant enough face to look at. He was in his late thirties. He had dark brown hair that was about two weeks overdue for a trim. His face was thin, his teeth were perfect, and his deep set green eyes had the penetrating gaze one expected of a romantic lead movie cop. Only this was no movie cop. This was an honest-to-goodness cop with a badge, and he wasn't in the least bit charming. He was studying her with a completely detached air, as though sizing up her reliability as a witness.

She gazed back at him, thinking, *Here I am, the rejected bride. He's probably wondering what's wrong with me. What terrible flaws I possess that led to my being stood up at the altar.*

She buried her fists in the white satin mounded on her lap. "I'm sure the smoke was white," she said tightly. "For whatever difference that makes."

"It makes a difference. It indicates a relative absence of carbon."

"Oh. I see." Whatever that told him.

"Were there any flames?"

"No. No flames."

"Did you smell anything?"

"You mean like gas?"

"Anything at all?"

She frowned. "Not that I remember. But I was outside the building."

"Where, exactly?"

"Reverend Sullivan and I were sitting in his car. In the parking lot around the side. So I wouldn't have smelled the gas. Anyway, natural gas is odorless. Isn't it?"

"It can be difficult to detect."

"So it doesn't mean anything. That I didn't smell it."

"Did you see anyone near the building prior to the explosion?"

"There was Reverend Sullivan. And some of my family. But they all left earlier."

"What about strangers? Anyone you don't know?"

"No one was inside when it happened."

"I'm referring to the time *prior* to the explosion, Miss Cormier."

"Prior?"

"Did you see anyone who shouldn't have been there?"

She stared at him. He gazed back at her, green eyes absolutely steady. "You mean—are you thinking—"

He didn't say anything.

"It wasn't a gas leak?" she said softly.

"No," he said. "It was a bomb."

She sank back, her breath escaping in a single shocked rush. Not an accident, she thought. Not an accident at all....

"Miss Cormier?"

Wordlessly she looked at him. Something about the way he was watching her, that flat, emotionless gaze of his, made her frightened.

"I'm sorry to have to ask you this next question," he said. "But you understand, it's something I have to pursue."

She swallowed. "What…what question?"

"Do you know of anyone who might want you dead?"

Two

"This is crazy," she said. "This is absolutely nuts."

"I have to explore the possibility."

"*What* possibility? That the bomb was meant for *me?*"

"Your wedding was scheduled for two o'clock. The bomb went off at 2:40. It exploded near the front row of pews. Near the altar. There's no doubt in my mind, judging by the obvious force of the blast, that you and your entire wedding party would have been killed. Or, at the very least, seriously maimed. This *is* a bomb we're talking about, Miss Cormier. Not a gas leak. Not an accident. A bomb. It was meant to kill someone. What I have to find out is, who was the target?"

She didn't answer. The possibilities were too horrible to even contemplate.

"Who was in your wedding party?" he asked.

She swallowed. "There was…there was…"

"You and Reverend Sullivan. Who else?"

"Robert—my fiancé. And my sister, Wendy. And Jeremy Wall, the best man…."

"Anyone else?"

"My father was going to give me away. And there was a flower girl and a ring bearer…"

"I'm only interested in the adults. Let's start with you."

Numbly she shook her head. "It—it wasn't me. It couldn't be me."

"Why couldn't it?"

"It's impossible."

"How can you be sure?"

"Because no one would want me dead!"

Her sharp cry seemed to take him by surprise. For a moment he was silent. Outside, on the street, a uniformed cop turned and glanced at them. Sam responded with an *everything's fine* wave of the hand, and the cop turned away again.

Nina sat clutching the rumpled hem of her gown. This man was horrid. Sam Spade without a trace of human warmth. Though it was getting hot in the car, she found herself shivering, chilled by the lack of obvious emotion displayed by the man sitting beside her.

"Can we explore this a little more?" he said.

She said nothing.

"Do you have any ex-boyfriends, Miss Cormier? Anyone who might be unhappy about your marriage?"

"No," she whispered.

"No ex-boyfriends at all?"

"Not—not in the last year."

"Is that how long you've been with your fiancé? A year?"

"Yes."

"His full name and address, please."

"Robert David Bledsoe, M.D., 318 Ocean View Drive."

"Same address?"

"We've been living together."

"Why was the wedding cancelled?"

"You'd have to ask Robert."

"So it was his decision? To call off the wedding?"

"As the expression goes, he left me at the altar."

"Do you know why?"

She gave a bitter laugh. "I've come to the earth-shattering conclusion, Detective, that the minds of men are a complete mystery to me."

"He gave you no warning at all?"

"It was just as unexpected as that…" She swallowed. "As that bomb. If that's what it was."

"What time was the wedding called off?"

"About one-thirty. I'd already arrived at the church, wedding gown and all. Then Jeremy—Robert's best man—showed up with the note. Robert didn't even have the nerve to tell me himself." She shook her head in disgust.

"What did the note say?"

"That he needed more time. And he was leaving town for a while. That's all."

"Is it possible Robert had any reason to—"

"No, it's *not* possible!" She looked him straight in the eye. "You're asking if Robert had something to do with it. Aren't you?"

"I keep an open mind, Miss Cormier."

"Robert's not capable of violence. For God's sake, he's a doctor!"

"All right. For the moment, we'll let that go. Let's look at other possibilities. I take it you're employed?"

"I'm a nurse at Maine Medical Center."

"Which department?"

"Emergency room."

"Any problems at work? Any conflicts with the rest of the staff?"

"No. We get along fine."

"Any threats? From your patients, for instance?"

She made a sound of exasperation. "Detective, wouldn't I know if I had enemies?"

"Not necessarily."

"You're trying your damn best to make me feel paranoid."

"I'm asking you to step back from yourself. Examine your personal life. Think of all the people who might not like you."

Nina sank back in the seat. *All the people who might not like me.* She thought of her family. Her older sister, Wendy, with whom she'd never been close. Her mother, Lydia, married to her wealthy snob of a husband. Her father, George, now on his fourth wife, a blond trophy bride who considered her husband's offspring a nuisance. It was one big, dysfunctional family, but there were certainly no murderers among them.

She shook her head. "No one, Detective. There's no one."

After a moment he sighed and closed his notebook. "All right, Miss Cormier. I guess that's all for now."

"For now?"

"I'll probably have other questions. After I talk to the rest of the wedding party." He opened the car door, got out, and pushed the door shut. Through the open window he said, "If you think of anything, anything at all, give me a call." He scribbled in his notebook and handed her the torn page with his name, Detective Samuel I. Navarro, and a phone number. "It's my direct line," he said. "I can also be

reached twenty-four hours a day through the police switch-
board."

"Then…I can go home now?"

"Yes." He started to walk away.

"Detective Navarro?"

He turned back to her. She had not realized how tall he
was. Now, seeing his lean frame at its full height, she
wondered how he'd ever fit in the seat beside her. "Is there
something else, Miss Cormier?" he asked.

"You said I could leave."

"That's right."

"I don't have a ride." She nodded toward the bombed-
out church. "Or a phone either. Do you think you could
give my mother a call? To come get me?"

"Your mother?" He glanced around, obviously anxious
to palm off this latest annoyance. Finally, with a look of resignation, he circled around to her side of the car and opened
the door. "Come on. We can go in my car. I'll drive you."

"Look, I was only asking you to make a call."

"It's no trouble." He extended his hand to help her out.
"I'd have to go by your mother's house anyway."

"My mother's house? Why?"

"She was at the wedding. I'll need to talk to her, too.
Might as well kill two birds with one stone."

What a gallant way to put it, she thought.

He was still reaching out to her. She ignored his out-
stretched hand. It was a struggle getting out of the car,
since her train had wrapped itself around her legs, and she
had to kick herself free of the hem. By the time she'd
finally extricated herself from the car, he was regarding her
with a look of amusement. She snatched up her train and
whisked past him in a noisy rustle of satin.

"Uh, Miss Cormier?"

"What?" she snapped over her shoulder.

"My car's in the other direction."

She halted, her cheeks flushing. Mr. Detective was actually smiling now, a full-blown ate-the-canary grin.

"It's the blue Taurus," he pointed out. "The door's unlocked. I'll be right with you." He turned and headed away, toward the gathering of cops.

Nina flounced over to the blue Taurus. There she peered in disgust through the window. She was supposed to ride in *this* car? With that mess? She opened the door. A paper cup tumbled out. On the passenger floor was a crumpled McDonald's bag, more coffee cups, and a two-day-old *Portland Press Herald*. The back seat was buried under more newspapers, file folders, a briefcase, a suit jacket, and—of all things—a baseball mitt.

She scooped up the debris from the passenger side, tossed it into the back, and climbed in. She only hoped the seat was clean.

Detective Cold Fish was walking toward the car. He looked hot and harassed. His shirtsleeves were rolled up now, his tie yanked loose. Even as he tried to leave the scene, cops were pulling him aside to ask questions.

At last he slid in behind the wheel and slammed the door. "Okay, where does your mother live?" he asked.

"Cape Elizabeth. Look, I can see you're busy—"

"My partner's holding the fort. I'll drop you off, talk to your mother, and swing by the hospital to see Reverend Sullivan."

"Great. That way you can kill *three* birds with one stone."

"I do believe in efficiency."

They drove in silence. She saw no point in trying to

dredge up polite talk. Politeness would go right over this man's head. Instead, she looked out the window and thought morosely about the wedding reception and all those finger sandwiches waiting for guests who'd never arrive. She'd have to call and ask for the food to be delivered to a soup kitchen before it all spoiled. And then there were the gifts, dozens of them, piled up at home. Correction—*Robert's* home. It had never really been *her* home. She had only been living there, a tenant. It had been her idea to pay half the mortgage. Robert used to point out how much he respected her independence, her insistence on a separate identity. In any good relationship, he'd say, privilege as well as responsibility was a fifty-fifty split. That's how they'd worked it from the start. First he'd paid for a date, then she had. In fact, she'd insisted, to show him that she was her own woman.

Now it all seemed so stupid.

I was never my own woman, she thought. I was always dreaming, longing for the day I'd be Mrs. Robert Bledsoe. It's what her family had hoped for, what her mother had expected of her: to marry well. They'd never understood Nina's going to nursing school, except as a way to meet a potential mate. A doctor. She'd met one, all right.

And all it's gotten me is a bunch of gifts I have to return, a wedding gown I can't return, and a day I'll never, ever live down.

It was the humiliation that shook her the most. Not the fact that Robert had walked out. Not even the fact that she could have died in the wreckage of that church. The explosion itself seemed unreal to her, as remote as some TV melodramas. As remote as this man sitting beside her.

"You're handling this very well," he said.

Startled that Detective Cold Fish had spoken, she looked at him. "Excuse me?"

"You're taking this very calmly. Calmer than most."

"I don't know how else to take it."

"After a bombing, hysteria would not be out of line."

"I'm an ER nurse, Detective. I don't do hysteria."

"Still, this had to be a shock for you. There could well be an emotional aftermath."

"You're saying this is the calm before the storm?"

"Something like that." He glanced at her, his gaze meeting hers. Just as quickly, he looked back at the road and the connection was gone. "Why wasn't your family with you at the church?"

"I sent them all home."

"I would think you'd want them around for support, at least."

She looked out the window. "My family's not exactly the supportive type. And I guess I just…needed to be alone. When an animal gets hurt, Detective, it goes off by itself to lick its wounds. That's what I needed to do…." She blinked away an unexpected film of tears and fell silent.

"I know you don't feel much like talking right now," he said. "But maybe you can answer this question for me. Can you think of anyone else who might've been a target? Reverend Sullivan, for instance?"

She shook her head. "He's the last person anyone would hurt."

"It was his church building. He would've been near the blast center."

"Reverend Sullivan's the sweetest man in the world! Every winter, he's handing out blankets on the street. Or scrounging up beds at the shelter. In the ER, when we see patients who have no home to go to, he's the one we call."

"I'm not questioning his character. I'm just asking about enemies."

"He has no enemies," she said flatly.

"What about the rest of the wedding party? Could any of them have been targets?"

"I can't imagine—"

"The best man, Jeremy Wall. Tell me about him."

"Jeremy? There's not much to say. He went to medical school with Robert. He's a doctor at Maine Med. A radiologist."

"Married?"

"Single. A confirmed bachelor."

"What about your sister, Wendy? She was your maid of honor?"

"Matron of honor. She's a happy homemaker."

"Any enemies?"

"Not unless there's someone out there who resents perfection."

"Meaning?"

"Let's just say she's the dream daughter every parent hopes for."

"As opposed to you?"

Nina gave a shrug. "How'd you guess?"

"All right, so that leaves one major player. The one who, coincidentally, decided not to show up at all."

Nina stared straight ahead. *What can I tell him about Robert,* she thought, *when I myself am completely in the dark?*

To her relief, he didn't pursue that line of questioning. Perhaps he'd realized how far he'd pushed her. How close to the emotional edge she was already tottering. As they drove the winding road into Cape Elizabeth, she felt her calm facade at last begin to crumble. Hadn't he warned her about it? The emotional aftermath. The pain creeping through the numbness. She had held together well, had weathered two devastating shocks with little more than a few spilt tears. Now her hands were beginning to shake, and she found that every breath she took was a struggle not to sob.

When at last they pulled up in front of her mother's house, Nina was barely holding herself together. She didn't wait for Sam to circle around and open her door. She pushed it open herself and scrambled out in a sloppy tangle of wedding gown. By the time he walked up the front steps, she was already leaning desperately on the doorbell, silently begging her mother to let her in before she fell apart completely.

The door swung open. Lydia, still elegantly coiffed and gowned, stood staring at her dishevelled daughter. "Nina? Oh, my poor Nina." She opened her arms.

Automatically Nina fell into her mother's embrace. So hungry was she for a hug, she didn't immediately register the fact that Lydia had drawn back to avoid wrinkling her green silk dress. But she did register her mother's first question.

"Have you heard from Robert yet?"

Nina stiffened. *Oh please,* she thought. *Please don't do this to me.*

"I'm sure this can all be worked out," said Lydia. "If you'd just sit down with Robert and have an honest discussion about what's bothering him—"

Nina pulled away. "I'm not going to sit down with Robert," she said. "And as for an honest discussion, I'm not sure we ever had one."

"Now, darling, it's natural to be angry—"

"But aren't you angry, Mother? Can't you be angry *for* me?"

"Well, yes. But I can't see tossing Robert aside just because—"

The sudden clearing of a male throat made Lydia glance up at Sam, who was standing outside the doorway.

"I'm Detective Navarro, Portland Police," he said. "You're Mrs. Cormier?"

"The name's now Warrenton." Lydia frowned at him. "What is this all about? What do the police have to do with this?"

"There was an incident at the church, ma'am. We're investigating.

"An incident?"

"The church was bombed."

Lydia stared at him. "You're not serious."

"I'm very serious. It went off at 2:40 this afternoon. Luckily no one was hurt. But if the wedding had been held…"

Lydia paled to a sickly white. She took a step back, her voice failing her.

"Mrs. Warrenton," said Sam, "I need to ask you a few questions."

Nina didn't stay to listen. She had heard too many questions already. She climbed upstairs to the spare bedroom, where she had left her suitcase—the suitcase she'd packed for St. John Island. Inside were her bathing suits and sundresses and tanning lotion. Everything she'd thought she needed for a week in paradise.

She took off the wedding dress and carefully draped it over an armchair where it lay white and lifeless.

Useless. She looked at the contents of her suitcase, at the broken dreams packed neatly between layers of tissue paper. That's when the last vestiges of control failed her. Dressed only in her underwear, she sat down on the bed. Alone, in silence, she finally allowed the grief to sweep over her.

And she wept.

LYDIA WARRENTON was nothing like her daughter. Sam had seen it the moment the older woman opened the front door. Flawlessly made up, elegantly coiffed, her slender frame shown to full advantage by the green gown, Lydia looked like no mother of the bride he'd ever seen. There was a physical resemblance, of course. Both Lydia and Nina had the same black hair, the same dark, thickly lashed eyes. But while Nina had a softness about her, a vulnerability, Lydia was standoffish, as though surrounded by some protective force field that would zap anyone who ventured too close. She was definitely a looker, not only thin but also rich, judging by the room he was now standing in.

The house was a veritable museum of antiques. He had noticed a Mercedes parked in the driveway. And the living room, into which he'd just been ushered, had a spectacular ocean view. A million-dollar view. Lydia sat down primly on a brocade sofa and motioned him toward a wing chair. The needlepoint fabric was so pristine-looking he had the urge to inspect his clothes before sinking onto the cushion.

"A bomb," murmured Lydia, shaking her head. "I just can't believe it. Who would bomb a church?"

"It's not the first bombing we've had in town."

She looked at him, bewildered. "You mean the warehouse? The one last week? I read that had something to do with organized crime."

"That was the theory."

"This was a church. How can they possibly be connected?"

"We don't see the link either, Mrs. Warrenton. We're trying to find out if there is one. Maybe you can help us. Do you know of any reason someone would want to bomb the Good Shepherd Church?"

"I know nothing about that church. It's not one I attend. It was my daughter's choice to get married there."

"You sound as if you don't approve."

She shrugged. "Nina has her own odd way of doing things. I'd have chosen a more…established institution. And a longer guest list. But that's Nina. She wanted to keep it small and simple."

Simple was definitely not Lydia Warrenton's style, thought Sam, gazing around the room.

"So to answer your question, Detective, I can't think of any reason to bomb Good Shepherd."

"What time did you leave the church?"

"A little after two. When it became apparent there wasn't anything I could do for Nina."

"While you were waiting, did you happen to notice anyone who shouldn't have been there?"

"There were just the people you'd expect. The florists, the minister. The wedding party."

"Names?"

"There was me. My daughter Wendy. The best man— I don't remember his name. My ex-husband, George, and his latest wife."

"Latest."

She sniffed. "Daniella. His fourth so far."

"What about your husband?"

She paused. "Edward was delayed. His plane was two hours late leaving Chicago."

"So he hadn't even reached town yet?"

"No. But he planned to attend the reception."

Again, Sam glanced around the room, at the antiques. The view. "May I ask what your husband does for a living, Mrs. Warrenton?"

"He's president of Ridley-Warrenton."

"The logging company?"

"That's right."

That explained the house and the Mercedes, thought Sam. Ridley-Warrenton was one of the largest landowners in northern Maine. Their forest products, from raw lumber to fine paper, were shipped around the world.

His next question was unavoidable. "Mrs. Warrenton," he asked, "does your husband have any enemies?"

Her response surprised him. She laughed. "Anyone with money has enemies, Detective."

"Can you name anyone in particular?"

"You'd have to ask Edward."

"I will," said Sam, rising to his feet. "As soon as your husband's back in town, could you have him give me a call?"

"My husband's a busy man."

"So am I, ma'am," he answered. With a curt nod, he turned and left the house.

In the driveway, he sat in his Taurus for a moment, gazing up at the mansion. It was, without a doubt, one of the most impressive homes he'd ever been in. Not that he was all that familiar with mansions. Samuel Navarro was the son of a Boston cop who was himself the son of a

Boston cop. At the age of twelve, he'd moved to Portland with his newly widowed mother. Nothing came easy for them, a fact of life which his mother resignedly accepted.

Sam had not been so accepting. His adolescence consisted of five long years of rebellion. Fistfights in the school yard. Sneaking cigarettes in the bathroom. Loitering with the rough-and-tumble crowd that hung out in Monument Square. There'd been no mansions in his childhood.

He started the car and drove away. The investigation was just beginning; he and Gillis had a long night ahead of them. There was still the minister to interview, as well as the florist, the best man, the matron of honor, and the groom.

Most of all, the groom.

Dr. Robert Bledsoe, after all, was the one who'd called off the wedding. His decision, by accident or design, had saved the lives of dozens of people. That struck Sam as just a little bit too fortunate. Had Bledsoe received some kind of warning? Had he been the intended target?

Was that the real reason he'd left his bride at the altar?

Nina Cormier's image came vividly back to mind. Hers wasn't a face he'd be likely to forget. It was more than just those big brown eyes, that kissable mouth. It was her pride that impressed him the most. The sort of pride that kept her chin up, her jaw squared, even as the tears were falling. For that he admired her. No whining, no self-pity. The woman had been humiliated, abandoned, and almost blown to smithereens. Yet she'd had enough spunk left to give Sam an occasional what-for. He found that both irritating and amusing. For a woman who'd probably grown up with everything handed to her on a silver platter, she was a tough little survivor.

Today she'd been handed a heaping dish of crow, and she'd eaten it just fine, thank you. Without a whimper.

Surprising, surprising woman.

He could hardly wait to hear what Dr. Robert Bledsoe had to say about her.

IT WAS AFTER five o'clock when Nina finally emerged from her mother's guest bedroom. Calm, composed, she was now wearing jeans and a T-shirt. She'd left her wedding dress hanging in the closet; she didn't even want to look at it again. Too many bad memories had attached themselves like burrs to the fabric.

Downstairs she found her mother sitting alone in the living room, nursing a highball. Detective Navarro was gone. Lydia raised the drink to her lips, and by the clinking of ice cubes in the glass, Nina could tell that Lydia's hands were shaking.

"Mother?" said Nina.

At the sound of her daughter's voice, Lydia's head jerked up. "You startled me."

"I think I'll be leaving now. Are you all right?"

"Yes. Yes, of course." Lydia gave a shudder. Then she added, almost as an afterthought, "How about you?"

"I'll be okay. I just need some time. Away from Robert."

Mother and daughter looked at each other for a moment, neither one speaking, neither one knowing what to say. This was the way things had always been between them. Nina had grown up hungry for affection. Her mother had always been too self-absorbed to grant it. And this was the result: the silence of two women who scarcely knew or understood each other. The distance between them couldn't be measured by years, but by universes.

Nina watched her mother take another deep swallow of her drink. "How did it go?" she asked. "With you and that detective?"

Lydia shrugged. "What's there to say? He asked questions, I answered them."

"Did he tell you anything? About who might have done it?"

"No. He was tight as a clam. Not much in the way of charm."

Nina couldn't disagree. She'd known ice cubes that were warmer than Sam Navarro. But then, the man was just doing his job. He wasn't paid to be charming.

"You can stay for dinner, if you'd like," said Lydia. "Why don't you? I'll have the cook—"

"That's all right, Mother. Thank you, anyway."

Lydia looked up at her. "It's because of Edward, isn't it?"

"No, Mother. Really."

"That's why you hardly ever visit. Because of him. I wish you *could* get to like him." Lydia sighed and looked down at her drink. "He's been very good to me, very generous. You have to grant him that much."

When Nina thought of her stepfather, *generous* was not the first adjective that came to mind. No, *ruthless* would be the word she'd choose. Ruthless and controlling. She didn't want to talk about Edward Warrenton.

She turned and started toward the door. "I have to get home and pack my things. Since it's obvious I'll be moving out."

"Couldn't you and Robert patch things up somehow?"

"After today?" Nina shook her head.

"If you just tried harder? Maybe it's something you could talk about. Something you could change."

"Mother. Please."

Lydia sank back. "Anyway," she said, "you *are* invited to dinner. For what it's worth."

"Maybe some other time," Nina said softly. "Bye, Mother."

She heard no answer as she walked out the front door.

Her Honda was parked at the side of the house, where she'd left it that morning. The morning of what should have been her wedding. How proudly Lydia had smiled at her as they'd sat together in the limousine! It was the way a mother *should* look at her daughter. The way Lydia never had before.

And probably never would again.

That ride to the church, the smiles, the laughter, seemed a lifetime away. She started the Honda and pulled out of her mother's driveway.

In a daze she drove south, toward Hunts Point. Toward Robert's house. What had been *their* house. The road was winding, and she was functioning on automatic pilot, steering without thought along the curves. What if Robert hadn't really left town? she thought. What if he's home? What would they say to each other?

Try: goodbye.

She gripped the steering wheel and thought of all the things she'd *like* to tell him. All the ways she felt used and betrayed. *A whole year* kept going through her head. *One whole bloody year of my life.*

Only as she swung past Smugglers Cove did she happen to glance in the rearview mirror. A black Ford was behind her. The same Ford that had been there a few miles back, near Delano Park. At any other time, she would have thought nothing of it. But today, after the possibilities Detective Navarro had raised...

She shook off a vague sense of uneasiness and kept driving. She turned onto Ocean House Drive.

The Ford did too. There was no reason for alarm. Ocean House Drive was, after all, a main road in the neighborhood. Another driver might very well have reason to turn onto it as well.

Just to ease her anxiety, she took the left turnoff, toward Peabbles Point. It was a lonely road, not heavily traveled. Here's where she and the Ford would surely part company.

The Ford took the same turnoff.

Now she was getting frightened.

She pressed the accelerator. The Honda gained speed. At fifty miles per hour, she knew she was taking the curves too fast, but she was determined to lose the Ford. Only she wasn't losing him. He had sped up, too. In fact, he was gaining on her.

With a sudden burst of speed, the Ford roared up right beside her. They were neck and neck, taking the curves in parallel.

He's trying to run me off the road! she thought.

She glanced sideways, but all she could see through the other car's tinted window was the driver's silhouette. *Why are you doing this?* she wanted to scream at him. *Why?*

The Ford suddenly swerved toward her. The thump of the other car's impact almost sent the Honda spinning out of control. Nina fought to keep her car on course.

Her fingers clamped more tightly around the wheel. Damn this lunatic! She had to shake him off.

She hit the brakes.

The Ford shot ahead—only momentarily. It quickly slowed as well and was back beside her, swerving, bumping.

She managed another sideways glance. To her surprise, the Ford's passenger window had been rolled down. She caught a glimpse of the driver—a male. Dark hair. Sunglasses.

In the next instant her gaze shot forward to the road, which crested fifty yards ahead.

Another car had just cleared the crest and was barreling straight toward the Ford.

Tires screeched. Nina felt one last violent thump, felt the sting of shattering glass against her face. Then suddenly she was soaring sideways.

She never lost consciousness. Even as the Honda flew off the road. Even as it tumbled over and over across shrubbery and saplings.

It came to a rest, upright, against a maple tree.

Though fully awake, Nina could not move for a moment. She was too stunned to feel pain, or even fear. All she felt was amazement that she was still alive.

Then, gradually, an awareness of discomfort seeped through the layers of shock. Her chest hurt, and her shoulder. It was the seat belt. It had saved her life, but it had also bruised her ribs.

Groaning, she pressed the belt release and felt herself collapse forward, against the steering wheel.

"Hey! Hey, lady!"

Nina turned to see a face anxiously peering through the window. It was an elderly man. He yanked open her door. "Are you all right?" he asked.

"I'm—I think so."

"I'd better call an ambulance."

"No, I'm fine. Really, I am." She took a deep breath. Her chest was sore, but that seemed to be her only injury. With the old man's help, she climbed out of the car. Though a little unsteady, she was able to stand. She was shocked by the damage.

Her car was a mess. The driver's door had been bashed in, the window was shattered, and the front fender was peeled off entirely.

She turned and glanced toward the road. "There was another car," she said. "A black one—"

"You mean that damn fool who tried to pass you?"

"Where is it?"

"Took off. You oughta report that fella. Probably drunk as a skunk."

Drunk? Nina didn't think so. Shivering, she hugged herself and stared at the road, but she saw no sign of another car.

The black Ford had vanished.

Three

Gordon Gillis looked up from his burger and fries. "Anything interesting?" he asked.

"Not a damn thing." Sam hung his jacket up on the coatrack and sank into a chair behind his desk, where he sat wearily rubbing his face.

"How's the minister doing?"

"Fine, so far. Doctors doubt it's a heart attack. But they'll keep him in for a day, just to be sure."

"He didn't have any ideas about the bombing?"

"Claims he has no enemies. And everyone I talked to seems to agree that Reverend Sullivan is a certifiable saint." Groaning, Sam leaned back. "How 'bout you?"

Gillis peeled off the hamburger wrapper and began to eat as he talked. "I interviewed the best man, the matron of honor and the florist. No one saw anything."

"What about the church janitor?"

"We're still trying to locate him. His wife says he usually gets home around six. I'll send Cooley over to talk to him."

"According to Reverend Sullivan, the janitor opens the front doors at 7:00 a.m. And the doors stay open all day. So anyone could've walked in and left a package."

"What about the night before?" asked Gillis. "What time did he lock the doors?"

"The church secretary usually locks up. She's a part-timer. Would've done it around 6:00 p.m. Unfortunately, she left for vacation this morning. Visiting family in Massachusetts. We're still trying to get hold of…" He paused.

Gillis's telephone was ringing. Gillis turned to answer it. "Yeah, what's up?"

Sam watched as his partner scribbled something on a notepad, then passed it across the desk. *Trundy Point Road* was written on the paper.

A moment later, Gillis said, "We'll be there," and hung up. He was frowning.

"What is it?" asked Sam.

"Report just came in from one of the mobile units. It's about the bride. The one at the church today."

"Nina Cormier?"

"Her car just went off the road near Trundy Point."

Sam sat up straight in alarm. "Is she all right?"

"She's fine. They wouldn't have called us at all, but she insisted they notify us."

"For an accident? Why?"

"She says it wasn't an accident. She says someone tried to run her off the road."

HER RIBS HURT, her shoulder was sore, and her face had a few cuts from flying glass. But at least her head was perfectly clear. Clear enough for her to recognize the man stepping out of that familiar blue Taurus that had just pulled up at the scene. It was that sullen detective, Sam Navarro. He didn't even glance in her direction.

Through the gathering dusk, Nina watched as he spoke to a patrolman. They conversed for a few moments. Then, together, the two men tramped through the underbrush to view the remains of her car. As Sam paced a slow circle around the battered Honda, Nina was reminded of a stalking cat. He moved with an easy, feline grace, his gaze focused in complete concentration. At one point he stopped and crouched to look at something on the ground. Then he rose to his feet and peered more closely at the driver's window. Or what was left of the window. He prodded the broken glass, then opened the door and climbed into the front seat. What on earth was he looking for? She could see his dark hair bobbing in and out of view. Now he seemed to be crawling all over the interior, and into the back seat. It was a good thing she had nothing to hide in there. She had no doubt that the sharp-eyed Detective Navarro could spot contraband a mile away.

At last he reemerged from her car, his hair tousled, his trousers wrinkled. He spoke again to the patrolman. Then he turned and looked in her direction.

And began to walk toward her.

At once she felt her pulse quickening. Something about this man both fascinated and frightened her. It was more than just his physical presence, which was impressive enough. It was also the way he looked at her, with a gaze that was completely neutral. That inscrutability unnerved her. Most men seemed to find Nina attractive, and they would at least make an attempt to be friendly.

This man seemed to regard her as just another homicide

victim in the making. Worth his intellectual interest, but that was all.

She straightened her back and met his gaze without wavering as he approached.

"Are you all right?" he asked.

"A few bruises. A few cuts. That's all."

"You're sure you don't want to go to the ER? I can drive you."

"I'm fine. I'm a nurse, so I think I'd know."

"They say doctors and nurses make the worst patients. I'll drive you to the hospital. Just to be sure."

She gave a disbelieving laugh. "That sounds like an order."

"As a matter of fact, it is."

"Detective, I really think I'd know if I was…"

She was talking to his back. The man had actually turned his *back* to her. He was already walking away, toward his car. *"Detective!"* she called.

He glanced over his shoulder. "Yes?"

"I don't— This isn't—" She sighed. "Oh, never mind," she muttered, and followed him to his car. There was no point arguing with the man. He'd just turn his back on her again. As she slid into the passenger seat, she felt a sharp stab of pain in her chest. Maybe he was right after all. She knew it could take hours, or even days, for injuries to manifest themselves. She hated to admit it, but Mr. Personality was probably right about this trip to the ER.

She was too uncomfortable to say much as they drove to the hospital. It was Sam who finally broke the silence.

"So, can you tell me what happened?" he asked.

"I already gave a statement. It's all in the police report. Someone ran me off the road."

"Yes, a black Ford, male driver. Maine license plate."

"Then you've been told the details."

"The other witness said he thought it was a drunk driver trying to pass you on the hill. He didn't think it was deliberate."

She shook her head. "I don't know what to think anymore."

"When did you first see the Ford?"

"Somewhere around Smugglers Cove, I guess. I noticed that it seemed to be following me."

"Was it weaving? Show any signs of driver impairment?"

"No. It was just…following me."

"Could it have been behind you earlier?"

"I'm not sure."

"Is it possible it was there when you left your mother's house?"

She frowned at him. He wasn't looking at her, but was staring straight ahead. The tenor of his questions had taken a subtle change of course. He had started out sounding noncommittal. Maybe even skeptical. But this last question told her he was considering a possibility other than a drunk driver. A possibility that left her suddenly chilled.

"Are you suggesting he was waiting for me?"

"I'm just exploring the possibilities."

"The other policeman thought it was a drunk driver."

"He has his opinion."

"What's your opinion?"

He didn't answer. He just kept driving in that maddeningly calm way of his. Did the man ever show any emotion? Once, just once, she'd like to see something get under that thick skin of his.

"Detective Navarro," she said. "I pay taxes. I pay your salary. I think I deserve more than just a brush-off."

"Oh. The old civil servant line."

"I'll use whatever line it takes to get an answer out of you!"

"I'm not sure you want to hear my answer."

"Why wouldn't I?"

"I made a brief inspection of your car. What I found there backs up quite a bit of what you just told me. There were black paint chips on the driver's side, indicating that the vehicle that rammed yours was, indeed, black."

"So I'm not color blind."

"I also noticed that the driver's window was shattered. And that the breakage was in a starburst pattern. Not what I'd expect for a rollover accident."

"That's because the window was already broken when I went off the road."

"How do you know?"

"I remember I felt flying glass. That's how I cut my face. When the glass hit me. That was *before* I rolled over."

"Are you sure?" He glanced at her. "Absolutely sure?"

"Yes. Does it make a difference?"

He let out a breath. "It makes a lot of difference," he said softly. "It also goes along with what I found in your car."

"*In* my car?" Perplexed, she shook her head. "What, exactly, did you find?"

"It was in the right passenger door—the door that was jammed against the tree. The metal was pretty crumpled; that's why the other cops didn't notice it. But I knew it was there somewhere. And I found it."

"Found what?"

"A bullet hole."

Nina felt the blood drain from her face. She couldn't speak; she could only sit in shocked silence, her world rocked by the impact of his words.

He continued talking, his tone matter-of-fact. Chillingly so. *He's not human,* she thought. *He's a machine. A robot.*

"The bullet must have hit your window," he said, "just to the rear of your head. That's why the glass shattered. Then the bullet passed at a slightly forward angle, missed you completely, and made a hole in the plastic molding of the opposite door, where it's probably still lodged. It'll be retrieved. By tonight, we'll know the caliber. And possibly the make of the gun. What I still don't know—what *you'll* have to tell me—is why someone's trying to kill you."

She shook her head. "It's a mistake."

"This guy's going to a lot of trouble. He's bombed a church. Tailed you. Shot at you. There's no mistake."

"There has to be!"

"Think of every possible person who might want to hurt you. Think, Nina."

"I told you, I don't have any enemies!"

"You must have."

"I don't! I don't…." She gave a sob and clutched her head in her hands. "I don't," she whispered.

After a long silence he said, gently, "I'm sorry. I know how hard it is to accept—"

"You *don't* know." She raised her head and looked at him. "You have no idea, Detective. I've always thought people liked me. Or—at least—they didn't *hate* me. I try so hard to get along with everyone. And now you're telling me there's someone out there—someone who wants to…" She swallowed and stared ahead, at the darkening road.

Sam let the silence stretch on between them. He knew she was in too fragile a state right now to press her with more questions. And he suspected she was hurting more, both physically and emotionally, than she was letting on. Judging by the condition of her car, her body had taken a brutal beating this afternoon.

In the ER, he paced the waiting room while Nina was examined by the doctor on duty. A few X rays later, she emerged looking even more pale than when she'd entered. It was reality sinking in, he thought. The danger was genuine, and she couldn't deny it any longer.

Back in his car, she sat in numb silence. He kept glancing sideways at her, waiting for her to burst into tears, into hysteria, but she remained unnervingly quiet. It concerned him. This wasn't healthy.

He said, "You shouldn't be alone tonight. Is there somewhere you can go?"

Her response was barely a shrug.

"Your mother's?" he suggested. "I'll take you home to pack a suitcase and—"

"No. Not my mother's," she murmured.

"Why not?"

"I…don't want to make things…uncomfortable for her."

"For *her?*" He frowned. "Pardon me for asking this, but isn't that what mothers are for? To pick us up and dust us off?"

"My mother's marriage isn't…the most supportive one around."

"She can't welcome her own daughter home?"

"It's not her home, Detective. It's her husband's. And he doesn't approve of me. To be honest, the feeling's mutual." She gazed straight ahead, and in that moment, she struck him as so very brave. And so very alone.

"Since the day they got married, Edward Warrenton has controlled every detail of my mother's life. He bullies her, and she takes it without a whimper. Because his money makes it all worthwhile for her. I just couldn't stand watching it any longer. So one day I told him off."

"Sounds like that's exactly what you should have done."

"It didn't do a thing for family harmony. I'm sure that's why he went on that business trip to Chicago. So he could conveniently skip my wedding." Sighing, she tilted her head back against the headrest. "I know I shouldn't be annoyed with my mother, but I am. I'm annoyed that she's never stood up to him."

"Okay. So I don't take you to your mother's house. What about dear old dad? Do you two get along?"

She gave a nod. A small one. "I suppose I could stay with him."

"Good. Because there's no way I'm going to let you be alone tonight." The sentence was scarcely out of his mouth when he realized he shouldn't have said it. It sounded too much as if he cared, as if feeling were getting mixed up with duty. He was too good a cop, too cautious a cop, to let that happen.

He could feel her surprised gaze through the darkness of the car.

In a tone colder than he'd intended, he said, "You may be my only link to this bombing. I need you alive and well for the investigation."

"Oh. Of course." She looked straight ahead again. And she didn't say another word until they'd reached her house on Ocean View Drive.

As soon as he'd parked, she started to get out of the car. He reached for her arm and pulled her back inside. "Wait."

"What is it?"

"Just sit for a minute." He glanced up and down the

road, scanning for other cars, other people. Anything at all suspicious. The street was deserted.

"Okay," he said. He got out and circled around to open her door. "Pack one suitcase. That's all we have time for."

"I wasn't planning to bring along the furniture."

"I'm just trying to keep this short and sweet. If someone's really looking for you, this is where they'll come. So let's not hang around, all right?"

That remark, meant to emphasize the danger, had its intended effect. She scooted out of the car and up the front walk in hyperspeed. He had to convince her to wait on the porch while he made a quick search of the house.

A moment later he poked his head out the door. "All clear."

While she packed a suitcase, Sam wandered about the living room. It was an old but spacious house, tastefully furnished, with a view of the sea. Just the sort of house one would expect a doctor to live in. He went over to the grand piano—a Steinway—and tapped out a few notes. "Who plays the piano?" he called out.

"Robert," came the answer from the bedroom. "Afraid I have a tin ear."

He focused on a framed photograph set on the piano. It was a shot of a couple, smiling. Nina and some blond, blue-eyed man. Undoubtedly Robert Bledsoe. The guy, it seemed, had everything: looks, money and a medical degree. And the woman. A woman he no longer wanted. Sam crossed the room to a display of diplomas, hanging on the wall. All of them Robert Bledsoe's. Groton prep. B.A. Dartmouth. M.D. Harvard. Dr. Bledsoe was Ivy League all the way. He was every mother's dream son-in-law. No wonder Lydia Warrenton had urged her daughter to patch things up.

The phone rang, the sound so abrupt and startling, Sam felt an instant rush of adrenaline.

"Should I get it?" Nina asked. She was standing in the doorway, her face drawn and tense.

He nodded. "Answer it."

She crossed to the telephone. After a second's hesitation, she picked up the receiver. He moved right beside her, listening, as she said, "Hello?"

No one answered.

"Hello?" Nina repeated. "Who is this? *Hello?*"

There was a click. Then, a moment later, the dial tone.

Nina looked up at Sam. She was standing so close to him, her hair, like black silk, brushed his face. He found himself staring straight into those wide eyes of hers, found himself reacting to her nearness with an unexpected surge of male longing.

This isn't supposed to happen. I can't let it happen.

He took a step back, just to put space between them. Even though they were now standing a good three feet apart, he could still feel the attraction. Not far enough apart, he thought. This woman was getting in the way of his thinking clearly, logically. And that was dangerous.

He looked down and suddenly noticed the telephone answering machine was blinking. He said, "You have messages."

"Pardon?"

"Your answering machine. It's recorded three messages."

Dazedly she looked down at the machine. Automatically she pressed the Play button.

There were three beeps, followed by three silences, and then dial tones.

Seemingly paralyzed, she stared at the machine. "Why?" she whispered. "Why do they call and hang up?"

"To see if you're home."

The implication of his statement at once struck her full force. She flinched away from the phone as if it had burned her. "I have to get out of here," she said, and hurried back into the bedroom.

He followed her. She was tossing clothes into a suitcase, not bothering to fold anything. Slacks and blouses and lingerie in one disorganized pile.

"Just the essentials," he said. "Let's leave."

"Yes. Yes, you're right." She whirled around and ran into the bathroom. He heard her rattling in the cabinets, collecting toiletries. A moment later she reemerged with a bulging makeup bag, which she tossed in the suitcase.

He closed and latched it for her. "Let's go."

In the car, she sat silent and huddled against the seat as he drove. He kept checking the rearview mirror, to see if they were being followed, but he saw no other headlights. No signs of pursuit.

"Relax, we're okay," he said. "I'll just get you to your dad's house, and you'll be fine."

"And then what?" she said softly. "How long do I hide there? For weeks, months?"

"As long as it takes for us to crack this case."

She shook her head, a sad gesture of bewilderment. "It doesn't make sense. None of this makes sense."

"Maybe it'll become clear when we talk to your fiancé. Do you have any idea where he might be?"

"It seems that I'm the last person Robert wanted to confide in…" Hugging herself, she stared out the window.

"His note said he was leaving town for a while. I guess he just needed to get away. From me…"

"From you? Or from someone else?"

She shook her head. "There's so much I don't know. So much he never bothered to tell me. God, I wish I understood. I could handle this. I could handle anything. If only I understood."

What kind of man is Robert Bledsoe? Sam wondered. What kind of man would walk away from this woman? Leave her alone to face the danger left in his wake?

"Whoever made that hang-up call may pay a visit to your house," he said. "I'd like to keep an eye on it. See who turns up."

She nodded. "Yes. Of course."

"May I have access?"

"You mean…get inside?"

"If our suspect shows up, he may try to break in. I'd like to be waiting for him."

She stared at him. "You could get yourself killed."

"Believe me, Miss Cormier, I'm not the heroic type. I don't take chances."

"But if he does show up—"

"I'll be ready." He flashed her a quick grin for reassurance. She didn't look reassured. If anything, she looked more frightened than ever.

For me? he wondered. And that, inexplicably, lifted his spirits. Terrific. Next thing he knew, he'd be putting his neck in a noose, and all because of a pair of big brown eyes. This was just the kind of situation cops were warned to avoid: assuming the role of hero to some fetching female. It got men killed.

It could get *him* killed.

"You shouldn't do this by yourself," she said.

"I won't be alone. I'll have backup."

"You're sure?"

"Yeah, I'm sure."

"You promise? You won't take any chances?"

"What are you, my mother?" he snapped in exasperation.

She took her keys out of her purse and slapped them on the dashboard. "No, I'm not your mother," she retorted. "But you're the cop in charge. And I need you alive and well to crack this case."

He deserved that. She'd been concerned about his safety, and he'd responded with sarcasm. He didn't even know why. All he knew was, whenever he looked in her eyes, he had the overwhelming urge to turn tail and run. Before he was trapped.

Moments later, they drove past the wrought iron gates of her father's driveway. Nina didn't even wait for Sam to open her door. She got out of the car and started up the stone steps. Sam followed, carrying her suitcase. And ogling the house. It was huge—even more impressive than Lydia Warrenton's home, and it had the Rolls-Royce of security systems. Tonight, at least, Nina should be safe.

The doorbell chimed like a church bell; he could hear it echoing through what must be dozens of rooms. The door was opened by a blonde—and what a blonde! Not much older than thirty, she was wearing a shiny spandex leotard that hugged every taut curve. A healthy sweat sheened her face, and from some other room came the thumpy music of an exercise video.

"Hello, Daniella," Nina said quietly.

Daniella assumed a look of sympathy that struck Sam as too automatic to be genuine. "Oh Nina, I'm so *sorry* about what happened today! Wendy called and told us about the church. Was anyone hurt?"

"No. No, thank God." Nina paused, as though afraid to ask the next question. "Do you think I could spend the night with you?"

The expression of sympathy faded. Daniella looked askance at the suitcase Sam was carrying. "I, uh…let me talk to your Dad. He's in the hot tub right now and—"

"Nina has no choice. She has to stay the night," said Sam. He stepped past Daniella, into the house. "It's not safe for her to be alone."

Daniella's gaze shifted to Sam, and he saw the vague spark of interest in those flat blue eyes. "I'm afraid I didn't catch your name," she said.

"This is Detective Navarro," said Nina. "He's with the Portland Bomb Squad. And this," she said to Sam, "is Daniella Cormier. My, uh…father's wife."

Stepmother was the appropriate term, but this stunning blonde didn't look like anybody's mother. And the look she was giving *him* was anything but maternal.

Daniella tilted her head, a gesture he recognized as both inquisitive and flirtatious. "So, you're a cop?"

"Yes, ma'am."

"Bomb Squad? Is that really what you think happened at the church? A bomb?"

"I'm not free to talk about it," he said. "Not while the investigation's underway." Smoothly he turned to Nina. "If you're okay for the night, I'll be leaving. Be sure to close those driveway gates. And activate the burglar alarm. I'll check back with you in the morning."

As he gave a nod of goodbye, his gaze locked with Nina's. It was only the briefest of looks, but once again he was taken by surprise at his instinctive response to this woman. It was an attraction so powerful he felt himself at once struggling to pull away.

He did. With a curt good-night, he walked out the front door.

Outside, in the darkness, he stood for a moment surveying the house. It seemed secure enough. With two other people inside, Nina should be safe. Still, he wondered whether those particular two people would be of much help in a crisis. A father soaking in a hot tub and a spandex-and-hormones stepmother didn't exactly inspire feelings of confidence. Nina, at least, was an intelligent woman; he knew she would be alert for signs of danger.

He drove back to Robert Bledsoe's house on Ocean View Drive and left the car on a side street around the corner.

With Nina's keys, he let himself in the front door and called Gillis to arrange for a surveillance team to patrol the area. Then he closed all the curtains and settled down to wait. It was nine o'clock.

At nine-thirty, he was already restless. He paced the living room, then roamed the kitchen, the dining room, the hallway. Any stalker watching the house would expect lights to go on and off in different rooms, at different times. Maybe their man was just waiting for the residents to go to bed.

Sam turned off the living room lights and went into the bedroom.

Nina had left the top dresser drawer hanging open. Sam, pacing the carpet, kept walking back and forth past that open drawer with its tempting glimpse of lingerie. Something black and silky lay on top, and one corner trailed partway out of the drawer. He couldn't resist the impulse. He halted by the dresser, picked up the item of lingerie, and held it up.

It was a short little spaghetti-strap thing, edged with lace, and designed to show a lot. An awful lot. He tossed it back in and slammed the drawer shut.

He was getting distracted again. This shouldn't be happening. Something about Nina Cormier, and his reaction to her, had him behaving like a damn rookie.

Before, in the line of duty, he'd brushed up against other women, including the occasional stunner. Women like that spandex bimbo, Daniella Cormier, Nina's stepmother. He'd managed to keep his trousers zipped up and his head firmly screwed on. It was both a matter of self-control as well as self-preservation. The women he met on the job were usually in some sort of trouble, and it was too easy for them to consider Sam their white knight, the masculine answer to all their problems.

It was a fantasy that never lasted. Sooner or later the knight gets stripped of his armor and they'd see him for what he really was: just a cop. Not rich, not brilliant. Not much of anything, in fact, to recommend him.

It had happened to him once. Just once. She'd been an aspiring actress trying to escape an abusive boyfriend; he'd been a rookie assigned to watch over her. The chemistry was right. The situation was right. But the girl was all wrong. For a few heady weeks, he'd been in love, had thought *she* was in love.

Then she'd dropped Sam like a hot potato.

He'd learned a hard but lasting lesson: romance and police work did not mix. He had never again crossed that line while on the job, and he wasn't about to do it with Nina Cormier, either.

He turned away from the dresser and was crossing to the opposite end of the room when he heard a thump.

It came from somewhere near the front of the house.

Instantly he killed the bedroom lights and reached for his gun. He eased into the hallway. At the doorway to the living room he halted, his gaze quickly sweeping the darkness.

The streetlight shone in dimly through the windows. He saw no movement in the room, no suspicious shadows.

There was a scraping sound, a soft jingle. It came from the front porch.

Sam shifted his aim to the front door. He was crouched and ready to fire as the door swung open. The silhouette of a man loomed against the backlight of the streetlamp.

"Police!" Sam yelled. *"Freeze!"*

Four

The silhouette froze.

"Hands up," ordered Sam. "Come on, *hands up!*"

Both hands shot up. "Don't hurt me!" came a terrified plea.

Sam edged over to the light switch and flipped it on. The sudden glare left both men blinking. Sam took one look at the man standing in front of him and cursed.

Footsteps pounded up the porch steps and two uniformed cops burst through the doorway, pistols drawn. "We got him covered, Navarro!" one of them yelled.

"You're right on time," muttered Sam in disgust. "Forget it. This isn't the guy." He holstered his gun and looked at the tall blond man, who was still wearing a look of terror on his face. "I'm Detective Sam Navarro, Portland Police. I presume you're Dr. Robert Bledsoe?"

Nervously Robert cleared his throat. "Yeah, that's me. What's going on? Why are you people in my house?"

"Where've you been all day, Dr. Bledsoe?"

"I've been—uh, may I put my hands down?"

"Of course."

Robert lowered his hands and glanced cautiously over his shoulder at the two cops standing behind him. "Do they, uh, really need to keep pointing those guns at me?"

"You two can leave," Sam said to the cops. "I'm all right here."

"What about the surveillance?" one of them asked. "Want to call it off?"

"I doubt anything's coming down tonight. But hang around the neighborhood. Just until morning."

The two cops left. Sam said, again, "Where've you been, Dr. Bledsoe?"

With two guns no longer pointed at his back, Robert's terror had given way to righteous anger. He glared at Sam. "First, you tell me why you're in my house! What is this, a police state? Cops breaking in and threatening homeowners? You have no authority to be trespassing on my property. I'll have your ass in a sling if you don't produce a search warrant right now!"

"I don't have a warrant."

"You don't?" Robert gave an unpleasantly triumphant laugh. "You entered my house without a warrant? You break in here and threaten me with your macho cop act?"

"I didn't break in," Sam told him calmly. "I let myself in the front door."

"Oh, sure."

Sam pulled out Nina's keys and held them up in front of Robert. "With these."

"Those—those keys belong to my fiancée! How did you get them?"

"She lent them to me."

"She *what?*" Robert's voice had risen to a yelp of

anger. "Where is Nina? She had no right to hand over the keys to my house."

"Correction, Doctor. Nina Cormier was living here with you. That makes her a legal resident of this house. It gives her the right to authorize police entry, which she did." Sam eyed the man squarely. "Now, I'll ask the question a third time. Where have you been, Doctor?"

"Away," snapped Robert.

"Could you be more specific?"

"All right, I went to Boston. I needed to get out of town for a while."

"Why?"

"What is this, an interrogation? I don't have to talk to you! In fact I *shouldn't* talk to you until I call my lawyer." He turned to the telephone and picked up the receiver.

"You don't need a lawyer. Unless you've committed a crime."

"A crime?" Robert spun around and stared at him. "Are you accusing me of something?"

"I'm not accusing you of anything. But I do need answers. Are you aware of what happened in the church today?"

Robert replaced the receiver. Soberly he nodded. "I...I heard there was some sort of explosion. It was on the news. That's why I came back early. I was worried someone might've been hurt."

"Luckily, no one was. The church was empty at the time it happened."

Robert gave a sigh of relief. "Thank God," he said softly. He stood with his hand still on the phone, as though debating whether to pick it up again. "Do the police—do you—know what caused it?"

"Yes. It was a bomb."

Robert's chin jerked up. He stared at Sam. Slowly he sank into the nearest chair. "All I'd heard was—the radio said—it was an explosion. There was nothing about a bomb."

"We haven't made a public statement yet."

Robert looked up at him. "Why the hell would anyone bomb a church?"

"That's what we're trying to find out. If the wedding had taken place, dozens of people might be dead right now. Nina told me you're the one who called it off. Why did you?"

"I just couldn't go through with it." Robert dropped his head in his hands. "I wasn't ready to get married."

"So your reason was entirely personal?"

"What else would it be?" Robert suddenly looked up with an expression of stunned comprehension. "Oh, my God. You didn't think the bomb had something to do with *me?*"

"It did cross my mind. Consider the circumstances. You cancelled the wedding without warning. And then you skipped town. Of course we wondered about your motives. Whether you'd received some kind of threat and decided to run."

"No, that's not at all what happened. I called it off because I didn't want to get married."

"Mind telling me why?"

Robert's face tightened. "Yes, as a matter of fact," he answered. Abruptly he rose from the chair and strode over to the liquor cabinet. There he poured himself a shot of Scotch and stood gulping it, not looking at Sam.

"I've met your fiancée," stated Sam. "She seems like a nice woman. Bright, attractive." *I'm sure as hell attracted to her,* he couldn't help adding to himself.

"You're asking why I left her at the altar, aren't you?" said Robert.

"Why did you?"

Robert finished off his drink and poured himself another.

"Did you two have an argument?"

"No."

"What was it, Dr. Bledsoe? Cold feet? Boredom?" Sam paused. "Another woman?"

Robert turned and glared at him. "This is none of your damn business. Get out of my house."

"If you insist. But I'll be talking to you again." Sam crossed to the front door, then stopped and turned back. "Do you know anyone who'd want to hurt your fiancée?"

"No."

"Anyone who'd want her dead?"

"What a ridiculous question."

"Someone tried to run her car off the road this afternoon."

Robert jerked around and stared at him. He looked genuinely startled. "*Nina?* Who did?"

"That's what I'm trying to find out. It may or may not be connected to the bombing. Do you have any idea at all what's going on? Who might try to hurt her?"

There was a split second's hesitation before Robert answered. "No. No one I can think of. Where is she?"

"She's in a safe place for tonight. But she can't stay in hiding forever. So if you think of anything, give me a call. If you still care about her."

Robert didn't say anything.

Sam turned and left the house.

Driving home, he used his car phone to dial Gillis. His partner, predictably, was still at his desk. "The bridegroom's back in town," Sam told him. "He claims he has no idea why the church was bombed."

"Why am I not surprised?" Gillis drawled.

"Anything new turn up?"

"Yeah. We're missing a janitor."

"What?"

"The church janitor. The one who unlocked the building this morning. We've been trying to track him down all evening. He never got home tonight."

Sam felt his pulse give a little gallop of excitement. "Interesting."

"We've already got an APB out. The man's name is Jimmy Brogan. And he has a record. Petty theft four years ago and two OUI's, that kind of stuff. Nothing major. I sent Cooley out to talk to the wife and check the house."

"Does Brogan have any explosives experience?"

"Not that we can determine. The wife swears up and down that he's clean. And he's always home for dinner."

"Give me more, Gillis. Give me more."

"That's all I have to give, unless you want me to slit open a vein. Right now I'm bushed and I'm going home."

"Okay, call it a day. I'll see you in the morning."

All the way home, Sam's mind was churning with facts. A cancelled wedding. A missing church janitor. An assassin in a black Ford.

And a bomb.

Where did Nina Cormier fit in this crazy thicket of events?

It was eleven-thirty when he finally arrived home. He let himself in the front door, stepped into the house, and turned on the lights. The familiar clutter greeted him. What a god-awful mess. One of these days he'd have to clean up the place. Or maybe he should just move; that'd be easier.

He walked through the living room, picking up dirty laundry and dishes as he went. He left the dishes in the kitchen sink, threw the laundry in the washing machine, and started the wash cycle. A Saturday night, and the swinging bachelor does his laundry. Wow. He stood in his kitchen, listening to the machine rumble, thinking about all the things he could do to make this house more of a home. Furniture, maybe? It was a good, sound little house, but he kept comparing it to Robert Bledsoe's house with its Steinway piano, the sort of house any woman would be delighted to call home.

Hell, Sam wouldn't know what to do with a woman even if one was crazy enough to move in with him. He'd been a bachelor too long, alone too long. There'd been the occasional woman, of course, but none of them had ever lasted. Too often, he had to admit, the fault lay with him. Or with his work. They couldn't understand why any man in his right mind would actually choose to stay with this insane job of bombs and bombers. They took it as a personal affront that he wouldn't quit the job and chose *them* instead.

Maybe he'd just never found a woman who made him *want* to quit.

And this is the result, he thought, gazing wearily at the basket of unfolded clothes. The swinging bachelor life.

He left the washing machine to finish its cycle and headed off to bed.

As usual, alone.

THE LIGHTS WERE ON at 318 Ocean View Drive. Someone was home. The Cormier woman? Robert Bledsoe? Or both of them?

Driving slowly past the house in his green Jeep Cherokee, he took a good long look at the house. He noted the dense shrubbery near the windows, the shadow of pine and birch trees ringing both edges of the property. Plenty of cover. Plenty of concealment.

Then he noticed the unmarked car parked a block away. It was backlit by a streetlamp, and he could see the silhouettes of two men sitting inside. *Police,* he thought. They were watching the house.

Tonight was not the time to do it.

He rounded the corner and drove on.

This matter could wait. It was only a bit of cleanup, a loose end that he could attend to in his spare time.

He had other, more important work to complete, and only a week in which to do it.

He drove on, toward the city.

AT 9:00 a.m., the guards came to escort Billy "The Snowman" Binford from his jail cell.

His attorney, Albert Darien, was waiting for him. Through the Plexiglas partition separating the two men, Billy could see Darien's grim expression and he knew that the news was not good. Billy sat down opposite his attorney. The guard wasn't standing close enough to catch their conversation, but Billy knew better than to speak freely. That stuff about attorney-client confidentiality was a bunch of bull. If the feds or the D.A. wanted you bad enough, they'd plant a bug on anyone, even your priest. It was outrageous, how they'd violate a citizen's rights.

"Hello, Billy," said Darien through the speaker phone. "How're they treating you?"

"Like a sultan. How the hell d'you *think* they're treating me? You gotta get me a few favors, Darien. A private TV. I'd like a private TV."

"Billy, we got problems."

Billy didn't like the tone of Darien's voice. "What problems?" he asked.

"Liddell's not even going to discuss a plea bargain. He's set on taking this to trial. Any other D.A.'d save himself the trouble, but I think Liddell's using you as a stepping stone to Blaine House."

"Liddell's running for governor?"

"He hasn't announced it. But if he puts you away, he'll be golden. And Billy, to be honest, he's got more than enough to put you away."

Billy leaned forward and glared through the Plexiglas at his attorney. "That's what I pay *you* for. So what the hell're you doing about the situation?"

"They've got too much. Hobart's turned state's witness."

"Hobart's a sleazeball. It'll be a piece of cake to discredit him."

"They've got your shipping records. It's all on paper, Billy."

"Okay, then let's try again with a plea bargain. Anything. Just keep my time in here short."

"I told you, Liddell's nixed a plea bargain."

Billy paused. Softly he said, "Liddell can be taken care of."

Darien stared at him. "What do you mean?"

"You just get me a deal. Don't worry about Liddell. I'm taking care of—"

"I don't want to know about it." Darien sat back, his hands suddenly shaking. "I don't want to know a damn thing, okay?"

"You don't have to. I got it covered."

"Just don't get me involved."

"All I want from you, Darien, is to keep this from going to trial. And get me out of here soon. You got that?"

"Yeah. Yeah." Darien glanced nervously at the guard, who wasn't paying the least bit of attention to their conversation. "I'll try."

"Just watch," said Billy. A cocky grin spread on his lips. "Next week, things'll be different. D.A.'s office will be happy to talk plea bargain."

"Why? What happens next week?"

"You don't want to know."

Darien exhaled a deep sigh and nodded. "You're right," he muttered. "I don't want to know."

NINA AWAKENED to the bass thump of aerobics dance music. Downstairs, she found Daniella stretched out on the polished oak floor of the exercise room. This morning Daniella was garbed in a shiny pink leotard, and her sleek legs knifed effortlessly through the air with every beat of the music. Nina stood watching in fascination for a moment, mesmerized by that display of taut muscles. Daniella worked hard at her body. In fact, she did little else. Since her marriage to George Cormier, Daniella's only goal in life seemed to be physical perfection.

The music ended. Daniella sprang to her feet with an easy grace. As she turned to reach for a towel, she noticed Nina standing in the doorway. "Oh. Good morning."

"Morning," said Nina. "I guess I overslept. Has Dad already left for work?"

"You know how he is. Likes to get started at the crack of dawn." With the towel, Daniella whisked away a delicate sheen of perspiration. A discomforting silence stretched between them. It always did. It was more than just the awkwardness of their relationship, the bizarre reality that this golden goddess was technically Nina's stepmother. It was also the fact that, except for their connection through George Cormier, the two women had absolutely nothing in common.

And never had that seemed more apparent to Nina than at this moment, as she stood gazing at the perfect face of this perfect blonde.

Daniella climbed onto an exercise bike and began pedaling away. Over the whir of the wheel, she said, "George had some board meeting. He'll be home for dinner. Oh, and you got two phone calls this morning. One was from that policeman. You know, the cute one."

"Detective Navarro?"

"Yeah. He was checking up on you."

So he's worried about me, thought Nina, feeling an unexpected lifting of her spirits. He'd cared enough to make sure she was alive and well. Then again, maybe he was just checking to make sure he didn't have a new corpse on his hands.

Yes, that was the likely reason he'd called.

Feeling suddenly glum, Nina turned to leave the room, then stopped. "What about the second call?" she asked. "You said there were two."

"Oh, right." Daniella, still pumping away, looked serenely over the handlebars. "The other call was from Robert."

Nina stared at her in shocked silence. "Robert called?"

"He wanted to know if you were here."

"Where is *he?*"

"At home."

Nina shook her head in disbelief. "You might have told me earlier."

"You were sound asleep. I didn't see the point of waking

you." Daniella leaned into the handlebars and began to pedal with singleminded concentration. "Besides, he'll call back later."

I'm not waiting till later, thought Nina. *I want answers now. And I want them face-to-face.*

Heart thudding, she left the house. She borrowed her father's Mercedes to drive to Ocean View Drive. He'd never miss it; after all, he kept a spare Jaguar and a BMW in the garage.

By the time she pulled into Robert's driveway, she was shaking from both anger and dread. What on earth was she going to say to him?

What was he going to say to *her?*

She climbed the porch steps and rang the doorbell. She didn't have her house keys. Sam Navarro did. Anyway, this wasn't her house any longer. It never had been.

The door swung open and Robert stood looking at her in surprise. He was wearing running shorts and a T-shirt, and his face had the healthy flush of recent exercise. Not exactly the picture of a man pining for his fiancée.

"Uh, Nina," he said. "I—I was worried about you."

"Somehow I have a hard time believing that."

"I even called your father's house—"

"What happened, Robert?" Her breath rushed out in a bewildered sigh. "Why did you walk out on me?"

He looked away. That alone told her how far apart they'd drifted. "It's not easy to explain."

"It wasn't easy for me, either. Telling everyone to go home. Not knowing why it fell apart. You could have told me. A week before. A *day* before. Instead you leave me there, holding the damn bouquet! Wondering if it was all *my* fault. Something *I* did wrong."

"It wasn't you, Nina."

"What was it, then?"

He didn't answer. He just kept looking away, unwilling to face her. Maybe afraid to face her.

"I lived with you for a whole year," she said with sad wonder. "And I don't have the faintest idea who you are." With a stifled sob, she pushed past him, into the house, and headed straight for the bedroom.

"What are you doing?" he yelled.

"Packing the rest of my things. And getting the hell out of your life."

"Nina, there's no need to be uncivilized about this. We tried to make it. It just didn't work out. Why can't we still be friends?"

"Is that what we are? Friends?"

"I like to think so. I don't see why we can't be."

She shook her head and laughed. A bitter sound. "*Friends* don't twist the knife after they stab you." She stalked into the bedroom and began yanking open drawers. She pulled out clothes and tossed them on the bed. She was beyond caring about neatness; all she wanted was to get out of this house and never see it again. Or him again. Up until a moment ago, she'd thought it still possible to salvage their relationship, to pick up the pieces and work toward some sort of life together. Now she knew there wasn't a chance of it. She didn't want *him*. She couldn't even recall what it was about Robert Bledsoe that had attracted her. His looks, his medical degree—those were things she'd considered nice but not that important. No, what she'd seen in Robert—or imagined she'd seen—was intelligence and wit and caring. He'd shown her all those things.

What an act.

Robert was watching her with a look of wounded nobility. As if this was all her fault. She ignored him and went to the closet, raked out an armful of dresses, and dumped them on the bed. The pile was so high it was starting to topple.

"Does it all have to be done right now?" he asked.

"Yes."

"There aren't enough suitcases."

"Then I'll use trash bags. And I need to take my books, too."

"Today? But you've got tons of them!"

"This week I've got tons of time. Since I skipped the honeymoon."

"You're being unreasonable. Look, I know you're angry. You have a right to be. But don't go flying off the damn handle."

"I'll fly off the handle if I *want* to!" she yelled.

The sound of a throat being cleared made them both turn in surprise. Sam Navarro stood in the bedroom doorway, looking at them with an expression of quiet bemusement.

"Don't you cops *ever* bother to knock?" snapped Robert.

"I did knock," said Sam. "No one answered. And you left the front door wide open."

"You're trespassing," said Robert. "*Again* without a warrant."

"He doesn't need a warrant," said Nina.

"The law says he does."

"Not if I invite him in!"

"You didn't invite him in. He *walked* in."

"The door was open," said Sam. "I was concerned." He looked at Nina. "That wasn't smart, Miss Cormier, driving here alone. You should have told me you were leaving your father's house."

"What am I, your prisoner?" she muttered and crossed back to the closet for another armload of clothes. "How did you track me down, anyway?"

"I called your stepmother right after you left the house. She thought you'd be here."

"Well, I am. And I happen to be busy."

"Yeah," muttered Robert. "She's really good at being busy."

Nina spun around to confront her ex-fiancé. "What's that supposed to mean?"

"I'm not the only one to blame in all this! It takes two people to screw up a relationship."

"I didn't leave *you* at the church!"

"No, but you left me. Every night, for months on end."

"What? *What?*"

"Every damn night, I was here on my own! I would have enjoyed coming home to a nice meal. But you were never here."

"They needed me on the evening shift. I couldn't change that!"

"You could've quit."

"Quit my *job?* To do what? Play happy homemaker to a man who couldn't even decide if he wanted to marry me?"

"If you loved me, you would have."

"Oh, my God. I can't believe you're turning this into my fault. I didn't *love* you enough."

Sam said, "Nina, I need to talk to you."

"Not now!" Nina and Robert both snapped at him.

Robert said to her, "I just think you should know I had my reasons for not going through with it. A guy has only so much patience. And then it's natural to start looking elsewhere."

"Elsewhere?" She stared at him with new comprehension. Softly she said, "So there was someone else."

"What do you think?"

"Do I know her?"

"It hardly makes a difference now."

"It does to *me*. When did you meet her?"

He looked away. "A while ago."

"How long?"

"Look, this is irrelevant—"

"For six months, we planned that wedding. Both of us. And you never bothered to tell me the minor detail that you were seeing another woman?"

"It's clear to me you're not rational at the moment. Until you are, I'm not discussing this." Robert turned and left the room.

"Not *rational?*" she yelled. "I'm more rational now than I was six months ago!"

She was answered by the thud of the front door as it slammed shut.

Another woman, she thought. *I never knew. I never even suspected.*

Suddenly feeling sick to her stomach, she sank down on the bed. The pile of clothes tumbled onto the floor, but she didn't even notice. Nor did she realize that she was crying, that the tears were dribbling down her cheeks and onto her shirt. She was both sick and numb at the same time, and oblivious to everything but her own pain.

She scarcely noticed that Sam had sat down beside her.

"He's not worth it, Nina," he soothed quietly. "He's not worth grieving over."

Only when his hand closed warmly over hers did she look up. She found his gaze focused steadily on her face. "I'm not grieving," she said.

Gently he brushed his fingers across her cheek, which was wet with tears. "I think you are."

"I'm not. I'm *not.*" She gave a sob and sagged against him, burying her face in his shirt. "I'm not," she whispered against his chest.

Only vaguely did she sense his arms folding around her back, gathering her against him. Suddenly those arms were holding her close, wrapping tightly around her. He didn't say a thing. As always, the laconic cop. But she felt his breath warming her hair, felt his lips brush the top of her head, and she heard the quickening of his heartbeat.

Just as she felt the quickening of her own.

It means nothing, she thought. He was being kind to her. Comforting her the way he would any hurt citizen. It was what she did every day in the ER. It was her job. It was his job.

Oh, but this felt so good.

It took a ruthless act of pure will to pull out of his arms. When she looked up, she found his expression calm, his green eyes unreadable. No passion, no desire. Just the public servant, in full control of his emotions.

Quickly she wiped away her tears. She felt stupid now, embarrassed by what he'd just witnessed between her and Robert. He knew it all, every humiliating detail, and she could scarcely bear to look him in the eye.

She stood up and began to gather the fallen clothes from the floor.

"You want to talk about it?" he asked.

"No."

"I think you need to. The man you loved leaves you for another woman. That must hurt pretty bad."

"Okay, I *do* need to talk about it!" She threw a handful of clothes on the bed and looked at him. "But not with some stone-faced cop who couldn't care less!"

There was a long silence. Though he looked at her without a flicker of emotion, she sensed that she'd just delivered a body blow. And he was too proud to show it.

She shook her head. "I'm sorry. Oh God, Navarro, I'm so sorry. You didn't deserve that."

"Actually," he said, "I think I did."

"You're just doing your job. And then I go and lash out at you." Thoroughly disgusted with herself, she sat down beside him on the bed. "I was just taking it out on you. I'm so—so angry at myself for letting him make me feel guilty."

"Why guilty?"

"That's the crazy part about it! I don't know why I should feel guilty! He makes it sound as if I neglected him. But I could never quit my job, even for him. I love my job."

"He's a doctor. He must've had long hours as well. Nights, weekends."

"He worked a lot of weekends."

"Did you complain?"

"Of course not. That's his job."

"Well?" He regarded her with a raised eyebrow.

"Oh." She sighed. "The old double standard."

"Exactly. I wouldn't expect my wife to quit a job she loved, just to make dinner and wait on me every night."

She stared down at her hands, clasped in her lap. "You wouldn't?"

"That's not love. That's possession."

"I think your wife's a very lucky woman," she said softly.

"I was only speaking theoretically."

She frowned at him. "You mean…it was just a theoretical wife?"

He nodded.

So he wasn't married. That piece of information made her flush with a strange and unexpected gladness. What on earth was the matter with her?

She looked away, afraid that he might see the confusion in her eyes. "You, uh, said you needed to talk to me."

"It's about the case."

"It must be pretty important if you went to all the trouble of tracking me down."

"I'm afraid we have a new development. Not a pleasant one."

She went very still. "Something's happened?"

"Tell me what you know about the church janitor."

She shook her head in bewilderment. "I don't know him at all. I don't even know his name."

"His name was Jimmy Brogan. We spent all yesterday evening trying to track Brogan down. We know he unlocked the church door yesterday. That he was in and out of the building all morning. But no one seems to know where he went after the explosion. We know he didn't turn up at the neighborhood bar where he usually goes every afternoon."

"You said *was*. That his name *was* Jimmy Brogan. Does that mean…"

Sam nodded. "We found his body this morning. He was in his car, parked in a field in Scarborough. He died from a gunshot wound to the head. The gun was in the car with him. It had his fingerprints on it."

"A suicide?" she asked softly.

"That's the way it looks."

She was silent, too shocked to say a thing.

"We're still waiting for the crime lab report. There are a number of details that bother me. It feels too neat, too packaged. It ties up every single loose end we've got."

"Including the bombing?"

"Including the bombing. There were several items in the car trunk that would seem to link Brogan to the bomb. Detonating cord. Green electrical tape. It's all pretty convincing evidence."

"You don't sound convinced."

"The problem is, Brogan had no explosives experience that we know of. Also, we can't come up with a motive for any bombing. Or for the attack on you. Can you help us out?"

She shook her head. "I don't know anything about the man."

"Are you familiar with the name Brogan?"

"No."

"He was familiar with *you*. There was a slip of paper with your address in his car."

She stared at him. His gaze was impenetrable. It frightened her, how little she could read in his eyes. How deeply the man was buried inside the cop. "Why would he have my address?" she asked.

"You must have some link to him."

"I don't know anyone named Brogan."

"Why would he try to kill you? Run you off the road?"

"How do you know *he* did it?"

"Because of his car. The one we found his body in."

She swallowed hard. "It was black?"

He nodded. "A black Ford."

Five

Sam drove her to the morgue. Neither one of them said much. He was being guarded about what information he told her, and she was too chilled to ask for the details. All the way there, she kept thinking, *Who was Jimmy Brogan and why did he want to kill me?*

In the morgue, Sam maintained a firm grip on her arm as they walked the corridor to the cold room. He was right beside her when the attendant led them to the bank of body drawers. As the drawer was pulled out she involuntarily flinched. Sam's arm came around her waist, a steady support against the terrible sight she was about to face.

"It ain't pretty," said the attendant. "Are you ready?"

Nina nodded.

He pulled aside the shroud and stepped back.

As an ER nurse, Nina had seen more than her share of grisly sights. This was by far the worst. She took one look at the man's face—what was left of it—and quickly turned away. "I don't know him," she whispered.

"Are you sure?" Sam asked.

She nodded and suddenly felt herself swaying. At once he was supporting her, his arm guiding her away from the drawers. Away from the cold room.

In the coroner's office she sat nursing a cup of hot tea while Sam talked on the phone to his partner. Only vaguely did she register his conversation. His tone was as matter-of-fact as always, betraying no hint of the horror he'd just witnessed.

"…doesn't recognize him. Or the name either. Are you sure we don't have an alias?" Sam was saying.

Nina cupped the tea in both hands but didn't sip. Her stomach was still too queasy. On the desk beside her was the file for Jimmy Brogan, open to the ID information sheet. Most of what she saw there didn't stir any memories. Not his address nor the name of his wife. Only the name of the employer was familiar: the Good Shepherd Church. She wondered if Father Sullivan had been told, wondered how he was faring in the hospital. It would be a double shock to the elderly man. First, the bombing of his church, and then the death of the janitor. She should visit him today and make sure he was doing all right…

"Thanks, Gillis. I'll be back at three. Yeah, set it up, will you?" Sam hung up and turned to her. Seeing her face, he frowned in concern. "You all right?"

"I'm fine." She shuddered and clutched the mug more tightly.

"You don't look fine. I think you need some recovery time. Come on." He offered his hand. "It's lunchtime. There's a café up the street."

"You can think about lunch?"

"I make it a point never to skip a chance at a meal. Or would you rather I take you home?"

"Anything," she said, rising from the chair. "Just get me out of this place."

NINA PICKED LISTLESSLY at a salad while Sam wolfed down a hamburger.

"I don't know how you do it," she said. "How you go straight from the morgue to a big lunch."

"Necessity." He shrugged. "In this job, a guy can get skinny real fast."

"You must see so many awful things as a cop."

"You're an ER nurse. I would think you've seen your share."

"Yes. But they usually come to us still alive."

He wiped his hands on a napkin and slid his empty plate aside. "True. If it's a bomb, by the time I get to the scene, we're lucky to find anyone alive. If we find much of them at all."

"How do you live with it? How do you stand a job like yours?"

"The challenge."

"Really, Navarro. How do you deal with the horror?"

"My name's Sam, okay? And as for how I deal with it, it's more a question of *why* I do it. The truth is, the challenge is a lot of it. People who make bombs are a unique breed of criminal. They're not like the guy who holds up your neighborhood liquor store. Bombers are craftier. A few of them are truly geniuses. But they're also cowards. Killers at a distance. It's that combination that makes those guys especially dangerous. And it makes my job all the more satisfying when I can nail them."

"So you actually enjoy it."

"*Enjoy* isn't the right word. It's more that I can't set the puzzle aside. I keep looking at the pieces and turning them around. Trying to understand the sort of mind that could do such a thing." He shook his head. "Maybe that makes me just as much a monster. That I find it so satisfying to match wits with these guys."

"Or maybe it means you're an outstanding cop."

He laughed. "Either that or I'm as screwy as the bombers are."

She gazed across the table at his smiling face and suddenly wondered why she'd ever considered those eyes of his so forbidding. One laugh and Sam Navarro transformed from a cop into an actual human being. And a very attractive man.

I'm not going to let this happen, she thought with sudden determination. *It would be such a mistake to rebound from Robert, straight into some crazy infatuation with a cop.*

She forced herself to look away, at anything but his face, and ended up focusing on his hands. At the long, tanned fingers. She said, "If Brogan was the bomber, then I guess I have nothing to worry about now."

"If he was the bomber."

"The evidence seems pretty strong. Why don't you sound convinced?"

"I can't explain it. It's just…a feeling. Instinct, I guess. That's why I still want you to be careful."

She lifted her gaze to meet his and found his smile was gone. The cop was back.

"You don't think it's over yet," she said.

"No. I don't."

SAM DROVE NINA BACK to Ocean View Drive, helped her load up the Mercedes with a few armloads of books and clothes, and made sure she was safely on her way back to her father's house.

Then he returned to the station.

At three o'clock, they held a catch-up meeting. Sam, Gillis, Tanaka from the crime lab, and a third detective on the Bomb Task Force, Francis Cooley, were in attendance. Everyone laid their puzzle pieces on the table.

Cooley spoke first. "I've checked and rechecked the records on Jimmy Brogan. There's no alias for the guy. That's his real name. Forty-five years old, born and raised in South Portland, minor criminal record. Married ten years, no kids. He was hired by Reverend Sullivan eight years ago. Worked as a janitor and handyman around the church. Never any problems, except for a few times when he showed up late and hung over after falling off the wagon. No military service, no education beyond the eleventh grade. Wife says he was dyslexic. I just can't see this guy putting together a bomb."

"Did Mrs. Brogan have any idea why Nina Cormier's address was in his car?" Sam asked.

"Nope. She'd never heard the name before. And she said the handwriting wasn't her husband's."

"Were they having any marital troubles?"

"Happy as clams, from what she told me. She's pretty devastated."

"So we've got a happily married, uneducated, dyslexic janitor as our prime suspect?"

"Afraid so, Navarro."

Sam shook his head. "This gets worse every minute." He looked at Tanaka. "Eddie, give us some answers. Please."

Tanaka, nervous as usual, cleared his throat. "You're not going to like what I have."

"Hit me anyway."

"Okay. First, the gun in the car was reported stolen a year ago from its registered owner in Miami. We don't know how Brogan got the gun. His wife says he didn't know the first thing about firearms. Second, Brogan's car *was* the black Ford that forced Miss Cormier's Honda off the road. Paint chips match, both ways. Third, the items in the trunk are the same elements used in the church bombing. Two-inch-wide green electrical tape. Identical detonator cord."

"That's Vincent Spectre's signature," said Gillis. "Green electrical tape."

"Which means we're probably dealing with an apprentice of Spectre's. Now here's something else you're not going to like. We just got back the preliminary report from the coroner. The corpse had no traces of gunpowder on his hand. Now, that's not necessarily conclusive, since powder can rub off, but it does argue against a self-inflicted wound. What clinches it, though, is the skull fracture."

"What?" Sam and Gillis said it simultaneously.

"A depressed skull fracture, right parietal bone. Because of all the tissue damage from the bullet wound, it wasn't immediately obvious. But it did show up on X ray. Jimmy Brogan was hit on the head. *Before* he was shot."

The silence in the room stretched for a good ten seconds. Then Gillis said, "And I almost bought it. Lock, stock and barrel."

"He's good," said Sam. "But not good enough." He looked at Cooley. "I want more on Brogan. I want you and your team to get the names of every friend, every acquaintance Brogan had. Talk to them all. It looks like our janitor got mixed up with the wrong guy. Maybe someone knows something, saw something."

"Won't the boys in Homicide be beating those bushes?"

"We'll beat 'em as well. They may miss something. And don't get into any turf battles, okay? We're not trying to steal their glory. We just want the bomber."

Cooley sighed and rose to his feet. "Guess it's back to the ol' widow Brogan."

"Gillis," said Sam, "I need you to talk to the best man and the matron of honor again. See if they have any links to Brogan. Or recognize his photo. I'll go back to the hospital and talk to Reverend Sullivan. And I'll talk to Dr. Bledsoe as well."

"What about the bride?" asked Gillis.

"I've pressed the questions a couple times already. She denies knowing anything about him."

"She seems to be the center of it all."

"I know. And she hasn't the foggiest idea why. But maybe her ex-bridegroom does."

The meeting broke up and everyone headed off to their respective tasks. It would take teamwork to find this bomber, and although he had good people working with him, Sam knew they were stretched thin. Since that rookie cop's death in the warehouse blast a week ago, Homicide had stepped into the investigation, and they were sucking up men and resources like crazy. As far as Homicide was concerned, the Bomb Task Force was little more than a squad of "techies"—the guys you called in when you didn't want your own head blown off.

The boys in Homicide were smart enough.

But the boys in Bombs were smarter.

That's why Sam himself drove out to Maine Medical

Center to reinterview Reverend Sullivan. This latest information on Jimmy Brogan's death had opened up a whole new range of possibilities. Perhaps Brogan had been a completely innocent patsy. Perhaps he'd witnessed something—and had mentioned it to the minister.

At the hospital, Sam learned that Reverend Sullivan had been transferred out of Intensive Care that morning. A heart attack had been ruled out, and Sullivan was now on a regular ward.

When Sam walked in the man's room, he found the minister sitting up in bed, looking glum. There was a visitor there already—Dick Yeats of Homicide. Not one of Sam's favorite people.

"Hey, Navarro," said Yeats in that cocky tone of his. "No need to spin your wheels here. We're on the Brogan case."

"I'd like to talk to Reverend Sullivan myself."

"He doesn't know anything helpful."

"Nevertheless," said Sam, "I'd like to ask my own questions."

"Suit yourself," Yeats said as he headed out the door. "Seems to me, though, that you boys in Bombs could make better use of your time if you'd let Homicide do its job."

Sam turned to the elderly minister, who was looking very unhappy about talking to yet another cop.

"I'm sorry, Reverend," said Sam. "But I'm afraid I'm going to have to ask you some more questions."

Reverend Sullivan sighed, the weariness evident in his lined face. "I can't tell you more than I already have."

"You've been told about Brogan's death?"

"Yes. That policeman—that Homicide person—"

"Detective Yeats."

"He was far more graphic than necessary. I didn't need all the…details."

Sam sat down in a chair. The minister's color was better today, but he still looked frail. The events of the last twenty-four hours must be devastating for him. First the destruction of his church building, and then the violent death of his handyman. Sam hated to flog the old man with yet more questions, but he had no choice.

Unfortunately, he could elicit no new answers. Reverend Sullivan knew nothing about Jimmy Brogan's private life. Nor could he think of a single reason why Brogan, or anyone else for that matter, would attack the Good Shepherd Church. There had been minor incidents, of course. A few acts of vandalism and petty theft. That's why he had started locking the church doors at night, a move that grieved him deeply as he felt churches should be open to those in need, day or night. But the insurance company had insisted, and so Reverend Sullivan had instructed his staff to lock up every evening at 6:00 p.m., and reopen every morning at 7:00 a.m.

"And there've been no acts of vandalism since?" asked Sam.

"None whatsoever," affirmed the minister. "That is, until the bomb."

This was a dead end, thought Sam. Yeats was right. He was just spinning his wheels.

As he rose to leave, there was a knock on the door. A heavyset woman poked her head in the room.

"Reverend Sullivan?" she said. "Is this a good time to visit?"

The gloom on the minister's face instantly transformed

to a look of relief. Thankfulness. "Helen! I'm so glad you're back! Did you hear what happened?"

"On the television, this morning. As soon as I saw it, I packed my things and started straight back for home." The woman, carrying a bundle of carnations, crossed to the bed and gave Reverend Sullivan a tearful hug. "I just saw the church. I drove right past it. Oh, what a mess."

"You don't know the worst of it," said Reverend Sullivan. He swallowed. "Jimmy's dead."

"Dear God." Helen pulled back in horror. "Was it…in the explosion?"

"No. They're saying he shot himself. I didn't even know he had a gun."

Helen took an unsteady step backward. At once Sam grasped her ample arm and guided her into the chair from which he'd just risen. She sat quivering, her face white with shock.

"Excuse me, ma'am," said Sam gently. "I'm Detective Navarro, Portland Police. May I ask your full name?"

She swallowed. "Helen Whipple."

"You're the church secretary?"

She looked up at him with dazed eyes. "Yes. Yes."

"We've been trying to contact you, Miss Whipple."

"I was—I was at my sister's house. In Amherst." She sat twisting her hands together, shaking her head. "I can't believe this. I saw Jimmy only yesterday. I can't believe he's gone."

"You saw Brogan? What time?"

"It was in the morning. Just before I left town." She began digging in her purse, desperately fishing for tissues. "I stopped in to pay a few bills before I left."

"Did you two speak?"

"Naturally. Jimmy's such…" She gave a soft sob. "*Was* such…a friendly man. He was always coming up to the office to chat. Since I was leaving on vacation, and Reverend Sullivan wasn't in yet. I asked Jimmy to do a few things for me."

"What things?"

"Oh, there was so much confusion. The wedding, you know. The florist kept popping in to use the phone. The men's bathroom sink was leaking and we needed some plumbing done quick. I had to give Jimmy some last minute instructions. Everything from where to put the wedding gifts to which plumber to call. I was so relieved when Reverend Sullivan arrived, and I could leave."

"Excuse me, ma'am," Sam cut in. "You said something about wedding gifts."

"Yes. It's a nuisance, how some people have gifts delivered to the church instead of the bride's home."

"How many gifts arrived at the church?"

"There was only one. Jimmy—oh, poor Jimmy. It's so unfair. A wife and all…"

Sam fought to maintain his patience. "What about the gift?"

"Oh. That. Jimmy said a man brought it by. He showed it to me. Very nicely wrapped, with all these pretty silver bells and foil ribbons."

"Mrs. Whipple," Sam interrupted again. "What happened to that gift?"

"Oh, I don't know. I told Jimmy to give it to the bride's mother. I assume that's what he did."

"But the bride's mother hadn't arrived yet, right? So what would Jimmy do with it?"

Helplessly Helen Whipple shrugged her shoulders. "I

suppose he'd leave it where she'd be sure to find it. In the front pew."

The front pew. The center of the blast.

Sam said, sharply, "Who was the gift addressed to?"

"The bride and groom, of course."

"Dr. Bledsoe and his fiancée?"

"Yes. That was on the card. Dr. and Mrs. Robert Bledsoe."

IT WAS STARTING to come together now, Sam thought as he got back in his car. The method of delivery. The time of planting. But the target wasn't quite clear yet. Was Nina Cormier or Robert Bledsoe supposed to die? Or was it both of them?

Nina, he knew, had no answers, no knowledge of any enemies. She couldn't help him.

So Sam drove to Ocean View Drive, to Robert Bledsoe's house. This time Bledsoe was damn well going to answer some questions, the first two being: Who was the other woman he'd been seeing, and was she jealous enough to sabotage her lover's wedding—and kill off a dozen people in the process?

Two blocks before he got there, he knew something was wrong. There were police lights flashing ahead and spectators gathered on the sidewalks.

Sam parked the car and quickly pushed his way through the crowd. At the edge of Bledsoe's driveway, a yellow police tape had been strung between wooden stakes. He flashed his badge to the patrolman standing guard and stepped across the line.

Homicide Detective Dick Yeats greeted him in the driveway with his usual I'm-in-charge tone of superiority.

"Hello again, Navarro. We have it all under control."

"You have *what* under control? What happened?"

Yeats nodded toward the BMW in the driveway.

Slowly Sam circled around the rear bumper. Only then did he see the blood. It was all over the steering wheel and the front seat. A small pool of it had congealed on the driveway pavement.

"Robert Bledsoe," said Yeats. "Shot once in the temple. The ambulance just left. He's still alive, but I don't expect he'll make it. He'd just pulled into his driveway and was getting out of his car. There's a sack of groceries in the trunk. Ice cream barely melted. The neighbor saw a green Jeep take off, just before she noticed Bledsoe's body. She thinks it was a man behind the wheel, but she didn't see his face."

"A man?" Sam's head snapped up. "Dark hair?"

"Yeah."

"Oh, God." Sam turned and started toward his car. *Nina,* he thought, and suddenly he was running. A dark-haired man had forced Nina off the road. Now Bledsoe was dead. Was Nina next?

Sam heard Yeats yell, "Navarro!" By then, he was already scrambling into his car. He made a screeching U-turn and headed away from Ocean View Drive.

He drove with his emergency lights flashing all the way to George Cormier's house.

It seemed he was ringing the bell forever before anyone answered the door. Finally it swung open and Daniella appeared, her flawless face arranged in a smile. "Why, hello, Detective."

"Where's Nina?" he demanded, pushing past her into the house.

"She's upstairs. Why?"

"I need to talk to her. *Now.*" He started for the stairway, then halted when he heard footsteps creak on the landing above. Glancing up, he saw Nina standing on the steps, her hair a tumble of black silk.

She's okay, he thought with relief. *She's still okay.*

She was dressed casually in jeans and a T-shirt, and she had a purse slung over her shoulder, as if she were just about to leave the house.

As she came down the stairs, she brought with her the elusive fragrance of soap and shampoo. Nina's scent, he thought with a pleasurable thrill of recognition. Since when had he committed her fragrance to memory?

By the time she reached the bottom step, she was frowning at him. "Has something happened?" she asked.

"Then no one's called you?"

"About what?"

"Robert."

She went very still, her dark eyes focused with sudden intensity on his face. He could see the questions in her eyes, and knew she was too afraid to ask them.

He reached for her hand. It was cold. "You'd better come with me."

"Where?"

"The hospital. That's where they took him." Gently he led her to the door.

"Wait!" called Daniella.

Sam glanced back. Daniella stood frozen, staring after them in panic. "What about Robert? What happened?"

"He's been shot. It happened a short while ago, just outside his house. I'm afraid it doesn't look good."

Daniella took a step backward, as though slapped. It was her reaction, that expression of horror in her eyes, that told Sam what he needed to know. *So she was the other woman,* he thought. *This blonde with her sculpted body and her perfect face.*

He could feel Nina's arm trembling in his grasp. He turned her toward the door. "We'd better go," he said. "There may not be much time."

Six

They spent the next four hours in a hospital waiting room.

Though Nina wasn't part of the medical team now battling to save Robert's life, she could picture only too vividly what was going on at that moment in the trauma suite. The massive infusions of blood and saline. The scramble to control the patient's bleeding, to keep his pressure up, his heart beating. She knew it all well because, at other times, on other patients, she had been part of the team. Now she was relegated to this useless task of waiting and worrying. Though her relationship with Robert was irrevocably broken, though she hadn't forgiven him for the way he'd betrayed her, she certainly didn't want him hurt.

Or dead.

It was only Sam's presence that kept her calm and sane during that long evening. Other cops came and went. As the hours stretched on, only Sam stayed next to her on the couch, his hand clasping hers in a silent gesture of support. She could see that he was tired, but he didn't leave her. He stayed right beside her as the night wore on toward ten o'clock.

And he was there when the neurosurgeon came out to inform them that Robert had died on the operating table.

Nina took the blow in numb silence. She was too stunned to shed any tears, to say much more than "Thank you for trying." She scarcely realized Sam had his arm around her. Only when she sagged against him did she feel his support, steadying her.

"I'm going to take you home," he said softly. "There's nothing more you can do here."

Mutely she nodded. He helped her to her feet and guided her toward the exit. They were halfway across the room when a voice called, "Miss Cormier? I need to ask you some more questions."

Nina turned and looked at the rodent-faced man who'd just spoken to her. She couldn't remember his name, but she knew he was a cop; he'd been in and out of the waiting room all evening. Now he was studying her closely, and she didn't like the look in his eyes.

"Not now, Yeats," said Sam, nudging her to the exit. "It's a bad time."

"It's the best time to ask questions," said the other cop. "Right after the event."

"She's already told me she knew nothing about it."

"She hasn't told *me.*" Yeats turned his gaze back to Nina. "Miss Cormier, I'm with Homicide. Your fiancé never regained consciousness, so we couldn't question him. That's why I need to talk to you. Where were you this afternoon?"

Bewildered, Nina shook her head. "I was at my father's house. I didn't know about it until…"

"Until I told her," filled in Sam.

"*You* did, Navarro?"

"I went straight from the crime scene to her father's house. Nina was there. You can ask Daniella Cormier to confirm it."

"I will." Yeats's gaze was still fixed on Nina. "I understand you and Dr. Bledsoe just called off the engagement. And you were in the process of moving out of his house."

Softly Nina said, "Yes."

"I imagine you must have been pretty hurt. Did you ever consider, oh…getting back at him?"

Horrified by his implication, she gave a violent shake of her head. "You don't really think that—that I had something to do with this?"

"Did you?"

Sam stepped between them. "That's enough, Yeats."

"What are you, Navarro? Her lawyer?"

"She doesn't have to answer these questions."

"Yes, she does. Maybe not tonight. But she does have to answer questions."

Sam took Nina's arm and propelled her toward the exit.

"Watch it, Navarro!" Yeats yelled as they left the room. "You're on thin ice!"

Though Sam didn't answer, Nina could sense his fury just by the way he gripped her arm all the way to the parking lot.

When they were back in his car, she said, quietly, "Thank you, Sam."

"For what?"

"For getting me away from that awful man."

"Eventually, you *will* have to talk to him. Yeats may be a pain in the butt, but he has a job to do."

And so do you, she thought with a twinge of sadness. She turned to look out the window. He was the cop again, always the cop, trying to solve the puzzle. She was merely one of the pieces.

"You're going to have to talk to him tomorrow," said Sam. "Just a warning—he can be a tough interrogator."

"There's nothing I have to tell him. I was at my father's house. You know that. And Daniella will confirm it."

"No one can knock your alibi. But murder doesn't have to be done in person. Killers can be hired."

She turned to him with a look of disbelief. "You don't think I'd—"

"I'm just saying that's the logic Yeats will use. When someone gets murdered, the number one suspect is always the spouse or lover. You and Bledsoe just broke up. And it happened in the most public and painful way possible. It doesn't take a giant leap of logic to come up with murderous intent on your part."

"I'm not a murderer. You know I'm not!"

He didn't answer. He just went on driving as though he had not registered a word.

"Navarro, did you hear me? I'm not a murderer!"

"I heard you."

"Then why aren't you saying anything?"

"Because I think something else just came up."

Only then did she notice that he was frowning at the rearview mirror. He picked up his car phone and dialed. "Gillis?" he said. "Do me a favor. Find out if Yeats has a tail on Nina Cormier. Yeah, right now. I'm in the car. Call me back." He hung up.

Nina turned and looked out the rear window, at a pair of headlights behind them. "Is someone following us?"

"I'm not sure. I do know that car pulled out behind ours when we left the hospital. And it's been there ever since."

"Your buddy in Homicide must really think I'm dangerous if he's having me followed."

"He's just keeping tabs on his suspect."

Me, she thought, and sank back against the seat, grateful that the darkness hid her face. *Am I your suspect as well?*

He drove calmly, making no sudden moves to alarm whoever was in the car behind them. In that tense stillness, the ringing of the phone was startling.

He picked up the receiver. "Navarro." There was a pause, then he said, "You're sure?" Again he glanced in the mirror. "I'm at Congress and Braeburn, heading west. There's a dark truck—looks like a Jeep Cherokee—right behind me. I'll swing around, make a pass by Houlton. If you can be ready and waiting, we'll sandwich this guy. Don't scare him off. For now, just move in close enough to get a good look. Okay, I'm making my turn now. I'll be there in five minutes." He hung up and shot Nina a tense glance. "You pick up what's happening?"

"What *is* happening?"

"That's not a cop behind us."

She looked back at the headlights. Not a cop. "Then who is it?"

"We're going to find out. Now listen good. In a minute I'll want you down near the floor. Not yet—I don't want to make him suspicious. But when Gillis pulls in behind him, things could get exciting. Are you ready for this?"

"I don't think I have much of a choice…"

He made his turn. Not too fast—a casual change of direction to make it seem as if he'd just decided on a different route.

The other car made the turn as well.

Sam turned again, back onto Congress Street. They were headed east now, going back the way they'd come.

The pair of headlights was still behind them. At 10:30 on a Sunday, traffic was light and it was easy to spot their pursuer.

"There's Gillis," Sam stated. "Right on schedule." He nodded at the blue Toyota idling near the curb. They drove past it.

A moment later, the Toyota pulled into traffic, right behind the Jeep.

"Perp sandwich," said Sam with a note of triumph. They were coming on a traffic light, just turning yellow. Purposely he slowed down, to keep the other two cars on his tail.

Without warning, the Cherokee suddenly screeched around them and sped straight through the intersection just as the light turned red.

Sam uttered an oath and hit the accelerator. They, too, lurched through the intersection just as a pickup truck barreled in from a side street. Sam swerved around it and took off after the sedan.

A block ahead, the Cherokee screeched around a corner.

"This guy's smart," muttered Sam. "He knew we were moving in on him."

"Watch out!" cried Nina as a car pulled out of a parking space, right in front of them.

Sam leaned on his horn and shot past.

This is crazy, she thought. *I'm riding with a maniac cop at the wheel.*

They spun around the corner into an alley. Nina, clutching the dashboard, caught a dizzying view of trash cans and Dumpsters as they raced through.

At the other end of the alley, Sam screeched to a halt.

There was no sign of the Cherokee. In either direction.

Gillis's Toyota squealed to a stop just behind them. "Which way?" they heard Gillis call.

"I don't know!" Sam yelled back. "I'll head east."

He turned right. Nina glanced back and saw Gillis turn left, in the other direction. A two-pronged search. Surely one of them would spot the quarry.

Four blocks later, there was still no sign of the Cherokee. Sam reached for the car phone and dialed Gillis.

"No luck here," he said. "How about you?" At the answer, he gave a grunt of disappointment. "Okay. At least you got the license number. I'll check back with you later." He hung up.

"So he did catch the number?" Nina asked.

"Massachusetts plate. APB's going out now. With any luck, they'll pick him up." He glanced at Nina. "I'm not so sure you should go back to your father's house."

Their gazes locked. What she saw, in his eyes, confirmed her fears.

"You think he was following me," she said softly.

"What I want to know is, why? There's something weird going on here, something that involves both you and Robert. You must have *some* idea what it is."

She shook her head. "It's a mistake," she whispered. "It must be."

"Someone's gone to a lot of trouble to ensure your deaths. I don't think he—or she—would mistake the target."

"She? Do you really think…"

"As I said before, murder needn't be done in person. It can be bought and paid for. And that could be what we're dealing with. I'm more and more certain of it. A professional."

Nina was shaking now, unable to answer him. Unable

to argue. The man next to her was talking so matter-of-factly. *His* life didn't hang in the balance.

"I know it's hard to accept any of this yet," he added. "But in your case, denial could be fatal. So let me lay it out for you. The brutal facts. Robert's already dead. And you could be next."

But I'm not worth killing! she thought. *I'm no threat to anyone.*

"We can't pin the blame on Jimmy Brogan," said Sam. "I think he's the innocent in all this. He saw something he shouldn't have, so he was disposed of. And then his death was set up to look like a suicide, to throw us off the track. Deflect our bomb investigation. Our killer's very clever. And very specific about his targets." He glanced at her, and she heard, in his voice, pure, passionless logic. "There's something else I learned today," he told her. "The morning of your wedding, a gift was delivered to the church. Jimmy Brogan may have seen the man who left it. We think Brogan put the parcel somewhere near the front pews. Right near the blast center. The gift was addressed specifically to you and Robert." He paused, as though daring her to argue that away.

She couldn't. The information was coming too fast, and she was having trouble dealing with the terrifying implications.

"Help me out, Nina," he urged. "Give me a name. A motive."

"I told you," she said, her voice breaking to a sob. "I don't know!"

"Robert admitted there was another woman. Do you know who that might be?"

She was hugging herself, huddling into a self-protective ball against the seat. "No."

"Did it ever seem to you that Daniella and Robert were particularly close?"

Nina went still. *Daniella?* Her father's wife? She thought back over the past six months. Remembered the evenings she and Robert had spent at her father's house. All the invitations, the dinners. She'd been pleased that her fiancé had been so quickly accepted by her father and Daniella, pleased that, for once, harmony had been achieved in the Cormier family. Daniella, who'd never been particularly warm toward her stepdaughter, had suddenly started including Nina and Robert in every social function.

Daniella and Robert.

"That's another reason," he said, "why I don't think you should go back to your father's house tonight."

She turned to him. "You think Daniella…"

"We'll be questioning her again."

"But why would she kill Robert? If she loved him?"

"Jealousy? If she couldn't have him, no one could?"

"But he'd already broken off our engagement! It was over between us!"

"Was it really?"

Though the question was asked softly, she sensed at once an underlying tension in his voice.

She said, "You were there, Sam. You heard our argument. He didn't love me. Sometimes I think he never did." Her head dropped. "For him it was definitely over."

"And for you?"

Tears pricked her eyes. All evening she'd managed not to cry, not to fall apart. During those endless hours in the hospital waiting room, she'd withdrawn so completely into numbness that when they'd told her Robert was dead, she'd registered that fact in some distant corner of her mind, but she hadn't *felt* it. Not the shock, nor the grief. She knew she *should* be grieving. No matter how much Robert had hurt her, how bitterly their affair had ended, he was still the man with whom she'd spent the last year of her life.

Now it all seemed like a different life. Not hers. Not Robert's. Just a dream, with no basis in reality.

She began to cry. Softly. Wearily. Not tears of grief, but tears of exhaustion.

Sam said nothing. He just kept driving while the woman beside him shed soundless tears. There was plenty he *wanted* to say. He wanted to point out that Robert Bledsoe had been a first-class rat, that he was scarcely worth grieving over. But women in love weren't creatures you could deal with on a logical level. And he was sure she did love Bledsoe; it was the obvious explanation for those tears.

He tightened his grip on the steering wheel as frustration surged through him. Frustration at his own inability to comfort her, to assuage her grief. The Roberts of the world didn't deserve any woman's tears. Yet they were the men whom women always seemed to cry over. The golden boys. He glanced at Nina, huddled against the door, and he felt a rush of sympathy. And something more, something that surprised him. Longing.

At once he quelled the feeling. It was yet another sign that he should not be in this situation. It was fine for a cop to sympathize, but when the feelings crossed that invisible line into more dangerous emotions, it was time to pull back.

But I can't pull back. Not tonight. Not until I make sure she's safe.

Without looking at her, he said, "You can't go to your father's. Or your mother's for that matter—her house isn't secure. No alarm system, no gate. And it's too easy for the killer to find you."

"I—I signed a lease on a new apartment today. It doesn't have any furniture yet, but—"

"I assume Daniella knows about it?"

She paused, then replied, "Yes. She does."

"Then that's out. What about friends?"

"They all have children. If they knew a killer was trying to find me…" She took a deep breath. "I'll go to a hotel."

He glanced at her and saw that her spine was suddenly stiff and straight. And he knew she was fighting to put on a brave front. That's all it was, a front. God, what was he supposed to do now? She was scared and she had a right to be. They were both exhausted. He couldn't just dump her at some hotel at this hour. Nor could he leave her alone. Whoever was stalking her had done an efficient job of dispatching both Jimmy Brogan and Robert Bledsoe. For such a killer, tracking down Nina would be no trouble at all.

The turnoff to Route 1 north was just ahead. He took it.

Twenty minutes later they were driving past thick stands of trees. Here the houses were few and far between, all the lots heavily forested. It was the trees that had first attracted Sam to this neighborhood. As a boy, first in Boston, then in Portland, he'd always lived in the heart of the city. He'd grown up around concrete and asphalt, but he'd always felt the lure of the woods. Every summer, he'd head north to fish at his lakeside camp.

The rest of the year, he had to be content with his home in this quiet neighborhood of birch and pine.

He turned onto his private dirt road, which wound a short way into the woods before widening into his gravel driveway. Only as he turned off the engine and looked at his house did the first doubts assail him. The place wasn't much to brag about. It was just a two-bedroom cottage of precut cedar hammered together three summers ago. And as for the interior, he wasn't exactly certain how presentable he'd left it.

Oh, well. There was no changing plans now.

He got out and circled around to open her door. She stepped out, her gaze fixed in bewilderment on the small house in the woods.

"Where are we?" she asked.

"A safe place. Safer than a hotel anyway." He gestured toward the front porch. "It's just for tonight. Until we can make other arrangements."

"Who lives here?"

"I do."

If that fact disturbed her, she didn't show it. Maybe she was too tired and frightened to care. In silence she waited while he unlocked the door. He stepped inside after her and turned on the lights.

At his first glimpse of the living room, he gave a silent prayer of thanks. No clothes on the couch, no dirty dishes on the coffee table. Not that the place was pristine. With newspapers scattered about and dust bunnies in the corners, the room had that unmistakable look of a sloppy bachelor. But at least it wasn't a major disaster area. A minor one, maybe.

He locked the door and turned the dead bolt.

She was just standing there, looking dazed. Maybe by the condition of his house? He touched her shoulder and she flinched.

"You okay?" he asked.

"I'm fine."

"You don't look so fine."

In fact she looked pretty pitiful, her eyes red from crying, her cheeks a bloodless white. He had the sudden urge to take her face in his hands and warm it with his touch. Not a good idea. He was turning into a sucker for women in distress, and this woman was most certainly in distress.

Instead he turned and went into the spare bedroom. One glance at the mess and he nixed that idea. It was no place to put up a guest. Or an enemy, for that matter. There was only one solution. He'd sleep on the couch and let her have his room.

Sheets. Oh Lord, did he have any clean sheets?

Frantically he rummaged in the linen closet and found a fresh set. He was on top of things after all. Turning, he found himself face-to-face with Nina.

She held out her arms for the sheets. "I'll make up the couch."

"These are for the bed. I'm putting you in my room."

"No, Sam. I feel guilty enough as it is. Let me take the couch."

Something in the way she looked at him—that upward tilt of her chin—told him she'd had enough of playing the object of pity.

He gave her the sheets and added a blanket. "It's a lumpy couch. You don't mind?"

"I've taken a lot of lumps lately. I'll hardly notice a few more."

Almost a joke. That was good. She was pulling herself together—an act of will he found impressive.

While she made up the couch, he went to the kitchen and called Gillis at home.

"We got the info on that Massachusetts plate," Gillis

told him. "It was stolen two weeks ago. APB hasn't netted the Cherokee yet. Man, this guy's quick."

"And dangerous."

"You think he's our bomber?"

"Our shooter, too. It's all tangled together, Gillis. It has to be."

"How does last week's warehouse bombing fit in? We figured that was a mob hit."

"Yeah. A nasty message to Billy Binford's rivals."

"Binford's in jail. His future's not looking so bright. Why would he order a church bombed?"

"The church wasn't the target, Gillis. I'm almost certain the target was Bledsoe or Nina Cormier. Or both."

"How does that tie in with Binford?"

"I don't know. Nina's never heard of Binford." Sam rubbed his face and felt the stubble of beard. God, he was tired. Too tired to figure anything out tonight. He said, "There's one other angle we haven't ruled out. The old crime of passion. You interviewed Daniella Cormier."

"Yeah. Right after the bombing. What a looker."

"You pick up anything odd about her?"

"What do you mean?"

"Anything that didn't sit right? Her reactions, her answers?"

"Not that I recall. She seemed appropriately stunned. What are you thinking?"

"I'm thinking Homicide should get their boys over there to question her tonight."

"I'll pass that message along to Yeats. What's your hunch?"

"She and Robert Bledsoe had a little thing going on the side."

"And she blew up the church out of jealousy?" Gillis laughed. "She didn't seem the type."

"Remember what they say about the female of the species."

"Yeah, but I can't imagine that gorgeous blonde—"

"Watch the hormones, Gillis."

His partner snorted. "If anyone better watch his hormones, it's you."

That's what I keep telling myself, thought Sam as he hung up. He paused for a moment in the kitchen, giving himself the same old lecture he'd given himself a dozen times since meeting Nina. *I'm a cop, I'm here to serve and protect. Not seduce.*

Not fall in love.

He went into the living room. At his first sight of Nina, he felt his resolve crumble. She was standing at the window, peering out at the darkness. He'd hung no curtains; here in the woods, he'd never felt the need for them. But now he realized just how open and vulnerable she was. And that worried him—more than he cared to admit.

He said, "I'd feel better if you came away from those windows."

She turned, a startled look in her eyes. "You don't think someone could have followed us?"

"No. But I'd like you to stay away from the windows all the same."

Shuddering, she moved to the couch and sat down. She'd already made the couch into a bed, and only now did he realize how tattered the blanket was. Tattered furniture, tattered linens. Those were details that had never bothered him before. So many things about his life as a bachelor had not bothered him, simply because he'd never stopped to think how much better, sweeter, his life could be. Only now, as he saw Nina sitting on his couch, did it occur to him how stark the room was. It was only the presence of this woman that gave it any life. Any warmth.

Too soon, she'd be gone again.

The sooner the better, he told himself. Before she grew on him. Before she slipped too deeply into his life.

He paced over to the fireplace, paced back toward the kitchen door, his feet restless, his instincts telling him to say something.

"You must be hungry," he said.

She shook her head. "I can't think about food. I can't think about anything except…"

"Robert?"

She lowered her head and didn't answer. Was she crying again? She had a right to. But she just sat very still and silent, as though struggling to hold her emotions in check.

He sat down in the chair across from her. "Tell me about Robert," he prompted. "Tell me everything you know about him."

She took a shaky breath, then said softly, "I don't know what to say. We lived together a year. And now I feel as if I never knew him at all."

"You met at work?"

She nodded. "The Emergency Room. Evening shift. I'd been working there for three years. Then Robert joined the ER staff. He was a good doctor. One of the best I'd ever worked with. And he was so fun to talk to. He'd traveled everywhere, done everything. I remember how surprised I was to learn he wasn't married."

"Never?"

"Never. He told me he was holding out for the best. That he just hadn't found the woman he wanted to spend his life with."

"At forty-one, he must've been more than a little picky."

Her glance held a trace of amusement. "*You're* not married, Detective. Does that make you more than a little picky?"

"Guilty as charged. But then, I haven't really been looking."

"Not interested?"

"Not enough time for romance. It's the nature of the job."

She gave a sigh. "No, it's the nature of the beast. Men don't really want to be married."

"Did I say that?"

"It's something I've finally figured out after years of spinsterhood."

"We're all rats, that kind of thing? Let's get back to one specific rat. Robert. You were telling me you two met in the ER. Was it love at first sight?"

She leaned back, and he could clearly see the remembered pain on her face. "No. No, it wasn't. At least, not for me. I thought he was attractive, of course."

Of course, thought Sam with an undeniable twinge of cynicism.

"But when he asked me out, that first time, I didn't really think it would go anywhere. It wasn't until I introduced him to my mother that I began to realize what a catch he was. Mom was thrilled with Robert. All these years, I'd been dating guys she considered losers. And here I show up with a doctor. It was more than she'd ever expected of me, and she was already hearing wedding bells."

"What about your father?"

"I think he was just plain relieved I was dating someone who wouldn't marry me for *his* money. That's always been Dad's preoccupation. His money. And his wives. Or rather, whichever wife he happens to be married to at the time."

Sam shook his head. "After what you've seen of your parents' marriages, I'm surprised you wanted to take the plunge at all."

"But that's exactly why I *did* want to be married!" She looked at him. "To make it *work*. I never had that stability in my family. My parents were divorced when I was eight, and after that it was a steady parade of stepmothers and mother's boyfriends. I didn't want to live my own life that way." Sighing, she looked down at her ringless left hand. "Now I wonder if it's just another urban myth. A stable marriage."

"My parents had one. A good one."

"Had?"

"Before my dad died. He was a cop, in Boston. Didn't make it to his twentieth year on the force." Now Sam was the one who wasn't looking at *her*. He was gazing, instead, at some distant point in the room, avoiding her look of sympathy. He didn't feel he particularly needed her sympathy. One's parents died, and one went on with life. There was no other choice.

"After my dad died, Mom and I moved to Portland," he continued. "She wanted a safer town. A town where she wouldn't have to worry about her kid being shot on the street." He gave a rueful smile. "She wasn't too happy when I became a cop."

"Why did you become a cop?"

"I guess it was in the genes. Why did you become a nurse?"

"It was definitely *not* in the genes." She sat back, thinking it over for a moment. "I guess I wanted that one-on-one sense of helping someone. I like the contact. The touching. That was important to me, that it be hands-on. Not some vague idea of service to humanity." She gave a wry smile. "You said your mother didn't want you to be a cop. Well, my mother wasn't too happy about *my* career choice, either."

"What does she have against nursing?"

"Nothing. Just that it's not an appropriate profession for her daughter. She thinks of it as manual labor, something other women do. I was expected to marry well, entertain with flair, and help humanity by hosting benefits. That's why she was so happy about my engagement. She thought I was finally on the right track. She was actually...*proud* of me for the first time."

"That's not why you wanted to marry Robert, was it? To please your mother?"

"I don't know." She looked at him with genuine puzzlement. "I don't know anymore."

"What about love? You must have loved him."

"How can I be sure of anything? I've just found out he was seeing someone else. And now it seems as if I were caught up in some fantasy. In love with a man I made up." She leaned back and closed her eyes. "I don't want to talk about him anymore."

"It's important you tell me everything you know. That you consider all the possible reasons someone wanted him dead. A man doesn't just walk up to a stranger and shoot him in the head. The killer had a reason."

"Maybe he didn't. Maybe he was crazy. Or high on drugs. Robert could have been in the wrong place at the wrong time."

"You don't really believe that. Do you?"

She paused. Then, softly, she said, "No, I guess I don't."

He watched her for a moment, thinking how very vulnerable she looked. Had he been any other man, he would be taking her in his arms, offering her comfort and warmth.

Suddenly he felt disgusted with himself. This was the wrong time to be pressing for answers, the wrong time to be doing the cop act. Yet that act was the only thing that kept him comfortably at a distance. It protected him, insulated him. From her.

He rose from the chair. "I think we both need to get some sleep."

Her response was a silent nod.

"If you need anything, my room's at the end of the hall. Sure you wouldn't rather take my bed? Give me the couch?"

"I'll be fine here. Good night."

That was his cue to retreat. He did.

In his bedroom, he paced between the closet and the dresser, unbuttoning his shirt. He felt more restless than tired, his brain moving a mile a minute. In the last two days, a church had been bombed, a man shot to death, and a woman run off the road in an apparent murder attempt. He felt certain it was all linked, perhaps even linked to that warehouse bombing a week ago, but he couldn't see the connection. Maybe he was too dense. Maybe his brain was too drunk on hormones to think straight.

It was all her fault. He didn't need or want this complication. But he couldn't seem to think about this case without lingering on thoughts of her.

And now she was in his house.

He hadn't had a woman sleeping under his roof since…well, it was longer than he cared to admit. His last fling had amounted to little more than a few weeks of lust with a woman he'd met at some party. Then, by mutual agreement, it was over. No complications, no broken hearts.

Not much satisfaction, either.

These days, what satisfaction he got came from the challenge of his work. That was one thing he could count on: the world would never run out of perps.

He turned off the lights and stretched out on the bed, but still he wasn't ready to sleep. He thought of Nina, just down the hall. Thought of what a mismatch they'd be together. And how horrified her mother would be if a cop started squiring around her daughter. If a cop even had a chance.

What a mistake, bringing her here. Lately it seemed he was making a lot of mistakes. He wasn't going to compound this one by falling in love or lust or whatever it was he felt himself teetering toward.

Tomorrow, he thought, *she's out of here.*

And I'm back in control.

Seven

Nina knew she ought to be crying, but she couldn't. In darkness she lay on the couch and thought about those months she'd lived with Robert. The months she'd thought of as stepping stones to their marriage. When had it fallen apart? When had he stopped telling her the truth? She should have noticed the signs. The avoided looks, the silences.

She remembered that two weeks ago, he'd suggested the wedding be postponed. She'd assumed it was merely bridegroom jitters. By then, the arrangements were all made, the date set in stone.

How trapped he must have felt.

Oh Robert. If only you'd come out and told me.

She could have dealt with the truth. The pain, the rejection. She was strong enough and adult enough. What she couldn't deal with was the fact that, all these months, she'd been living with a man she scarcely knew.

Now she'd never know what he really felt about her. His death had cut off any chance she had to make peace with him.

At last she did fall asleep, but the couch was lumpy and the dreams kept waking her up.

Dreams not of Robert, but of Sam Navarro.

He was standing before her, silent and unsmiling. She saw no emotion in his eyes, just that flat, unreadable gaze of a stranger. He reached out to her, as though to take her hand. But when she looked down, there were handcuffs circling her wrists.

"You're guilty," he said. And he kept repeating the word. *Guilty. Guilty.*

She awakened with tears in her eyes. Never had she felt so alone. And she *was* alone, reduced to the pitiful state of seeking refuge in the home of a cop who cared nothing at all about her. Who considered her little more than an added responsibility. An added bother.

It was a flicker of shadow across the window that drew her attention. She would not have noticed it at all, save for the fact it had passed just to the right of her, a patch of darkness moving across her line of vision. Suddenly her heart was thudding. She stared at the curtainless squares of moonlight, watching for signs of movement.

There it was again. A shadow, flitting past.

In an instant she was off the couch and running blindly up the hallway to Sam's room. She didn't stop to knock, but pushed right inside.

"Sam?" she whispered. He didn't answer. Frantic to wake him, she reached down to give him a shake, and her hands met warm, bare flesh. "Sam?"

At her touch, he awoke with such a violent start she jerked away in fright. "What?" he said. "What is it?"

"I think there's someone outside!"

At once he seemed to snap fully awake. He rolled off

the bed and grabbed his trousers from a chair. "Stay here," he whispered. "Don't leave the room."

"What are you going to do?"

She was answered by a metallic click. A gun. Of course he had a gun. He was a cop.

"Just stay here," he ordered, and slipped out of the room.

She wasn't crazy; she wasn't going to go wandering around a dark house when there was a cop with a loaded gun nearby. Chilled and shivering, she stood by the door and listened. She heard Sam's footsteps creak down the hall toward the living room. Then there was silence, a silence so deep it made every breath she took seem like a roar. Surely he hadn't left the house? He wouldn't go outside, would he?

The creak of returning footsteps made her back away from the door. She scurried to the far side of the bed. At the first glimpse of a figure entering the room, she ducked behind the mattress. Only when she heard Sam say, "Nina?" did she dare raise her head.

"Here," she whispered, suddenly feeling ridiculous as she emerged from her hiding place.

"There's no one out there."

"But I saw someone. Something."

"It could have been a deer. An owl flying past." He set his gun down on the nightstand. The solid clunk of metal on wood made her flinch. She hated guns. She wasn't sure she wanted to be anywhere near a man who owned one. Tonight, though, she didn't have a choice.

"Nina, I know you're scared. You have a right to be. But I've checked, and there's no one out there." He reached toward her. At the first touch of his hand on her arm, he gave a murmur of alarm. "You're freezing."

"I'm scared. Oh God, Sam. I'm so scared…"

He took her by the shoulders. By now she was shaking so hard she could barely form any words. Awkwardly, he drew her against him, and she settled, trembling, against his chest. If only he'd hold her. If only he'd put his arms around her. When at last he did, it was like being welcomed home. Enclosed in warmth and safety. This was not the man she'd dreamed about, not the cold, unsmiling cop. This was a man who held her and murmured comforting sounds. A man whose face nuzzled her hair, whose lips, even now, were lowering toward hers.

The kiss was gentle. Sweet. Not the sort of kiss she ever imagined Sam Navarro capable of. Certainly she never imagined being hugged by him, comforted by him. But here she was, in his arms, and she had never felt so protected.

He coaxed her, still shivering, to the bed. He pulled the covers over them both. Again, he kissed her. Again the kiss was gently undemanding. The heat of the bed, of their bodies, banished her chill. And she became aware of so many other things: the scent of his bare skin, the bristly plane of his chest. And most of all, the touch of his lips, lingering against hers.

They had their arms wrapped around each other now, and their legs were slowly twining together. The kiss had gone beyond sweetness, beyond comfort. This was transforming to lust, pure and simple, and she was responding with such a rush of eagerness it astonished her. Her lips parted, welcoming the thrust of his tongue. Through the tangle of sheets, the barrier of her clothes, she felt the undeniable evidence of his arousal burgeoning against her.

She had not meant for this to happen, had not expected

this to happen. But as their kiss deepened, as his hand slid hungrily down the curve of her waist, the flare of her hips, she knew that this had been inevitable. That for all his cool, unreadable looks, Sam Navarro harbored more passion than any man she'd ever known.

He regained control first. Without warning, he broke off the kiss. She heard his breathing, harsh and rapid, in the darkness.

"Sam?" she whispered.

He pulled away from her and sat up on the side of the bed. She watched his silhouette in the darkness, running his hands through his hair. "God," he murmured. "What am I doing?"

She reached out toward the dark expanse of his back. As her fingers brushed his skin, she felt his shudder of pleasure. He wanted her—that much she was certain of. But he was right, this was a mistake, and they both knew it. She'd been afraid and in need of a protector. He was a man alone, in need of no one, but still a man with needs. It was natural they'd seek each other's arms for comfort, however temporary it might be.

Staring at him now, at the shadow huddled at the side of the bed, she knew she still wanted him. The longing was so intense it was a physical ache.

She said, "It's not so awful, is it? What just happened between us?"

"I'm not getting sucked into this again. I can't."

"It doesn't have to mean anything, Sam. Not if you don't want it to."

"Is that how you see it? Quick and meaningless?"

"No. No, that's not at all what I said."

"But that's how it'd end up." He gave a snort of self-disgust. "This is the classic trap, you know. I want to keep you safe. You want a white knight. It's good only as long as that lasts. And then it falls apart." He rose from the bed and moved to the door. "I'll sleep on the couch."

He left the room.

She lay alone in his bed, trying to sort out the confusing whirl of emotions. Nothing made sense to her. Nothing was under her control. She tried to remember a time when her life was in perfect order. It was before Robert. Before she'd let herself get caught up in those fantasies of the perfect marriage. That was where she'd gone wrong. Believing in fantasies.

Her reality was growing up in a broken home, living with a succession of faceless stepparents, having a mother and father who despised each other. Until she'd met Robert, she hadn't expected to marry at all. She'd been content enough with her life, her job. That's what had always sustained her: her work.

She could go back to that. She *would* go back to that.

That dream of a happy marriage, that fantasy, was dead.

SAM WAS UP AT DAWN. The couch had been even more uncomfortable than he'd expected. His sleep had been fitful, his shoulder ached, and at 7:00 a.m., he was unfit for human companionship. So when the phone rang, he was hard-pressed to answer with a civil "Hello."

"Navarro, you've got some explaining to do," said Abe Coopersmith.

Sam sighed. "Good morning, Chief."

"I just got an earful from Yeats in Homicide. I shouldn't have to tell you this, Sam. Back off the Cormier woman."

"You're right. You shouldn't have to tell me. But you did."

"Anything going on between you two?"

"I felt she was in danger. So I stepped in."

"Where is she right now?"

Sam paused. He couldn't avoid this question; he had to answer it. "She's here," he admitted. "My house."

"Damn."

"Someone was following us last night. I didn't think it was prudent to leave her alone. Or unprotected."

"So you brought her to *your* house? Where, exactly, did you happen to park your common sense?"

I don't know, thought Sam. *I lost track of it when I looked into Nina Cormier's big brown eyes.*

"Don't tell me you two are involved. Please don't tell me that," said Coopersmith.

"We're not involved."

"I hope to God you're not. Because Yeats wants her in here for questioning."

"For Robert Bledsoe's murder? Yeats is fishing. She doesn't know anything about it."

"He wants to question her. Bring her in. One hour."

"She has an airtight alibi—"

"*Bring her in,* Navarro." Coopersmith hung up.

There was no way around this. Much as he hated to do it, he'd have to hand Nina over to the boys in Homicide. Their questioning might be brutal, but they had their job to do. As a cop, he could hardly stand in their way.

He went up the hall to the bedroom door and knocked. When she didn't answer, he cautiously cracked open the door and peeked inside.

She was sound asleep, her hair spread across the pillow in a luxurious fan of black. Just the sight of her, lying so peacefully in his bed, in his house, sent a rush of yearning through him. It was so intense he had to grip the doorknob just to steady himself. Only when it had passed, when he had ruthlessly suppressed it, did he dare enter the room.

She awakened with one gentle shake of the shoulder. Dazed by sleep, she looked at him with an expression of utter vulnerability, and he cleared his throat just to keep his voice steady.

"You'll have to get up," he told her. "The detectives in Homicide want to see you downtown."

"When?"

"One hour. You have time to take a shower. I've already got coffee made."

She didn't say anything. She just looked at him with an expression of bewilderment. And no wonder. Last night they had held each other like lovers.

This morning, he was behaving like a stranger.

This was a mistake, coming into her room. Approaching the bed. At once he put distance between them and went to the door. "I'm sure it'll just be routine questions," he said. "But if you feel you need a lawyer—"

"Why should I need a lawyer?"

"It's not a bad idea."

"I don't need one. I didn't do anything." Her gaze was direct and defiant. He'd only been trying to protect her rights, but she had taken his suggestion the wrong way, had interpreted it as an accusation.

He didn't have the patience right now to set her straight. "They'll be waiting for us," was all he said, and he left the room.

While she showered, he tried to scrounge together a breakfast, but could come up with only frozen French bread and a months-old box of cornflakes. Both the pantry and the refrigerator looked pretty pathetic; bachelorhood was showing, and he wasn't at all proud of it.

In disgust, he went outside to fetch the newspaper, which had been delivered to its usual spot at the end of the driveway. He was walking back toward the house when he abruptly halted and stared at the ground.

There was a footprint.

Or, rather, a series of footprints. They tracked through the soft dirt, past the living room window, and headed off among the trees. A man's shoes, thick soled. Size eleven at least.

He glanced toward the house and thought about what the man who'd made those prints could have seen last night, through the windows. Only darkness? Or had he seen Nina, a moving target as she walked around the living room?

He went to his car, parked near the front porch. Slowly, methodically, he examined it from bumper to bumper. He found no signs of tampering.

Maybe I'm paranoid. Maybe those footprints mean nothing.

He went back inside, into the kitchen, and found Nina finishing up her cup of coffee. Her face was flushed, her hair still damp from the shower. At her first look at him, she frowned. "Is something wrong?" she asked.

"No, everything's fine." He carried his cup to the sink. There he looked out the window and thought about how isolated this house was. How open those windows were to the sight of a gunman.

He turned to her and said, "I think it's time to leave."

I SHOULD HAVE TAKEN Sam's advice. I should have hired a lawyer.

That was the thought that now crossed Nina's mind as she sat in an office at the police station and faced the three Homicide detectives seated across the table from her. They were polite enough, but she sensed their barely restrained eagerness. Detective Yeats in particular made her think of an attack dog—leashed, but only for the moment.

She glanced at Sam, hoping for moral support. He gave her none. Throughout the questioning, he hadn't even looked at her. He stood at the window, his shoulders rigid, his gaze focused outside. He'd brought her here, and now he was abandoning her. The cop, of course, had his duty to perform. And at this moment, he was playing the cop role to the hilt.

She said to Yeats, "I've told you everything I know. There's nothing else I can think of."

"You were his fiancée. If anyone would know, you would."

"I don't. I wasn't even there. If you'd just talk to Daniella—"

"We have. She confirms your alibi," Yeats admitted.

"Then why do you keep asking me these questions?"

"Because murder doesn't have to be done in person," one of the other cops said.

Now Yeats leaned forward, his gaze sympathetic, his voice quietly coaxing. "It must have been pretty humiliating for you," he persisted. "To be left at the altar. To have the whole world know he didn't want you."

She said nothing.

"Here's a man you trusted. A man you loved. And for weeks, maybe months, he was cheating on you. Probably laughing at you behind your back. A man like that doesn't deserve a woman like you. But you loved him anyway. And all you got for it was pain."

She lowered her head. She still didn't speak.

"Come on, Nina. Didn't you want to hurt him back? Just a little?"

"Not—not that way," she whispered.

"Even when you found out he was seeing someone else? Even when you learned it was your own step-mother?"

She looked up sharply at Yeats.

"It's true. We spoke to Daniella and she admitted it. They'd been meeting on the sly for some time. While you were at work. You didn't know?"

Nina swallowed. In silence she shook her head.

"I think maybe you *did* know. Maybe you found out on your own. Maybe he told you."

"No."

"And how did it make you feel? Hurt? Angry?"

"I didn't know."

"Angry enough to strike back? To find someone who'd strike back *for* you?"

"I didn't know!"

"That's simply not believable, Nina. You expect us to accept your word that you knew nothing about it?"

"I didn't!"

"You *did*. You—"

"That's *enough*." It was Sam's voice that cut in. "What the hell do you think you're doing, Yeats?"

"My job," Yeats shot back.

"You're badgering her. Interrogating without benefit of counsel."

"Why should she need a lawyer? She claims she's innocent."

"She *is* innocent."

Yeats glanced smugly at the other Homicide detectives. "I think it's pretty obvious, Navarro, that you no longer belong on this investigation."

"You don't have the authority."

"Abe Coopersmith's given me the authority."

"Yeats, I don't give a flying—"

Sam's retort was cut off by the beeping of his pocket pager. Irritably he pressed the Silence button. "I'm not through here," he snapped. Then he turned and left the room.

Yeats turned back to Nina. "Now, Miss Cormier," he said. All trace of sympathy was gone from his expression. In its place was the razor-tooth smile of a pit bull. "Let's get back to the questions."

THE PAGE WAS FROM Ernie Takeda in the crime lab, and the code on the beeper readout told Sam it was an urgent message. He made the call from his own desk.

It took a few dialings to get through; the line was busy. When the usually low-key Takeda finally answered, there was an uncharacteristic tone of excitement in his voice.

"We've got something for you, Sam," said Takeda. "Something that'll make you happy."

"Okay. Make me happy."

"It's a fingerprint. A partial, from one of the device fragments from the warehouse bomb. It could be enough to ID our bomber. I've sent the print off to NCIC. It'll take a few days to run it through the system. So be patient. And let's hope our bomber is on file somewhere."

"You're right, Ernie. You've made me a happy man."

"Oh, one more thing. About that church bomb."

"Yes?"

"Based on the debris, I'd say the device had some sort of gift wrapping around it. Also, since it had no timing elements, my guess is, it was designed to be triggered on opening. But it went off prematurely. Probably a short circuit of some kind."

"You mentioned gift wrapping."

"Yeah. Silver-and-white paper."

Wedding wrap, thought Sam, remembering the gift that had been delivered that morning to the church. If the bomb was meant to explode on opening, then there was no longer any doubt who the intended victims were.

But why kill Nina? he wondered as he headed back to the conference room. Could this whole mess be attributed to another woman's jealousy? Daniella Cormier had a motive, but would she have gone so far as to hire a bomber?

What was he missing here?

He opened the office door and halted. The three homicide detectives were still sitting at the table. Nina wasn't. She was gone.

"Where is she?" Sam asked.

Yeats shrugged. "She left."

"What?"

"She got fed up with our questions, so she walked out."

"You *let* her leave?"

"We haven't charged her with anything. Are you saying we should have, Navarro?"

Sam's reply was unrepeatable. With a sudden sense of anxiety, he left Yeats and headed out the front entrance of police headquarters. He stood on the sidewalk, looking up and down the street.

Nina was nowhere in sight.

Someone's trying to kill her, he thought as he headed for his car. *I have to reach her first.*

From his car phone, he called Nina's father's house. She wasn't there. He called Robert Bledsoe's house. No answer. He called Lydia Warrenton's house. Nina wasn't there either.

On a hunch, he drove to Lydia's Cape Elizabeth home anyway. People in distress often flee home for comfort, he reasoned. Eventually, Nina might wind up at her mother's.

He found Lydia at home. But no Nina—not yet, at least.

"I haven't spoken to her since yesterday morning," said Lydia, ushering Sam into the seaview room. "I'm not sure she *would* come here."

"Do you know where she might go?" Sam asked. "Someone she might turn to?"

Lydia shook her head. "I'm afraid my daughter and I aren't very close. We never were. The truth is, she wasn't the easiest child."

"What do you mean, Mrs. Warrenton?"

Lydia seated herself on the white couch. Her silk pantsuit was a startling slash of purple against the pale cushions. "What I mean to say—I know it sounds awful— is that Nina was something of a disappointment to me. We offered her so many opportunities. To study abroad, for instance. At a boarding school in Switzerland. Her sister Wendy went and benefited wonderfully. But Nina refused to go. She insisted on staying home. Then there were the other things. The boys she brought home. The ridiculous outfits she'd wear. She could be doing so much with her life, but she never achieved much."

"She earned a nursing degree."

Lydia gave a shrug. "So do thousands of other girls."

"She's not any other girl, Mrs. Warrenton. She's your daughter."

"That's why I expected more. Her sister speaks three languages and plays the piano and cello. She's married to an attorney who's in line for a judicial seat. While Nina…" Lydia sighed. "I can't imagine how sisters could be so different."

"Maybe the real difference," said Sam, rising to his feet, "was in how you loved them." He turned and walked out of the room.

"Mr. Navarro!" he heard Lydia call as he reached the front door.

He looked back. She was standing in the hallway, a woman of such perfectly groomed elegance that she didn't seem real or alive. Or touchable.

Not like Nina at all.

"I think you have entirely the wrong idea about me and my daughter," Lydia said.

"Does it really matter what I think?"

"I just want you to understand that I did the best I could, under the circumstances."

"Under the circumstances," replied Sam, "so did she." And he left the house.

Back in his car, he debated which way to head next. Another round of phone calls came up empty. Where the hell was she?

The only place he hadn't checked was her new apartment. She'd told him it was on Taylor Street. There was probably no phone in yet; he'd have to drive there to check it out.

On his way over, he kept thinking about what Lydia Warrenton had just told him. He thought about what it must

have been like for Nina to grow up the black sheep, the un-
favored child. Always doing the wrong thing, never
meeting Mommy's approval. Sam had been fortunate to
have a mother who'd instilled in him a sense of his own
competence.

I understand now, he thought, *why you wanted to marry
Robert.* Marrying Robert Bledsoe was the one sure way to
gain her mother's approval. And even that had collapsed
in failure.

By the time he pulled up at Nina's new apartment
building, he was angry. At Lydia, at George Cormier and
his parade of wives, at the entire Cormier family for its bat-
tering of a little girl's sense of self-worth.

He knocked harder at the apartment door than he had
to.

There was no response. She wasn't here, either.

Where are you, Nina?

He was about to leave when he impulsively gave the
knob a turn. It was unlocked.

He pushed the door open. "Nina?" he called.

Then his gaze focused on the wire. It was almost invisible, a tiny line of silver that traced along the door-
frame and threaded toward the ceiling.

Oh, my God...

In one fluid movement he pivoted away and dived
sideways, down the hallway.

The force of the explosion blasted straight through the
open door and ripped through the wall in a flying cloud of
wood and plaster.

Deafened, stunned by the blast, Sam lay facedown in
the hallway as debris rained onto his back.

Eight

"Man, oh man," said Gillis. "You sure did bring down the house."

They were standing outside, behind the yellow police line, waiting for the rest of the search team to assemble. The apartment house—what was left of it—had been cleared of any second devices, and now it was Ernie Takeda's show. Takeda was, at that moment, diagramming the search grid, handing out evidence bags, and assigning his lab crew to their individual tasks.

Sam already knew what they'd find. Residue of Dupont label dynamite. Scraps of green two-inch-wide electrical tape. And Prima detonating cord. The same three components as the church bomb and the warehouse bomb.

And every other bomb put together by the late Vincent Spectre.

Who's your heir apparent, Spectre? Sam wondered. *To whom did you bequeath your tricks of the trade? And why is Nina Cormier the target?*

Just trying to reason it through made his head pound.

He was still covered in dust, his cheek was bruised and swollen, and he could barely hear out of his left ear. But he had nothing to complain about. He was alive.

Nina would not have been so fortunate.

"I've got to find her," he said. "Before he does."

"We've checked with the family again," said Gillis. "Father, mother, sister. She hasn't turned up anywhere."

"Where the hell could she have gone?" Sam began to pace along the police line, his worry turning to agitation. "She walks out of headquarters, maybe she catches a cab or a bus. Then what? What would she do?"

"Whenever my wife gets mad, she goes shopping," Gillis offered helpfully.

"I'm going to call the family again." Sam turned to his car. "Maybe she's finally shown up somewhere."

He was about to reach inside the Taurus for the car phone when he froze, his gaze focused on the edge of the crowd. A small, dark-haired figure stood at the far end of the street. Even from that distance, Sam could read the fear, the shock, in her pale face.

"Nina," he murmured. At once he began to move toward her, began to push, then shove his way through the crowd. "Nina!"

She caught sight of him, struggling to reach her. Now she was moving as well, frantically plunging into the gathering of onlookers. They found each other, fell into each other's embrace. And at that moment, there was no one else in the world for Sam, no one but the woman he was holding. She felt so very precious in his arms, so easily taken from him.

With a sudden start, he became acutely aware of the crowd. All these people, pressing in on them. "I'm getting you out of here," he said. Hugging her close to his side, he guided her toward his car. The whole time, he was scanning faces, watching for any sudden movements.

Only when he'd bundled her safely into the Taurus did he allow himself a deep breath of relief.

"Gillis!" he called. "You're in charge here!"

"Where you going?"

"I'm taking her somewhere safe."

"But—"

Sam didn't finish the conversation. He steered the car out of the crowd and they drove away.

Drove north.

Nina was staring at him. At the bruise on his cheek, the plaster dust coating his hair. "My God, Sam," she murmured. "You've been hurt—"

"A little deaf in one ear, but otherwise I'm okay." He glanced at her and saw that she didn't quite believe him. "I ducked out just before it blew. It was a five-second delay detonator. Set off by opening the door." He paused, then added quietly, "It was meant for you."

She said nothing. She didn't have to; he could read the comprehension in her gaze. This bombing was no mistake, no random attack. She was the target and she could no longer deny it.

"We're chasing down every lead we have," he said. "Yeats is going to question Daniella again, but I think that's a dead end. We did get a partial fingerprint off the warehouse bomb, and we're waiting for an ID. Until then, we've just got to keep you alive. And that means you have to cooperate. Do exactly what I tell you to do." He gave an exasperated sigh and clutched the steering wheel tighter. "That was *not* smart, Nina. What you did today."

"I was angry. I needed to get away from all you cops."

"So you storm out of headquarters? Without telling me where you're going?"

"You threw me to the wolves, Sam. I expected Yeats to clap the handcuffs on me. And you delivered me to him."

"I had no choice. One way or the other, he was going to question you."

"Yeats thinks I'm guilty. And since *he* was so sure of it, I thought…I thought you must have your doubts as well."

"I have no doubts," he said, his voice absolutely steady. "Not about you. And after this latest bomb, I don't think Yeats'll have any doubts either. You're the target."

The turnoff to Route 95—the Interstate—was just ahead. Sam took it.

"Where are we going?" she asked.

"I'm getting you out of town. Portland isn't a safe place for you. So I have another spot in mind. A fishing camp on Coleman Pond. I've had it for a few years. You'll be roughing it there, but you can stay as long as you need to."

"You won't be staying with me?"

"I have a job to do, Nina. It's the only way we'll get the answers. If I do my job."

"Of course, you're right." And she looked straight ahead at the road. "I forget sometimes," she said softly, "that you're a cop."

ACROSS THE STREET from the police line, he stood in the thick of the crowd, watching the bomb investigators scurry about with their evidence bags and their notebooks. Judging by the shattered glass, the debris in the street, the blast had been quite impressive. But of course he'd planned it that way.

Too bad Nina Cormier was still alive.

He'd spotted her just moments before, being escorted through the crowd by Detective Sam Navarro. He'd recognized Navarro at once. For years he'd followed the man's career, had read every news article ever written about the Bomb Squad. He knew about Gordon Gillis and Ernie Takeda as well. It was his business to know. They were the enemy, and a good soldier must know his enemy.

Navarro helped the woman into a car. He seemed unusually protective—not like Navarro at all, to be succumbing to romance on the job. Cops like him were supposed to be professionals. What had happened to the quality of civil servants these days?

Navarro and the woman drove away.

There was no point trying to follow them; another opportunity would arise.

Right now he had a job to do. And only two days in which to finish it.

He gave his gloves a little tug. And he walked away, unnoticed, through the crowd.

BILLY "THE SHOWMAN" Binford was happy today. He was even grinning at his attorney, seated on the other side of the Plexiglas barrier.

"It's gonna be all right, Darien," said Billy. "I got everything taken care of. You just get ready to negotiate that plea bargain. And get me out of here, quick."

Darien shook his head. "I told you, Liddell's not in a mood to cut any deals. He's out to score big with your conviction."

"Darien, Darien. You got no faith."

"What I got is a good grip on reality. Liddell's aiming for a higher office. For that, he's got to put you away."

"He won't be putting anyone away. Not after Saturday."

"What?"

"You didn't hear me say nothing, okay? I didn't say nothing. Just believe me, Liddell won't be a problem."

"I don't want to know. Don't tell me about it."

Billy regarded his attorney with a look of both pity and amusement. "You know what? You're like that monkey with his paws over his ears. Hear no evil. That's you."

"Yeah," Darien agreed. And he nodded miserably. "That's me exactly."

A FIRE CRACKLED in the hearth, but Nina felt chilled to the bone. Outside, dusk had deepened, and the last light was fading behind the dense silhouettes of pine trees. The cry of a loon echoed, ghostlike, across the lake. She'd never been afraid of the woods, or the darkness, or of being alone. Tonight, though, she *was* afraid, and she didn't want Sam to leave.

She also knew he had to.

He came tramping back into the cottage, carrying an armload of firewood, and began to stack it by the hearth. "This should do you for a few days," he said. "I just spoke to Henry Pearl and his wife. Their camp's up the road. They said they'd check up on you a few times a day. I've known them for years, so I know you can count on them. If you need anything at all, just knock on their door."

He finished stacking the wood and clapped the dirt from his hands. With his shirtsleeves rolled up and sawdust clinging to his trousers, he looked more like a woodsman than a city cop. He threw another birch log on the fire and the flames shot up in a crackle of sparks. He turned to look at her, his expression hidden against the backlight of fire.

"You'll be safe here, Nina. I wouldn't leave you alone if I had even the slightest doubt."

She nodded. And smiled. "I'll be fine."

"There's a fishing pole and tackle box in the kitchen, if you feel like wrestling with a trout. And feel free to wear anything you find in the closet. None of it'll fit, but at least you'll be warm. Henry's wife'll drop by some, uh, women's wear tomorrow." He paused and laughed. "Those probably won't fit either. Since she's twice *my* size."

"I'll manage, Sam. Don't worry about me."

There was a long silence. They both knew there was nothing more to say, but he didn't move. He glanced around the room, as though reluctant to leave. Almost as reluctant as she was to see him go.

"It's a long drive back to the city," she said. "You should eat before you go. Can I interest you in dinner? Say, a gourmet repast of macaroni and cheese?"

He grinned. "Make it anything else and I'll say yes."

In the kitchen, they rummaged through the groceries they'd bought at a supermarket on the way. Mushroom omelets, a loaf of French bread, and a bottle of wine soon graced the tiny camp table. Electricity had not yet made it to this part of the lake, so they ate by the light of a hurricane lamp. Outside, dusk gave way to a darkness alive with the chirp of crickets.

She gazed across the table at him, watching the way his face gleamed in the lantern light. She kept focusing on that bruise on his cheek, thinking about how close he'd come to dying that afternoon. But that was exactly the sort of work he did, the sort of risk he took all the time. Bombs.

Death. It was insane, and she didn't know why any man in his right mind would take those risks. *Crazy cop,* she thought. *And I must be just as insane, because I think I'm falling for this guy.*

She took a sip of wine, the whole time intensely, almost painfully aware of his presence. And of her attraction toward him, an attraction so strong she was having trouble remembering to eat.

She had to remind herself that he was just doing his job, that to him, she was nothing more than a piece of the puzzle he was trying to solve, but she couldn't help picturing other meals, other nights they might spend together. Here, on the lake. Candlelight, laughter. Children. She thought he'd be good with children. He'd be patient and kind, just as he was with her.

How would I know that? I'm dreaming. Fantasizing again.

She reached across to pour him more wine.

He put his hand over the glass. "I have to be driving back."

"Oh. Of course." Nervously she set the bottle down again. She folded and refolded her napkin. For a whole minute they didn't speak, didn't look at each other. At least, she didn't look at him.

But when she finally raised her eyes, she saw that he was watching her. Not the way a cop looks at a witness, at a piece of a puzzle.

He was watching her the way a man watches a woman he wants.

He said, quickly, "I should leave now—"

"I know."

"—before it gets too late."

"It's still early."

"They'll need me, back in the city."

She bit her lip and said nothing. Of course he was right. The city did need him. Everyone needed him. She was just one detail that required attending to. Now she was safely tucked away and he could go back to his real business, his real concerns.

But he didn't seem at all eager to leave. He hadn't moved from the chair, hadn't broken eye contact. She was the one who looked away, who nervously snatched up her wineglass.

She was startled when he reached over and gently caught her hand. Without a word he took the glass and set it down. He raised her hand, palm side up, and pressed a kiss, ever so light, to her wrist. The lingering of lips, the tickle of his breath, was the sweetest torture. If he could wreak such havoc kissing that one square inch of skin, what could he do with the rest of her?

She closed her eyes and gave a small, soft moan. "I don't want you to leave," she whispered.

"It's a bad idea. For me to stay."

"Why?"

"Because of this." He kissed her wrist again. "And this." His lips skimmed up her arm, his beard delightfully rough against her sensitive skin. "It's a mistake. You know it. I know it."

"I make mistakes all the time," she replied. "I don't always regret them."

His gaze lifted to hers. He saw both her fear and her fearlessness. She was hiding nothing now, letting him read all. Her hunger was too powerful to hide.

He rose from the table. So did she.

He pulled her toward him, cupped her face in his hands, and pressed his lips to hers. The kiss, sweet with the taste of wine and desire, left her legs unsteady. She swayed against him, her arms reaching up to clutch his shoulders. Before she could catch her breath, he was kissing her again, deeper. As their mouths joined, so did their bodies. His hands slid down her waist, to her hips. He didn't need to pull her against him; she could already feel him, hard and aroused. And that excited her even more.

"If we're going to stop," he breathed, "it had better be now…."

She responded with a kiss that drowned out any more words between them. Their bodies did all the talking, all the communicating.

They were tugging at each other's clothes, feverish for the touch of bare skin. First her sweater came off, then his shirt. They kissed their way into the next room, where the fire had quieted to a warm glow. Still kissing her, he pulled the afghan off the couch and let it fall onto the floor by the hearth.

Facing each other, they knelt before the dying fire. His bare shoulders gleamed in the flickering light. She was eager, starved for his touch, but he moved slowly, savoring every moment, every new experience of her. He watched with longing as she unhooked her bra and shrugged the straps off her shoulders. When he reached out to cup her breast, to tug at her nipple, she let her head sag back with a moan. His touch was ever so gentle, yet it left her feeling weak. Conquered. He tipped her back and lowered her onto the afghan.

Her body was pure liquid now, melting under his touch. He unzipped her jeans, eased them off her hips. Her underwear slid off with the hiss of silk. She lay unshielded to his gaze now, her skin rosy in the firelight.

"I've had so many dreams about you," he whispered as

his hand slid exploringly down her belly, toward the dark triangle of hair. "Last night, when you were in my house, I dreamed of holding you. Touching you just the way I am now. But when I woke up, I told myself it could never happen. That it was all fantasy. All longing. And here we are…" He bent forward, his kiss tender on her lips. "I shouldn't be doing this."

"I want you to. I want us to."

"I want it just as much. More. But I'm afraid we're going to regret it."

"Then we'll regret it later. Tonight, let's just be you and me. Let's pretend there's nothing else, no one else."

He kissed her again. And this time his hand slipped between her thighs, his finger dipping into her wetness, sliding deep into her warmth. She groaned, helpless with delight. He slid another finger in, and felt her trembling, tightening around him. She was ready, so ready for him, but he wanted to take his time, to make this last.

He withdrew his hand, just long enough to remove the rest of his clothes. As he knelt beside her, she couldn't help drawing in a sharp breath of admiration. What a beautiful man he was. Not just his body, but his soul. She could see it in his eyes: the caring, the warmth. Before it had been hidden from her, concealed behind that tough-cop mask of his. Now he was hiding nothing. Revealing everything.

As she was revealing everything to him.

She was too lost in pleasure to feel any modesty, any shame. She lay back, whimpering, as his fingers found her again, withdrew, teased, plunged back in. Already she was slick with sweat and desire, her hips arching against him.

"Please," she murmured. "Oh, Sam. I—"

He kissed her, cutting off any protest. And he continued his torment, his fingers dipping, sliding, until she was wound so tight she thought she'd shatter.

Only then, only as she reached the very edge, did he take away his hand, fit his hips to hers, and thrust deep inside her.

She gripped him, crying out as he swept her, and himself, toward climax. And when it came, when she felt herself tumbling into that wondrous free fall, they clung to each other and they tumbled together, to a soft and ever-so-gentle landing.

She fell asleep, warm and safe, in his arms.

It was later, much later, when she awakened in the deepest chill of night.

The fire had died out. Although she was cocooned in the afghan, she found herself shivering.

And alone.

Hugging the afghan to her shoulders, she went into the kitchen and peered out the window. By the light of the moon, she could see that Sam's car was gone. He had returned to the city.

Already I miss him, she thought. Already his absence was like a deep, dark gulf in her life.

She went into the bedroom, climbed under the blankets, and tried to stop shivering, but she could not. When Sam had left, he had taken with him all the warmth. All the joy.

It scared her, how much she felt his absence. She was not going to fall in love with him; she could not afford to. What they'd experienced tonight was pleasure. The enjoyment of each other's bodies. As a lover, he was superb.

But as a man to love, he was clearly wrong for her.

No wonder he'd stolen away like a thief in the night. He'd known it was a mistake, just as she did. At this moment, he was probably regretting what they'd done.

She burrowed deeper under the blankets and waited for sleep, for dawn—whichever came first. Anything to ease the ache of Sam's departure.

But the night, cold and lonely, stretched on.

IT WAS A MISTAKE. A stupid, crazy mistake.

All the way back to Portland, on the drive down that long, dark highway, Sam kept asking himself how he could have let it happen.

No, he *knew* how it happened. The attraction between them was just too strong. It had been pulling them together from the first day they'd met. He'd fought it, had never stopped reminding himself that he was a cop, and she was an important element in his investigation. Good cops did not fall into this trap.

He used to think he was a good cop. Now he knew he was far too human, that Nina was a temptation he couldn't resist, and that the whole investigation would probably suffer because he'd lost his sense of objectivity.

All because she'd come to mean too much to him.

Not only would the investigation suffer, *he* would as well, and he had only himself to blame. Nina was scared and vulnerable; naturally she'd turn to her protector for comfort. He should have kept her at arm's length, should have kept his own urges in check. Instead he'd succumbed, and now she was all he could think about.

He gripped the steering wheel and forced himself to focus on the road. On the case.

By 1:00 a.m., he was back in the city. By 1:30, he was at his desk, catching up on the preliminary reports from Ernie Takeda. As he'd expected, the bomb in Nina's apartment was similar to the devices that blew up the church

and the warehouse. The difference between the three was
in the method of detonation. The warehouse device had
had a simple timer. The church device was a package
bomb, designed to explode on opening. Nina's apartment
had been wired to blow after the door opened. This bomber
was a versatile fellow. He could trigger a blast in any
number of ways. He varied his device according to the
situation, and that made him both clever and extremely
dangerous.

He went home at 5:00 a.m., caught a few hours of sleep,
and was back at headquarters for an eight o'clock meeting.

With three bombings in two weeks, the pressure was on,
and the tension showed in the faces around the conference
table. Gillis looked beat, Chief Coopersmith was testy,
and even the normally unemotional Ernie Takeda was
showing flashes of irritation. Part of that irritation was due
to the presence of two federal agents from Alcohol,
Tobacco and Firearms. Both the men from ATF wore expressions of big-time experts visiting Hicksville.

But the most annoying source of irritation was the
presence of their esteemed D.A. and perpetual pain in the
neck, Norm Liddell.

Liddell was waving the morning edition of the *New
York Times*. "Look at the headline," he said. "'Portland,
Maine, the new bombing capital?' New York's saying that
about us? *Us?*" He threw the newspaper down on the table.
"What the hell is going on in this town? Who *is* this
bomber?"

"We can give you a likely psychological profile," said
one of the ATF agents. "He's a white male, intelligent—"

"I already know he's intelligent!" snapped Liddell. "A
hell of a lot more intelligent than we are. I don't want some

psychological profile. I want to know who he *is*. Does anyone have any idea about his identity?"

There was a silence at the table. Then Sam said, "We know who he's trying to kill."

"You mean the Cormier woman?" Liddell snorted. "So far, no one's come up with a single good reason why she's the target."

"But we know she is. She's our one link to the bomber."

"What about the warehouse bomb?" said Coopersmith. "How's that connect to Nina Cormier?"

Sam paused. "That I don't know," he admitted.

"I'd lay ten-to-one odds that Billy Binford's people ordered that warehouse bombing," said Liddell. "It was a logical move on his part. Scare off a prosecution witness. Does the Cormier woman have any connection to Binford?"

"All she knows about him is what she's read in the newspapers," said Sam. "There's no link."

"What about her family? Are they linked at all to Binford?"

"No link there, either," spoke up Gillis. "We've checked into the finances of the whole family. Nina Cormier's father, mother, stepfather, stepmother. No connection to Binford. Her ex-fiancé was just as clean."

Liddell sat back. "Something's coming. I can feel it. Binford's got something big planned."

"How do you know?" asked Coopersmith.

"I have sources." Liddell shook his head in disgust. "Here I finally get The Snowman behind bars, and he's still pulling strings, still making mincemeat of the court system. I'm convinced that warehouse bomb was an intimidation tactic. He's trying to scare all my witnesses. If

I don't get a conviction, he'll be a free man in a few months. And he'll be scaring them in person."

"But chances are good you'll get that conviction," Coopersmith reassured him. "You've got credible witnesses, financial records. And you've drawn a law-and-order judge."

"Even so," countered Liddell, "Binford's not finished maneuvering. He's got something up his sleeve. I just wish I knew what it was." He looked at Sam. "Where are you hiding Nina Cormier?"

"A safe place," said Sam.

"You keeping it top secret or something?"

"Under the circumstances, I'd prefer to keep it known only to myself and Gillis. If you have questions to ask her, I can ask them for you."

"I just want to know what her connection is to these bombings. Why The Snowman wants her dead."

"Maybe this has nothing to do with Binford," suggested Sam. "He's in jail, and there's another party involved here. The bomber."

"Right. So find him for me," snapped Liddell. "Before Portland gets known as the American Beirut." He rose from his chair, his signal that the meeting was over. "Binford goes to trial in a month. I don't want my witnesses scared off by any more bombs. So *get* this guy, before he destroys my case." With that, Liddell stalked out.

"Man, election year is hell," muttered Gillis.

As the others filed out of the room, Coopersmith said, "Navarro, a word with you."

Sam waited, knowing full well what was coming. Coopersmith shut the door and turned to look at him.

"You and Nina Cormier. What's going on?"

"She needs protection. So I'm looking out for her."

"Is that all you're doing?"

Sam let out a weary sigh. "I…may be more involved than I should be."

"That's what I figured." Coopersmith shook his head. "You're too smart for this, Sam. This is the sort of mistake rookies make. Not you."

"I know."

"It could put you both in a dangerous situation. I ought to yank you off the case."

"I need to stay on it."

"Because of the woman?"

"Because I want to nail this guy. I'm *going* to nail him."

"Fine. Just keep your distance from Nina Cormier. I shouldn't have to tell you this. This kind of thing happens, someone always gets hurt. Right now she thinks you're John Wayne. But when this is all over, she's gonna see you're human like the rest of us. Don't set yourself up for this, Sam. She's got looks, she's got a daddy with lots of money. She doesn't want a cop."

I know he's right, thought Sam. *I know it from personal experience. Someone's going to get hurt. And it'll be me.*

The conference room door suddenly swung open and an excited Ernie Takeda stuck his head in the room. "You're not gonna believe this," he said, waving a sheet of fax paper.

"What is it?" asked Coopersmith.

"From NCIC. They just identified that fingerprint off the bomb fragment."

"And?"

"It's a match. With Vincent Spectre."

"That's impossible!" exclaimed Sam. He snatched the

sheet from Ernie's grasp and stared at the faxed report. What he read there left no doubt that the ID was definite.

"There has to be a mistake," said Coopersmith. "They found his body. Spectre's been dead and buried for months."

Sam looked up. "Obviously not," he growled.

Nine

The rowboat was old and well used, but the hull was sound. At least, it didn't leak as Nina rowed it out into the lake. It was late afternoon and a pair of loons were paddling lazily through the water, neither one alarmed by the presence of a lone rower. The day was utter stillness, utter peace, as warm as a summer day should be.

Nina guided the boat to the center of the pond, where sunlight rippled on the water, and there she let the boat drift. As it turned lazy circles, she lay back and stared up at the sky. She saw birds winging overhead, saw a dragonfly hover, iridescent in the slanting light.

And then she heard a voice, calling her name.

She sat up so sharply the boat rocked. She saw him then, standing at the water's edge, waving to her.

As she rowed the boat back to shore, her heart was galloping, more from anticipation than exertion. Why had he returned so soon? Last night he'd left without a word of goodbye, the way a man leaves a woman he never intends to see again.

Now here he was, standing silent and still on the shore, his gaze as unreadable as ever. She couldn't figure him out. She'd never be able to figure him out. He was a man designed to drive her crazy, and as she glided across the last yards of water, she could already feel that lovely insanity take hold of her. It required all her willpower to suppress it.

She tossed him the painter rope. He hauled the rowboat up onto the shore and helped her step out. Just the pressure of his hand grasping her arm gave her a thrill of delight. But one look at his face quelled any hopes that he was here as a lover. This was the cop, impersonal, businesslike. Not at all the man who'd held her in his arms.

"There's been a new development," he said.

Just as coolly, she met his gaze. "What development?"

"We think we know who the bomber is. I want you to take a look at some photographs."

On the couch by the fireplace—the same fireplace that had warmed them when they'd made love the night before—Nina sat flipping through a book of mug shots. The hearth was now cold, and so was she, both in body and in spirit. Sam sat a good foot away, not touching her, not saying a word. But he was watching her expectantly, waiting for some sign that she recognized a face in that book.

She forced herself to concentrate on the photos. One by one she scanned the faces, carefully taking in the features of each man pictured there. She reached the last page. Shaking her head, she closed the cover.

"I don't recognize anyone," she declared.

"Are you certain?"

"I'm certain. Why? Who am I supposed to recognize?"

His disappointment was apparent. He opened the book

to the fourth page and handed it back to her. "Look at this face. Third one down, first column. Have you ever seen this man?"

She spent a long time studying the photo. Then she said, "No. I don't know him."

With a sigh of frustration, Sam sank back against the couch. "This doesn't make any sense at all."

Nina was still focused on the photograph. The man in the picture appeared to be in his forties, with sandy hair, blue eyes, and hollow, almost gaunt, cheeks. It was the eyes that held her attention. They stared straight at her, a look of intimidation that burned, lifelike, from a mere two-dimensional image. Nina gave an involuntary shiver.

"Who is he?" she asked.

"His name is—or was—Vincent Spectre. He's five foot eleven, 180 pounds, forty-six years old. At least, that's what he would be now. If he's still alive."

"You mean you don't know if he is?"

"We thought he was dead."

"You're not sure?"

"Not any longer." Sam rose from the couch. It was getting chilly in the cabin; he crouched at the hearth and began to arrange kindling in the fireplace.

"For twelve years," he said, "Vincent Spectre was an army demolitions expert. Then he got booted out of the service. Dishonorable discharge, petty theft. It didn't take him long to launch a second career. He became what we call a specialist. Big bangs, big bucks. Hired himself out to anyone who'd pay for his expertise. He worked for terrorist governments. For the mob. For crime bosses all over the country.

"For years he raked in the money. Then his luck ran out.

He was recognized on a bank security camera. Arrested, convicted, served only a year. Then he escaped."

Sam struck a match and lit the kindling. It caught fire in a crackle of sparks and flames. He lay a log on top and turned to look at her.

"Six months ago," he continued, "Spectre's remains were found in the rubble after one of his bombs blew up a warehouse. That is, authorities *thought* it was his body. Now we think it might have been someone else's. And Spectre's still alive."

"How do you know that?"

"Because his fingerprint just turned up. On a fragment of the warehouse bomb."

She stared at him. "You think he also blew up the church?"

"Almost certainly. Vincent Spectre's trying to kill you."

"But I don't know any Vincent Spectre! I've never even heard his name before!"

"And you don't recognize his photo."

"No."

Sam stood up. Behind him, the flames were now crackling, consuming the log. "We've shown Spectre's photo to the rest of your family. They don't recognize him, either."

"It must be a mistake. Even if the man's alive, he has no reason to kill me."

"Someone else could have hired him."

"You've already explored that. And all you came up with was Daniella."

"That's still a possibility. She denies it, of course. And she passed the polygraph test."

"She let you hook her up to a *polygraph?*"

"She consented. So we did it."

Nina shook her head in amazement. "She must have been royally ticked off."

"As a matter of fact, I think she rather enjoyed giving the performance. She turned every male head in the department."

"Yes, she's good at that. She certainly turned my father's head. And Robert's, too," Nina added softly.

Sam was moving around the room now, pacing a slow circle around the couch. "So we're back to the question of Vincent Spectre," he said. "And what his connection is to you. Or Robert."

"I told you, I've never heard his name before. I don't remember Robert ever mentioning the name, either."

Sam paced around the couch, returned to stand by the fireplace. Against the background of flames, his face was unreadable. "Spectre *is* alive. And he built a bomb intended for you and Robert. Why?"

She looked down again at the photo of Vincent Spectre. Try as she might, she could conjure up no memory of that face. The eyes, perhaps, seemed vaguely familiar. That stare was one she might have seen before. But not the face.

"Tell me more about him," she suggested.

Sam went to the couch and sat down beside her. Not quite close enough to touch her, but close enough to make her very aware of his presence.

"Vincent Spectre was born and raised in California. Joined the army at age nineteen. Quickly showed an aptitude for explosives work, and was trained in demolitions. Saw action in Grenada and Panama. That's where he lost his finger—trying to disarm a terrorist explosive. At that point, he could have retired on disability but—"

"Wait. Did you just say he was missing a finger?"

"That's right."

"Which hand?"

"The left. Why?"

Nina went very still. Thinking, remembering. A missing finger. Why did that image seem so vividly familiar?

Softly she said, "Was it the left middle finger?"

Frowning, Sam reached for his briefcase and took out a file folder. He flipped through the papers contained inside. "Yes," he said. "It was the middle finger."

"No stump at all? Just…missing entirely."

"That's right. They had to amputate all the way back to the knuckle." He was watching her, his eyes alert, his voice quiet with tension. "So you *do* know him."

"I—I'm not sure. There was a man with an amputated finger—the left middle finger—"

"What? Where?"

"The Emergency Room. It was a few weeks ago. I remember he was wearing gloves, and he didn't want to take them off. But I had to check his pulse. So I pulled off the left glove. And I was so startled to see he was missing a finger. He'd stuffed the glove finger with cotton. I think I…I must have stared. I remember I asked him how he lost it. He told me he'd caught it in some machinery."

"Why was he in the ER?"

"It was—I think an accident. Oh, I remember. He was knocked down by a bicycle. He'd cut his arm and needed stitches put in. The strange part about it all was the way he vanished afterward. Right after the cut was sutured, I left the room to get something. When I came back, he was gone. No thank you, nothing. Just—disappeared. I thought he was trying to get away without paying his bill. But I found out later that he did pay the clerk. In cash."

"Do you remember his name?"

"No." She gave a shrug. "I'm terrible with names."

"Describe him for me. Everything you remember."

She was silent for a moment, struggling to conjure up the face of a man she'd seen weeks ago, and only once. "I remember he was fairly tall. When he lay down on the treatment table, his feet hung over the edge." She looked at Sam. "He'd be about your height."

"I'm six feet. Vincent Spectre's five-eleven. What about his face? Hair, eyes?"

"He had dark hair. Almost black. And his eyes…" She sat back, frowning in concentration. Remembered how startled she'd been by the missing finger. That she'd looked up and met the patient's gaze. "I think they were blue."

"The blue eyes would match Spectre's. The black hair doesn't. He could've dyed it."

"But the face was different. It didn't look like this photo."

"Spectre has resources. He could've paid for plastic surgery, completely changed his appearance. For six months we assumed he was dead. During that time he could've remade himself into an entirely different man."

"All right, what if it *was* Spectre I saw in the ER that day? Why does that make me a target? Why would he want to kill me?"

"You saw his face. You could identify him."

"A lot of people must have seen his face!"

"You're the only one who could connect that face with a man who was missing a finger. You said he was wearing gloves, that he didn't want to remove them."

"Yes, but it was part of his uniform. Maybe the only reason for the gloves was—"

"What uniform?"

"Some sort of long-sleeved jacket with brass buttons. White gloves. Pants with this side stripe. You know, like an elevator operator. Or a bellhop."

"Was there a logo embroidered on the jacket? A building or hotel name?"

"No."

Sam was on his feet now, pacing back and forth with new excitement. "Okay. Okay, he has a minor accident. Cuts his arm, has to go to the ER for stitches. You see that he's missing a finger. You see his face. And you see he's wearing some sort of uniform…."

"It's not enough to make me a threat."

"Maybe it is. Right now, he's operating under a completely new identity. The authorities have no idea what he looks like. But that missing finger is a giveaway. You saw it. And his face. You could identify him for us."

"I didn't know anything about Vincent Spectre. I wouldn't have thought to go to the police."

"We were already raising questions about his so-called death. Wondering if he was still alive and operating. Another bombing, and we might have figured out the truth. All we had to do was tell the public we were looking for a man missing his left middle finger. You would have come forward. Wouldn't you?"

She nodded. "Of course."

"That may be what he was afraid of. That you'd tell us the one thing we didn't know. What he looks like."

For a long moment she was silent. She was staring down at the book of mug shots, thinking about that day in the ER. Trying to remember the patients, the crises. Sore throats and sprained ankles. She'd been a nurse for eight years, had treated so many patients, that the days all seemed to blend together. But she did remember one more detail about that visit from the man with the gloves. A detail that left her suddenly chilled.

"The doctor," she said softly. "The doctor who sutured the cut—"

"Yes? Who was it?"

"Robert. It was Robert."

Sam stared at her. In that instant, he understood. They both did. Robert had been in the same room as well. He'd seen the patient's face, had seen the mutilated left hand. He, like Nina, could have identified Vincent Spectre.

Now Robert was dead.

Sam reached down to take Nina's hand. "Come on." He pulled her to her feet.

They were standing face-to-face now, and she felt her body respond immediately to his nearness, felt her stomach dance that little dance of excitement. Arousal.

"I'm driving you back to Portland," he said.

"Tonight?"

"I want you to meet with our police artist. See if you two can come up with a sketch of Spectre's face."

"I'm not sure I can. If I saw him, I'd recognize him. But just to describe his face—"

"The artist will walk you through it. The important thing is that we have something to work with. Also, I need you to help me go through the ER records. Maybe there's some information you've forgotten."

"We keep a copy of all the encounter forms. I can find his record for you." *I'll do anything you want me to do,* she thought, *if only you'll stop this tough-cop act.*

As they stood gazing at each other, she thought she saw a ripple of longing in his eyes. Too quickly, he turned away to get a jacket from the closet. He draped it over her shoulders. Just the brushing of his fingers against her skin made her quiver.

She shifted around to face him. To confront him.

"Has something happened between us?" she asked softly.

"What do you mean?"

"Last night. I didn't imagine it, Sam. We made love, right here in this room. Now I'm wondering what I did wrong. Why you seem so…indifferent."

He sighed, a sound of weariness. And perhaps regret. "Last night," he began, "shouldn't have happened. It was a mistake."

"I didn't think so."

"Nina, it's always a mistake to fall in love with the investigating cop. You're scared, you're looking for a hero. I happen to fall into the role."

"But you're not playing a role! Neither am I. Sam, I care about you. I think I'm falling in love with you."

He just looked at her without speaking, his silence as cutting as any words.

She turned away, so that she wouldn't have to see that flat, emotionless gaze of his. With a forced laugh she said, "God, I feel like such an idiot. Of course, this must happen to you all the time. Women throwing themselves at you."

"It's not like that."

"Isn't it? The hero cop. Who could resist?" She turned back to him. "So, how do I compare with all the others?"

"There aren't any others! Nina, I'm not trying to shove you away. I just want you to understand that it's the situation that's pulled us together. The danger. The intensity. You look at me and you completely miss all the flaws. All the reasons I'm not the right guy for you. You were engaged to Robert Bledsoe. Ivy League. Medical degree. House on the water. What the hell am I but a civil servant?"

She shook her head, tears suddenly filling her eyes. "Do you really think that's how I see you? As just a civil servant? Just a cop?"

"It's what I am."

"You're so much more." She reached up to touch his face. He flinched, but didn't pull away as her fingers caressed the roughness of his jaw. "Oh, Sam. You're kind. And gentle. And brave. I haven't met any other man like you. Okay, so you're a cop. It's just part of who you are. You've kept me alive. You've watched over me…."

"It was my job."

"Is that all it was?"

He didn't answer right away. He just looked at her, as though reluctant to tell the truth.

"Is it, Sam? Just a part of your job?"

He sighed. "No," he admitted. "It was more than that. You're more than that."

Pure joy made her smile. Last night she'd felt it—his warmth, his caring. For all his denials, there was a living, breathing man under that mask of indifference. She wanted so badly to fall into his arms, to coax the real Sam Navarro out from his hiding place.

He reached up for her hand and gently but firmly lowered it from his face. "Please, Nina," he said. "Don't make this hard for both of us. I have a job to do, and I can't be distracted. It's dangerous. For you and for me."

"But you do care. That's all I need to know. That you care."

He nodded. It was the most she could hope for.

"It's getting late. We should leave," he mumbled. And he turned toward the door. "I'll be waiting for you in the car."

NINA FROWNED at the computer-generated sketch of the suspect's face. "It's not quite right," she said.

"What's not right about it?" asked Sam.

"I don't know. It's not easy to conjure up a man's face. I saw him only that one time. I didn't consciously register the shape of his nose or jaw."

"Does he look anything like this picture?"

She studied the image on the computer screen. For an hour, they'd played with different hairlines, noses, shapes of jaws and chins. What they'd come up with seemed generic, lifeless. Like every other police sketch she'd ever seen.

"To be honest," she admitted with a sigh, "I can't be sure this is what he looks like. If you put the real man in a lineup, I think I'd be able to identify him. But I'm not very good at re-creating what I saw."

Sam, obviously disappointed, turned to the computer technician. "Print it up anyway. Send copies to the news stations and wire services."

"Sure thing, Navarro," the tech replied and he flipped on the printer switch.

As Sam led Nina away, she said miserably, "I'm sorry. I guess I wasn't much help."

"You did fine. And you're right, it's not easy to re-create a face. Especially one you saw only once. You really think you'd know him if you saw him?"

"Yes. I'm pretty sure of it."

He gave her arm a squeeze. "That may be all we'll need from you. Assuming we ever get our hands on him. Which leads to the next item on our agenda."

"What's that?"

"Gillis is already at the hospital, pulling those treatment records. He'll need you to interpret a few things on the encounter form."

She nodded. "*That* I know I can do."

They found Gillis sitting in a back room of the ER, papers piled up on the table in front of him. His face was pasty with fatigue under the fluorescent lights. It was nearly midnight, and he'd been on the job since 7:00 a.m. So had Sam.

For both of them, the night was just beginning.

"I pulled what I think is the right encounter form," said Gillis. "May 29, 5:00 p.m. Sound about right, Miss Cormier?"

"It could be."

Gillis handed her the sheet. It was the one-page record of an ER visit. On top was the name Lawrence Foley, his address, and billing information. On the line Chief Complaint, she recognized her own handwriting: Laceration, left forearm. Below that, she had written: forty-six-year-old white male hit by bicycle in crosswalk. Fell, cut arm on fender. No loss of consciousness."

She nodded. "This is the one. Here's Robert's signature, on the bottom. Treating physician. He sutured the cut—four stitches, according to his notes."

"Have we checked out this name, Lawrence Foley?" Sam asked Gillis.

"No one by that name living at that address," Gillis informed him. "And that's a nonexistent phone number."

"Bingo," said Sam. "False address, false identity. This is our man."

"But we're no closer to catching him," stressed Gillis.

"He left no trail, no clues. Where are we supposed to look?"

"We have a sketch of his face circulating. We know he was wearing some sort of uniform, possibly a bellhop's. So we check all the hotels. Try to match the sketch with any of their employees." Sam paused, frowning. "A hotel. Why would he be working at a hotel?"

"He needed a job?" Gillis offered.

"As a bellhop?" Sam shook his head. "If this is really Vincent Spectre, he had a reason to be there. A contract. A target…" He sat back and rubbed his eyes. The late hour, the stress, was showing in his face. All those shadows, all those lines of weariness. Nina longed to reach out to him, to stroke away the worry she saw there, but she didn't dare. Not in front of Gillis. Maybe not ever. He'd made it perfectly clear she was a distraction to him, to his work, and that distractions were dangerous. That much she accepted.

Yet how she ached to touch him.

Sam rose to his feet and began to move about, as though forcing himself to stay awake. "We need to check all the hotels. Set up a lineup of bellhops. And we need to check police reports. Maybe someone called in that bicycle accident."

"Okay, I'll get Cooley on it."

"What we really need to know is—who is he after? Who's the target?"

"We're not going to figure that out tonight," said Gillis. "We need more to go on." He yawned, and added, "And we need some sleep. Both of us."

"He's right," said Nina. "You can't function without rest, Sam. You need to sleep on this."

"In the meantime, Spectre's at work on God knows what catastrophe. So far we've been lucky. Only one bombing casualty. But the next time..." Sam stopped pacing. Stopped because he'd simply run out of steam. He was standing in one spot, his shoulders slumped, his whole body drooping.

Gillis looked at Nina. "Get him home, will ya? Before he keels over and I have to drag him."

Nina rose from her chair. "Come on, Sam," she said softly. "I'll drive you home."

Heading out to the car, he kept insisting he could drive, that he was in perfectly good shape to take the wheel. She, just as insistently, pointed out that he was a menace on the road.

He let her drive.

Scarcely after she'd pulled out of the hospital parking lot, he was sound asleep.

At his house, she roused him just long enough to climb out of the car and walk in the front door. In his bedroom, he shrugged off his gun holster, pulled off his shoes, and collapsed on the bed. His last words were some sort of apology. Then he was fast asleep.

Smiling, she pulled the covers over him and went out to check the windows and doors. Everything was locked tight; the house was secure—as secure as it could be.

Back in Sam's room, she undressed in the dark and climbed into bed beside him. He didn't stir. Gently she stroked her fingers through his hair and thought, *My poor, exhausted Sam. Tonight, I'll watch over you.*

Sighing, he turned toward her, his arm reaching out to hug her against him. Even in his sleep, he was trying to protect her.

Like no other man I've ever known.
Nothing could hurt her. Not tonight, not in his arms.
She'd stake her life on it.

THEY WERE SHOWING his picture on the morning news.

Vincent Spectre took one look at the police sketch on the TV screen and he laughed softly. What a joke. The picture looked nothing like him. The ears were too big, the jaw was too wide, and the eyes looked beady. He did not have beady eyes. How had they gotten it so wrong? What had happened to the quality of law enforcement?

"Can't catch me, I'm the gingerbread man," he murmured.

Sam Navarro was slipping, if that drawing was the best he could come up with. A pity. Navarro had seemed such a clever man, a truly worthy opponent. Now it appeared he was as dumb a cop as all the others. Though he *had* managed to draw one correct conclusion.

Vincent Spectre was alive and back in the game.

"Just wait till you see how alive I am," he said.

That Cormier woman must have described his face to the police artist. Although the sketch wasn't anything for him to worry about, Nina Cormier did concern him. Chances were, she'd recognize him in a room of anonymous strangers. She was the only one who could link his face to his identity, the only one who could ruin his plan. She would have to be disposed of.

Eventually.

He turned off the TV and went into the apartment bedroom, where the woman was still asleep. He'd met Marilyn Dukoff three weeks ago at the Stop Light Club, where he'd gone to watch the topless dance revue. Marilyn had been the blonde in the purple-sequined G-string. Her face was coarse, her IQ a joke, but her figure was a marvel of nature and silicone. Like so many other women on the exotic dance circuit, she was in desperate need of money and affection.

He'd offered her both, in abundance.

She'd accepted his gifts with true gratitude. She was like a puppy who'd been neglected too long, loyal and hungry for approval. Best of all, she asked no questions. She knew enough not to.

He sat down beside her on the bed and nudged her awake. "Marilyn?"

She opened one sleepy eye and smiled at him. "Good morning."

He returned her smile. And followed it with a kiss. As usual, she responded eagerly. Gratefully. He removed his clothes and climbed under the sheets, next to that architecturally astonishing body. It took no coaxing at all to get her into the mood.

When they had finished, and she lay smiling and satisfied beside him, he knew it was the right time to ask.

And he said, "I need another favor from you."

TWO HOURS LATER, a blond woman in a gray suit presented her ID to the prison official. "I'm an attorney with Frick and Darien," she said. "Here to see our client, Billy Binford."

Moments later she was escorted to the visiting room. Billy "The Snowman" took a seat on the other side of the Plexiglas. He regarded her for a moment, then said, "I been watching the news on TV. What the hell's all this other stuff going on?"

"He says it's all necessary," said the blonde.

"Look, I just wanted the job done like he promised."

"It's being taken care of. Everything's on schedule. All you have to do is sit back and wait."

Billy glanced at the prison guard, who was standing off to the side and obviously bored. "I got everything riding on this," he muttered.

"It will happen. But he wants to make sure you keep up your end of the bargain. Payment, by the end of the week."

"Not yet. Not till I'm sure it's done. I got a court date coming up fast—too fast. I'm counting on this."

The blonde merely smiled. "It'll happen," she said. "He guarantees it."

Ten

Sam woke up to the smell of coffee and the aroma of something cooking, something delicious. It was Saturday. He was alone in the bed, but there was no question that someone else was in the house. He could hear the bustle in the kitchen, the soft clink of dishes. For the first time in months, he found himself smiling as he rose from bed and headed to the shower. There was a woman in the kitchen, a woman who was actually cooking breakfast. Amazing how different that made the whole house feel. Warm. Welcoming.

He came out of the shower and stood in front of the mirror to shave. That's when his smile faded. He suddenly wondered how long he'd been asleep. He'd slept so heavily he hadn't heard Nina get out of bed this morning, hadn't even heard her take a shower. But she'd been in here; the shower curtain had already been damp when he stepped in.

Last night someone could have broken into the house, and he would have slept right through it.

I'm useless to her, he thought. He couldn't track down

Spectre and keep Nina safe at the same time. He didn't have the stamina or the objectivity. He was worse than useless; he was endangering her life.

This was exactly what he'd been afraid would happen.

He finished shaving, got dressed, and went into the kitchen.

Just the sight of her standing at the stove was enough to shake his determination. She turned and smiled at him.

"Good morning," she murmured, and wrapped her arms around him in a sweetly scented hug. Lord, this was every man's fantasy. Or, at least, it was *his* fantasy: a gorgeous woman in his kitchen. The good morning smile. Pancakes cooking in the skillet.

A woman in the house.

Not just any woman. Nina. Already he felt his resistance weakening, felt the masculine urges taking over again. This was what always happened when he got too close to her.

He took her by the shoulders and stepped away. "Nina, we have to talk."

"You mean…about the case?"

"No. I mean about you. And me."

All at once that radiant smile was gone from her face. She'd sensed that a blow was about to fall, a blow that would be delivered by *him*. Mutely she turned, lifted the pancake from the skillet, and slid it onto a plate. Then she just stood there, looking at it lying on the countertop.

He hated himself at that moment. At the same time he knew there was no other way to handle this—not if he really cared about her.

"Last night shouldn't have happened," he said.

"But nothing *did* happen between us. I just brought you home and put you to bed."

"That's exactly what I'm talking about. Nina, I was so exhausted last night, someone could've driven a damn train through my bedroom and I wouldn't have moved a muscle. How am I supposed to keep you safe when I can't even keep my eyes open?"

"Oh, Sam." She stepped toward him, her hands rising to caress his face. "I don't expect you to be my guardian. Last night, I wanted to take care of *you*. I was so happy to do it."

"I'm the cop, Nina. I'm responsible for your safety."

"For once, can't you stop being a cop? Can't you let me take care of *you?* I'm not so helpless. And you're not so tough that you don't need someone. When I was scared, you were there for me. And I want to be here for *you*."

"I'm not the one who could get killed." He took both her hands and firmly lowered them from his face. "This isn't a good idea, getting involved, and we both know it. I can't watch out for you the way I should. Any other cop could do a better job."

"I don't trust any other cop. I trust you."

"And that could be a fatal mistake." He pulled away, gaining himself some breathing space. Anything to put distance between them. He couldn't think clearly when she was so near; her scent, her touch, were too distracting. He turned and matter-of-factly poured himself a cup of coffee, noting as he did it that his hand wasn't quite steady. Her effect, again. Not looking at her, he said, "It's time to focus on the case, Nina. On finding Spectre. That's the best way to ensure your safety. By doing my job and doing it right."

She said nothing.

He turned and saw that she was gazing listlessly at the table. It had already been set with silverware and napkins, glasses of juice, and a small crock of maple syrup. Again he felt that stab of regret. *I've finally found a woman I care about, a woman I could love, and I'm doing my best to push her away.*

"So," she said softly. "What do you propose, Sam?"

"I think another man should be assigned to protect you. Someone who has no personal involvement with you."

"Is that what we have? A personal involvement?"

"What else would you call it?"

She shook her head. "I'm beginning to think we have no involvement at all."

"For God's sake, Nina. We slept with each other! How can two people get more involved than that?"

"For some people, sex is purely a physical act. And that's all it is." Her chin tilted up in silent inquiry. *For some people.*

Meaning me?

Damn it, he refused to get caught up in this hopeless conversation. She was baiting him, trying to get him to admit there was more to that act of lovemaking than just sex. He was not about to admit the truth, not about to let her know how terrified he was of losing her.

He knew what had to be done.

He crossed the kitchen to the telephone. He'd call Coopersmith, ask him to assign a man to pull guard duty. He was about to pick up the receiver when the phone suddenly rang.

He answered it with a curt "Navarro."

"Sam, it's me."

"Morning, Gillis."

"Morning? It's nearly noon. I've already put in a full day here."

"Yeah, I'm hanging my head in shame."

"You should. We've got that lineup scheduled for one o'clock. Bellhops from five different hotels. You think you can bring Nina Cormier down here to take a look? That is, if she's there with you."

"She's here," admitted Sam.

"That's what I figured. Be here at one o'clock, got it?"

"We'll be there." He hung up and ran his hand through his damp hair. God. Nearly noon? He was getting lazy. Careless. All this agonizing over him and Nina, over a relationship that really had nowhere to go, was cutting into his effectiveness as a cop. If he didn't do his job right, *she* was the one who'd suffer.

"What did Gillis say?" he heard her ask.

He turned to her. "They've scheduled a lineup at one o'clock. Want you to look at a few hotel bellhops. You up to it?"

"Of course. I want this over with as much as you do."

"Good."

"And you're right about turning me over to another cop. It's all for the best." She met his gaze with a look of clear-eyed determination. "You have more important things to do than baby-sit me."

He didn't try to argue with her. In fact, he didn't say a thing. But as she walked out of the kitchen, leaving him standing alone by that cozily set breakfast table, he thought, *You're wrong. There's no more important job in the world to me than watching over you.*

EIGHT MEN STOOD on the other side of the one-way mirror. All of them were facing forward. All of them looked a little sheepish about being there.

Nina carefully regarded each man's uniform in turn, searching for any hint of familiarity. Any detail at all that might trip a memory.

She shook her head. "I don't see the right uniform."

"You're absolutely certain?" asked Gillis.

"I'm certain. It wasn't any of those."

She heard an undisguised snort of disappointment. It came from Norm Liddell, the D.A. who was standing next to Gillis. Sam, poker-faced, said nothing.

"Well, this was a big waste of my time," muttered Liddell. "Is this all you've come up with, Navarro? A bellhop roundup?"

"We know Spectre was wearing some sort of uniform similar to a bellhop's," said Sam. "We just wanted her to look over a few."

"We did track down a police report of that bike accident," said Gillis. "The bicyclist himself called it in. I think he was worried about a lawsuit, so he made a point of stating that he hit the man outside a crosswalk. Apparently, Spectre was jaywalking when he was hit on Congress Street."

"Congress?" Liddell frowned.

"Right near the Pioneer Hotel," said Sam. "Which, we've found out, is where the Governor plans to stay day after tomorrow. He's the guest speaker at some small business seminar."

"You think Spectre's target is the Governor?"

"It's a possibility. We're having the Pioneer checked and double-checked. Especially the Governor's room."

"What about the Pioneer's bellhops?"

"We eliminated all of them, just based on height and age. No one's missing any fingers. That one there—number three—is the closest to Spectre's description. But he has all his fingers, too. We just wanted Nina to take a look at the uniform, see if it jogged a memory."

"But no one in that lineup is Spectre."

"No. We've looked at everyone's hands. No missing fingers."

Nina's gaze turned to number three in the lineup. He was dressed in a bellhop's red jacket and black pants. "Is that what all the Pioneer's bellhops wear?" she asked.

"Yeah," said Gillis. "Why?"

"I don't think that's the uniform I saw."

"What's different about it?"

"The man I saw in the ER—I'm just remembering it—his jacket was green. Sort of a forest green. It was definitely not red."

Gillis shook his head. "We got us a problem then. The Holiday Inn's uniform is red, too. Marriott's green, but it's not located anywhere near the bicycle accident."

"Check out their staff anyway," Liddell ordered. "If you have to interview every bellhop in town, I want this guy caught. And I sure as hell want him caught before he blows up some high-muck-a-muck. When's the Governor arriving tomorrow?"

"Sometime in the afternoon," said Gillis.

Liddell glanced at his watch. "We have a full twenty-four hours. If anything comes up, I get called. Got it?"

"Yes, sir, your highness," muttered Gillis.

Liddell glanced sharply at him, but obviously decided to drop it. "My wife and I'll be at the Brant Theater tonight. I'll have my beeper with me, just in case."

"You'll be first on our list to call," said Sam.

"We're in the spotlight on this. So let's not screw up." It was Liddell's parting shot, and the two cops took it in silence.

Only after Liddell had left the room did Gillis growl, "I'm gonna get that guy. I swear, I'm gonna get him."

"Cool it, Gillis. He may be governor someday."

"In which case, I'll help Spectre plant the damn bomb myself."

Sam took Nina's arm and walked her out of the room. "Come on. I have my hands full today. I'll introduce you to your new watchdog."

Passing me off already, she thought. Was she such a nuisance to him?

"For now, we're keeping you in a hotel," he said. "Officer Pressler's been assigned to watch over you. He's a sharp cop. I trust him."

"Meaning I should, too?"

"Absolutely. I'll call you if we turn up any suspects. We'll need you to identify them."

"So I may not be seeing you for a while."

He stopped in the hallway and looked at her. "No. It may be a while."

They faced each other for a moment. The hallway was hardly private; certainly this wasn't the time or the place to confess how she felt about him. *She* wasn't even sure how she felt about him. All she knew was that it hurt to say goodbye. What hurt even worse was to look in his eyes and see no regret, no distress. Just that flat, unemotional gaze.

So it was back to Mr. Civil Servant. She could deal with that. After the trauma of this last week, she could deal with anything, including the realization that she had, once again, gotten involved with the wrong man.

She met his gaze with one just as cool and said, "You find Spectre. I'll identify him. Just do it soon, okay? So I can get on with my life."

"We're working on it round the clock. We'll keep you informed."

"Can I count on that?"

He answered with a curt dip of the head. "It's part of my job."

OFFICER LEON PRESSLER was not a conversationalist. In fact, whether he could converse at all was in question. For the past three hours, the muscular young cop had done a terrific sphinx imitation, saying nary a word as he roamed the hotel room, alternately checking the door and glancing out the third floor window. The most he would say was "Yes, ma'am," or "No, ma'am," and that was only in response to a direct question. Was the strong, silent bit some kind of cop thing? Nina wondered. Or was he under orders not to get too chatty with the witness?

She tried to read a novel she'd picked up in the hotel gift shop, but after a few chapters she gave up. His silence made her too nervous. It was simply not natural to spend a day in a hotel room with another person and not, at the very least, talk to each other. Lord knew, she tried to draw him out.

"Have you been a cop a long time, Leon?" she asked.

"Yes, ma'am."

"Do you enjoy it?"

"Yes, ma'am."

"Does it ever scare you?"

"No, ma'am."

"Never?"

"Sometimes."

Now they were getting somewhere, she thought.

But then Officer Pressler crossed the room and peered out the window, ignoring her.

She put her book aside and launched another attempt at conversation.

"Does this sort of assignment bore you?" she asked.

"No, ma'am."

"It would bore me. Spending all day in a hotel room doing nothing."

"Things could happen."

"And I'm sure you'll be ready for it." Sighing, she reached for the remote and clicked on the TV. Five minutes of channel surfing turned up nothing of interest. She clicked it off again. "Can I make a phone call?" she asked.

"Sorry."

"I just want to call my nursing supervisor at Maine Medical. To tell her I won't be coming in next week."

"Detective Navarro said no phone calls. It's necessary for your safety. He was very specific on that."

"What else did the good detective tell you?"

"I'm to keep a close eye. Not let my guard down for a minute. Because if anything happened to you…" He paused and gave a nervous cough.

"What?"

"He'd, uh, have my hide."

"That's quite an incentive."

"He wanted to make sure I took special care. Not that I'd let anything happen. I owe him that much."

She frowned at him. He was at the window again, peering down at the street. "What do you mean, you owe him?"

Officer Pressler didn't move from the window. He stood looking out, as though unwilling to meet her gaze. "It was a few years back. I was on this domestic call. Husband didn't much like me sticking my nose into his business. So he shot me."

"My god."

"I radioed for help. Navarro was first to respond." Pressler turned and looked at her. "So you see, I do owe him." Calmly he turned back to the window.

"How well do you know him?" she asked softly.

Pressler shrugged. "He's a good cop. But real private. I'm not sure anyone knows him very well."

Including me, she thought. Sighing, she clicked on the boob tube again and channel surfed past a jumble of daytime soaps, a TV court show and a golf tournament. She could almost feel another few brain cells collapse into mush.

What was Sam doing right now? she wondered.

And ruthlessly suppressed the thought. Sam Navarro was his own man. That much was perfectly clear.

She would have to be her own woman.

I WONDER WHAT Nina's doing right now. At once Sam tried to suppress the thought, tried to concentrate instead on what was being said at the meeting, but his mind kept drifting back to the subject of Nina. Specifically, her safety. He had every reason to trust Leon Pressler. The young cop was sharp and reliable, and he owed his life to Sam. If anyone could be trusted to keep Nina out of harm's way, it would be Pressler.

Still, he couldn't shake that lingering sense of uneasiness. And fear. It was one more indication that he'd lost his objectivity, that his feelings were way out of control. To the point of affecting his work…

"…the best we can do? Sam?"

Sam suddenly focused on Abe Coopersmith. "Excuse me?"

Coopersmith sighed. "Where the hell are you, Navarro?"

"I'm sorry. I let my attention drift for a moment."

Gillis said, "Chief asked if we're following any other leads."

"We're following every lead we have," Sam informed him. "The sketch of Spectre is circulating. We've checked all the hotels in Portland. So far, no employees with a missing finger. Problem is, we're operating blind. We don't know Spectre's target, when he plans to strike, or where he plans to strike. All we have is a witness who's seen his face."

"And this bit about the bellhop's uniform."

"That's right."

"Have you shown all those uniforms to Miss Cormier? To help us identify which hotel we're talking about?"

"We're getting together a few more samples for her to look at," said Gillis. "Also, we've interviewed that bicyclist. He doesn't remember much about the man he hit. It happened so fast, he didn't really pay attention to the face. But he does back up Miss Cormier's recollection that the uniform jacket was green. Some shade of it, anyway. And he confirms that it happened on Congress Street, near Franklin Avenue."

"We've combed that whole area," said Sam. "Showed the sketch to every shopkeeper and clerk within a five-block radius. No one recognized the face."

Coopersmith gave a grunt of frustration. "We've got the Governor arriving tomorrow afternoon. And a bomber somewhere in the city."

"We don't know if there's a connection. Spectre could be targeting someone else entirely. It all depends on who hired him."

"He may not even plan a hit at all," suggested Gillis. "Maybe he's finished his job. Maybe he's left town."

"We have to assume he's still here," cautioned Cooper-smith. "And up to no good."

Sam nodded in agreement. "We have twenty-four hours before the Governor's meeting. By then, something's bound to turn up."

"God, I hope so," said Coopersmith, and he rose to leave. "If there's one thing we don't need, it's another bomb going off. And a dead Governor."

"LET'S TAKE IT from the top. Measure 36." The conductor raised his baton, brought it down again. Four beats later, the trumpets blared out the opening notes of "Wrong Side of the Track Blues," to be joined seconds later by wood-winds and bass. Then the sax slid in, its plaintive whine picking up the melody.

"Never did understand jazz," complained the Brant Theater manager, watching the rehearsal from the middle aisle. "Lotta sour notes if you ask me. All the instruments fighting with each other."

"I like jazz," said the head usher.

"Yeah, well, you like rap, too. So I don't think much of your taste." The manager glanced around the theater, sur-veying the empty seats. He noted that everything was clean, that there was no litter in the aisles. The audience tonight would be a discriminating crowd. Bunch of lawyer types. They wouldn't appreciate sticky floors or wadded up programs in the chairs.

Just a year ago, this building had been a porn palace, showing X-rated films to an audience of nameless, faceless men. The new owner had changed all that. Now, with a little private money from a local benefactor, the Brant Theater had been rehabilitated into a live performance center, featuring stage plays and musical artists. Unfortunately, the live performances brought in fewer crowds than the porn had. The manager wasn't surprised.

Tonight, at least, a big audience was assured—five hundred paid and reserved seats, with additional walk-ins expected, to benefit the local Legal Aid office. Imagine that. All those lawyers actually paying to hear jazz. He didn't get it. But he was glad these seats would be filled.

"Looks like we may be short a man tonight," said the head usher.

"Who?"

"That new guy you hired. You know, the one from the Agency. Showed up for work two days ago. Haven't heard from him since. I tried calling him, but no luck."

The manager cursed. "Can't rely on these agency hires."

"That's for sure."

"You just gotta work the crowd with four men tonight."

"Gonna be a bear. Five hundred reserved seats and all."

"Let some of 'em find their own seats. They're lawyers. They're supposed to have brains." The manager glanced at his watch. It was six-thirty. He'd have just enough time to wolf down that corned beef sandwich in his office. "Doors open in an hour," he said. "Better get your supper now."

"Sure thing," replied the head usher. He swept up the green uniform jacket from the seat where he'd left it. And, whistling, he headed up the aisle for his dinner.

AT SEVEN-THIRTY, Officer Pressler escorted Nina back to police headquarters. The building was quieter than it had been that afternoon, most of the desks deserted, and only an occasional clerk circulating in the halls. Pressler brought Nina upstairs and ushered her into an office.

Sam was there.

He gave her only the most noncommittal of greetings: a nod, a quiet hello. She responded in kind. Pressler was in the room too, as were Gillis and another man in plain-clothes, no doubt a cop as well. With an audience watching, she was not about to let her feelings show. Obviously Sam wasn't, either.

"We wanted you to take a look at these uniforms," Sam said, gesturing to the long conference table. Laid out on the table were a half dozen uniform jackets of various colors. "We've got bellhops, an elevator operator, and an usher's uniform from the downtown Cineplex. Do any of them strike you as familiar?"

Nina approached the table. Thoughtfully she eyed each one, examining the fabrics, the buttons. Some of them had embroidered hotel logos. Some were trimmed with gold braid or nametags.

She shook her head. "It wasn't one of these."

"What about that green one, on the end?"

"It has gold braid. The jacket I remember had black braid, sort of coiled up here, on the shoulder."

"Geez," murmured Gillis. "Women remember the weirdest things."

"Okay," Sam said with a sigh. "That's it for this session. Thanks, everyone. Pressler, why don't you take a break and get some supper. I'll bring Miss Cormier back to her hotel. You can meet us there in an hour or so."

The room emptied out. All except Sam and Nina.

For a moment, they didn't speak to each other. They didn't even look at each other. Nina almost wished that the earnest Officer Pressler was back with her again; at least *he* didn't make her feel like turning tail and running.

"I hope your hotel room's all right," he finally said.

"It's fine. But I'll be going stir crazy in another day. I have to get out of there."

"It's not safe yet."

"When will it be safe?"

"When we have Spectre."

"That could be never." She shook her head. "I can't live this way. I have a job. I have a life. I can't stay in a hotel room with some cop who drives me up a wall."

Sam frowned. "What's Pressler done?"

"He won't sit still! He never stops checking the windows. He won't let me touch the phone. And he can't carry on a decent conversation."

"Oh." Sam's frown evaporated. "That's just Leon doing his job. He's good."

"Maybe he is. But he still drives me crazy." Sighing, she took a step toward him. "Sam, I can't stay cooped up. I have to get on with my life."

"You will. But we have to get you through this part alive."

"What if I left town? Went somewhere else for a while—"

"We might need you here, Nina."

"You don't. You have his prints. You know he's missing a finger. You could identify him without any question—"

"But we need to spot him first. And for that, we might need you to pick him out of a crowd. So you have to stay in town. Available. We'll keep you safe, I promise."

"I suppose you'll have to. If you want to catch your man."

He took her by the shoulders. "That's not the only reason, and you know it."

"Do I?"

He leaned closer. For one astonishing moment she thought he was going to kiss her. Then a rap on the door made them both jerk apart.

Gillis, looking distinctly ill at ease, stood in the doorway. "Uh...I'm heading over to get a burger. You want I should get you something, Sam?"

"No. We'll pick something up at her hotel."

"Okay." Gillis gave an apologetic wave. "I'll be back here in an hour." He departed, leaving Sam and Nina alone once again.

But the moment was gone forever. If he'd intended to kiss her, she saw no hint of it in his face.

He said, simply, "I'll drive you back now."

In Sam's car, she felt as if they'd reverted right back to the very first day they'd met, to the time when he'd been the stone-faced detective and she'd been the bewildered citizen. It was as if all the events of the past week—their nights together, their lovemaking—had never happened. He seemed determined to avoid any talk of feelings tonight, and she was just as determined not to broach the subject.

The only safe topic was the case. And even on that topic, he was not very forthcoming.

"I notice you've circulated the police sketch," she said.

"It's been everywhere. TV, the papers."

"Any response?"

"We've been inundated by calls. We've spent all day chasing them down. So far, nothing's panned out."

"I'm afraid my description wasn't very helpful."

"You did the best you could."

She looked out the window, at the streets of downtown

Portland. It was already eight o'clock, the summer dusk just slipping into night. "If I saw him again, I'd know him. I'm sure I would."

"That's all we need from you, Nina."

All you want from me, too, she thought sadly. She asked, "What happens tomorrow?"

"More of the same. Chase down leads. Hope someone recognizes that sketch."

"Do you know if Spectre's even in the city?"

"No. He may be long gone. In which case we're just spinning our wheels. But my instincts are telling me he's still here somewhere. And he's got something planned, something big." He glanced at her. "*You* could be the wrench in the works. The one person who can recognize him. That's why we have to keep you under wraps."

"I can't stand much more of this. I'm not even allowed to make a phone call."

"We don't want people to know your whereabouts."

"I won't tell anyone. I promise. It's just that I feel so cut off from everyone."

"Okay." He sighed. "Who do you want to call?"

"I could start with my sister, Wendy."

"I thought you two didn't get along."

"We don't. But she's still my sister. And she can tell the rest of the family I'm okay."

He thought it over for a moment, then said, "All right, go ahead and call her. You can use the car phone. But don't—"

"I know, I know. Don't tell her where I am." She picked up the receiver and dialed Wendy's number. She heard three rings, and then a woman's voice answered—a voice she didn't recognize.

"Hayward residence."

"Hello, this is Nina. I'm Wendy's sister. Is she there?"

"I'm sorry, but Mr. and Mrs. Hayward are out for the evening. I'm the baby-sitter."

That's how worried she is about me, thought Nina with an irrational sense of abandonment.

"Would you like her to call you back?" asked the baby-sitter.

"No, I, uh, won't be available. But maybe I can call her later. Do you know what time she'll be home?"

"They're at the Brant Theater for that Legal Aid benefit. I think it runs till ten-thirty. And then they usually go out for coffee and dessert, so I'd expect them home around midnight."

"Oh. That's too late. I'll call tomorrow, thanks." She hung up and gave a sigh of disappointment.

"Not home?"

"No. I should have guessed they'd be out. In Jake's law firm, the business day doesn't end at five. The evenings are taken up by business affairs, too."

"Your brother-in-law's an attorney?"

"With ambitions of being a judge. And he's only thirty years old."

"Sounds like a fast-tracker."

"He is. Which means he needs a fast-track wife. Wendy's perfect that way. I'll bet you that right at this moment, she's at the theater charming the socks off some judge. And she can do it without even trying. She's the politician in the family." She glanced at Sam and saw that he was frowning. "Is something wrong?" she asked.

"What theater? Where did they go tonight?"

"The Brant Theater. That's where the benefit is."

"Benefit?"

"The baby-sitter said it was for Legal Aid. Why?"

Sam stared ahead at the road. "The Brant Theater. Didn't it just reopen?"

"A month ago. It was a disgrace before. All those porn flicks."

"Damn. Why didn't I think of it?"

Without warning, he made a screeching U-turn and headed the car the way they'd come, back toward the downtown district.

"What are you doing?" she demanded.

"The Brant Theater. A Legal Aid benefit. Who do you suppose'll be there?"

"A bunch of lawyers?"

"Right. As well as our esteemed D.A., Norm Liddell. Now, I'm not particularly fond of lawyers, but I'm not crazy about picking up their dead bodies, either."

She stared at him. "You think that's the target? The Brant Theater?"

"They'll need ushers tonight. Think about it. What does an usher wear?"

"Sometimes it's just black pants and a white shirt."

"But in a grand old theater like the Brant? They just might be dressed in green jackets with black braid…."

"That's where we're going?"

He nodded. "I want you to take a look. Tell me if we're warm. Tell me if that uniform you saw could've been a theater usher's."

By the time they pulled up across the street from the Brant Theater, it was 8:20. Sam didn't waste his time looking for a parking space; he left the car angled against the red-painted curb. As he and Nina climbed out, they heard a doorman yell, "Hey, you can't park there!"

"Police!" Sam answered, waving his badge. "We need to get in the theater."

The doorman stepped aside and waved them in.

The lobby was deserted. Through the closed aisle doors, they could hear the bluesy wail of clarinets, the syncopated beats of a snare drum. No ushers were in sight.

Sam yanked open an aisle door and slipped into the theater. Seconds later, he reemerged with a short and loudly protesting usher in tow. "Look at the uniform," he said to Nina. "Look familiar?"

Nina took one glance at the short green jacket, the black braid and brass buttons, and she nodded. "That's it. That's the one I saw."

"*What's* the one?" demanded the usher, yanking himself free.

"How many ushers working here tonight?" snapped Sam.

"Who are you, anyway?"

Again Sam whipped out his badge. "Police. There's a chance you have a bomb somewhere in there. So tell me quick. How many ushers?"

"A bomb?" The man's gaze darted nervously toward the lobby exit. "Uh, we got four working tonight."

"That's it?"

"Yeah. One didn't show up."

"Did he have a missing finger?"

"Hell, I don't know. We all wear gloves." The usher looked again toward the exit. "You really think there could be a bomb in there?"

"We can't afford to make a wrong guess. I'm evacuating the building." He glanced at Nina. "Get out of here. Wait in the car."

"But you'll need help—"

He was already pushing through the door, into the darkened theater. From the open doorway, she watched him walk swiftly down the aisle. He climbed up to the stage and crossed to the conductor, who regarded him with a look of startled outrage.

The musicians, just as startled, stopped playing.

Sam grabbed the conductor's microphone. "Ladies and gentlemen," he said curtly. "This is the Portland Police. We have had a bomb threat. Calmly, but without delay, will everyone please evacuate the building. I repeat, stay calm, but please evacuate the building."

Almost immediately the exodus began. Nina had to scramble backward out of the doorway to avoid the first rush of people heading up the aisle. In the confusion, she lost sight of Sam, but she could still hear his voice over the speaker system.

"Please remain calm. There is no immediate danger. Exit the building in an orderly fashion."

He's going to be the last one out, she thought. *The one most likely hurt if a bomb does go off.*

The exodus was in full force now, a rush of frightened men and women in evening clothes. The first hint of disaster happened so quickly Nina didn't even see it. Perhaps someone had tripped over a long hem; perhaps there were simply too many feet storming the doorway. Suddenly people were stumbling, falling over each other. A woman screamed. Those still backed up in the aisle instantly panicked.

And rushed for the door.

Eleven

Nina watched in horror as a woman in a long evening gown fell beneath the stampede. Struggling to reach her, Nina shoved through the crowd, only to be swept along with them and forced out the lobby doors and into the street. To get back inside the building was impossible; she'd be moving against the crowd, against the full force of panic.

Already the street was filling up with evacuees, everyone milling about looking dazed. To her relief, she caught sight of Wendy and Jake among the crowd; at least her sister was safe and out of the building. The flood of people out the doors gradually began to ebb.

But where was Sam? Had he made it out yet?

Then, through the crowd, she spotted him emerging from the lobby door. He had his arm around an elderly man, whom he hauled to the sidewalk and set down against the lamppost.

As Nina started toward him, Sam spotted her and yelled, "This one needs attention. Take care of him!"

"Where are you going?"

"Back inside. There are a few more in there."

"I can help you—"

"Help me by staying *out* of the building. And see to that man."

He has his job to do, she thought, watching Sam head back into the theater. *So do I.*

She turned her attention to the elderly man propped up against the lamppost. Kneeling beside him she asked, "Sir, are you all right?"

"My chest. It hurts…"

Oh, no. A coronary. And no ambulance in sight. At once she lowered his head onto the sidewalk, checked his pulse, and unbuttoned his shirt. She was so busy attending to her patient she scarcely noticed when the first patrol car pulled up in front of the theater. By then the crowd was a mass of confusion, everyone demanding to know what was going on.

She looked up to see Sam push out the lobby door again, this time carrying the woman in the evening dress. He lay the woman down beside Nina.

"One more inside," he said, turning back to the building. "Check the lady out."

"Navarro!" yelled a voice.

Sam glanced back as a man in a tuxedo approached.

"What the hell is going on?"

"Can't talk, Liddell. I've got work to do."

"Was there a bomb call or not?"

"Not a call."

"Then why'd you order an evacuation?"

"The usher's uniform." Again Sam turned toward the building.

"Navarro!" Liddell yelled. "I want an explanation! People have been hurt because of this! Unless you can justify it—"

Sam had vanished through the lobby doors.

Liddell paced the sidewalk, waiting to resume his harangue. At last, in frustration, he shouted, "I'm going to have your ass for this, Navarro!"

Those were the last words out of Liddell's mouth before the bomb exploded.

The force of the blast threw Nina backward, onto the street. She landed hard, her elbows scraping across the pavement, but she felt no pain. The shock of the impact left her too stunned to feel anything at all except a strange sense of unreality. She saw broken glass pelt the cars in the street. Saw smoke curl through the air and scores of people lying on the road, all of them just as stunned as she was. And she saw that the lobby door of the Brant Theater was tilted at a crazy angle and hanging by one hinge.

Through the pall of silence, she heard the first moan. Then another. Then came sobs, cries from the injured. Slowly she struggled to sit up. Only then did she feel the pain. Her elbows were torn and bleeding. Her head ached so badly she had to clutch it just to keep from throwing up. But as the awareness of pain crept into her consciousness, so too did the memory of what had happened just before the blast.

Sam. Sam had gone into the building.

Where was he? She scanned the road, the sidewalk, but her vision was blurry. She saw Liddell, sitting up now and groaning by the lamppost. Next to him was the elderly man whom Sam had dragged out of the theater. He, too, was conscious and moving. But there was no Sam.

She stumbled to her feet. A wave of dizziness almost sent her back down to her knees. Fighting it, she forced herself to move toward that open door and stepped inside.

It was dark, too dark to see anything. The only light was

the faint glow from the street, shining through the doorway. She stumbled across debris and landed on her knees. Quickly she rose back to her feet, but she knew it was hopeless. It was impossible to navigate, much less find anyone in this darkness.

"Sam?" she cried, moving deeper into the shadows. *"Sam?"*

Her own voice, thick with despair, echoed back at her.

She remembered that he'd stepped into the lobby a moment before the blast. He could be anywhere in the building, or he could be somewhere nearby. Somewhere she could reach him.

Again she cried out, "Sam!"

This time, faintly, she heard a reply. "Nina?" It didn't come from inside the building. It came from the outside. From the street.

She turned and felt her way back toward the exit, guided by the glow of the doorway. Even before she reached it, she saw him standing there, silhouetted in the light from the street.

"Nina?"

"I'm here. I'm here…." She stumbled through the last stretch of darkness dividing them and was instantly swept into an embrace that was too fierce to be gentle, too terrified to be comforting.

"What the hell were you doing in *there?*" he demanded.

"Looking for you."

"You were supposed to stay outside. Away from the building. When I couldn't find you…" His arms tightened around her, drawing her so close she felt as though it were his heart hammering in her chest. "Next time, you *listen* to me."

"I thought you were inside—"

"I came out the other door."

"I didn't see you!"

"I was dragging the last man out. I'd just got out when the bomb went off. It blew us both out onto the sidewalk." He pulled back and looked at her. Only then did she see the blood trickling down his temple.

"Sam, you need to see a doctor—"

"We have a lot of people here who need a doctor." He glanced around at the street. "I can wait."

Nina, too, focused on the chaos surrounding them. "We've got to get people triaged for the ambulances. I'll get to work."

"You feeling up to it?"

She gave him a nod. And a quick smile. "This is my forte, Detective. Disasters." She waded off into the crowd.

Now that she knew Sam was alive and safe, she could concentrate on what needed to be done. And one glance at the scene told her this was the start of a busy night. Not just here, in the street, but in the ER as well. All the area hospitals would need to call in every ER nurse they had to attend to these people.

Her head was starting to ache worse than ever, her scraped elbows stung every time she bent her arms. But at this moment, as far as she knew, she was the only nurse on the scene.

She focused on the nearest victim, a woman whose leg was cut and bleeding. Nina knelt down, ripped a strip of fabric from the victim's hem, and quickly wrapped a make-shift pressure bandage around the bleeding limb. When she'd finished tying it off, she noted to her satisfaction that the flow of blood had stopped.

That was only the first, she thought, and she looked around for the next patient. There were dozens more to go....

ACROSS THE STREET, his face hidden in the shadows, Vincent Spectre watched the chaos and muttered a curse. Both Judge Stanley Dalton and Norm Liddell were still alive. Spectre could see the young D.A. sitting against the lamppost, clutching his head. The blond woman sitting beside him must be Liddell's wife. They were right in the thick of things, surrounded by dozens of other injured theater patrons. Spectre couldn't just walk right over and dispatch Liddell, not without being seen by a score of witnesses. Sam Navarro was just a few yards from Liddell, and Navarro would certainly be armed.

Another humiliation. This would destroy his reputation, not to mention his back account. The Showman had promised four hundred thousand dollars for the deaths of Dalton and Liddell. Spectre had thought this an elegant solution: to kill both of them at once. With so many other victims, the identity of the targets might never be pinpointed.

But the targets were still alive, and there'd be no payment forthcoming.

The job had become too risky to complete, especially with Navarro on the scent. Thanks to Navarro, Spectre would have to bow out. And kiss his four hundred thousand goodbye.

He shifted his gaze, refocusing on another figure in the crowd. It was that nurse, Nina Cormier, bandaging one of the injured. This fiasco was her fault, too; he was sure of it. She must've given the police just enough info to tip them off to the bomb. The usher's uniform, no doubt, had been the vital clue.

She was another detail he hadn't bothered to clean up, and look at the result. No hit, no money. Plus, she could identify him. Though that police sketch was hopelessly generic, Spectre had a feeling that, if Nina Cormier ever saw his face, she would remember him. That made her a threat he could no longer ignore.

But now was not the opportunity. Not in this crowd, in this street. The ambulances were arriving, siren after siren whooping to a stop. And the police had cordoned off the street from stray vehicles.

Time to leave.

Spectre turned and walked away, his frustration mounting with every step he took. He'd always prided himself on paying attention to the little things. Anyone who worked with explosives had to have a fetish for details, or they didn't last long. Spectre intended to hang around in this business, which meant he would continue to fuss over the details.

And the next detail to attend to was Nina Cormier.

SHE WAS MAGNIFICENT. Sam paused wearily amid the broken glass and shouting voices and he gazed in Nina's direction. It was ten-thirty, an hour and a half since the explosion, and the street was still a scene of confusion. Police cars and ambulances were parked haphazardly up and down the block, their lights flashing like a dozen strobes. Emergency personnel were everywhere, picking through the wreckage, sorting through the victims. The most seriously injured had already been evacuated, but there were dozens more still to be transported to hospitals.

In the midst of all that wreckage, Nina seemed an island of calm efficiency. As Sam watched, she knelt down beside a groaning man and dressed his bleeding arm with a make-shift bandage. Then, with a reassuring pat and a soft word, she moved on to the next patient. As though sensing she was being watched, she suddenly glanced in Sam's direction. Just for a moment their gazes locked across the chaos, and she read the question in his eyes: *Are you holding up okay?*

She gave him a wave, a nod of reassurance. Then she turned back to her patient.

They both had their work cut out for them tonight. He focused his attention, once again, on the bomb scene investigation.

Gillis had arrived forty-five minutes ago with the personal body armor and mask. The rest of the team had straggled in one by one—three techs, Ernie Takeda, Detective Cooley. Even Abe Coopersmith had appeared, his presence more symbolic than practical. This was Sam's show, and everyone knew it. The bomb disposal truck was in place and parked nearby. Everyone was waiting.

It was time to go in the building. Time to search for any second device.

Sam and Gillis, both of them wearing headlamps, entered the theater.

The darkness made the search slow and difficult. Stepping gingerly over debris, Sam headed down the left aisle, Gillis the right. The back rows of seats had sustained damage only to the upholstery—shredded fabric and stuffing. The further they advanced the more severe the damage.

"Dynamite," Gillis noted, sniffing the air.

"Looks like the blast center's near the front."

Sam moved slowly toward the orchestra pit, the beam

of his headlamp slicing the darkness left and right as he scanned the area around the stage—or what had once been the stage. A few splintered boards was all that remained.

"Crater's right here," observed Gillis.

Sam joined him. The two men knelt down for a closer inspection. Like the church bomb a week before, this one was shallow—a low-velocity blast. Dynamite.

"Looks like the third row, center stage," said Sam. "Wonder who was sitting here."

"Assigned seating, you figure?"

"If so, then we'll have ourselves a convenient list of potential targets."

"Looks all clear to me," Gillis declared.

"We can call in the searchers." Sam rose to his feet and at once felt a little dizzy. The aftereffects of the blast. He'd been in so many bombs lately, his brain must be getting scrambled. Maybe some fresh air would clear his head.

"You okay?" asked Gillis.

"Yeah. I just need to get out of here for a moment." He stumbled back up the aisle and through the lobby doors. Outside he leaned against a lamppost, breathing gulps of night air. His dizziness faded and he became aware, once again, of the activity in the street. He noticed that the crowds had thinned, and that the injured had all been evacuated. Only one ambulance was still parked in the road.

Where was Nina?

That one thought instantly cleared his head. He glanced up and down the street, but caught no glimpse of her. Had she left the scene? Or was she taken from it?

A young cop manning the police line glanced up as Sam approached. "Yes, sir?"

"There was a woman—a nurse in street clothes—working out here. Where'd she go?"

"You mean the dark-haired lady? The pretty one?"

"That's her."

"She left in one of the ambulances, about twenty minutes ago. I think she was helping with a patient."

"Thanks." Sam went to his car and reached inside for his cellular phone. He was not taking any chances; he had to be sure she was safe. He dialed Maine Med ER.

The line was busy.

In frustration he climbed in the car. "I'm heading to the hospital!" he yelled to Gillis. "Be right back."

Ignoring his partner's look of puzzlement, Sam lurched away from the curb and steered through the obstacle course of police vehicles. Fifteen minutes later, he pulled into a parking stall near the hospital's emergency entrance.

Even before he walked in the doors, he could hear the sounds of frantic activity inside. The waiting area was mobbed. He pushed his way through the crowd until he'd reached the triage desk, manned by a clearly embattled nurse.

"I'm Detective Navarro, Portland Police," he said. "Is Nina Cormier working here?"

"Nina? Not tonight, as far as I know."

"She came in with one of the ambulances."

"I might have missed her. Let me check." She punched the intercom button and said, "There's a policeman out here. Wants to speak to Nina. If she's back there, can you ask her to come out?"

For a good ten minutes, he waited with growing impatience. Nina didn't appear. The crowd in the ER seemed to grow even larger, packing into every available square inch of the waiting area. Even worse, the reporters had shown up, TV cameras and all. The triage nurse had her hands full; she'd forgotten entirely about Sam.

Unable to wait any longer, he pushed past the front desk. The nurse was calming down a hysterical family member; she didn't even notice Sam had crossed into the inner sanctum and was heading up the ER corridor.

Treatment rooms lined both sides of the halls. He glanced in each one as he passed. All were occupied and overflowing with victims from the bombing. He saw stunned faces, bloodied clothes. But no Nina.

He turned, retraced his steps down the hall, and paused outside a closed door. It was the trauma room. From beyond the door came the sound of voices, the clang of cabinets. He knew that a crisis was in full swing, and he was reluctant to intrude, but he had no alternative. He had to confirm that Nina was here, that she'd made it safely to the ER.

He pushed open the door.

A patient—a man—was lying on the table, his body white and flaccid under the lights. Half a dozen medical personnel were laboring over him, one performing CPR, the others scurrying about with IV's and drugs. Sam paused, momentarily stunned by the horror of the scene.

"Sam?"

Only then did he notice Nina moving toward him from the other side of the room. Like all the other nurses, she was dressed in scrub clothes. He hadn't even noticed her in that first glimpse of blue-clad personnel.

She took his arm and quickly tugged him out of the room. "What are you doing here?" she whispered.

"You left the blast site. I wasn't sure what happened to you."

"I rode here in one of the ambulances. I figured they needed me." She glanced back at the door to the trauma room. "I was right."

"Nina, you can't just take off without telling me! I had no idea if you were all right."

She regarded him with an expression of quiet wonder, but didn't say a thing.

"Are you listening to me?" he said.

"Yes," she replied softly. "But I don't believe what I'm hearing. You actually sound scared."

"I wasn't scared. I was just— I mean—" He shook his head in frustration. "Okay, I was worried. I didn't want something to happen to you."

"Because I'm your witness?"

He looked into her eyes, those beautiful, thoughtful eyes. Never in his life had he felt so vulnerable. This was a new feeling for him and he didn't like it. He was not a man who was easily frightened, and the fact that he had experienced such fear at the thought of losing her told him he was far more deeply involved than he'd ever intended to be.

"Sam?" She reached up and touched his face.

He grasped her hand and gently lowered it. "Next time," he instructed, "I want you to tell me where you're going. It's *your* life at stake. If you want to risk it, that's your business. But until Spectre's under arrest, your safety's my concern. Do you understand?"

She withdrew her hand from his. The retreat was more than physical; he could feel her pulling away emotionally as well, and it hurt him. It was a pain of his own choosing, and that made it even worse.

She said, tightly, "I understand perfectly well."

"Good. Now, I think you should go back to the hotel where we can keep an eye on you tonight."

"I can't leave. They need me here."

"I need you, too. Alive."

"Look at this place!" She waved toward the waiting area, crowded with the injured. "These people all have to be examined and treated. I can't walk out now."

"Nina, I have a job to do. And your safety is part of that job."

"I have a job to do, too!" she asserted.

They faced each other for a moment, neither one willing to back down.

Then Nina snapped, "I don't have time for this," and she turned back toward the trauma room.

"Nina!"

"I'll do my job, Sam. You do yours."

"Then I'm sending a man over to keep an eye on you."

"Do whatever you want."

"When will you be finished here?"

She stopped and glanced at the waiting patients. "My guess? Not till morning."

"Then I'll be back to get you at 6:00 a.m."

"Whatever you say, Detective," she retorted and pushed into the trauma room. He caught a fleeting glimpse of her as she rejoined the surgical team, and then the door closed behind her.

I'll do my job. You do yours, she'd told him.

She's right, he thought. *That's exactly what I should be focusing on. My job.*

From his car phone, he put in a call to Officer Pressler and told him to send his relief officer down to Maine Med ER, where he'd be the official baby-sitting service for the

night. Then, satisfied that Nina was in good hands, he
headed back to the bomb scene.

It was eleven-thirty. The night was just beginning.

NINA MADE IT THROUGH the next seven hours on sheer
nerve. Her conversation with Sam had left her hurt and
angry, and she had to force herself to concentrate on the
work at hand—tending to the dozens of patients who now
filled the waiting area. Their injuries, their discomfort,
had to take priority. But every so often, when she'd pause
to collect her thoughts or catch her breath, she'd find
herself thinking about Sam, about what he'd said.

I have a job to do. And your safety is part of that job.

Is that all I am to you? she wondered as she signed her
name to yet another patient instruction sheet. A job, a
burden? And what had she expected, anyway? From the
beginning, he'd been the unflappable public official, Mr.
Cool himself. There'd been flashes of warmth, of course,
even the occasional glimpse of the man inside, a man of
genuine kindness. But every time she thought she'd
touched the real Sam Navarro, he'd pull away from her as
though scalded by the contact.

What am I to do with you, Sam? she wondered sadly. And
what was she to do with all the feelings she had for him?

Work was all that kept her going that night. She never
even noticed when the sun came up.

By the time 6:00 a.m. rolled around, she was so tired
she could scarcely walk without weaving, but at last the
waiting room was empty and the patients all sent home.
Most of the ER staff had gathered, shell-shocked, in the
employee lounge for a well-deserved coffee break. Nina
was about to join them when she heard her name called.

She turned. Sam was standing in the waiting room.

He looked every bit as exhausted as she felt, his eyes bleary, his jaw dark with a day's growth of beard. At her first sight of his face, all the anger she'd felt the night before instantly evaporated.

My poor, poor Sam, she thought. *You give so much of yourself. And what comfort do you have at the end of the day?*

She went to him. He didn't speak; he just looked at her with that expression of weariness. She put her arms around him. For a moment they held each other, their bodies trembling with fatigue. Then she heard him say, softly, "Let's go home."

"I'd like that," she said. And smiled.

She didn't know how he managed to pilot the car to his house. All she knew was that a moment after she dozed off, they were in his driveway, and he was gently prodding her awake. Together they dragged themselves into the house, into his bedroom. No thoughts of lust crossed her mind, even as they undressed and crawled into bed together, even as she felt his lips brush her face, felt his breath warm her hair.

She fell asleep in his arms.

SHE FELT SO WARM, so perfect, lying beside him. As if she belonged here, in his bed.

Sam gazed through drowsy eyes at Nina, who was still sound asleep. It was already afternoon. He should have been up and dressed hours ago, but sheer exhaustion had taken its toll.

He was getting too old for this job. For the past eighteen years, he'd been a cop through and through. Though there were times when he hated the work, when the ugly side of it seemed to overwhelm his love for the job, he'd never once doubted that a cop was exactly what he was meant to be. And so it dismayed him now that, at this moment, being a cop was the furthest thing from his mind.

What he wanted, really wanted, was to spend eternity in this bed, gazing at this woman. Studying her face, enjoying the view. Only when Nina was asleep did he feel it was safe to really look at her. When she was awake, he felt too vulnerable, as though she could read his thoughts, could see past his barriers, straight to his heart. He was afraid to admit, even to himself, the feelings he harbored there.

As he studied her now, he realized there was no point denying it to himself: he couldn't bear the thought of her walking out of his life. Did that mean he loved her? He didn't know.

He did know this was not the turn of events he'd wanted or expected.

But last night he'd watched her at work in the wreckage of the bomb site, and he'd admired a new dimension of Nina, one he saw for the first time. A woman with both compassion and strength.

It would be so easy to fall in love with her. It would be such a mistake.

In a month, a year, she'd come to see him for what he was: no hero with a badge, but an everyday guy doing his job the best way he knew how. And there she'd be in that hospital, working side by side with men like Robert Bledsoe. Men with medical degrees and houses on the water. How long would it take for her to grow weary of the cop who just happened to love her?

He sat up on the side of the bed and ran his hands through his hair, trying to shake off the last vestiges of sleep. His brain wasn't feeling alert yet. He needed coffee, food, anything to snap him back into gear. There were so many details to follow up on, so many leads still to check out.

Then he felt a touch, soft as silk, caress his bare back. All at once, work was the last thing on his mind.

He turned and met her gaze. She was looking drowsily at him, her smile relaxed and contented. "What time is it?" she murmured.

"Almost three."

"We slept that long?"

"We needed it. Both of us. It was okay to let our guard down. Pressler was watching the house."

"You mean he was outside all day?"

"I made the arrangements last night. Before he went off duty. I knew I wanted to bring you home with me."

She opened her arms to him. That gesture of invitation was too tempting to resist. With a groan of surrender, he lay down beside her and met her lips with a kiss. At once his body was responding, and so was she. Their arms were entwined now, their warmth mingling. He couldn't stop, couldn't turn back; he wanted her too badly. He wanted to feel their bodies join, just one last time. If he couldn't have her for the rest of his life, at least he would have her for this moment. And he'd remember, always, her face, her smile, her sweet moans of desire as he thrust, hard and deep, inside her.

They both took. They both gave.

But even as he reached his climax, even as he felt the first glorious release, he thought, *This is not enough. This could never be enough.* He wanted to know more than just her body; he wanted to know her soul.

His passion was temporarily sated, yet he felt both unsatisfied and depressed as he lay beside her afterward. Not at all what the carefree bachelor should expect to feel after a conquest. If anything, he was angry at himself for sliding into this situation. For allowing this woman to become so important to him.

And here she was, smiling, working her way even deeper into his life.

His response was to pull away, to rise from the bed and head into the shower. When he reemerged, clean and still damp, she was sitting up on the side of the bed, watching him with a look of bewilderment.

"I have to get back to work," he said, pulling on a clean shirt. "I'll invite Pressler inside to sit with you."

"The bombing's over and done with. Spectre's probably a thousand miles away by now."

"I can't take that chance."

"There are others who know his face. The theater ushers. They could identify him."

"One of them hit his head on the sidewalk. He's still in and out of consciousness. The other one can't even decide on the color of Spectre's eyes. That's how helpful the ushers are."

"Nevertheless, you've got other witnesses and Spectre knows it." She paused. "I'd say that lets both of us off the hook."

"What do you mean?"

"I can stop worrying about being a target. And you can stop worrying about keeping me alive. And go back to your real job."

"This is part of my job."

"So you've told me." She tilted her chin up, and he saw

the brief gleam of tears in her eyes. "I wish I was more than that. God, I wish…"

"Nina, please. This doesn't help either one of us."

Her head drooped. The sight of her, hurt, silent, was almost more than he could stand. He knelt down before her and took her hands in his. "You know I'm attracted to you."

She gave a softly ironic laugh. "That much, I guess, is obvious to us both."

"And you also know that I think you're a terrific woman. If I ever get hauled to the ER in an ambulance, I hope you're the nurse who takes care of me."

"But?"

"But…" He sighed. "I just don't see us together. Not for the long haul."

She looked down again, and he could sense her struggle for composure. He'd hurt her, and he hated himself for it, hated his own cowardice. That's what it was, of course. He didn't believe hard enough in their chances. He didn't believe in *her*.

All he was certain of was that he'd never, ever get over her.

He rose to his feet. She didn't react, but just sat on the bed, staring down. "It's not you, Nina," he said. "It's *me*. It's something that happened to me years ago. It convinced me that this situation we're in—it doesn't last. It's artificial. A scared woman. And a cop. It's a setup for all kinds of unrealistic expectations."

"Don't give me the old psychology lecture, Sam. I don't need to hear about transference and misplaced affections."

"You have to hear it. And understand it. Because the effect goes both ways. How you feel about me, and how I feel about you. My wanting to take care of you, protect you. It's something I can't help, either." He sighed, a sound of both frustration and despair. *It's too late,* he thought. *We both feel things we shouldn't be feeling. And it's impossible to turn back the clock.*

"You were saying something happened to you. Years ago," she said. "Was it…another woman?"

He nodded.

"The same situation? Scared woman, protective cop?"

Again he nodded.

"Oh." She shook her head and murmured in a tone of self-disgust, "I guess I fell right into it."

"We both did."

"So who left whom, Sam? The last time this happened?"

"It was the only time it happened. Except for you." He turned away, began to move around the room. "I was just a rookie patrolman. Twenty-two years old. Assigned to protect a woman being stalked. She was twenty-eight going on forty when it came to sophistication. It's not surprising I got a little infatuated. The surprising part was that she seemed to return the sentiment. At least, until the crisis was over. Then she decided I wasn't so impressive after all. And she was right." He stopped and looked at her. "It's that damn thing called reality. It has a way of stripping us all down to what we really are. And in my case, I'm just a hardworking cop. Honest for the most part. Brighter than some, dumber than others. In short, I'm not anyone's hero. And when she finally saw that, she turned right around and walked out, leaving behind one sadder but wiser rookie."

"And you think that's what I'm going to do."

"It's what you should do. Because you deserve so much, Nina. More than I can ever give you."

She shook her head. "What I really want, Sam, has nothing to do with what a man can *give* me."

"Think about Robert. What you could have had with him."

"Robert was the perfect example! He had it all. Everything except what I wanted from him."

"What did you want, Nina?"

"Love. Loyalty." She met his gaze. "Honesty."

What he saw in her eyes left him shaken. Those were the things he wanted to give her. The very things he was afraid to give her.

"Right now you think it's enough," he remarked. "But maybe you'll find out it's not."

"It's more than I ever got from Robert." *More than I'll ever get from you, too,* was what her eyes said.

He didn't try to convince her otherwise. Instead, he turned toward the door.

"I'm going to call Pressler inside," he told her. "Have him stay with you all day today."

"There's no need."

"You shouldn't be alone, Nina."

"I won't be." She looked up at him. "I can go back to my father's house. He has that fancy security system. Not to mention a few dogs. Now that we know Daniella isn't the one running around planting bombs, I should be perfectly safe there." She glanced around the room. "I shouldn't be staying here, anyway. Not in your house."

"You can. As long as you need to."

"No." She met his gaze. "I don't really see the point, Sam. Since it's so apparent to us both that this is a hopeless relationship."

He didn't argue with her. And that, more than anything else, was what hurt her. He could see it in her face.

He simply said, "I'll drive you there." Then he turned and left the room. He had to.

He couldn't bear to see the look in her eyes.

Twelve

"We think we know who the target was," reported Sam. "It was our wonderful D.A., Liddell."

Chief Coopersmith stared across the conference table at Sam and Gillis. "Are you certain?"

"Everything points that way. We pinpointed the bomb placement to somewhere in Row Three, Seats G through J. The seating last night was reserved weeks in advance. We've gone over the list of people sitting in that row and section. And Liddell and his wife were right smack in the center. They would've been killed instantly."

"Who else was in that row?"

"Judge Dalton was about six seats away," said Gillis. "Chances are, he would've been killed, too. Or at least seriously maimed."

"And the other people in that row?"

"We've checked them all out. A visiting law professor from California. A few relatives of Judge Dalton's. A pair of law clerks. We doubt any of them would've attracted the interest of a hired killer. Oh, and you may be interested to hear Ernie Takeda's latest report. He called it in from the lab this afternoon. It was dynamite, Dupont label. Prima detonating cord. Green electrical tape."

"Spectre," said Coopersmith. He leaned back and exhaled a loud sigh of weariness. They were all tired. Every one of them had worked straight through the night, caught a few hours of sleep, and then returned to the job. Now it was 5:00 p.m., and another night was just beginning. "God, the man is back with a vengeance."

"Yeah, but he's not having much luck," commented Gillis. "His targets keep surviving. Liddell. Judge Dalton. Nina Cormier. I'd say that the legendary Vincent Spectre must be feeling pretty frustrated about now."

"Embarrassed, too," added Sam. "His reputation's on the line, if it isn't already shot. After this fiasco, he's washed up as a contract man. Anyone with the money to hire will go elsewhere."

"Do we know who *did* hire him?"

Sam and Gillis glanced at each other. "We can make a wild guess," said Gillis.

"Billy Binford?"

Sam nodded. "The Snowman's trial is coming up in a month. And Liddell was dead set against any plea bargains. Rumor has it, he was going to use a conviction as a jumping-off place for some political campaign. I think The Snowman knows he's in for a long stay in jail. I think he wants Liddell off the prosecution team. Permanently."

"If Sam hadn't cleared that theater," added Gillis, "we could have lost half our prosecutors. The courts would've been backed up for months. In that situation, Binford's lawyers could've written the plea bargain for him."

"Any way we can pin this down with proof?"

"Not yet. Binford's attorney, Albert Darien, denies any knowledge of this. We're not going to be able to shake a word out of him. ATF's going over the videotapes from the prison surveillance cameras, looking over all the visitors that Binford had. We may be able to identify a go-between."

"You think it's someone other than his attorney?"

"Possibly. If we can identify that go-between, we may have a link to Spectre."

"Go for it," said Coopersmith. "I want this guy, and I want him bad."

At five-thirty, the meeting broke up and Sam headed for the coffee machine in search of a caffeine boost that would keep him going for the next eight hours. He was just taking his first sip when Norm Liddell walked into the station. Sam couldn't help feeling a prick of satisfaction at the sight of the bruises and scrapes on Liddell's face. The injuries were minor, but last night, after the bomb, Liddell had been among those screaming the loudest for medical assistance. His own wife, who'd sustained a broken arm, had finally told her husband to shut up and act like a man.

Now here he was, sporting a few nasty scrapes on his face as well as a look of—could it be? Contrition?

"Afternoon, Navarro," said Liddell, his voice subdued.

"Afternoon."

"I, uh…" Liddell cleared his throat and glanced around the hall, as though to check if anyone was listening. No one was.

"How's the wife doing?" asked Sam.

"Fine. She'll be in a cast for a while. Luckily, it was just a closed fracture."

"She handled herself pretty well last night, considering her injury," Sam commented. *Unlike you.*

"Yes, well, my wife's got a spine of steel. In fact, that's sort of why I want to talk to you."

"Oh?"

"Look, Navarro. Last night…I guess I jumped on you prematurely. I mean, I didn't realize you had information about any bomb."

Sam didn't say a word. He didn't want to interrupt this enjoyable performance.

"So when I got on your case last night—about evacuating the building—I should've realized you had your reasons. But damn it, Navarro, all I could see was all those people hurt in the stampede. I thought you'd gotten them panicked for nothing, and I—" He paused, obviously struggling to bite back his words. "Anyway, I apologize."

"Apology accepted."

Liddell gave a curt nod of relief.

"Now you can tell your wife you're off the hook."

The look on Liddell's face was all Sam needed to know that he'd guessed right. This apology had been Mrs. Liddell's idea, bless her steely spine. He couldn't help grinning as he watched the other man turn and walk stiffly toward Chief Coopersmith's office. The good D.A., it appeared, was not the one wearing the pants in the family.

"Hey, Sam!" Gillis was heading toward him, pulling on his jacket. "Let's go."

"Where?"

"Prison's got a surveillance videotape they want us to look at. It's The Snowman and some unknown visitor from a few days ago."

Sam felt a sudden adrenaline rush. "Was it Spectre?"

"No. It was a woman."

"THERE. THE BLONDE," said Detective Cooley.

Sam and Gillis leaned toward the TV screen, their gazes fixed on the black-and-white image of the woman. The view of her face was intermittently blocked by other visitors moving in the foreground, but from what they could see, the woman was indeed a blonde, twenties to thirties, and built like a showgirl.

"Okay, freeze it there," Cooley said to the video tech. "That's a good view of her."

The woman was caught in a still frame, her face turned to the surveillance camera, her figure momentarily visible between two passersby. She was dressed in a skirt suit, and she appeared to be carrying a briefcase. Judging by her attire, she might be an attorney or some other professional. But two details didn't fit.

One was her shoes. The camera's angle, facing downward, captured a view of her right foot, perched atop a sexy spike-heeled sandal with a delicate ankle strap.

"Not the kind of shoes you wear to court," noted Sam.

"Not unless you're out to give the judge a thrill," Gillis said. "And look at that makeup."

It was the second detail that didn't fit. This woman was made up like no lawyer Sam had ever seen. Obviously false eyelashes. Eyeshadow like some tropical fish. Lipstick painted on in bold, broad smears.

"Man, she sure ain't the girl next door," Gillis observed.

"What's the name on the visitor log?" asked Sam.

Cooley glanced at a sheet of paper. "She signed in as Marilyn Dukoff. Identified her purpose for visiting The Snowman as attorney-client consultation."

Gillis laughed. "If she's an attorney, then I'm applying to law school."

"Which law firm did she say she was with?" asked Sam.

"Frick and Darien."

"Not true?"

Cooley shook his head. "She's not on the firm's list of partners, associates or clerks. But…" He leaned forward, a grin on his face. "We think we know where she *did* work."

"Where?"

"The Stop Light."

Gillis shot Sam a look of *Didn't I tell ya?* No one had to explain a thing. They knew all about the Stop Light and its stage shows, pasties optional.

"Let me guess," said Sam. "Exotic dancer."

"You got it," affirmed Cooley.

"Are we sure we're talking about the right Marilyn Dukoff?"

"I think we are," Cooley answered. "See, all visitors to the prison have to present ID, and that's the name she gave, backed up by a Maine driver's license. We've pulled the license file. And here's the photo." Cooley passed a copy of the photo to Sam and Gillis.

"It's her," said Gillis.

"Which means we're talking about the right Marilyn Dukoff," said Cooley. "I think she just waltzed in under her own name and didn't bother with fake IDs. All she faked was her profession."

"Which is obviously not in the legal field," Gillis drawled.

Sam gave a nod to Cooley. "Good work."

"Unfortunately," added the younger detective, "I can't seem to locate the woman herself. We know where she *was* employed, but she left the job two weeks ago. I sent a man to the address listed on her license. She doesn't answer the door. And her phone's just been disconnected." He paused. "I think it's time for a search warrant."

"Let's get it." Sam rose to his feet and glanced at Gillis. "Meet you in the car, ten minutes."

"The blonde's?"

"Unless you've got somewhere better to go."

Gillis looked back at the video screen. At that still shot of a slim ankle, a sexy shoe. "Better than *that?*" He laughed. "I don't think so."

THE POLICE WERE getting too close for comfort.

Spectre slouched in the doorway of an apartment building half a block away and watched the cops come out of Marilyn's old building. Only moments before, Spectre had been inside that apartment, checking to make sure Marilyn hadn't left behind any clues to her current whereabouts. Luckily for him, he'd slipped out just ahead of Navarro's arrival.

They'd been inside almost an hour. They were good, all right—but Spectre was cleverer. Hours after the theater bombing, he'd hustled Marilyn into a different apartment across town. He'd known that his target might become apparent once they'd pinpointed the bomb placement in the theater. And that Marilyn would inevitably come under their scrutiny. Luckily, she'd been cooperative.

Unfortunately, her usefulness was just about over, and the time had come to end their association. But first, he needed her for one more task.

His face tightened as he spotted a familiar figure emerge from the building. Navarro again. The detective had come to represent all the failures that Spectre had suffered over the past week. Navarro was the brains behind the investigation, the one man responsible for Liddell still being alive.

No hit. No fee. Navarro had cost him money—a lot of it.

Spectre watched the cops confer on the sidewalk. There were five of them, three in plain clothes, two in uniform, but it was Navarro on whom he focused his rage. This had turned into a battle of wits between them, a test of determination. In all his years as a "fuse" man, Spectre had never matched skills with such a wily opponent.

The safe thing to do was merely to slip away from this town and seek out contracts elsewhere. Miami or New Orleans. But his reputation had suffered a serious blow here; he wasn't sure he could land a job in Miami. And he had the feeling Navarro wouldn't give up the pursuit, that, wherever Spectre went, the detective would be dogging his trail.

And then, there was the matter of getting even. Spectre wasn't going to walk away without exacting some kind of payback.

The three plainclothes cops climbed into an unmarked car and drove away. A moment later, the uniformed cops were gone as well. They had found nothing in Marilyn's apartment; Spectre had seen to it.

Catch me if you can, Navarro, he thought. *Or will I catch you first?*

He straightened and stamped his feet, feeling the blood return to his legs. Then he left the doorway and walked around the corner, to his car.

Navarro. Once and for all, he had to take care of Navarro. And he had the perfect plan. It would require Marilyn's help. One little phone call—that's all he'd ask. And then he'd ask no more of her.

Ever again.

THE DINNER WAS EXCELLENT. The company was wretched.

Daniella, dressed in an iridescent green leotard and a slinky wraparound skirt, sullenly picked at her salad, ignoring the platter of roast duckling and wild rice. She was not speaking to her husband, and he was not speaking to her, and Nina was too uncomfortable to speak to either one of them.

After all those questions by the police, the matter of Daniella's affair with Robert had come to light. While Nina would never forgive Daniella for that betrayal, at least she could manage to pull off a civil evening with the woman.

Nina's father could not. He was still in a state of shock from the revelation. His showpiece wife, the stunning blonde thirty years his junior, had not been satisfied with marrying mere wealth. She'd wanted a younger man. After four marriages, George Cormier still didn't know how to choose the right wife.

Now it looks like this will be his fourth divorce, Nina thought. She glanced at her father, then at Daniella. Though she loved her father, she couldn't help feeling that he and Daniella deserved each other. In the worst possible way.

Daniella set down her fork. "If you'll excuse me," she said, "I don't really have much of an appetite. I think I'll skip out for a movie."

"What about me?" snapped George. "I know I'm just your husband, but a few evenings a week with your boring old spouse isn't too much to ask, is it? Considering all the benefits you get in exchange."

"Benefits? *Benefits?*" Daniella drew herself to her feet

in anger. "All the money in the world can't make up for being married to an old goat like you."

"Goat?"

"An old goat. Do you hear me? *Old.*" She leaned across the table. "In every sense of the word."

He, too, rose to his feet. "Why, you bitch…"

"Go ahead. Call me names. I can think of just as many to call you back." With a whisk of her blond hair, she turned and walked out of the dining room.

George stared after her for a moment. Slowly, he sank back in his chair. "God," he whispered. "What was I thinking when I married her?"

You weren't thinking at all, Nina felt like saying. She touched her father's arm. "Seems like neither one of us is any good at picking spouses. Are we, Dad?"

He regarded his daughter with a look of shared misery. "I sincerely hope you haven't inherited my bad luck with love, sweetheart."

They sat for a moment without speaking. Their supper lay, almost untouched, on the table. In another room, music had started up, the fast and thumping rhythm of an aerobics tape. Daniella was at it again, working off her anger by sculpting a new and better body. Smart girl; she was going to come out of a divorce looking like a million bucks.

Nina sighed and leaned back. "Whether it's bad luck or character flaws, Dad, maybe some people are just meant to be single."

"Not you, Nina. You *need* to love someone. You always have. And that's what makes you so easy to love."

She gave a sad laugh but said nothing. *Easy to love, easy to leave,* she thought.

Once again, she found herself wondering what Sam

was doing. What he was thinking. Not about her, surely; he was too much the cop to be bothered by minor distractions.

Yet when the phone rang, she couldn't suppress the sudden hope that he was calling. She sat at the table, heart thumping hard as she listened to Daniella's voice in the next room talking on the phone.

A moment later, Daniella appeared in the doorway and said, "It's for you, Nina. The hospital. They said they've been trying to reach you."

Disappointed, Nina rose to take the call. "Hello?"

"Hi, this is Gladys Power, the night nursing supervisor. Sorry to bother you—we got your phone number from your mother. We have a number of staff out sick tonight, and we were wondering if you could come in to cover for the ER."

"Night shift?"

"Yes. We could really use you."

Nina glanced toward Daniella's exercise room, where the music was playing louder than ever. She had to get out of this house. Away from this emotional battleground.

She said, "Okay, I'll take the shift."

"See you at eleven o'clock."

"Eleven?" Nina frowned. The night shift usually started at midnight. "You want me there an hour early?"

"If you could manage it. We're shorthanded on the evening shift as well."

"Right. I'll be there, eleven o'clock." She hung up and breathed a soft sigh of relief. Work was exactly what she needed. Maybe eight hours of crises, major and minor, would get her mind back on track.

And off the subject of Sam Navarro.

MARILYN HUNG UP THE PHONE. "She said she'd be there."

Spectre gave a nod of approval. "You handled it well."

"Of course." Marilyn favored him with that satisfied smile of hers. A smile that said, *I'm worth every penny you pay me.*

"Did she seem at all suspicious?" he asked.

"Not a bit. I'm telling you, she'll be there. Eleven o'clock, just like you wanted." Marilyn tilted back her head and gave her lips a predatory lick. "Now, do I get what I want?"

He smiled. "What *do* you want?"

"You know." She sidled toward him and unbuckled his belt. His breath caught in an involuntary gasp as that hot little hand slid inside his trousers. Her touch was delicious, expert, her technique designed to reduce a man to begging. Oh yes, he knew exactly what she was asking for.

And it wasn't sex.

Why not enjoy the moment? he thought. She was willing, and he still had the time to spare. Three hours until Nina Cormier showed up for her shift at the hospital. Some quick amusement with Marilyn, and then on to more serious business.

She dropped to her knees before him. "You said you'd pay me what I was worth," she whispered.

He groaned. "I promised…"

"I'm worth a lot. Don't you think?"

"Absolutely."

"I can be worth even more to you."

He gave a jerk of pleasure and grasped her face. Breathing heavily, he stroked down her cheek, her jaw, to her neck. Such a long, slender neck. How easy it should be to finish it. First, though, he'd let *her* finish…

"Oh, yes," she murmured. "You're ready for me."

He pulled her, hard, against him. And he thought, *A pity you won't be ready for me.*

IT WAS TEN-THIRTY by the time a weary Sam stepped through his front door. The first thing he noticed was the silence. The emptiness. It was a house that had somehow lost its soul.

He turned on the lights, but even the glow of all those lamps couldn't seem to dispel the shadows. For the past three years, this was the house he'd called home, the house he'd returned to every evening after work. Now the place felt cold to him, like the house of a stranger. Not a home at all.

He poured himself a glass of milk and drank it in a few thirsty gulps. So much for supper; he didn't have the energy to cook. He poured a second glass and carried it over to the telephone. All evening, he'd been itching to make this call, but something had always interrupted him. Now that he had a few blessed moments of peace, he was going to call Nina. He was going to tell her what he'd been afraid to tell her, what he could no longer deny to her, or to himself.

It had come to him this afternoon, a realization that had struck him, oddly enough, in the midst of searching Marilyn Dukoff's apartment. He'd stood in the woman's bedroom and gazed at the empty bureau drawers, the stripped mattress. And without warning, he'd been struck by a sense of loneliness so intense it made his chest ache. Because that abandoned room had suddenly come to represent his life. It had a purpose, a function, but it was nevertheless empty.

I've been a cop too long, he'd thought. *I've let it take over my life.* Only at that moment, standing in that empty bedroom, did it occur to him how little of his own life he really had. No wife, no kids, no family.

Nina had opened his eyes to the possibilities. Yes, he was scared. Yes, he knew just how much, how deeply, he would be hurt if she ever left him. But the alternative was just as bleak; that he would never even give it a chance.

He'd been a coward. But no longer.

He picked up the phone and dialed Nina's father's house.

A few rings later, the call was answered by a bland "Hello?" Not Nina but Daniella, the fitness freak.

"This is Sam Navarro," he said. "Sorry to call so late. May I speak to Nina?"

"She's not here."

His immediate pang of disappointment was quickly followed by a cop's sense of dismay. How could she not be there? She was supposed to stay in a safe place tonight, not run around unprotected.

"Mind telling me where she went?" he asked.

"The hospital. They called her in to work the night shift."

"The Emergency Room?"

"I guess so."

"Thanks." He hung up, his disappointment so heavy it felt like a physical weight on his shoulders. What the hell. He was not going to hold off any longer. He was going to tell her now. Tonight.

He dialed Maine Medical ER.

"Emergency Room."

"This is Detective Sam Navarro, Portland Police. May I speak with Nina Cormier?"

"Nina's not here tonight."

"Well, when she gets there, could you ask her to call me at home?"

"She's not scheduled to come in."

"Excuse me?"

"I have the time sheet right in front of me. Her name's not down here for tonight."

"I was told someone called her in to work the night shift."

"I don't know anything about that."

"Well, can you find out? This is urgent."

"Let me check with the supervisor. Can you hold?"

In the silence that followed, Sam could hear his own blood rushing through his ears. Something was wrong. That old instinct of his was tingling.

The woman came back on the line. "Detective? I've checked with the supervisor. She says she doesn't know anything about it, either. According to her schedule, Nina isn't listed for any shifts until next week."

"Thank you," said Sam softly.

For a moment he sat thinking about that phone call from the hospital. Someone had known enough to locate Nina at her father's house. Someone had talked her into leaving those protective gates at an hour of night when there'd be few witnesses to see what was about to happen.

Not just someone. Spectre.

It was 10:45.

In a heartbeat, he was out the door and running to his car. Even as he roared out of his driveway, he knew he might already be too late. Racing for the freeway, he steered with one hand and dialed his car phone with the other.

"Gillis here," answered a weary voice.

"I'm on my way to Maine Med," Sam said. "Spectre's there."

"What?"

"Nina got a bogus call asking her to come in to work. I'm sure it was him. She's already left the house—"

Gillis replied, "I'll meet you there," and hung up.

Sam turned his full attention to the road. The speedometer hit seventy. Eighty.

Don't let me be too late, he prayed.

He floored the accelerator.

THE HOSPITAL PARKING garage was deserted, a fact that scarcely concerned Nina as she drove through the automatic gate. She had often been in this garage late at night, either coming to, or leaving from, her shifts in the ER, and she'd never encountered any problems. Portland, after all, was one of the safest towns in America.

Provided you're not on someone's hit list, she reminded herself.

She pulled into a parking stall and sat there for a moment, trying to calm her nerves. She wanted to start her shift with her mind focused clearly on the job. Not on death threats. Not on Sam Navarro. Once she walked in those doors, she was first and foremost a professional. People's lives depended on it.

She opened the door and stepped out of the car.

It was still an hour before the usual shift change. Come midnight, this garage would be busy with hospital staff coming or going. But at this moment, no one else was around. She quickened her pace. The hospital elevator was just ahead; the way was clear. Only a dozen yards to go.

She never saw the man step out from behind the parked car.

But she felt a hand grasp her arm, felt the bite of a gun barrel pressed against her temple. Her scream was cut off by the first words he uttered.

"Not a sound or you're dead." The gun at her head was all the emphasis needed to keep her silent.

He yanked her away from the elevator, shoved her toward a row of parked cars. She caught a fleeting glimpse of his face as she was spun around. *Spectre.* They were moving now, Nina sobbing as she stumbled forward, the man gripping her arm with terrifying strength.

He's going to kill me now, here, where no one will see it....

The pounding of her own pulse was so loud at first, she didn't hear the faint squeal of tires across pavement.

But her captor did. Spectre froze, his grip still around her arm.

Now Nina heard it, too: car tires, screeching up the garage ramp.

With savage force, Spectre wrenched her sideways, toward the cover of a parked car. *This is my only chance to escape,* she thought.

In an instant she was fighting back, struggling against his grip. He was going to shoot her anyway. Whether it happened in some dark corner or out here, in the open, she would not go down without a fight. She kicked, flailed, clawed at his face.

He swung at her, a swift, ugly blow that slammed against her chin. The pain was blinding. She staggered, felt herself falling. He grasped her arm and began dragging her across the pavement. She was too stunned to fight now, to save herself.

Light suddenly glared in her eyes, a light so bright it seemed to stab straight through her aching head. She heard tires screech and realized she was staring at a pair of headlights.

A voice yelled, *"Freeze!"*

Sam. It was Sam.

"Let her go, Spectre!" Sam shouted.

The gun barrel was back at Nina's head, pressing harder than ever. "What superb timing, Navarro," Spectre drawled without a trace of panic in his voice.

"I said, *let her go.*"

"Is that a command, Detective? I certainly hope not. Because, considering the young woman's situation—" Spectre grabbed her by the chin and turned her face toward Sam "—offending me could prove hazardous to her health."

"I know your face. So do the ushers at the Brant Theater. You have no reason to kill her now!"

"No reason? Think again." Spectre, still holding the gun to Nina's head, nudged her forward. Toward Sam. "Move out of the way, Navarro."

"She's worthless to you—"

"But not to you."

Nina caught a glimpse of Sam's face, saw his look of helpless panic. He was gripping his gun in both hands, the barrel aimed, but he didn't dare shoot. Not with her in the line of fire.

She tried to go limp, tried to slump to the ground. No good; Spectre was too strong and he had too firm a grip around her neck. He simply dragged her beside him, his arm like a vise around her throat.

"Back off!" Spectre yelled.

"You don't want her!"

"Back off or it ends here, with her brains all over the ground!"

Sam took a step back, then another. Though his gun was still raised, it was useless to him. In that instant, Nina's gaze locked with his, and she saw more than fear, more than panic in his eyes. She saw despair.

"Nina," he said. "Nina—"

It was her last glimpse of Sam before Spectre pulled her into Sam's car. He slammed the door shut and threw the car in Reverse. Suddenly they were screeching backward down the ramp. She caught a fast-moving view of parked cars and concrete pillars, and then they crashed through the arm of the security gate.

Spectre spun the car around to face forward and hit the accelerator. They roared out of the driveway and onto the road.

Before she could recover her wits, the gun was back at her head. She looked at him, and saw a face that was frighteningly calm. The face of a man who knows he's in complete control.

"I have nothing to lose by killing you," he said.

"Then why don't you?" she whispered.

"I have plans. Plans that happen to include you."

"What plans?"

He gave a low, amused laugh. "Let's just say they involve Detective Navarro, his Bomb Squad, and a rather large amount of dynamite. I like spectacular endings, don't you?" He smiled at her.

That's when she realized whom she was looking at. What she was looking at.

A monster.

Thirteen

Sam raced down the parking garage ramp, his legs pumping with desperate speed. He emerged from the building just in time to see his car, Spectre at the wheel, careening out of the driveway and taking off down the road.

I've lost her, he thought as the taillights winked into the night. *My God. Nina...*

He sprinted to the sidewalk and ran halfway down the block before he finally came to a stop. The taillights had vanished.

The car was gone.

He gave a shout of rage, of despair, and heard his voice echo in the darkness. Too late. He was too late.

A flash of light made him spin around. A pair of headlights had just rounded the corner. Another car was approaching—one he recognized.

"Gillis!" he shouted.

The car braked to a stop near the curb. Sam dashed to the passenger door and scrambled inside.

"Go. *Go!*" he barked.

A perplexed Gillis stared at him. "What?"

"Spectre's got Nina! Move it!"

Gillis threw the car into gear. They screeched away from the curb. "Which way?"

"Left. Here!"

Gillis swerved around the corner.

Sam caught a glimpse of his own car, two blocks ahead, as it moved into an intersection and turned right.

"There!"

"I see it," Gillis said, and made the same turn.

Spectre must have spotted them, too. A moment later he accelerated and shot through a red light. Cars skidded to a stop in the intersection.

As Gillis steered through the maze of vehicles and pressed his pursuit, Sam picked up the car phone and called for assistance from all available patrol cars. With a little help, they could have Spectre boxed in.

For now, they just had to keep him in sight.

"This guy's a maniac," Gillis muttered.

"Don't lose her."

"He's gonna get us all killed. Look!"

Up ahead, Spectre swerved into the left lane, passed a car, and swerved back to the right just as a truck barreled down on him.

"Stay with them!" Sam ordered.

"I'm trying, I'm trying," Gillis, too, swerved left to pass. Too much traffic was heading toward them; he swerved back.

Seconds were lost. Seconds that Spectre pushed to his advantage.

Gillis tried again, this time managing to scoot back into his lane before colliding head-on with an oncoming van.

Spectre was nowhere in sight.

"What the hell?" muttered Gillis.

They stared at the road, saw stray taillights here and there, but otherwise it was an empty street. They drove on, through intersection after intersection, scanning the side roads. With every block they passed, Sam's panic swelled.

A half mile later, he was forced to accept the obvious. They had lost Spectre.

He had lost Nina.

Gillis was driving in grim silence now. Sam's despair had rubbed off on him as well. Neither one said it, but both of them knew. Nina was as good as dead.

"I'm sorry, Sam," murmured Gillis. "God, I'm sorry."

Sam could only stare ahead, wordless, his view blurring in a haze of tears. Moments passed. An eternity.

Patrol cars reported in. No trace of the car. Or Spectre.

Finally, at midnight, Gillis pulled over and parked at the curb. Both men sat in silence.

Gillis said, "There's still a chance."

Sam dropped his head in his hands. *A chance.* Spectre could be fifty miles away by now. Or he could be right around the corner. *What I would give for one, small chance….*

His gaze fell and he focused on Gillis's car phone.

One small chance.

He picked up the phone and dialed.

"Who're you calling?" asked Gillis.

"Spectre."

"What?"

"I'm calling my car phone." He listened as it rang. Five, six times.

Spectre answered, his voice raised in a bizarre falsetto. "Hello, you have reached the Portland Bomb Squad. No one's available to answer your call, as we seem to have misplaced our damn telephone."

"This is Navarro," growled Sam.

"Why hello, Detective Navarro. How *are* you?"

"Is she all right?"

"Who?"

"Is she all right?"

"Ah, you must be referring to the young lady. Perhaps I'll let her speak for herself."

There was a pause. He heard muffled voices, some sort of scraping sound. A soft, distant whine. Then Nina's voice came on, quiet, frightened. "Sam?"

"Are you hurt?"

"No. No, I'm fine."

"Where are you? Where's he taken you?"

"Oops," cut in Spectre. "Forbidden topic, Detective. Afraid I must abort this phone call."

"Wait. *Wait!*" cried Sam.

"Any parting words?"

"If you hurt her, Spectre—if anything happens to her— I swear I'll kill you."

"Is this a *law* enforcement officer I'm speaking to?"

"I mean it. I'll *kill* you."

"I'm shocked. *Shocked,* I tell you."

"Spectre!"

He was answered by laughter, soft and mocking. And then, abruptly, the line went dead.

Frantically Sam redialed and got a busy signal. He hung up, counted to ten, and dialed once more.

Another busy signal. Spectre had taken the phone off the hook.

Sam slammed the receiver down. "She's still alive."

"Where are they?"

"She never got the chance to tell me."

"It's been an hour. They could be anywhere within a fifty-mile radius."

"I know, I know." Sam sat back, trying to think through his swirl of panic. During his years as a cop, he'd always managed to keep his head cool, his thoughts focused. But tonight, for the first time in his career, he felt paralyzed by fear. By the knowledge that, with every moment that passed, every moment he did nothing, Nina's chances for survival faded.

"Why hasn't he killed her?" murmured Gillis. "Why is she still alive?"

Sam looked at his partner. At least Gillis still had a functioning brain. And he was thinking. Puzzling over a question that should've been obvious to them both.

"He's keeping her alive for a reason," said Gillis.

"A trump card. Insurance in case he's trapped."

"No, he's already home free. Right now, she's more of a liability than a help. Hostages slow you down. Complicate things. But he's allowed her to live."

So far, thought Sam with a wave of helpless rage. *I'm losing it, losing my ability to think straight. Her life depends on me. I can't afford to blow it.*

He looked at the phone again, and a memory echoed in his head. Something he'd heard over the phone during that brief pause between hearing Spectre's voice and Nina's. That distant wail, rising and falling.

A siren.

He reached for the phone again and dialed 911.

"Emergency operator," answered a voice.

"This is Detective Sam Navarro, Portland Police. I need

a list of all emergency dispatches made in the last twenty minutes. Anywhere in the Portland-South Portland area."

"Which vehicles, sir?"

"Everything. Ambulance, fire, police. All of them."

There was a brief silence, then another voice came on the line. Sam had his notepad ready.

"This is the supervisor, Detective Navarro," a woman said. "I've checked with the South Portland dispatcher. Combined, we've had three dispatches in the last twenty minutes. At 11:55, an ambulance was sent to 2203 Green Street in Portland. At 12:10, the police were dispatched to a burglar alarm at 751 Bickford Street in South Portland. And at 12:13, a squad car was called to the vicinity of Munjoy Hill for a report of some disturbance of the peace. There were no fire trucks dispatched during that period."

"Okay, thanks." Sam hung up and rifled through the glove compartment for a map. Quickly he circled the three dispatch locations.

"What now?" asked Gillis.

"I heard a siren over the phone, when I was talking to Spectre. Which means he had to be within hearing distance of some emergency vehicle. And these are the only three locations vehicles were dispatched to."

Gillis glanced at the map and shook his head. "We've got dozens of city blocks covered there! From point of dispatch to destination."

"But these are starting points."

"Like a haystack's a starting point."

"It's all we have to go on. Let's start at Munjoy Hill."

"This is crazy. The APB's out on your car. We've got people looking for it already. We'd be running ourselves ragged trying to chase sirens."

"Munjoy Hill, Gillis. Go."

"You're beat. I'm beat. We should go back to HQ and wait for things to develop."

"You want me to drive? Then move the hell over."

"Sam, are you *hearing* me?"

"Yes, damn you!" Sam shouted back in a sudden outburst of rage. Then, with a groan, he dropped his head in his hands. Quietly he said, "It's my fault. My fault she's going to die. They were right there in front of me. And I couldn't think of any way to save her. Any way to keep her alive."

Gillis gave a sigh of comprehension. "She means that much to you?"

"And Spectre knows it. Somehow he knows it. That's why he's keeping her alive. To torment me. Manipulate me. He has the winning hand and he's using it." He looked at Gillis. "We have to find her."

"Right now, he has the advantage. He has someone who means a lot to you. And *you're* the cop he seems to be focused on. The cop he wants to get back at." He glanced down at his car phone. It was ringing.

He answered it. "Gillis here." A moment later he hung up and started the car. "Jackman Avenue," he said, pulling into the road. "It could be our break."

"What's on Jackman Avenue?"

"An apartment, unit 338-D. They just found a body there."

Sam went very still. A sense of dread had clamped down on his chest, making it difficult to breathe. He asked, softly, "Whose body?"

"Marilyn Dukoff's."

HE WAS SINGING "Dixie!" as he worked, stringing out wire in multicolored lengths along the floor. Nina, hands and feet bound to a heavy chair, could only sit and watch helplessly. Next to Spectre was a toolbox, a soldering iron, and two dozen dynamite sticks.

"In Dixieland where I was born, early on a frosty mornin'…"

Spectre finished laying out the wire and turned his attention to the dynamite. With green electrical tape, he neatly bundled the sticks together in groups of three and set the bundles in a cardboard box.

"In Dixieland we'll make our stand, to live and die in Dixie. Away, away, away down south, in DIXIE!" he boomed out, and his voice echoed in the far reaches of the vast and empty warehouse. Then, turning to Nina, he dipped his head in a bow.

"You're crazy," whispered Nina.

"But what is madness? Who's to say?" Spectre wound green tape around the last three dynamite sticks. Then he gazed at the bundles, admiring his work. "What's that saying? 'Don't get mad, get even'? Well, I'm not mad, in any sense of the word. But I *am* going to get even."

He picked up the box of dynamite and was carrying it toward Nina when he seemed to stumble. Nina's heart almost stopped as the box of explosives tilted toward the floor. Toward her.

Spectre gave a loud gasp of horror just before he caught the box. To Nina's astonishment, he suddenly burst out laughing. "Just an old joke," he admitted. "But it never fails to get a reaction."

He really was crazy, she thought, her heart thudding.

Carrying the box of dynamite, he moved about the warehouse, laying bundles of explosives at measured intervals around the perimeter. "It's a shame, really," he said, "to waste so much quality dynamite on one building. But I do want to leave a good impression. A lasting impression. And I've had quite enough of Sam Navarro and his nine lives. This should take care of any extra lives he still has."

"You're laying a trap."

"You're so clever."

"Why? Why do you want to kill him?"

"Because."

"He's just a policeman doing his job."

"*Just* a policeman?" Spectre turned to her, but his expression remained hidden in the shadows of the warehouse. "Navarro is more than that. He's a challenge. My nemesis. To think, after all these years of success in cities like Boston and Miami, I should find my match in a small town like this. Not even Portland, Oregon, but Portland, *Maine*." He gave a laugh of self-disgust. "It ends here, in this warehouse. Between Navarro and me."

Spectre crossed toward her, carrying the final bundle of dynamite. He knelt beside the rocking chair where Nina sat with hands and ankles bound. "I saved the last blast for you, Miss Cormier," he said. And he taped the bundle under Nina's chair. "You won't feel a thing," he assured her. "It will happen so fast, why, the next thing you know, you'll be sprouting angel's wings. So will Navarro. If he gets his wings at all."

"He's not stupid. He'll know you've set a trap."

Spectre began stringing out more color-coded wire now, yards and yards of it. "Yes, it should be quite obvious this isn't any run-of-the-mill bomb. All this wire, tangled up to confuse him. Circuitry that makes no sense…" He snipped a white wire, then a red one. With his soldering iron, he connected the ends. "And the time ticking away.

Minutes, then seconds. Which is the detonator wire? Which wire should he cut? The wrong one, and it all goes up in smoke. The warehouse. You. And him—if he has nerve enough to see it to the end. It's a hopeless dilemma, you see. He stays to disarm it and you could both die. He chickens out and runs, and *you* die, leaving him with guilt he'll never forget. Either way, Sam Navarro suffers. And I win."

"You can't win."

"Spare me the moralistic warnings. I have work to do. And not much time to do it." He strung the wires out to the other dynamite bundles, crisscrossing colors, splicing ends to blasting caps.

Not much time to do it, he had said. How much time was he talking about?

She glanced down at the other items laid out on the floor. A digital timer. A radio transmitter. It was to be a timed device, she realized, the countdown triggered by that transmitter. Spectre would be safely out of the building when he armed the bomb. Out of harm's way when it exploded.

Stay away, Sam, she thought. *Please stay away. And live.*

Spectre rose to his feet and glanced at his watch. "Another hour and I should be ready to make the call." He looked at her and smiled. "Three in the morning, Miss Cormier. That seems as good an hour as any to die, don't you think?"

THE WOMAN WAS NUDE from the waist down, her body crumpled on the wood floor. She had been shot once, in the head.

"The report came in at 10:45," said Yeats from Homicide. "Tenant below us noticed bloodstains seeping across the ceiling and called the landlady. She opened the door, saw the body and called us. We found the victim's ID in her purse. That's why we called you."

"Any witnesses? Anyone see anything, hear anything?" asked Gillis.

"No. He must've used a silencer. Then slipped out without being seen."

Sam gazed around at the sparsely furnished room. The walls were bare, the closets half empty, and there were boxes of clothes on the floor—all signs that Marilyn Dukoff had not yet settled into this apartment.

Yeats confirmed it. "She moved in a day ago, under the name Marilyn Brown. Paid the deposit and first month's rent in cash. That's all the landlady could tell me."

"She have any visitors?" asked Gillis.

"Next-door tenant heard a man's voice in here yesterday. But never saw him."

"Spectre," said Sam. He focused once again on the body. The criminalists were already combing the room, dusting for prints, searching for evidence. They would find none, Sam already knew; Spectre would've seen to it.

There was no point hanging around here; they'd be better off trying to chase sirens. He turned to the door, then paused as he heard one of the detectives say, "Not much in the purse. Wallet, keys, a few bills—"

"What bills?" asked Sam.

"Electric, phone. Water. Look like they're to the old apartment. The name Dukoff's on them. Delivered to a PO box."

"Let me see the phone bill."

At his first glance at the bill, Sam almost uttered a groan

of frustration. It was two sheets long and covered with long distance calls, most of them to Bangor numbers, a few to Massachusetts and Florida. It would take hours to track all those numbers down, and the chances were it would simply lead them to Marilyn Dukoff's bewildered friends or family.

Then he focused on one number, at the bottom of the bill. It was a collect call charge, from a South Portland prefix, dated a week and a half ago at 10:17 p.m. Someone had called collect and Marilyn Dukoff had accepted the charges.

"This could be something," Sam noted. "I need the location of this number."

"We can call the operator from my car," said Gillis. "but I don't know what it's going to get you."

"A hunch. That's what I'm going on," Sam admitted.

Back in Gillis's car, Sam called the Directory Assistance supervisor.

After checking her computer, she confirmed it was a pay phone. "It's near the corner of Calderwood and Hardwick, in South Portland."

"Isn't there a gas station on that corner?" asked Sam. "I seem to remember one there."

"There may be, Detective. I can't tell you for certain."

Sam hung up and reached for the South Portland map. Under the dome light, he pinpointed the location of the pay phone. "Here it is," he said to Gillis.

"There's just some industrial buildings out there."

"Yeah, which makes a collect call at 10:17 p.m. all the more interesting."

"Could've been anyone calling her. Friends, family. For all we know—"

"It was Spectre," Sam said. His head jerked up in sudden excitement. "South Portland. Let's *go*."

"What?"

Sam thrust the map toward Gillis. "Here's Bickford Street. A squad car was dispatched there at 12:10. And here's Calderwood and Hardwick. The squad car would've gone right through this area."

"You think Spectre's holed up around there?"

Sam scrawled a circle on the map, a three-block radius around Calderwood and Hardwick. "He's here. He's got to be around here."

Gillis started the car. "I think our haystack just got a hell of a lot smaller."

Twenty minutes later, they were at the corner of Hardwick and Calderwood. There was, indeed, a gas station there, but it had been closed down and a For Sale—Commercial Property sign was posted in the scraggly strip of a garden near the road. Sam and Gillis sat in their idling car for a moment, scanning the street. There was no other traffic in sight.

Gillis began to drive up Hardwick. The neighborhood was mostly industrial. Vacant lots, a boating supply outlet. A lumber wholesaler. A furniture maker. Everything was closed for the night, the parking lots empty, the buildings dark. They turned onto Calderwood.

A few hundred yards later, Sam spotted the light. It was faint, no more than a yellowish glow from a small window—the only window in the building. As they pulled closer, Gillis cut his headlights. They stopped half a block away.

"It's the old Stimson warehouse," said Sam.

"No cars in the lot," Gillis noted. "But it looks like someone's home."

"Didn't the Stimson cannery close down last year?"

Sam didn't answer; he was already stepping out of the car.

"Hey!" whispered Gillis. "Shouldn't we call for backup?"

"You call. I'm checking it out."

"Sam!" Gillis hissed. "Sam!"

Adrenaline pumping, Sam ignored his partner's warnings and started toward the warehouse. The darkness was in his favor; whoever was inside wouldn't be able to spot his approach. Through the cracks in the truck bay doors, he saw more light, vertical slivers of yellow.

He circled the building, but spotted no ground floor windows, no way to look inside. There was a back door and a front door, but both were locked.

At the front of the building, he met up with Gillis.

"Backup's on the way," Gillis informed him.

"I have to get in there."

"We don't know what we'll find in there—" Gillis suddenly paused and glanced at his car.

The phone was ringing.

Both men scurried back to answer it.

Sam grabbed the receiver. "Navarro here."

"Detective Navarro," said the police operator. "We have an outside phone call for you. The man says it's urgent. I'll put it through."

There was a pause, a few clicks, and then a man's voice said, "I'm so glad to reach you, Detective. This car phone of yours is coming in handy."

"Spectre?"

"I'd like to issue a personal invitation, Detective. To you and you alone. A reunion, with a certain someone who's right here beside me."

"Is she all right?"

"She's perfectly fine." Spectre paused and added with a soft tone of threat. "For the moment."

"What do you want from me?"

"Nothing at all. I'd just like you to come and take Miss Cormier off my hands. She's becoming an inconvenience. And I have other places to go to."

"Where is she?"

"I'll give you a clue. Herring."

"What?"

"Maybe the name *Stimson* rings a bell? You can look up the address. Sorry I won't be here to greet you, but I really *must* be going."

SPECTRE HUNG UP the phone and smiled at Nina. "Time for me to go. Lover boy should be here any minute." He picked up his toolbox and set it in the car, which he'd driven through the loading bay to keep it out of sight.

He's leaving, she thought. *Leaving me as bait for the trap.*

It was cool in the warehouse, but she felt a drop of sweat slide down her temple as she watched Spectre reach down for the radio transmitter. All he had to do was flick one switch on that radio device, and the bomb would be armed, the countdown started.

Ten minutes later, it would explode.

Her heart gave a painful thud as she saw him reach for the radio switch. Then he smiled at her.

"Not yet," he said. "I wouldn't want things to happen prematurely."

Turning, he walked toward the truck bay door. He gave Nina a farewell salute. "Say goodbye to Navarro for me. Tell him I'm so sorry to miss the big kaboom." He unlatched the bay door and gave the handle a yank. It slid up with the sound of grating metal. It was almost open when Spectre suddenly froze.

Right in front of him, a pair of headlights came on.

"Freeze, Spectre!" came a command from somewhere in the darkness. "Hands over your head!"

Sam, thought Nina. *You found me….*

"Hands up!" yelled Sam. "Do it!"

Silhouetted against the headlights, Spectre seemed to hesitate for a few seconds. Then, slowly, he raised his hands over his head.

He was still holding the transmitter.

"Sam!" cried Nina. "There's a bomb! He's got a transmitter!"

"Put it down," Sam ordered. "Put it down or I shoot!"

"Certainly," agreed Spectre. Slowly he dropped to a crouch and lowered the transmitter toward the floor. But as he lay it down, there was a distinct *click* that echoed through the warehouse.

My God, he's armed the bomb, thought Nina.

"Better run," said Spectre. And he dived sideways, toward a stack of crates.

He wasn't fast enough. In the next instant, Sam squeezed off two shots. Both bullets found their target.

Spectre seemed to stumble. He dropped to his knees and began to crawl forward, but his limbs were moving drunkenly, like a swimmer trying to paddle across land. He was making gurgling sounds now, gasping out curses with his last few breaths.

"Dead," wheezed Spectre, and it was almost a laugh. "You're all dead…."

Sam stepped over Spectre's motionless body and started straight toward Nina.

"No!" she cried. "Stay away!"

He stopped dead, staring at her with a look of bewilderment. "What is it?"

"He's wired a bomb to my chair," sobbed Nina. "If you try to cut me loose it'll go off!"

At once Sam's gaze shot to the coils of wire ringing her chair, then followed the trail of wire to the warehouse wall, to the first bundle of dynamite, lying in plain view.

"He has eighteen sticks planted all around the building," she said. "Three are under my chair. It's set to go off in ten minutes. Less, now."

Their gazes met. And in that one glance she saw his look of panic. It was quickly suppressed. He stepped across the wire and crouched by her chair.

"I'm getting you out of here," he vowed.

"There's not enough time!"

"Ten minutes?" He gave a terse laugh. "That's loads of time." He knelt down and peered under the seat. He didn't say a thing, but when he rose again, his expression was grim. He turned and called, "Gillis?"

"Right here," Gillis answered, stepping gingerly over the wires. "I got the toolbox. What do we have?"

"Three sticks under the chair, and a digital timer." Sam gently slid out the timing device, bristling with wires, and set it carefully on the floor. "It looks like a simple series-parallel circuit. I'll need time to analyze it."

"How long do we have?"

"Eight minutes and forty-five seconds and counting."

Gillis cursed. "No time to get the bomb truck."

A wail of a siren suddenly cut through the night. Two police cruisers pulled up outside the bay door.

"Backup's here," Gillis said. He hurried over to the doors, waving at the other cops. "Stay back!" he yelled. "We got a bomb in here! I want a perimeter evac *now!* And get an ambulance here on standby."

I won't need an ambulance, thought Nina. *If this bomb goes off, there'll be nothing left of me to pick up.*

She tried to calm her racing heart, tried to stop her slide toward hysteria, but sheer terror was making it hard for her to breathe. There was nothing she could do to save herself. Her wrists were tightly bound; so were her ankles. If she so much as shifted too far in her chair, the bomb could be triggered.

It was all up to Sam.

Fourteen

Sam's jaw was taut as he studied the tangle of wires and circuitry. There were so many wires! It would take an hour just to sort them all out. But all they had were minutes. Though he didn't say a word, she could read the urgency in his face, could see the first droplets of sweat forming on his forehead.

Gillis returned to his partner's side. "I checked the perimeter. Spectre's got the building wired with fifteen or more sticks. No other action fuses as far as I can see. The brain to this whole device is right there in your hands."

"It's too easy," muttered Sam, scanning the circuitry. "He *wants* me to cut this wire."

"Could it be a double feint? He knew we'd be suspicious. So he made it simple on purpose—just to throw us?"

Sam swallowed. "This looks like the arming switch right here. But over here, he's got the cover soldered shut. He could have a completely different switch inside. Magnetic reed or a Castle-Robins device. If I pry off that cap, it could fire."

Gillis glanced at the digital timer. "Five minutes left."

"I know, I know." Sam's voice was hoarse with tension, but his hands were absolutely steady as he traced the circuitry. One tug on the wrong wire, and all three of them could be instantly vaporized.

Outside, more sirens whined to a stop. Nina could hear voices, the sounds of confusion.

But inside, there was silence.

Sam took a breath and glanced up at her. "You okay?"

She gave a tense nod. And she saw, in his face, the first glimpse of panic. *He won't figure this out in time, and he knows it.*

This was just what Spectre had planned. The hopeless dilemma. The fatal choice. Which wire to cut? One? None? Does he gamble with his own life? Or does he make the rational choice to abandon the building—and her?

She knew the choice he would make. She could see it in his eyes.

They were both going to die.

"Two and a half minutes," said Gillis.

"Go on, get out of here," Sam ordered.

"You need an extra pair of hands."

"And your kids need a father. Get the hell out."

Gillis didn't budge.

Sam picked up the wire cutters and isolated a white wire.

"You're guessing, Sam. You don't know."

"Instinct, buddy. I've always had good instincts. Better leave. We're down to two minutes. And you're not doing me any good."

Gillis rose to his feet, but lingered there, torn between leaving and staying. "Sam—"

"Move."

Gillis said, softly, "I'll have a bottle of Scotch waiting for you, buddy."

"You do that. Now get out of here."

Without another word, Gillis left the building.

Only Sam and Nina remained. *He doesn't have to stay,* she thought. *He doesn't have to die.*

"Sam," she whispered.

He didn't seem to hear her; he was concentrating too hard on the circuit board, his wire cutters hovering between a life-and-death choice.

"Leave, Sam," she begged.

"This is my job, Nina."

"It's not your job to die!"

"We're not going to die."

"You're right. *We* aren't. *You* aren't. If you leave now—"

"I'm not leaving. You understand? I'm *not.*" His gaze rose to meet hers. And she saw, in those steady eyes, that he had made up his mind. He'd made the choice to live— or die—with her. This was not the cop looking at her, but the man who loved her. The man *she* loved.

She felt tears trickle down her face. Only then did she realize she was crying.

"We're down to a minute. I'm going to make a guess here," he said. "If I'm right, cutting this wire should do the trick. If I'm wrong…" He let out a breath. "We'll know pretty quick one way or the other." He slipped the teeth of the cutter around the white wire. "Okay, I'm going with this one."

"Wait."

"What is it?"

"When Spectre was putting it together, he soldered a white wire to a red one, then he covered it all up with green tape. Does that make a difference?"

Sam stared down at the wire he'd been about to cut. "It does," he said softly. "It makes a hell of a lot of difference."

"Sam!" came Gillis's shout through a megaphone. "You've got ten seconds left!"

Ten seconds to run.

Sam didn't run. He moved the wire cutter to a black wire and positioned the jaws to cut. Then he stopped and looked up at Nina.

They stared at each other one last time.

"I love you," he said.

She nodded, the tears streaming down her face. "I love you too," she whispered.

Their gazes remained locked, unwavering, as he slowly closed the cutter over the wire. Even as the jaws came together, even as the teeth bit into the plastic coating, Sam was looking at her, and she at him.

The wire snapped in two.

For a moment neither one of them moved. They were still frozen in place, still paralyzed by the certainty of death.

Then, outside, Gillis yelled, "Sam? You're past count-down! *Sam!*"

All at once, Sam was cutting the bonds from her hands, her ankles. She was too numb to stand, but she didn't need to. He gathered her up into his arms and carried her out of the warehouse, into the night.

Outside, the street was ablaze with the flashing lights of emergency vehicles: squad cars, ambulances, fire trucks. Sam carried her safely past the yellow police tape and set her down on her feet.

Instantly they were surrounded by a mob of officials, Chief Coopersmith and Liddell among them, all clamoring to know the bomb's status. Sam ignored them all. He just stood there with his arms around Nina, shielding her from the chaos.

"Everyone back!" shouted Gillis, waving the crowd away. "Give 'em some breathing space!" He turned to Sam. "What about the device?"

"It's disarmed," said Sam. "But be careful. Spectre may have left us one last surprise."

"I'll take care of it." Gillis started toward the warehouse, then turned back. "Hey, Sam?"

"Yeah?"

"I'd say you just earned your retirement." Gillis grinned. And then he walked away.

Nina looked up at Sam. Though the danger was over, she could still feel his heart pounding, could feel her own heart beating just as wildly.

"You didn't leave me," she whispered, new tears sliding down her face. "You could have—"

"No, I couldn't."

"I told you to go! I *wanted* you to go."

"And I wanted to stay." He took her face in his hands. Firmly, insistently. "There was no other place I'd be but right there beside you, Nina. There's no other place I ever want to be."

She knew a dozen pairs of eyes were watching them. Already the news media had arrived with their camera flashbulbs and their shouted questions. The night was alive with voices and multicolored lights. But at that moment, as he held her, as they kissed, there was no one else but Sam.

When dawn broke, he would still be holding her.

Epilogue

The wedding was on. No doubt about it.

Accompanied by a lilting Irish melody played by flute and harp, Nina and her father walked arm in arm into the forest glade. There, beneath the fiery brilliance of autumn foliage, stood Sam. Just as she knew he would be.

He was grinning, as nervous as a rookie cop on his first beat. Beside him stood his best man, Gillis, and Reverend Sullivan, both wearing smiles. A small circle of friends and family stood gathered under the trees: Wendy and her husband. Chief Coopersmith. Nina's colleagues from the hospital. Also among the guests was Lydia, looking quietly resigned to the fact her daughter was marrying a mere cop.

Some things in life, thought Nina, cannot be changed. She had accepted that. Perhaps Lydia, some day, would learn to be as accepting.

The music faded, and the leaves of autumn drifted down in a soft rain of red and orange. Sam reached out to her. His smile told her all she needed to know. This was right; this was meant to be.

She took his hand.

#1 *NEW YORK TIMES*
BESTSELLING AUTHOR
DEBBIE MACOMBER

What do you want most in the world?

Anne Marie Roche wants to find happiness again. At 38, she's childless, a recent widow and alone. On Valentine's Day, Anne Marie and several other widows get together to celebrate...what? Hope, possibility, the future. They each begin a list of twenty wishes.

Anne Marie's list includes learning to knit, doing good for someone else and falling in love again. She begins to act on her wishes, and when she volunteers at a school, little Ellen enters her life. It's a relationship that becomes far more important than she ever imagined, one in which they both learn that wishes can come true.

Twenty Wishes

"These involving stories...continue the Blossom Street themes of friendship and personal growth that readers find so moving."—*Booklist* on *Back on Blossom Street*

Available the first week of May 2008 wherever books are sold!

MIRA®

NEW YORK TIMES
BESTSELLING AUTHOR

ANNE STUART

Talk about lost in translation....

In the wake of a failed love affair, Jilly Lovitz takes off for
Tokyo. She's expecting to cry on her sister Summer's shoulder,
then spend a couple months blowing off steam in Japan.
Instead, she's snatched away on the back of a motorcycle,
narrowly avoiding a grisly execution attempt meant for her
sister and brother-in-law.

Her rescuer is Reno. They'd met before and the attraction was
odd but electric. Now Reno and Jilly are pawns in a deadly
tangle of assassination attempts, kidnappings and prisoner
swaps that could put their steamy partnership on ice.

FIRE AND ICE

"Anne Stuart delivers exciting stuff for those of us who like
our romantic suspense dark and dangerous."
—*New York Times* bestselling author Jayne Ann Krentz

MIRA®

*Available the first week of May 2008
wherever paperbacks are sold!*

www.MIRABooks.com

MAS2536

REQUEST YOUR FREE BOOKS!

2 FREE NOVELS
FROM THE ROMANCE/SUSPENSE
COLLECTION PLUS 2 FREE GIFTS!

YES! Please send me 2 FREE novels from the Romance/Suspense Collection and my 2 FREE gifts (gifts are worth about $10). After receiving them, if I don't wish to receive any more books, I can return the shipping statement marked "cancel." If I don't cancel, I will receive 4 brand-new novels every month and be billed just $5.49 per book in the U.S. or $5.99 per book in Canada, plus 25¢ shipping and handling per book plus applicable taxes, if any*. That's a savings of at least 20% off the cover price! I understand that accepting the 2 free books and gifts places me under no obligation to buy anything. I can always return a shipment and cancel at any time. Even if I never buy another book from the Reader Service, the two free books and gifts are mine to keep forever.

185 MDN EF5Y   385 MDN EF6C

Name _____ (PLEASE PRINT)

Address _____ Apt. #

City _____ State/Prov. _____ Zip/Postal Code

Signature (if under 18, a parent or guardian must sign)

Mail to **The Reader Service:**
IN U.S.A.: P.O. Box 1867, Buffalo, NY 14240-1867
IN CANADA: P.O. Box 609, Fort Erie, Ontario L2A 5X3

Not valid to current subscribers to the Romance Collection,
the Suspense Collection or the Romance/Suspense Collection.

Want to try two free books from another line?
Call 1-800-873-8635 or visit www.morefreebooks.com.

* Terms and prices subject to change without notice. N.Y. residents add applicable sales tax. Canadian residents will be charged applicable provincial taxes and GST. This offer is limited to one order per household. All orders subject to approval. Credit or debit balances in a customer's account(s) may be offset by any other outstanding balance owed by or to the customer. Please allow 4 to 6 weeks for delivery. Offer available while quantities last.

Your Privacy: Harlequin is committed to protecting your privacy. Our Privacy Policy is available online at www.eHarlequin.com or upon request from the Reader Service. From time to time we make our lists of customers available to reputable third parties who may have a product or service of interest to you. If you would prefer we not share your name and address, please check here. ☐

BOB08